SCARRED WORLD

Written by: S. Sexton

Contents

Chapter 1

Thunder rolled over and through the hills, as Billy walked. The hill he was climbing was not steep, but it did cut back and forth a few times, with long drops on the side occasionally showing off the lowland area below. The walk was not far but it was rough on Billy, who was now approaching 30 years of mountain living. Billy was on his way to work at the old hardware store his uncle had owned for the last 50 years or so. He didn't like his uncle much, but he did enjoy the work and paycheck provided through his labors.

While Billy was hiking alongside the road, he kept an eye out for anything interesting-looking that may have fallen from the mountain above. Sometimes, he found a lovely quartz crystal or a piece of pyrite. Most often he found interesting shards of flint, which he collected as a kind of hobby. This particular part of the road was in shadow for several more hours as the mountain blocked the early morning sunlight. Something sparkly caught Billy's eye in the shallow runoff ditch beside the road, and he bent to pick it up when he heard a thump. Just before Billy was unwittingly covered in tons of stoney death, he picked up the sparkly thing from the ground and stood.

"What was that noise?" Billy said aloud as he stood and turned around.

Instead of seeing the road running along the mountainside, he found himself in a park. The sky was clear, the air warm, and the smell of freshness permeated his senses. A few feet away, Billy saw there was a bench, and on that bench sat an old man wearing a white robe and feeding some colorful birds. Curious, Billy walked over to the man on the bench and watched him for a while.

Not wanting to interrupt the man, Billy busied himself with looking at the thing he had just picked up a moment ago. It looked like a clear glass cube. As he turned it in his hand, the light did weird things as it passed through, creating beautiful rainbow lines that seemed to spiral inward forever. Caught up in the optical illusion, Billy had not noticed when the old man spoke to him.

"What was that?" He asked, turning his head to look at the old man. The sight took his breath away. He knew this old man. He couldn't say how he knew him, but something deep in the recesses of his memory sparked some sort of recognition.

"I said good morning, Billy." The old man smiled as he spoke. His deep blue eyes sparkled strangely as Billy looked at them, and for another moment, he thought he recognized the pattern in them.

"Uh, yes. Good morning," Billy stammered, momentarily confused by where he was standing.

The old man just sat and continued to smile warmly at Billy. He seemed to be waiting for something but was in no real rush.

"I, uh, found this a minute ago, and I can't help but think it looks just like your eyes. Does this belong to you by chance?" Carefully so as not to chance dropping the strange crystal, Billy held it out to the old man on the bench.

"Yes, I know. And no, it is not mine. It's yours, Billy," The old man said calmly.

Not knowing what else to do with the strange thing, Billy let his arm drop while maintaining his hold on it. He moved over to the bench and sat down, and the old man handed Billy a bag full of bird seed. Billy took out a handful and scattered it on the grass for the birds to peck at. He spent some time doing this. He and the old man shared the silence of the park, together feeding the lovely birds as they began to flock in.

"You know, Billy, most people I meet here do a lot more talking than you." The old man paused in his feeding and watching the birds to look over at Billy, who just sat forward a little, admiring the myriad birds and their ever more colorful plumage as more and more birds showed up for the feast.

"Yeah, I guess it's because most people don't know much about themselves." Casually, Billy tossed out some more seeds, and the birds began to quietly peck at them. "I think it's because they have a certain expectation in life and are surprised when it turns out to be something different."

"And you, Billy? Do you know yourself? Do you not have expectations when it comes to life?"

Billy looked over to the old man, who was sitting back and looking up at the clouds in the sky above.

"I know myself as much as anyone else can, I suppose. And by 'expectations in life,' I think it is folly to expect some meaning to it. Sometimes," Billy tossed more seeds out for the birds, "Sometimes things happen regardless of anyone's expectations."

The old man grunted, seeming to agree with Billy. Then, after a few more minutes of quiet birds rustling and clouds being admired, the old man spoke again.

"So, what do you expect to happen now?"

Billy sat there for a time, pondering the question. He had already reached the conclusion he was likely dead from a rockslide and that this was probably what came next in the cycle of existence. Deciding he was done and gone from the world he had recently existed in, Billy looked over to the old man with a question.

"Can you send me somewhere else, maybe? I'd like another go at it if that's possible." He did not sound sad or upset, he was simply ready for what comes next.

The old man chuckled and said, "Another go, huh? Those who come through here get to do this, yes."

Billy looked over to the old man to see him still looking up at the clouds in the sky, no real worry or concern on his face. Billy wrinkled his brow, then, and asked, "Why haven't you gone, then?"

"That, Billy, is an excellent question. I can, of course, go elsewhere. However, during times such as this, I find it far better to give a personal touch to the issues at hand. You see, you were not supposed to stop there on your way to work. You were supposed to keep walking and carry on with your life. But for some reason I do not know, you stopped where you did at just the right time and picked up that prompt there in your hand."

Billy looked at the "prompt" in his hand, and only saw it to be a very pretty crystal cube. "This thing?" He asked, holding it up.

"Yes, Billy, that is a prompt. It was not meant to be in your world at this time, but somehow you managed to not only call out to it, you even managed to pick it up. Truly marvelous, indeed," The old man said as he looked over to Billy.

"What does it do?" Billy asked, trying to more closely examine the crystal.

"It is a prompt, of course. More accurately, it is a Quest Prompt."

Billy froze when the old man said those words. Quest Prompt. He could feel the capital letters. This was something important.

"Quest Prompt? Like, video game quest prompt?"

"Yes, like that. Only this one is not meant for just anyone. It is one which gives a quest to a certain caliber of individual. It is one to save a world."

Billy almost dropped the small crystal. He had read books where people were given roles in other worlds where they would inevitably save a world or destroy it. This was one of those things, apparently. What was it called, iziki, useki? He, he couldn't remember right now. What it meant was that he could reincarnate into another world, another reality, with game-like mechanics running in the background. It meant his world, probably all worlds, are simulations running on some cosmic mainframe somewhere. Or gods existed and messed with mortal souls for fun. In either case, this truly was his call to adventure.

"Where will this take me?" Billy asked, holding up the crystal to the sunlight to watch its infinite interior facets sparkle.

"I cannot say, exactly. Only that you will go not as you are, but as something else. These things are usually random in nature, designed to fill a niche role in that world, but not an alien one. You will be uploaded into a new form to perform tasks in another reality in the hopes that you can save it."

"And will I have access to some kind of interface? Something that would help me track stats, and experience points and stuff like that?" Billy seemed fit to burst with all kinds of questions now. But he was not overly excited. He had also read manga and watched anime where the individuals who went to different realities died almost immediately upon arrival or suffered greatly in some unfair or near-impossible tasks. However, this crystal he held in his hand already told him whatever he was to do would be hard, probably impossible. But it also meant it could likely be done and that he could do it.

"Yes and no. The Great Simulation is full of worlds that cannot utilize its interface, but I am fairly certain this Quest Prompt will take you to a world where it is possible. There are many worlds out there, Billy, and each has its own rules."

"Do I get to take anything with me on this quest?" Billy asked, bouncing the crystal in his palm. He was starting to get pretty excited about this.

"You get to take your memories, Billy."

Billy looked up at this, "My memories?"

"Yes. Normally, people who come here and move along do not take their past life experiences with them. However, those few individuals who stumble across the Quest Prompts can choose to take their memories with them or try without. Some choose to go in blind, as the traumas from life were too much to keep a hold of. Some succeed in doing this, ; some don't. The simulation moves along either way."

Billy watched the old man as he spoke, and his words made sense. Some people would have seen or been through some stuff they would rather forget. He could get behind that. But he himself had a good life. He would prefer to take his memories with him on this new adventure.

"Can I take anything else?" Billy asked the old man.

"What would you take if you could?" The old man smiled at Billy's enthusiasm.

Billy was taken aback for a moment, then blurted, "Can I take my smartphone?"

Pausing for a moment, the old man looked down at the birds and then back over to Billy. "Sure, why not? I'll even hook you up to the simulation itself to get information and access its delivery system, and various stores. Unfortunately, I can't let you take the device itself. I can, however, append it to your personal folder."

Billy scratched his chin in thought. "What does that mean?"

"Ah, well, it means that it will be integrated into your matrix. From your perspective, it will be more like an overlay you can interact with directly using thought, which more or less will look like interacting with your smartphone, but it will be happening in your mind." He tapped the side of his temple as he said this.

Intrigued, Billy nodded. "Yeah, that'd be neat. I think I'll take that with me, then."

The two sat there for a while, the old man slowly looking around at the park, Billy looking nervous as he held the strange crystal Quest Prompt. After a moment, Billy had a question pop into his head, "Will I be hum.." The world went blank before he could finish asking.

The first thing Billy recognized as he came to was the sound of clinking metal chains on metal pipes. He couldn't see anything, but he got the feeling it was dark wherever he was. He tried to stand up, and the clanking and rattle of metal and other things could be heard echoing off nearby walls.

Billy couldn't feel his arms or legs, but he could sense he was rocking all around as he tried to move them. He also felt a rumbling pressure building inside himself as he became more aware. Carefully, Billy tried to move his arms over his head to see if something was holding him up. For some reason or another, his arms didn't want to bend properly. And he had the strange feeling something else was happening.

He could feel more than two arms. He could feel more than two legs as well. And still, he could not see. Forgoing any of the confusing thoughts running around in his head, Billy focused on manipulating his limbs to try and grab on to whatever was holding him. He realized he was hanging in some sort of apparatus but was unable to determine the points of contact so he could try and escape.

Eventually, one of his arms managed to grab something and he gripped onto it as tightly as he could; clanking and creaking metal resounded in the room. Contorting himself, Billy tried to get more hands on this thing, probably a cable of some sort, so he could try and pull himself upright. He felt as if he were both lying down and standing upright, which was quite disorienting.

"Dammit," Billy tried to say aloud, "Where are the lights in this place so I can see what I'm doing?" His voice sounded strange, but he ignored this. There was no reaction from his environment, though he had managed to get two more hands on the thing he was hanging from. He was getting concerned the noise he was making would attract unwanted attention.

Using this one cable, Billy was able to almost flip himself upside down while he felt around the air to see if those pesky chains were nearby. They were not. Finally, desperate to get free of this thing stuck to him, Billy pulled his face forward and tried to bite onto this cable. His arms knew their business and brought the cable to his mouth.

To his surprise, he felt his mouth clamp down, then chomp right through the material of the cable. Without time to shout, Billy fell a short distance to crash onto the floor.

Strange instincts told him he was on his back, and that this was not the safest position for him to be in. That same instinct guided him into righting himself onto his feet. The noise he was making was horrible, and if anyone were nearby, they would undoubtedly know where he was. It sounded to himself like he was encased in metal, with metal feet, hands and body all making their own ruckus.

It did not take him long to right himself, and when he stood, Billy did his best to take stock of himself. As he calmed, he could feel a pressure building up inside his stomach area, and then as he relaxed further, he felt another something release and he heard a small "pssssssshhh" of compressed air. It had to be steam, though, because he could feel how hot it was on two of his legs. He also felt much more stable all of a sudden.

One by one, Billy lifted and tapped on the ground each of the limbs he felt. He heard one tap after another, and when the count was done, he had reached eight. Eight feet was how many limbs spiders had. He also had two arms, which he thought he recalled being the "feelers." These had hands on them, from what he could feel.

"But did spiders sound like they were made of metal and belched steam?" He thought. He was sure they weren't, but he knew that was what his predicament was looking like. He was a metal-covered spider that farted steam.

After further contemplation, Billy tried to feel around his body. He had an abdomen, and that seemed to be the largest part of his body, big and bulbous. The front part of his body is where all the legs were connected to. That meant he probably had eyes on his head, and if memory serves correct, he could have as many as eight of those as well.

Being very careful not to poke himself in the eyes, Billy felt around his head. He felt something with bumps on it, and after slowly moving over all of them, he could feel eight of them. Then, as he was moving his hand over the rest of his head, he felt something else and he paused.

"What's this?" He thought to himself.

With as much care as he could manage, Billy felt something encasing the front of his head. He could feel everywhere he touched himself as if the metal covering his body were skin, but this part he could not feel at all. It must be some sort of covering,

As careful as he could manage, Billy tried to grab the thing on the top of his head and pulled slowly. A tearing sound could just be made out as the metal thing covering his head pulled away. All of a sudden, Billy's world was filled with light.

He was worried for a little bit that if he was a spider and had eight eyes, it would be difficult for him to use them without getting dizzy. However, when the time came for him to use those eyes, Billy learned he had no problems at all.

The first thing Billy saw was something being pulled from his eyes, looking like strange blue lines contrasted by other darker or lighter blue lines and curves. Once off, Billy inspected the thing with his spidery arms, the feelers, and thought that whatever it was, it had protected his eyes for some reason. Not knowing what else to do with it, Billy carefully set it aside as he slowly looked around the room he was in.

There seemed to be no lights on as everything Billy saw was pitch black. When using his eyes to look around, Billy saw a strange contrasting of many blue lines that formed general shapes, as if this was a computer screen showing the layout of a room that had no lights, but anyone looking at the monitor could see all of the shapes. Part of the giant rectangular room he was in had collapsed. He himself had been in some sort of large pod. Suspended nearby were machines that had been connected to him. Around the pod were other ancient-looking machines that probably monitored this body while it was suspended.

Ancient machines covered in inches of now-disturbed dust were everywhere. None of the lights functioned on anything. Most of the things that were probably glass had long since shattered. Nothing else moved in the room except Billy.

As Billy took stock of the situation he recalled he was allowed to use an interface. Not sure how that would work he spoke the only word that came immediately to mind.

"Menu."

Suddenly, portions of his vision had overlapping screens, similar to holographic ones portrayed in movies. He had what looked like a targeting circle, and other information portrayed in different corners of the various screens. As Billy looked at these screens, he could still make out what was happening in the background through them as he moved around.

For a moment, all of the screens contained gibberish, nothing that made any sense to Billy. For no reason he understood, the screens began to blink on and off rapidly, showing more and stranger symbols, shapes and colors. Eventually, one set of symbols that he recognized froze into place, and Billy found he had access to an English translation of the interface. Now, he might have a chance to see what it all said.

Before he could get into anything in particular, a digital envelope floated into his field of view and tore itself open to reveal a message addressed to him directly.

Billy,

Congratulations on locating and activating the Quest Prompt! You're well on your way to high adventure. As you may be aware, you were uploaded into the housing of a magically improved, steam-powered spider mechanism called a Mechanoid. You have eight feet, two pedipalps, eight eyes, and all you need to venture forth to SAVE A WORLD! (The last words were flashing gold and fluttering on the screen in Billy's mind.)

To aid you in this quest, we have provided you with an interface and a digital assistant to aid you in redirecting this dystopian world to a brighter future! We have also sent you a small Welcome Package, which will provide you with some Experience crystals for you to consume. The amount and quality have been determined by the accolades you have from your previous incarnation. The more that you have accomplished, the greater the rewards!

Also contained within this Welcome Package is a Map Icon, which will integrate with your matrix. This Map Icon will help track quest objectives and provide other topographical information you may find useful. This function is available once your personal assistant becomes activated.

Your personal assistant has been successfully uploaded, but it may take some time to fully integrate into your psyche. We estimate the time required before full operation to be approximately four hours. Please stand by for your new assistant.

Now, as for the Quest. This world has been invaded by a diabolical force that has twisted the minds of its people. The foreordained fate of the fey and the humes has been altered beyond their original plan. The world is dying. You must discover why, and save those you can. Good luck, Billy. We are cheering for you out here.

Billy found he now had four hours before he could examine his map. His screens were available, but he could not yet interact with them. For now, the only information they had were gibberish words, but with English lexicon. He figured his incoming assistant would help rearrange things to make sense for him whenever it came online.

In the meantime, Billy thought it best to have a look around. He did not dwell on the fact he was now some kind of mechanical spider monster. He was not really bothered by such things as physical appearance. Billy was more of a thinker, planner and doer. When dealing with things like logistics, he was a wiz at organizing, and when it came time to get the work done, he was only too happy to get into the tasks. The feeling of accomplishing tasks was one he rather enjoyed, as it meant he was successful in both his planning and execution.

Managing eight limbs, each of which also had its own appendages, as well as two shorter arms, was not too difficult to do. He found that as he wanted to "walk" forward, his legs would just perform the task, not unlike when he was human and wanted to walk forward and his legs obeyed his will. When he wanted to touch something, his pedipalp would reach out. After a moment, Billy decided to think of his pedipalps as manipulators instead. They had hands on them. What was new to him was how accurately he could place each limb while he moved.

Despite being a rather large machine, he learned that if he moved slower, he could be nearly totally silent in his steps. With two legs, moving slowly meant placing one leg forward while the other one balanced, but with eight legs, he could move several legs at a time and maintain perfect balance the whole time. This also meant that as he was sneaking around the old dusty room he could hear everything else without drowning it out with his own footsteps.

As Billy moved around, he could hear the mechanisms of his body making strange sounds. Clicks, whirs, and the slight squeal of pistons low on lubricant were prominent as he tested his new body. Billy's eyes could also see quite well, even though there were no lights, as far as he could tell. Everything was the same strange blue color, but with a vast degree of contrast. He could see the shape and contour of dust mounds in what was essentially total darkness. He was quite happy about this, but he was also concerned that such light sensitivity might mean he would be blind during full daylight. Just in case, he returned to his awakening place and, grabbed the face cover that had protected his eyes and laid it on his back. Hopefully, it would stay there while he explored. He would just have to wait and see.

Two of Billy's front feet contained four finger-like appendages carefully collapsed into the pad of the foot. When he saw what looked like a tablet, he reached out with a foot and was fascinated as he watched the limb carefully and quietly separate into several digits with one more joint than he was used to. He used these digits to search through the debris and pick things up. His manipulators were too short to reach some of the stuff without disturbing the thick layer of dust on it.

After a time of moving around the room, checking the various dust-covered tables for anything useful, Billy finally gave up as the third tablet-looking device crumbled in one of his feet-hands while trying to pick it up. With care, he had tried to pick up the device but it had simply cracked into pieces. A few more attempts preceded his last, but no amount of control could stop things from falling apart. It looked like the material they were made of had decayed completely, and their own weight caused them to fall apart as he lifted them.

Undeterred, Billy was interested in finding that Welcome Package, wherever it was. It had to be here somewhere, he just needed to locate it. He made his way around the room, carefully inspecting everything, sometimes moving large clumps of rusted material to the side to check beneath. After some time, he had managed to circle the whole room, and ended back where he had first released himself from the harness which had suspended him. Curious, Billy carefully scanned the area where he had been housed, and suddenly, a small section of the wall, looking like every other section of the ancient wall, showed a bright red outline in the shape of a rectangle.

Billy scampered over to the part of the wall that was highlighted and carefully reached out to touch the wall. There was a little give as he pushed, then it clicked. He withdrew his hand quickly, and a small drawer hissed open. The light in it tried to flicker on, as if its capacitor held just the tiniest bit of power, but ultimately remained dark. Billy moved a little closer and could make out a set of boxes perfectly preserved within, each with a spider symbol embossed in some kind of metallic blue material.

Reaching forward, Billy slowly picked up the two boxes and flipped each lid open. Inside were clear glass keys with strange lines made of some unknown materials running through them. As soon as his eyes lit upon the keys, Billy felt something inside his mouth adjust and move forward, not unlike a tongue. To his surprise, a small green circle overlaid the keys and arrows which strobed to the direction of his mouth in his field of view.

Billy moved first one key, then the other, to his mouth and slid them into the device that was there. He had no idea how he knew what to do exactly, but instinct guided him with the insertion and application process.

Billy felt the glass keys, almost credit card-sized, move around down his throat to his abdomen. Once there, the two keys were moved around and within a minute of inserting them into his mouth, Billy had a screen open up showing a new prompt.

The prompt flashed what looked like computer code almost too fast for Billy to read. What he could make out, as it was happening, was some sort of release for his weapon systems and tactical capabilities. There were also many schemas for how to make various tools and devices using what was termed his "Dissembler" and his "Assembler," whatever those were. The information was not very distracting to him, as it seemed to be running in the background of his mind. After half an hour of waiting, Billy got bored and decided to check out the caved-in section of this room a second time while whatever was going on in his backside did its thing.

It looked like stone and dirt had caved in from outside the room and filled into it through a doorway in the wall. Deciding he had nothing better to do, Billy set to work removing the rubble, stacking it down in a pile further in the room. He moved carefully but quickly, taking this time to get used to having so many extra limbs moving all at once. The eight eyes he now had helped immensely with keeping track of everything, both while handling heavy boulders and watching the pile in case it collapsed further.

In around two hours, he guessed, he had opened up a large enough hole that he could move out of the room for the first time and discovered the passage only let out into a hallway. It was when he moved through the opening in the wall that Billy got some perspective of his own size, as well. As best he could tell, the doorway was made for humans, and when he stood normally he calculated his head was about four feet off the ground. A little quick math and he guessed each of his middle legs were about six feet long, and each of his front and rear legs about four and a half feet long. His body was that of a sleek spider, similar to that of a large jumping spider. If he lay down and spread out his legs, front to back, he would be almost nine feet long, and side to side, he would be only a little more.

Billy stretched out and maneuvered through the doorway and looked left. The right hallway was blocked. His eyes showed the ceiling was similar to commercial buildings back on Earth, as it had some kind of acoustical ceiling. A little poking, and one of the tiles came out. A quick peek, and he found the low clearance expected in a multi-story building of concrete and steel stuffed with cables, pipes and ductwork. Standing on tiptoes, Billy got the corner of his head up above the ceiling and saw the ceiling going to the left went as far as he could make out, disappearing off into the distance. The hallway, of course, did the same. Turning back to the room, taking one last look at his birthplace, Billy took a picture of the place, in case he returned one day in the future. That done, he turned and began carefully moving down the hallways into the darkness. As he walked, he occasionally plucked a tile from the ceiling and chewed on it, the soft metal they were made of crunching quietly.

Several hours, and many an empty room or dusty closet later, Billy was jolted out of his exploration by a new overlay appearing in his vision. Stopping suddenly caused him to emit a small belch of steam from his legs as they locked in place.

Congratulations! You have acquired two Experience tokens.

Experience points: +10,000.

These points are spent to modify your Attributes, Abilities and Disciplines.

Access your personal digital assistant to process upgrade requests and apply changes to your Attributes, Abilities and Disciplines.

"Ah, that must be what those key things were earlier." He thought for a minute, but before he could articulate his thoughts, another prompt appeared.

Your personal digital map is now available. Access your personal digital assistant to utilize its various functions.

Yep, that was it. Now, all he needed to do was wait for his digital assistant to integrate or whatever, and he could make use of those lovely Experience points. Excited about his new prospects, Billy continued to explore his abyssal birth place.

Only another hour or so passed when Billy finally located what looked like a passage upwards. Crunching on yet another ceiling tile, Billy poked his head into what looked to be the shaft for an elevator system of some sort. There was no visible method of ascension or descension, but the square stone vertical shaft plummeted down and rose up into total darkness.

Chapter 2

For the first time since awakening as a mechanoid, Billy got the chance to practice climbing as a spider. To his surprise and disappointment, it was simple and not at all unlike walking along a flat floor. He easily scampered up and down the stone shaft, never fearing his grip would slip. The clicking of gears, and popping of springs echoing strangely in the shaft as his feet gripped the walls while he climbed.

Pausing to look at the pads of his "feet," Billy got to wondering where he was, and what kind of place it was. Obviously, this was some sort of research and development facility, buried deep in the bedrock of the world, wherever that was, and he was somewhere in the middle of it. Giving himself a mental shrug, he reoriented himself and descended into the darkness. Maybe he will luck out and find something useful down there and he could make use of it. He had a hunch something interesting would be down there. If nothing, it would be passing the time until his digital assistant showed up.

It didn't take Billy long, only another hour or so of delving deep into the shaft, before he reached the bottom. He was worried, however, that there were no other exit portals the entire way down. He must be something like five or six miles straight down at this point, and there seemed to be only one destination at the bottom. The doors at the bottom of the shaft were closed tightly, but having eight appendages to settle himself with, Billy managed to force them open with ease.

With a *WOOOOF* of air that nearly broke his grip, air blasted past him as he clung to the inner shaft to fill the room in front of him.

"Negative pressure," he said to himself. His voice echoed up the shaft. This negative pressure is usually indicative of some sort of contagion that could be trapped inside. It only took a minute or two for the pressure to equalize, but already Billy could sense dust from far above slowly drifting down the shaft, knocked loose by the sudden changes.

Cautiously, Billy moved his bulbous body through the doorway into the large open area. It looked like an underground aircraft hangar, and the only thing he could see in it was a tall box a few hundred yards away in the center of the empty space. Except for himself, all was silent now, with dust kicked up earlier, slowly settling out of the air and blocking most sound. The scrubbers weren't on, meaning if anything toxic or virus-y were in-house, it was liable to spread now the seal was broken. Hopefully, it was nothing dangerous.

Billy looked around while he slowly approached the tall box. It looked to be a cube about 10 feet on the side. As he approached, he could make out several bundles of cabling stretching down from the high ceiling down to the top of it, where it penetrated the interior. Walking around it, Billy could see no doors, but on one side, the side opposite the elevator was what looked like a hand scanner.

On impulse, Billy leaned forward to blow off the dust before he remembered he was a robot spider, but to his surprise, a controlled burst of compressed air shot out and blew the dust from the pad.

"That's convenient," he said to himself while he studied the pad. It looked as ancient as the rest of the devices in the facility, and as he thought it would, it disintegrated as soon as he touched it, the decayed material clattering to the ground.

"Maybe I can stick my hand in there and pry something loose," Billy thought, examining the hole in the side of the box. A casual tap with one of his limbs showed the material it was made of was sturdier than whatever the pad was made of, for it thunked with the sound of a hollow metal box. Fortunately, nothing knocked back.

Giving a mental shrug, Billy brought up one of his manipulators and, plunged it into the hole and fiddled around until his finger tripped something and he heard a soft pop. Right after that, he heard a series of clunks as something was released inside the box.

Taking a step back, Billy watched as one of the sides popped loose and started to lower before halting. Billy moved forward and helped the thing open the rest of the way after a minute of waiting. Part way down, something broke and the 10 by 10 wall section slammed to the ground, making the dust on the floor blast up all over the place.

After waiting impatiently for the dust to settle again, Billy finally moved closer to the contents of the box. Inside, there was some sort of machine with many sides, and around all of the faces of the thing were wires and cables plugged into it. Interestingly, there were lights on. Several were steady, and one was blinking.

Getting in even closer, something inside Billy resonated with the device, and he felt himself emit a low hum, followed by a few clicking sounds. The lights immediately brightened, and a tiny drawer opened up. It looked like a slot for a plug. Tentatively, Billy raised one of his front arms and touched it. Something else resonated in Billy and he felt the tip of one of his digits click open and gently slotted into the port.

A simple screen popped up in Billy's field of view.

Downloading Data...

He waited as his mind began changing shape. He could feel memories moving around in his headspace and saw files of information arrange themselves. There were not many, but from the glimpses he got as they moved through his conscience, he knew he absolutely needed them and would protect them at all costs.

It only took a minute to download everything that was going to be downloaded, and once done, all of the glowing lights blinked off. He pulled his digit from the port, and it encapsulated itself. The screen also disappeared. He was glad he had taken the time to come down here, but now that this was done, he wanted to get out and take care of this quest. He did not know what it would entail, but he wanted to begin. As far as he was concerned, this introduction was stretching on too long, and he wanted to see what the world looked like aboveground.

With the important data compiled and stored, it was time to get moving. Before he turned to leave, however, a new screen popped up in his view.

Please Dissemble the device. The components will be assimilated to provide the Assembler with the necessary materials for maintenance.

Scratching his spider chin with his spider digit, Billy gave himself a mental shrug and reached in to pull the strange device out. The cables and wires snapped off with almost no effort. The thing itself was dense, and he rolled it around with his manipulators, but all the sides looked the same, more or less. Giving another mental shrug, Billy turned to the elevator shaft, device in hand.

Placing the device in the small set of manipulators that weren't feet-hands, Billy began the walk back up the shaft as his Dissembler… Dissembled. Disassembled. Whatever it was doing. He wasn't chewing this time, his mouth parts were painstakingly taking it apart while his manipulators rotated it on their own. It went fast, almost like taking bites, but he was steadily taking it apart with his mouth.

The whole way back up the shaft, Billy continued to gnaw on the device, and once he passed the point where he entered the shaft, he was almost done with it. The extra sensitive paw things Billy used to handle the device were intriguing. He knew spiders had these things, but he never really thought that he would have them also. He did know that as he was this mechanoid spider thing, his front feet could act as hands in a pinch but after hours of handling this block of material, he knew these things were far better manipulators. His feet were his feet, and his manipulators were his hands.

At long last, after what seemed like half a day of climbing, Billy finally got the prompt he was waiting for.

Looking forward to seeing how far he had left to go and finding no end in sight, Billy moved himself into a corner and settled in to do some reading. It was also fortuitous that he had finished the device just now. He could put his full attention into learning about himself and this new world. Thus, settled down, he thought, "Menu."

Something wiggled suddenly in his stomach. Well, it wasn't his stomach; it was his spider abdomen. Something began moving around in there. Feeling unsettled by this sensation but not fearful, he waited as patiently as possible. After a moment, the wriggling stopped and he felt something on his back pop loose. Having eyes on top of his head allowed Billy to watch as a tiny critter popped out of the hatch, turned and closed the hatch, then it began clambering over him to mount on his head.

Billy followed it to his head and got the feeling he was going cross-eyed with eight eyes, and had to look somewhere else to clear his head. In short order, the little critter settled down on a spot in front of his eyes, above his Dissembler, and clamped onto his face. As soon as he heard the click of it settling down, a new window popped up in his view.

"Hello there! Nice to meet you, dear." The sense he got from the message was almost grandmotherly.

Billy moved to scratch his chin as he read this. A little burp of steam emitted from his back end and sputtered out as a valve stuttered closed.

"Um, hello there. Are you the thing that just climbed out of me?" As Billy thought the words, they appeared on the little screen in his mind, like a chat box.

"Yes. I exited your Assembler after my construction was finished. This place here, on the front of your head, has an access port specifically for me and those like me, to plug in so we can communicate on the internal communications relay."

"Uh, right. So, you are my new Digital Assistant? Aren't you a bit too... tangible to be digital?" He thought at the text box where his words were typed and watched the question appear. It was kind of neat watching his thoughts make words on computer screens, even if they weren't in English but some machine language he could read.

"I have a digital avatar I am uploading right now!" And with that, a smaller, holographic version of itself popped into view and moved around. The screens using text winked out, and the little blue holographic avatar of his assistant climbed all over the place.

"You are in rough shape, buddy," The tiny holographic spider said to Billy in a cheery old lady voice. It didn't speak out loud, but somehow, Billy could hear it speaking directly into his head. "You need some serious maintenance before we get outside. You need lubrication, and some parts replaced, and others polished. Oh, but this is a joy indeed. I never thought I'd live to see the day you would walk this world." The tiny holo wandered around, checking each limb carefully, inspecting ports, grease packing joints, fittings, bushings, bearings, gears, and cogs, its tiny feet making no sound as it moved around.

"Well," Billy spoke internally, "I don't think I got to pick where I ended up when I acquired the Quest Prompt. Speaking of which, do you know anything about that?"

The tiny holo continued to inspect Billy, choosing not to answer immediately, so Billy settled in for a good long wait. Every once in a while the little holo would request he move this limb or that limb, to roll this way or that, and to do a number of strange tasks with his body. In only a few minutes, the little thing had completely gone over Billy's frame and a small screen popped up in front of Billy for his inspection.

The list was quite detailed, and required a number of things to be done, none of which he had any clue as to how to accomplish. Fortunately, his assistant.

"Hey, what can I call you? I can't keep thinking of you as "Assistant" or "Holo." Do you have a name?"

The eerie blue holo clambered in front of Billy and rubbed its abdomen with its rear legs for some reason. It was very spider-like.

"Hmm, I think you can call me Charlotte."

"LIke the book?" Billy asked.

"Exactly like the book," Charlotte said.

"How do we get these maintenance things checked off?" Billy hoped this personal assistant was literally that, but he wasn't sure.

"Well, I put in a request to the Assembler to make a few things. It shouldn't take me long to get you back into ship-shape once you approve them. It was a good thing you Dissembled that device earlier; it had many of the components necessary to build the tools and parts I need to work on you."

"What does "Dissemble" mean? I have seen a couple notes on this, but shouldn't it be called a Disassembler?" Internally, Billy signed off on the parts request and soon, the Assembler in his abdomen began processing each line item. The sensation was quite unique.

Charlotte took a few minutes to explain this part of his anatomy, and for that, Billy was thankful. The little old granny manner of Charlotte came across as very caring, and much like an elementary school teacher. He got the feeling she would be eternally patient with him until he understood whatever it was they were talking about or doing.

"Okay, that makes sense to me. It takes raw materials and makes things. Do you have access to my memories? I mean, you pulled the name Charlotte from my past."

Charlotte's avatar crawled up and around the walls while they talked, and finally, she replied. "Yes and no, Billy. I have access to some of your memories, enough to put together points of reference for your language and create an image of who you are and what some of your needs may be. Nothing more, I promise." She seemed genuine in this answer, and Billy felt a little better. She was unaware of some of his more private moments.

"Alright, then, Charlotte, how long before this maintenance is completed?"

WIthout saying a word, a screen popped up with a list of estimated times for the long list of tasks to be completed. Most are grayed out, and have a little arrow beside them. Mentally tapping on an arrow, Billy found it was a list of raw materials. He needed to do this sidequest first, in order to ensure he was in top form once he got out of this ancient catacomb, dungeon, place. Without a fuss, Billy stood up and moved to the next door up the shaft.

As Billy explored, he had Charlotte explain the mapping functions he was supposed to have. She even walked him through accessing the last 24 hours in order to process his locations until they were current. In his mind, Billy pieced together a picture of many layers and lines forming the innumerable passageways and rooms he had explored since awakening. Using this mapping ability, Billy was easily able to search several floors with rooms and hallways crisscrossing without worry of becoming lost or turned around. He had slowly ticked off the items required to fulfill his maintenance needs, and in what felt like half a day, what he thought was about 12 hours, he had finally found the last of the things he needed: purified lithium grease.

The number of things he had to locate and dissemble was far more than he thought would be normal for something his size, but Charlotte was adamant she required every item in order to fully repair Billy and bring him back to optimal condition. Why did he need to eat 45 decomposing chairs. Who knew? He would just have to wait and see.

"Now, Billy, I need you to shut down for about three days while I perform repairs. I need to remove parts and reconstruct others. Online, you will essentially feel all of the parts being removed and reinstalled, but offline, you will not. Before you go offline, I need you to finally open your Menu, access your Status, and apply the Experience points you have. With those selections, I will be able to incorporate any substantial changes directly afterward, so we can combine two maintenance cycles into one big one." During this speech, Billy had watched Charlotte walk back and forth in the room as a holo, where she marked out a spot on the floor of the room.

"And I need you to settle down right here, so that I have enough space to work and be in close proximity to other essential minerals and materials should those be required." Her little holo moved just outside the marked area and vanished.

Curious about what he would find on his Status page, Billy opened up his Menu and mentally selected it to open. Immediately, he found out why Charlotte had wanted to do this maintenance as soon as possible and before leaving this underground facility. All of his Attributes were grayed out. He was unable to determine how strong he was or how much health he had, among other things.

Carefully positioning himself on the spot on the floor, Billy arranged his limbs just the way Charlotte had wanted while he pondered his Status. The cost of raising any given stat had a requisite Experience expenditure attached. The higher the stat rose, the greater the cost. His initial Experience point pool was not small by any means, but it definitely limited Billy in choices for his own personal improvement.

After an hour of crawling through the veritable library of information describing each of his Attributes, Talents, Skills, Database, Construction Schema, and so on, Billy had decided he most needed to determine how he wanted to grow from now on. He would be limited to these maintenance cycles in the future in order to enhance his capabilities, and he would need time to perform these upgrades, so he searched for the various means he could mitigate the downtime or bypass it entirely. He did not want to be vulnerable for such long periods of time if he did not have to.

He also decided that as the ancient mechanoid spider-robot hybrid being that he was, he would need to be very careful in how he moved through the world. So he sought out things that would help him travel many terrains as well as things that would lessen the damages incurred from traveling unique pastures, such as total vacuum or the bottom of an ocean. He located a few interesting Talents and ordered some upgrades there.

Billy also knew that, in the future, his ability to create things from other things would get to the point where he would be continually hunting down raw minerals and such to repurpose, so he located a schema that would produce smaller bots that would attach to his undercarriage. These little critters would detach on command to scavenge whatever he selected. The selections would be highlighted wherever he looked and produce a holographic marker, and the things would travel to them and work.

Last, Billy decided he needed to manage his Attributes. These included things like Durability, Speed, Stability and Structural Strength, as well as a few other things such as Processing Capacity, Steam Pressure Regulation, Pressure Capacity, Exhaust Management, and so on. The cost of raising these Attributes was not high initially, but it did climb quickly when points began piling on them. As most of them were grayed out right now, Billy had figured he'd put at least a point in everything available before focusing on his particular build, removing the grayed-out status of them as he did so.

After he had finished purchasing and distributing all of his points, leaving himself with only a few dozen remaining Experience points, Billy took one last look around. If all went well, in three days, he would wake up to a far stronger, faster, and sleeker body, with much more utility and capacity. "While I'm asleep, Charlotte, if you have any questions about my selections, feel free to make the best choices you can for me. I trust you have my best interest in mind."

'I will, of course, do my best, Billy. Now select the Apply button, and I will see you soon," The little holo of Charlotte looked almost excited to begin as Billy mentally chose Accept, and he fell into darkness yet again.

The darkness did not last very long, however, and soon Billy was blinking away bright sunlight as he found himself once again in a park. Looking around, he spotted the old man from the last time he was here, and he was sitting on the grass some distance away.

Billy moved to the old man and saw him sitting beside a small stream, throwing bits of something in, which was being eaten by the fish residing therein.

While feeding the fish, the old man said, "I see you have located the things you needed to begin your journey, young man. I should say, young mechanoid. Your humanity is now behind you."

Billy paused for a moment, examining how he felt about the mention of his former life and his former body. He found he did not have any regrets there and so shrugged off the old man's words in his spidery way. "I have no regrets. I rather enjoy being what I am now," he said as he sat down beside the old fellow. Even his body here was that of the mechanical spider he was now.

"I took a look at some of the things you have done so far, and I must say I am impressed. You did not dwell long on your predicament and have striven forward into your destiny with no complaints." The old man chuckled at these words and Billy looked over at him to see a small smile playing on his lips.

"Why? Do many people cling to the past or something?"

"No, they simply cannot cope with the pressure of something so different or die before accomplishing much."

Billy felt only a little uncomfortable at this. He hadn't been aware he would be in any serious danger upon arrival in the new world. After a few more minutes of quietude Billy had thought to ask a question he wanted to ask last time he was here.

"Did I die on Earth?" He was very curious to discover the answer. He didn't recall any dying, but he did know that his presence here preceded a landslide happening right by his face.

"No. You did not die. We cannot select candidates who have died to go on these quests. Once the spirit leaves a body, it, well, that is not for you to know right now, Billy."

Billy once again looked at the old man and saw that he was not upset by the question, only firm in not answering it fully.

"Fair enough. So, I did not die, and I managed to begin this quest. I had a little time before I went into my maintenance cycle to review some of the information you gave me, and I did not find anything that linked me to the internet there. I did locate a Special Ability that would allow me to do the same thing. Was that what I was given, the chance to choose the ability?" Billy had chosen to utilize that particular ability, it was a special one and had only cost a single Experience point, so that had been a no-brainer for him.

"I suppose so. The link embedded in the Experience crystals you incorporated into yourself seems not to have worked out as planned. It appeared you were in much rougher shape than I had previously thought." The old man grabbed some more of the things he was feeding the fish and tossed them into the water.

"I figured it was something like that, honestly. Once I gained access to my Status and saw how damaged I was, I thought it might have been processed wrong. My Assembler was heavily damaged and was only able to process about 2% of the total Experience you gave me."

"I can do nothing, unfortunately, to recover the lost Experience. I think, however," He looked over to Billy, "You will have little problems adapting."

Billy nodded at this as best he could as a spider. He knew he had chosen as well as he could with his Status so that he could be as adaptable as possible without forfeiting durability. He knew, at some point, he would have to fight something and that being as tough as possible would be necessary. He also knew he needed to be strong and all the requisite things necessary for a machine to meet those needs, even if he was new at being the machine. He knew he would indeed have little trouble adapting to events in the future, assuming he survived long enough, thanks to his planning.

Billy asked the old man, pointing down into the water with one of his many feet, "Are those fish?" He saw the things casually consuming the bits of stuff the old man tossed into the water, not fighting each other but greedily eating whatever came their way.

"What do you think, Billy? Are these fish?" The old man tossed more of the stuff into the water, and the fish moved to consume it.

As Billy focused on the fish, the sunlight from above played on the water and off the animal's intricate scales. This distorted the shape of the fish somewhat, but as far as he could tell, they were only that: fish.

"They look like fish to me," he said to the old man, who nodded.

"I wasn't sure. When you came here, this place came into being at the same time and I thought I'd feed them. They seemed hungry."

"I see," Billy said, watching the fish be fish. "Do you know how lo…"

Billy snapped awake before he could finish his question. That seemed to be the theme with the old man, apparently.

Billy could both feel and hear his new and improved self waking up as the various magical and mechanical components which he knew acted as his organs cranked up. The quiet but powerful magical furnace he had for a heart burned much more efficiently and hotter than before, making heat boil the water inside him faster. This produced the steam which moved his turbines and pistons with more power. His gears and bearings moved almost silently. His suspension much improved, his balance more profound. He could even think more clearly. All of this would allow Billy to function as this mechanoid being and explore the world more efficiently. And possibly save it. That was the plan, anyways.

Billy had many screens up in his vision a few moments after waking up from his maintenance cycle. Charlotte had informed him it had taken several additional days due to some of the more eccentric changes he had applied to his Status upgrades coupled with a lack of necessary minerals nearby. His bulbous abdomen had been entirely reshaped and reworked to reflect his new Attributes and Abilities. He was more compact and far lighter than he had been now that he had replaced or upgraded ancient parts with slightly newer ones.

One thing Billy had brought back with him was knowledge of plastics, which he had used to search through some logs and embedded schematics prior to shutting down to incorporate into his new form. He knew that most of the things he needed were parts that would be easily replaceable or ablative, and by using the schema for plastics he had managed to combine several of his upgrades with parts made of the stuff.

The new plastic covers provided his parts with protection from the environment and were designed to be easily removed for quick repairs and maintenance. He was pretty happy about this because most of those parts acted as small storage areas, camouflage surfaces, and simple armor. It also made him much lighter. His interior framework was able to be modified much easier thanks to other upgrades he had, and primary to that was a small horde of scavenger bots made of different kinds of plastics and a minimum of necessary metals.

Some aspect of his anatomy provided a magical force to animate these bots with the turn of a key each had, and he was limited to only two, so he had taken a moment or three while he was deciding on his Attributes to doodle out a schematic of his own for them. They worked out quite well, and he managed to bypass some size limitations by using plastics and the anatomy of a crab from earth with one tiny claw and one giant one. This let him mirror them for easy side storage and low drag on his overall form.

"Charlotte, I love what you've done with this! I feel great, like I could run forever, or punch through a brick wall." Billy's excitement did nothing to curb Charlotte's stoicism, for she only stood where she had been when he reactivated and watched him clamber all over the room.

"Well, I had to make some changes when I got to the scavengers, but your notes helped me figure out what to do there. Also, the duration was longer than initial estimations were made. I had to locate additional materials to complete some of your upgrades. Your choice to use the titan metal was a wise one, but unfortunately, most of the remaining metal in this place is a composite of the stuff, and processing it took some time longer than other materials. How you knew about that stuff," She shuddered her little holo body, which Billy understood to be the equivalent of a human head shake.

"I knew you could handle the changes, Charlotte. You're the best," he said to her little holo. She did not respond, but he took that in stride. "Alright, Charlotte, let's get out of here and see what's out there in the world."

With that, Charlotte's holo vanished. The pile of trash surrounding the space Billy had occupied for maintenance was presumably useless. He checked his internal stores and found he did have one tiny little problem.

"Charlotte," he began.

"I know, Billy. I could not locate any," She said, expecting the question.

"Right, so now we head straight out. No dilly-dallying." Billy pulled up his map and set it to overlay in an out-of-the-way spot in his mind. He quickly maneuvered to the elevator shaft and began climbing upward. His lightened weight and new Attributes made moving practically effortless and orders of magnitude more quiet. Before, he was clicking and clacking, hissing, squealing and screeching. Now he was all super-quiet whooshes, and barely detectable gear rotations, and screwing motions, and little wastewater expulsion. He had been low on water days ago, but now it was worse. His upgraded system required more to cool other parts, and it being so low meant he was still operating at less than 30% efficiency.

Unconcerned with the running clock, Billy focused on locating water as fast as possible. He used his new map function to filter out as much of the noise his other senses detected to try and sniff out moisture. He had been in an area with a cave-in, and if he were underground, it was likely water had tried to get in from somewhere at some point in time.

As Billy came upon elevator doors, he would pry them open and give a furtive "sniff" to see if water was nearby. There were no signs on any of the dozen or so floors he had stopped at, and he was getting a little nervous. He only had a couple more hours of time left before he would have to cut power to 10%, and this would only serve to slow him down even further.

Still, Billy strove upward. He checked his map once more and counted the distance from where he had awoken, and was mildly surprised to learn he had traveled nearly 20 miles straight up. What was so astonishing about that was how not on fire everything was. On Earth, going a few miles down meant an incredible increase in heat. But this world seemed not to suffer from this particular issue. Or there was something else going on.

Billy continued to climb, forgoing stopping and checking other floors. His only goal now was the top floor. He required a particular molecule, and he hoped once he popped out of the top of this place, there would be some he could collect. His boiler was operating at incredible efficiency when compared to how rough he had been prior to his maintenance cycle. He hadn't been aware, but he had been limited both on power and efficiency for more than half a day, and he had wasted a large portion of water he had managed to have stored in his reserves on processing garbage.

Now, he was borderline critically low. He only hoped, as he put several feet in front of several others, that he would escape. Otherwise, he would end up like those side characters in those izuchi anime who died on arrival.

Fortunately, Billy only had to climb for a couple more hours before reaching a point where going up was no longer an option. The top of the shaft was marked with a large set of doors, which he spent a few minutes forcing open. As soon as he pried the doors open a crack, his sensing organs detected copious amounts of water nearby. The smells of this world were somewhat muffled to Billy. As a human, he had the use of the combination of a nose and a mouth to provide the taste of things. Smell was an important part of the flavor perception. As a mechanoid, he had special magical and mechanical parts that interpreted his environment and fed him a magical stream of sensations matching what he was familiar with as best as could be done.

When the doors finally separated as far as they could go, Billy got his first real look at what life could be like in an alien world. He knew that he was and was not an alien, but he found it exciting to see life in a world humans had never seen before. Humans from Earth anyways.

The hallway this elevator shaft had opened up to had large mounds of stuff blocking it. Large, stinky piles of stuff ran along the walls, leaving a narrow pathway for him to navigate. His very large primary eyes took in all the details of the tunnel far better than they had earlier, as there was now a decent addition of natural sunlight filtering in from a number of breaks in the ceiling.

Billy carefully avoided walking on any of the goop on the floor while also avoiding exposure to direct sunlight, but this became more complicated as larger holes above let in more light.

"Charlotte, do you have any idea what this stuff is?" Billy asked his little assistant while hoping she might know something.

Billy reached out one of his feet and poked the goop gently, and it came away with a bit of the substance on it. Charlotte popped out of her little niche and scampered down the leg to inspect the goo. After a moment, she said, "It is excrement."

"Gross," Billy said, carefully scraping the stuff off his foot while Charlotte returned to her port to plug back in.

Billy was very grateful he had made some physical changes to himself. His previous bulbous body would have been forced to scrape against one side or another of the piles. His new, thinner body fit easily in the hallway and he more easily avoided the piles of poo along the walls.

Not far through the temple of poo, Billy had found a large section of missing ceiling and reached up with several feet to pull himself out. He was very careful to do so, not knowing what would be there. His concern was mirrored in Charlotte, for he thought he felt here wiggling in the port on his face. It almost tickled.

"Charlotte, you are starting to tickle my nose," Billy said, doing his best to resist the urge to scratch her off.

"Oh dear, I am sorry, Billy. I am just so excited to see the world!" Her little old lady's voice in his head was filled with wonder as he saw the sky above, with thick white clouds slowly blowing in a strange blue sky.

"Yeah, I am too, Charlotte." Billy ended up having to pull himself up by placing four of his front feet along the hole to carefully lift himself up. He popped his head up quickly to look about, then ducked back down. Quickly, he scuttled around 180 degrees to look the other way. The next time he popped up and saw it was clear, he pulled himself all the way out in one smooth motion, then hunkered down over the hole to make as low a profile as possible while his nerves calmed down.

Already, he could feel his thirst. To his utter delight, not a mile away, there was what looked like the edges of a gigantic lake, short waves lapping along a sandy beach.

"Charlotte, we are lucky I woke up when I did. If I hadn't, it's likely that lakewater would have eventually worked its way through the ground and made a hole into the facility. Once that happened, it would have filled it in and buried us down there forever." Billy saw on his map that there were also several rivers or creeks nearby. From what he could tell, they all moved to the lake.

Spinning slowly around to get the best view of his surroundings possible, Billy turned to the nearest tributary creek and moved forward. With quick bursts of speed, he dashed across the open ground, dropping down every few dozen feet to look for danger. He remembered seeing something online about spiders doing this. It was easier for them on Earth, however, being as small as they were. Here, he was large and heavy and with being covered in dark plastic plates, quite visible against the bright green grass. His frame was made of metal, and being the size he was, he had to be careful not to step down too hard, or he risked sinking into the soft soil with each step.

Chapter 3

In no time at all, Billy had arrived at the creek. He moved away from the lake, however, to find a place he could safely nestle down into and set Charlotte out to gather the water he needed. The process was simple enough though, and it only took half an hour to slowly pull water up a hose to his purifier before dumping the pure water into his water storage systems. He carried about 15 gallons of water, which was far more than he wanted to carry around in himself. However, this will be the first time his new body is at 100% efficiency.

Once he was topped off, Charlotte helped him retract his gathering hose and stored it. Afterward, she did a quick clamber over his body to inspect the plates covering him, checking for damage and adjusting anything that had come loose or shifted. She made sure he was in perfect shape in less than five minutes, then sent him the very short list of completed tasks for him to view after she returned to her port.

While Charlotte busied herself with her inspection, Billy carefully ramped up the internal furnace in himself, and occasionally, he would release small jets of steam from multiple ports along his underside. The large number of ports helped to muffle the hiss of steam. The alternative was a far larger exhaust port, but Billy preferred a more dispersed pattern to a large hole that led straight to his heart. He had seen those Star Wars movies and knew such ports were only weak spots.

Once the furnace had produced proper steam power and Charlotte plugged in, Billy stood up and did something he had always wanted to do since he awoke as a spider but couldn't because he was stuck in narrow concrete tunnels underground, and he jumped. A blast of power hammered in his legs as heat and vapor slammed down through them. The power was so great that it not only launched Billy forward nearly 20 feet, but was able to get him more than 10 feet off the ground as well.

Even as his feet left the ground, springs pulled powerfully on them to prepare them for his landing. He had known instinctively how they needed to be arranged to get them to absorb all of his momentum in one go, but he had never actually done it before. His optical overlay showed the location he had chosen to land and highlighted the best places for his feet to be for the best landing. It only took a little more than a second for the jump to occur, but to Billy, it took many more than that.

His processing power accelerated when he jumped, and while he was flying through the air, thanks to the blast of power from his abdomen and his legs, he had done a rapid scan of the area around him to check for danger. He had seen nothing that stuck out, so he turned to focus on the landing. Strong shocks compressed air as they spread out the weight of his landing. He noticed they sounded exactly like brand new car shocks when they moved fresh off the line, but he had quite a few more than cars had inside himself.

Billy had not landed at a dead stop. He moved forward immediately to preserve some of the momentum. This allowed him to shoot off like a bullet across the ground. A few miles away was a wooded area. He thought it may provide more cover than the tall, whipping grass he was dashing through. His legs moved with literal mechanical repetitiveness, and the grass only made scratching sounds on his undercarriage and across his legs as he tore through the grass towards the trees.

Glancing at his map, which he kept transparent and off to the side of where he focused, he could see he was traveling much faster than a horse overland. He was dealing with tough dirt and grass, but as best he could tell, he was hurtling along at a cool 35 miles per hour.

In what felt like no time at all, Billy cleared the edge of the woods and slowed rapidly as he tried to process the more complex environment. He could feel his internal flywheels consume his forward motion and turn it into centripetal force to slow him. He was vibrating slightly until his braking system quietly slowed the rapidly rotating metal discs. In moments, he was standing still.

His hyper-sensitive eyes took in the local vegetation quickly, and he saw there was no motion other than a few birds he had startled when he'd dashed into the shade of these trees. Billy had hoped these things would be large enough to support his weight so that he could get a view from higher up. They weren't, so he would just have to resort to his plan B.

Angling up slightly, Billy placed one of his targeting points on the open sky, and a small hatch on his back popped loose. A wide, flat flying drone was shot forward on the steam catapult it had been settled in and zipped up through the canopy. Billy held still while he studied his surroundings and waited for the small drone to return. He did not share the powerful communication link with the drone as he had with Charlotte, but the drone was capable of taking a few images for a few minutes before its momentum was lost and it fell back in his direction. Right on cue, the little flat drone floated through the tree branches to bounce lightly on the ground a few feet away. He carefully reached over and grabbed it up, then positioned it back on the spot on his back where it docked back in.

A few seconds later, Billy had images pulled from the drone and he was excited to see that not far off was what looked like smoke from chimneys. They were a few miles out, but all of that distance was through the woods.

"Charlotte, do you think we can get there before the sun changes in the sky too much?" He asked her, scratching his chin with a manipulator.

Charlotte's holo blipped into existence in front of him and scratched its little spider head very cutely with a long leg. "I am sure we can make it there with time to spare. From what I can tell, it looks like it is still early morning."

"Do you think there will be people in the woods here? We seem to be between this village and the great lake behind us." Billy was only a little concerned with interacting with whatever lay ahead. He was very fast and quite strong. More importantly, he was very difficult to see in this shadowy place, thanks to his armor.

He had planned out a number of possible color palettes for his plating, and he had gone with a standard green, dark green, and brown pixel style. It was a static design, but it helped break up his profile.

"What do you think they will look like, Charlotte?" Billy asked while carefully skittering through the forest floor. The sparse trees had many open places for foot travel, but there were many strange fruit-bearing bushes that scattered all over the place, breaking up trails.

"I am not sure, Billy. My logs do not indicate what any particular thing looks like. It seems to not contain much information on biological life here. It is very strange," She said, her holo doing some sort of little spider dance while Billy walked.

"Strange how? Like the data was deleted? Or do you think it was corrupted?" A few minutes into the woods and, the fauna became more abundant. There appeared to be mammals of various types, not much unlike Earth animals. There were also a number of insects. He did not see any indication of reptiles, no snakes or lizards, or salamanders.

Back home, Billy had often found lizards in his house when the weather turned cold. They would cram into anywhere they could to find warmth when things got chilly to hibernate. He had a natural eye out for them, and he could see nothing that showed they were present. He was curious about how the ecology here was balanced when he heard the deep-chested growl of something nearby.

Instantly, Billy froze. He muffled his exhaust and prepared to move at the first sign of trouble. He slowly scanned the area around him with all his senses. He had been sniffing the air for anything recognizable, but everything he came across was a new scent to him. His eyes were his biggest sensory organ, and he cranked up the contrasts to 11.

He then clearly saw there was something big a dozen yards to his left. He had stopped right next to a tree when he heard the growl, so Billy carefully and ever so slowly readjusted his legs to hide more of his form. The internal stresses of silencing all of his movement would not allow him to be totally silent for very long, but he only needed a moment to conceal himself from whatever was there.

The one major benefit Billy had over that of his previous human life was that he was large, but he was also irregularly shaped. His only real weakness was his eyes. They were very hard acrylic-like lenses of some good size, and those things reflected light quite nicely. It was likely he had reflected something and that is what caught this thing's attention. He made a mental note to devise some shutters to protect his eyes. Not having the ability to feel how sensitive they were to touch made it hard for him to treat them as anything other than camera lenses, which he saw in his mind as computer screen images of immeasurable clarity.

Once his legs were arranged just so, Billy very slowly lowered himself and prepared to dash up this tree or leap off of it if necessary. The growl continued while he positioned himself. It was all for naught, however, as just before he began the motion to dash away, a shadow fell across him. His array of eyes saw the silhouette of the shape, but he had to turn to actually see what it was.

To his delight, it appeared to be a bipedal being wearing strangely colored clothing. It had a spear held at the ready in his direction. It looked like it was pointed directly at his large eyes.

The being before him looked masculine, but he was unsure. The features were not that of a human that much was sure. The "skin" was something more akin to bark than skin, with its dark woody textures and stiff appearance. He had a long, wide snout similar to a dog, and strange, horizontal goat-shaped eyes. The figure and he looked at each other for a solid minute before Billy decided to make the first move.

Slowly and carefully, Billy raised his manipulator hand and waved. "Hello," he tried to say.

At the first motion of his small appendage, the being took a single step back. The speartip never wavered from Billy's eyes, however.

In an effort to appear less harmless than he thought he might look, Billy rubbed his two manipulator hands together in what could be interpreted as nervousness. "Do you understand me?" Billy asked aloud. He was not sure how he was speaking, but it sounded very close to what he recalled himself sounding like back on Earth, though he was not speaking English.

The being in front of him lowered the spear slightly. It whistled a series of notes and the growling beast stopped growling. Billy could hear it make its way through the bushes towards them.

Billy tried to remember that he was a living person in the body of a machine and had to make small motions that made him look more alive purposely. He knew that totally stationary objects would not be considered alive, and so by acting alive, he would not be treated as a thing, hopefully. A few seconds passed with the two staring at each other when a large, grumpy-looking boar stomped through the bush and trundled over to the being in front of Billy. It snorted at the person's leg and a hand gently patted its head. It turned to look back at Billy then plopped down right there. The being lifted its spear and settled the butt into the dirt and squatted down. It took its hand and smoothed out a patch of ground, then used a finger to draw a symbol on the dirt. Billy dipped his body down carefully to get a look at what the symbol was and could not make heads or tails of it.

He rotated his body left and right a little bit, hoping to get across the idea that he did not know what it said. Instead, he tapped himself with his manipulator hand and said, "My name is Billy."

The being looked at him as he did this but did not tense. Billy tapped himself again and repeated his name. He then moved his hand to indicate the other fellow and cocked his whole front half in a questioning manner.

The being did not respond to Billy, instead running a hand through its pale green hair. It looked almost like running a hand through very soft, floppy, narrow feathers that acted exactly like hair. The being let out a sigh, and in response, Billy had too, although unintentionally; a pressure release valve let off some steam and it stuttered closed.

The fellow in front of him hopped back when he'd done this, but Billy was careful not to move himself. He tried to remain as harmless looking as possible while not giving off vibes that screamed steampunk spider-bot murder-machine.

After a moment of staring at each other again, the being straightened and hefted its spear as if prepared to leave. It waved Billy to follow and turned to leave. The boar scrambled up and quickly followed the fellow, and Billy scratched his spider head.

"Any ideas, Charlotte?" He asked her on the internal communications relay.

"Not precisely. I have some information about the history of this place, but nothing in my records matches what we are observing. They are vastly out of date. None of the flora is recognizable. I do not know what that brown animal is. I do not recognize the tree-skinned creature." She did not sound very concerned. She just provided the information he required. Not even her little holo was out now.

"Think it could be a trap?" Billy asked. He moved to follow the being when it had paused a dozen feet away, then turned to continue as he saw Billy moving.

"I don't know, Billy. I only hope we have some time to do a quick maintenance check to see how the systems behaved during your jaunt." She seemed only a little annoyed at his rough treatment of his systems, but he'd needed to test what his limits would be and only by doing something could he collect any data.

"You're no fun, Charlotte. We are out of that abyssal hole, and out in a world full of wonder. We get to explore the whole of everything and see it for the first time." His exuberance almost affected the tiny assistant, but she was far too professional for his rashness.

"I am your assistant, Billy, not your sense of adventure." She did not sound upset, but she did seem a little worried about what work she may have to do later if things turn sideways.

"It'll be fine, Charlotte," Billy said placatingly. "It looks like the people here only have spears and swords and stuff. I think we could handle those."

"It isn't about their threat level, Billy. I am concerned because you have not encoded your translator. I am certain part of the startup process involved its activation. And I am sure the component was installed. I even upgraded it after your Status updated." She turned a little from her port to look around.

"Besides," She continued, "I think we are fine. I do not detect any other complex life forms within a mile of our current position."

Billy thought about the translator issue as he walked behind his new friend. He didn't actually think of this as a friend, really. They had only just met. A quick glance at his Status confirmed he had indeed chosen a translator device installed, expanding his Knowledge Database storage capacity. He quickly recalled everything his audio and visual sensors recorded of his first interactions with this fellow and found only a few points where there could have been language spoken.

He also reviewed the message scribed in the dirt. He did a quick search through his memories and could not place any specific meaning on the lines. They could be language or not.

Billy was the first to react when the forest suddenly went silent. His mechanical body immediately dropped as low to the ground as possible as he let out a quick hiss of steam to alert his friend ahead. Straining, Billy pushed his audio sensors to their limit to try and pick out what had set him off to begin with. Then he felt it. A thump he barely perceived in his torso. It would be like feeling a thump deep in his chest, were he still human, laying flat on the ground.

On this thump, the being Billy had been following let out a sound, probably a curse of some sort, and dropped to the ground with their boar. They wrapped an arm around the animal and dragged it and himself under a rather large fungus that looked exactly like an old log at first glance. It was tube-shaped, like a straw, but a couple feet wide, and it drooped a little under its own weight. Its cap was more than wide enough to cover the being and his boar.

Billy, however, lay hunkered down with all of his legs pulled tight to his body. They stuck up regularly, however, the plating he had provided a visual camouflage, which broke up his profile very effectively. From above he imagined he would look not much different from a large mound of dirt and grass.

Minutes went by in total silence as the two hid. Internally, Billy's magically powered steam heart was preparing to vaporize water into steam in an instant. His pressure chamber was slowly filling with compressed air to aid if necessary.

The cracking of trees snapping echoed far off in the woods as if they were being rolled over by some silent bulldozer, moving closer by the second. Billy was watching the strange being to get some sense of how screwed they were when he noticed that they weren't showing any signs of fear. Since closing his eyes in reality was not an option, exactly, Billy closed his eyes inwardly and focused on the source of the sound and its motion. He felt the ground to try and detect the way in which the impact waves rolled through the ground. It took him moments to discover whatever was doing this was much further away already and continuing to move away.

Billy cautiously stood up and, walked over to the figure and used his manipulator arms to indicate they were not in danger at the moment. The person stood up and looked around as the sound slowly faded and the nearby trees stopped their shuddering. Few leaves fell, which Billy noted simply because of the absence.

"It looks safe, for now," Billy tried to say before forgetting that this being probably did not speak the machine language he knew. Being this close, Billy could make out bizarre whispering sounds coming from the bark-skinned being. They looked up when it recognized Billy was looking at him intently. There must be something in Billy's spidery eyes that gave him away, so he backed up a step to try and reassure the person he meant no harm.

To his surprise, the being gave a curt nod, picked up its dropped spear, and urged the boar to follow with a short whistle. The cracking of wood and the low rumble faded entirely as the two continued to head to wherever they were going.

Billy carefully cataloged the route he was taking through these woodlands. The trees sometimes formed odd clusters of three or four at seemingly regular intervals. This led to the strange lower vegetation making almost natural-looking paths all around, and as the trio traveled and Billy watched his map, he realized the path was perfectly navigating a maze. The bushes and trees created an intentional maze.

Every few minutes of silent walking, Billy had to release some of the steam built up in his system. Thanks to his Status upgrade, his new body more efficiently retained the water that would have otherwise been wasted with the exhaust. The little spurts of compressed air would, in the beginning, cause the strange figure he was following to glance back at him, but after a couple of hours of walking, they finally stopped reacting to it. Billy barely noticed it himself anymore. He knew he was decompressing occasionally, but it began to feel more like exhaling the longer he experienced life as this mechanoid.

Long hours passed and as the light in the sky continued to burn. Billy began to take note of new kinds of plants growing. The trees were also growing in a more random pattern, more natural. Small animals were often seen ducking away behind other plants or sticks, too, unlike the strange woodland, which held next to little else except the clustered trees, the weird bushes, and the occasional fungus clump. Billy also saw the fellow he was following looking more relaxed in their stride, almost happy to be returning to something more familiar than the strange maze of wood.

All of a sudden, coming around a roll in the ground, a large hill they had been slowly circling, Billy was met with a small open space surrounded by trees. There was a pair of 10-foot rods planted near the center of the clearing, about six feet apart from one another. There were beings going in and out from between them, and they would vanish going in or appear as they came out. They all arrived empty-handed and left loaded up with hunting successes. A path had been walked into the ground leading between them.

Checking his map to make sure he had this location marked, Billy followed the fellow between the pair of rods on either side of the pathway. There was a feeling of fuzzing around the edges of everything, and then it was gone. Once through, Billy paused and the person he had been following turned to him, waving a hand, but Billy was caught up in the city that practically appeared out of nowhere.

"Billy, pay attention. That strange fellow seems to want us to follow him over to that post by the wall." Charlotte's voice brought Billy out of his shock and he lurched forward to investigate the thing the fellow was placing his hand on.

It looked alot like a hand scanner you would find anywhere on Earth that used palm scanning technology just sticking out of the ground. As he watched, a nimbus of light surrounded the being's hand and a small beetle sitting on the top of the panel blinked green. It looked like a large lightning bug, with its strange orange and black wings, but it was almost two inches long.

Intrigued by what this thing was, Billy moved forward and placed his manipulator hand on the panel. It produced a nimbus of light for a moment, then it vanished. Then another light, this time a harsh orange, surrounded his hand. It, too, vanished. Then, a strange blue light surrounded Billy's hand, and he noticed he had received a prompt.

Register this as your current Resurrection point? Yes. No.

Billy mentally selected *Yes* and the prompt vanished. Right afterwards, the strange bug lit up green and Billy removed his manipulator hand, almost fidgeting in nervousness.

He turned to thank the person he had been following for hours and hours, only to see the being holding out a hand as if to shake his.

"Uh, hello there," Billy stuttered as he shook the person's hand. Doing so caused another prompt to pop up in Billy's view.

Ageel has invited you to learn the Knowledge: Language: Common Elven.

Do you accept the education for the cost of 10 Experience points? Yes. No.

Scratching his spidery chin with his other manipulator hand, Billy inwardly shrugged and selected *Yes*. Instantly, he got an update that his Knowledge Database for the Language Common Elven was learned successfully and that he had exchanged 10 Experience points with the elf by the name of Ageel Husker, the Swift.

"There we go, fella," Billy heard the elf, Ageel, say to him. The elf had a very rough-sounding Australian accent and it took Billy aback when he heard the translator apply the accent to him. He watched the elf form the words with his mouth, and heard the sounds coming from his mouth, but he couldn't place where the accent came from. "Now we can talk to one another without havin' to spend 10 times the rate for learnin' Knowledges out in the field." He'd said this as if it were common knowledge the cost was something to avoid.

"Yes, thank you for the help, uh, Ageel." Billy let go of the elf's hand and looked around at his surroundings. For all the people not 20 feet away, there was no sound to be heard whatsoever. "Why can't I hear the people over there?" He asked, pointing.

"Ah, you must have never been to a city before, fella. All cities have their own Zones. Once you cross into the Zone, you can get the full effect of the place. Come on, I'll show you around," Husker said, beginning to walk toward the city.

As soon as they stepped away from the poles, Billy's map changed entirely. It was as if he were no longer on the same planet. His area map vanished and a new map was being generated based on what he was seeing right now. He turned around and looked back to the woods he had just come from and saw the trees right over there. They just did not show up on his map.

The sound of a multitude of voices drowned out any questions Billy had about the sudden spatial shift, but this was nothing compared to the variety of beings that populated this place.

Everywhere he looked, there were what looked like shipping containers made of wood, but to the same dimensions and stacked in interesting pyramids. Each of the containers was differently personalized, even though they were the same size in every other way. Units were not placed side by side, but alternated being offset with stairs built on the side of the place sticking out furthest leading upward. This allowed the exteriors to be accessed without compromising interior spaces.

Billy was intrigued by the arrangement. It was as if some wood production facility had made thousands of these things in bulk, and people were buying them as housing. The efficient off-set stacking made multi-story structures that were always stable and accessible from any point along the base. The walls of the whole structure were basically one container thick. This left room on the interior of the pyramid for other structures that were protected by the houses, creating giant market areas where he saw creatures of fantasy selling all kinds of things.

Seeing not a single human as Billy followed Ageel past pyramid after pyramid, but seeing a myriad variety of fantasy creatures, characters, and what could be considered monsters put Billy at ease as to why his particular appearance did not put off this elf. He looked like a giant spider being. There were other insectoid beings all over, some flying, some crawling, others creeping along silken threads they produced that connected between pyramids, but none of them seemed interested in the least with Billy himself, even with the occasional pressure release.

Billy's map was exploding with prompts as every place of interest he walked past, dozens at a time, was being marked with information tags on his map. After a few minutes he'd had to minimize his map so it would stop blinding him with the flashing messages.

Tall, elven folk wearing a variety of clothes walked the streets with packs of heavily laden animals. Groups of short, stocky, bearded folk tromped around, making their own ruckus. Their heavy mail shirts and short-bladed axes clattered against their hardened leather leg covers as they moved past him, a few even ducking under him not to be slowed down by the traffic.

Billy flinched as one of them ran a hand along his belly and down the length of his abdomen, the sudden touch to such a sensitive place nearly causing him to kick the dwarf who'd done it. To his surprise, he also received a *Friend Request* from the dwarf who had touched him. Shrugging, he accepted and Orgar, The Oaken Stump, joined Ageel Husker, the Swift on his growing Friends List.

"Charlotte, pay attention to the places we can get some interesting items from, okay?" Billy sent the message to her via their internal relay. She managed to turn somehow and give him a look that said, "Duh," without actually saying anything.

Chuckling to himself, Billy set about following Ageel through the city outskirts. For the next hour they walked, and Ageel would occasionally point out a particular merchant that sold certain goods, or a farmer who sold some particularly good meat, and others he had pointed out to avoid. On several occasions Ageel had stopped by a couple of other elves to say something to them before continuing further into the pyramid city.

Each block of the city held one of the intricately arranged pyramids, and the interiors of all of them held different layouts for their occupants. Hundreds, maybe thousands of people lived in them. Many of the blocks they had passed looked to be doing well economically. However, the further Ageel took Billy, the worse the area began to look. Many of the places Billy now walked looked run down, or purposefully made to look uninviting. Most of the corners of the blocks had groups of armed citizens who seemed to be keeping the peace.

Between the pyramids, there were rope bridges of varying quality leading from one terrace of the housing to those on another block. The foot traffic on those bridges was nearly as great as that of the street level. The air was also filled with a variety of flying folk taking off or landing, yelling at this or that, and otherwise creating quite a ruckus. Oddly, Billy had seen few wagons despite the population density and standard of living.

When Billy had asked about this, Ageel had said, "The war with the humes has put a severe strain on the Kingdom of Flowers and the Lair of the Fey. The two groups were never really friendly, but with the humes running around slaughtering anything not like themselves, the people had been forced together here. This city, The Lair of the Fey, is one of the last bastions along the eastern coast of the continent for beings that aren't humes. And sometimes they do not all get along."

Billy took this information in stride. Back on Earth, even when there were only humans who held sway in the intellectual world, not all of them agreed with one another. He could see why the different people here might act similarly.

Just outside one particular pyramidal structure, which was painted mostly with purples and oranges, Ageel had stopped and turned to Billy. He had a pensive look on his face, but after a quick shake of his head, he put on a smile.

"Over there is where I live. I stay with a group of outlaws and outcasts who practice what the Council here deems taboo. A couple of fellas might be interested in asking you a few questions. It would go well if you answered them as best you can."

Billy looked around, taking note of the large number of similarly attired folk, all armed, paying quite a bit of attention to this conversation. He tried not to let it bother him, so he turned back to Ageel and bobbed his head. "Alright. I'll do what I can."

Billy gave the appearance of total calm as he followed behind Ageel into the interior structure of the pyramid compound. This particular one was almost walled off entirely to keep people out and was fortified.

"I didn't think to ask you earlier, but do you, by chance, need anything to eat?"

Ageel's question almost caught Billy off guard, but he was more than prepared for just such inquiries. "I could go for a bite to eat. Is there anything in particular you would recommend?"

Husker paused mid-step and scratched his head, thinking for a moment. "I can get ya something before the boss talks to ya. Can ya stomach spirits?"

Inwardly, Billy grinned. He had been hoping this would come up. "The stronger, the better, if you got it."

This seemed to calm Ageel further as the elf chuckled and ran a hand through his feathery hair, which had at some point changed color to a dirty black. His boar, which had followed closely to Ageel the whole way through the city, snorted a squeal and trotted ahead to disappear into one of the housing units. As soon as it entered the building, other squeals were heard, probably in greeting.

Doing his best to shrug as he looked back to Ageel, Billy carefully followed the elf between the gate guards into the compound. The place was well-lit and looked much larger from the inside than the outside. The bottom level was open all the way up to the seventh level, which is where the top level of units met and was supported by a four-way leaf column settled in the center of the irregular square.

All of the housing units had open access to the interior from the sixth level down to the ground level, and each of them had either ropes or ladders leading from their porch to the ground. As the lower floor was placed further away from the column than the one above, this let the higher floors have plenty of space to have a way down without tangling with their lower-level neighbors.

Billy was busy looking up and around at all of the people here. Many had gone quiet as the two of them entered the gates, and he saw that the hundreds of creatures here, elves, faerie, gnomes, dwarves, and more that he did not recognize stood in groups of threes and fours watching him and Ageel.

Ahead of them, Billy saw a rather heavily armed group lounging around the center column, and one of them looked quite mean. She wore some kind of shiny leather body armor. It was all black and very form-fitting. She had on black gloves, wore black boots, and had a black flower done up in her rich white, feathery hair that lay back over her head all the way down to the middle of her back.

"Ageel, you wiley old liar. What did you bring me today?" The woman, for clearly she was that veritably dripped sexiness, sauntered up to Ageel and got right in his personal space. She ran a gloved finger down the side of the elf's face and pinched his chin, shaking his head a little.

Before he could answer her, she pushed his chin away from her as he leaned to, probably, kiss her, and turned toward Billy as he watched the exchange. She advanced on Billy the same she had with Ageel, and ran her fingers over his legs as she closed on Billy's face. His very large eyes were filled with her red-lipped smile as she moved to look very closely at her reflection in his eyes.

"What have we here?" She said, raising a finger to tap on one of Billy's eyes, but he had backed up before she could touch the lenses.

"Uh, hi. I'm Billy. And I'm new to the area. I," he trailed off as he reviewed a prompt that had popped up.

Aurora has attempted to bind your spirit to her will.

Mental Reflex successful. You have resisted Aurora. Your will is your own.

As he read this, he saw Aurora make a pouting face. "Oh, boo. It seems you are not quite like the other ones. Very well!" She says and spins around, throwing a thumb over her shoulder toward Billy. "Cage it before it escapes."

Billy heard a loud clunk sound and felt the floor near him begin to shift. Having been prepared for this particular trap, Billy simply moved forward along the floor Aurora had just crossed. She heard him follow and Billy watched her look over her shoulder with a devilish smile. That was when he realized he had made a mistake.

As Billy watched Aurora turn, Ageel backed up a step, and a half dozen other fellows began approaching Billy from all around.

"Can we talk about this at least?" Billy asked, hoping that he would not have to go to war with the local underground immediately. "I don't know why you think I would enjoy being caged, but I assure you, Aurora, I will not be kept in one."

At the mention of her name Aurora's face grew ugly. "Don't call me that, hume trash. How dare you come into our sanctuary so boldly. We will take you and have you provide us some entertainment. And when we have had our fill, we will dismantle you before you have the chance to escape and report back to your hume masters."

Chapter 4

Aurora snapped her fingers, and the half dozen elves around Billy threw weighted nets over him. They all overlapped his body while he stood still and let them land. Charlotte gave him a quick update on the position of all of the nets, and Billy gave an internal shake of his head. The things were only rope, weighted with lead. At best, they would snap while just walking and would not hinder him.

Still, he did not wish to harm anyone here. Instead of fighting back, he simply squatted down, and used every other leg to lift all of the nets over himself. Stunned, the elves around him watched as he easily removed, folded and laid the weighted nets down on the ground around him.

"I do not wish to harm anyone here. I have important business elsewhere and would prefer to go in peace." One of the men went to approach Billy with a hammer in hand, and Billy let the man come.

The fellow brought back his arm, and let swing with the weapon, and it just clunked off the plating on Billy's leg. As far as he could tell, it did no damage. Before the elf could blink, Billy brought one of his legs up, opened its digits, and grabbed the tool. Be brought it around to his manipulator hand, and grabbed it, then he began chewing on it.

The entire block was silent as he ate the hammer, head and all. "Thanks for the snack."

"Uh," The elf stuttered.

Several other elves began to surround Billy with more exotic weapons. He got the feeling some of the weapons were not normal ones, either.

"Do not damage it," Aurora said as she walked back toward the column. Billy watched as several of her lieutenants followed her along with Ageel, who glanced back at Billy with a *'Ya do what ya gotta do,'* look.

"Alright, if you want a fight, a fight you have," Billy had quietly begun raising his magical boiler fire and stockpiling pressure during the netting. He had slowly increased his clockwork flywheel's speeds as he built up energy. He had even prepared his mind as he selected targets to strike one after another. Instead of doing any of that, however, he released his pent-up pressure and blasted backwards, right through the gate he had come in here with, to the astonishment of everyone.

Billy smashed through the shoddy iron gate that kept passersby out and rolled several times to slow himself down quickly. Popping back onto his feet, Billy saw he was easily 30 feet away from where he had been a moment ago. Without pausing, Billy spun and dashed up the street, back the way he had come not even five minutes ago, the shouts of dozens of voices calling out for his capture.

"Charlotte, I think we should avoid this particular part of the city," Billy said to his assistant as he climbed up a housing unit a few blocks away. He practically vaulted up the one side in near total silence thanks to his well-thought-out build. He knew at the beginning, he would need to escape or advance quickly and quietly, primarily playing into the role of all hunting spiders.

At the top of the unit, Billy turned to face the next building over and launched himself up and forward. To his dismay, his powerful launch knocked over one of the units he was standing on, and he heard it crash down onto a lower level as he caught himself on the side of a unit with a solid *THUMP*. Before too many voices called out, he whipped around to the opposite side of the building, snatching up a large tarp on the way, tossed it over his back like a giant cloak, and made his way down to the streets.

People saw him clambering down to the roadways, but as he was going carefully, nobody really said anything. There were any number of other creatures crawling and walking around and he did his best to blend into the masses heading towards the edge of the city.

Several hours later, and after taking a very winding path, the sun suddenly vanished. The instant night was a boon for Billy, even though he had no idea why the sky went instantly from day to night. He would not pass up this opportunity, however, and used the darkness to make his way through dense crowds of people in the streets, who were slowly making their way under the pyramids in droves while others were going about lighting lamps to stave off the darkness.

Once the sun had vanished, storm clouds rolled in, and rain began falling in fits and starts all throughout the city as Billy did his best to mix in with the crowds.

At long last Billy had made it back to near where he had entered the city and located one of the blocks that had a healthy number of dwarves who had arranged their units to house several smithies. Deep red-orange light lit the roads where the inner vestibule opened up to them, and high above, pipes could be seen poking out of spaces and letting out the smoke from the forges.

Hundreds of short, stocky dwarves with beefy little arms and hairy chests were all over the place working iron with their tiny efforts. Billy paused in a deep shadow across the street and watched them at work.

The dwarves were all less than three feet tall but were almost two feet wide and a foot thick. Their arms were all as thick as their short legs. They looked like a society of six-year-olds on steroids, with beards and solid black eyes. They all seemed to chant a lot while they performed their jobs at the various stages of the forging processes.

It seemed to Billy they were in the process of turning piles of rocks into ingots of metal. The furnaces they used were all underground, and Billy watched a nearly continuous line of people bringing in loads of wood in long lines that weaved throughout the city. People would trudge in with backs loaded with bundles of wood and exit counting the few coins they got in exchange for their efforts.

"I wonder why they are working day and night here," Billy said to himself while he chewed on a bit of metal he had picked up on the way here.

The rain pounded down around him, but thanks to his pilfered tarp, most of the water stayed off of him. Unfortunately, this did not prevent moisture from steaming off of his body. He had turned his boiler down so as not to look so out of place, but he saw plenty of strange creatures walking around that had their own reactions to the water. Some steamed, others seemed to funnel it around them. Others still repelled it. He was not special in his body's reaction either, as there were some rather large, three-armed folks walking around with large logs on each shoulder who were also steaming. Either they were very cold, and the air was fogging around them, or they were as hot-blooded as Billy, and the water was boiling off of their skin. The difference was in which direction the fog went.

Whatever the case, Billy was able to stay huddled up beside one of the container-buildings left along the road for folks to rest at or to set up street vendors. The unit he was against sold alcohol for some metal coins, but Billy did not have any such coins, and he really wanted some of that pure alcohol. Billy had tried to make a coin and exchange it; however, when the vendor touched the coin, he scoffed, saying this wasn't money, and told Billy to come back when he had some. He had decided he would need to wait and find some work in order to get some of those coins.

After hours of waiting, Billy finally saw what he was looking for. It was a short, stocky dwarf who was washing soot from his hands and face that was coming out to take a break. He had pulled what looked like a cigarette from one of his little pockets and lit it on a nearby torch. He took a few puffs on it and sighed as he looked up at the dark sky from under the awning he stood beneath. After a few minutes of puffing on his smoke, the dwarf looked over to Billy and paused. He flicked his ashes and looked around the smithy and back to Billy.

Billy watched Orgar watch him. Finally, the dwarf had finished his smoke, put it out, grabbed a cloak from a nearby hook, and tossed it over his head. He trumped across the muddy street and stepped under the canopy of the unit where Billy sat.

The dwarf said something to Billy, but he couldn't understand what was said. Sighing, Orgar held out a hand, and Billy reached out with his manipulator arm and shook it. A prompt popped up.

Orgar has invited you to learn the Knowledge: Language: Common Dwarven.

Do you accept the education for the cost of 1 Experience point? Yes. No.

Billy scratched his chin with his other manipulator and mentally selected *Yes*.

A moment later, he received the notification that he had successfully learned the Language, Common Dwarven.

"Yer wanton' work I s'pose?" Orgar asked.

"What's available?" Billy asked.

The dwarf grunted then. "It's good yer not botherin' bout wage rates. I'll pay yer 10 silver per hunnerd weight. That'd be a whole tree, logs chopped to my height. Can yer do it?"

Billy scratched his other manipulator's elbow and rolled a little side to side while he thought of a response. "Does it matter where I get the wood from?"

Orgar chuckled at this. "I like yer. Don't waste no time with the details. Straight ter the point. Back where yer came in earlier this morn, out there before yer get ter the maze. Take anything down a mile out, chop it, drop it off here and you'll get paid. We're always open," Orgar said, trying to look under the cloak at Billy.

"Wet or dry alright?" Billy asked.

"Dry is preferred."

"Right. I'll get started then." Billy started to get up but Orgar held up a hand and Billy paused.

"That feller yer came in town with, bad sort. I won't tell em yer here, but keep yer head down. Come morning, if yer can get me a few good loads, I'll let yer crash at my place. I wan' ter ask yer some things." Orgar looked serious with his invitation, and not knowing anyone else in the area, Billy simply nodded his body as best as possible.

"Alright," Was all he said.

Orgar turned back into the rain and across the road. He stomped off the rainwater and mud at the entrance and went back inside. The sounds of hammering and dwarves calling out to each other never ceased.

Billy looked at the quest he had received from Orgar, and it looked just like a standard fetch quest.

New quest! Collect 100 weight of wood.

Reward: 10 silver coins, or 1 Experience point per 100 weight.

This quest is repeatable.

"Good news, Charlotte," Billy sent to his assistant. "Looks like we have ourselves a fetch quest. And it's repeatable."

Unimpressed, Charlotte said nothing as she went about the business of monitoring his maintenance needs. She had no trouble working under the makeshift cloak and made no complaints. His joints were lubricated, and any dirt or debris was meticulously removed. She was done soon after Orgar had returned to his forges and plugged herself back into her port up front.

Billy glanced at the report she provided and he noted the need for the alcohol still blinking glaringly at the top of the list. With any luck, he would have that taken care of in the next couple of hours.

Crossing the line where the city ended and the forest began came with quite a nice surprise for Billy. In the city, it had been pouring rain pretty hard. Once he crossed the line marking the beginning of the forest, he seemed to have entered a totally different zone, and it was not raining here. It was still night, but it wasn't raining.

Billy mentally switched to his night vision, and instantly, the world around him tinted green. Down in the underworld, he had woken up in, the underground facility, Billy had used a different sort of vision. Outside, he had not needed it, so he subconsciously disabled it. Now, outside, where starlight lit the world, he got an opportunity to make use of his sophisticated night vision.

He easily navigated away from the strange poles, choosing a direction almost at random. He did not follow the path he had taken before as there were other people moving in and out of it now, performing their own tasks. During the daylight, it seemed few people went about outside the city, but come night, there were lines of people looking to go out.

Billy made sure nobody followed him as he slipped into the woods. He carefully packed up his tarp and stowed it in one of his abdominal compartments for later. He then picked up speed to head a mile away from the poles, picked a new direction, and traveled for almost an hour.

Billy loved walking through these woods. He was able to turn down his light sensitivity a little to see what the woods looked like naturally, and he noticed there were many forms of life operating in the dark. Insects and birds flew around in the never-ending war of survival of the fittest. Off in the distance, predators hunted prey. Life and death encounters were happening everywhere, and Billy was careful not to include himself in those encounters.

Finally, Billy stopped by a number of trees that looked good enough for chopping and collecting. They all looked like they could be hardwood, but a few gentle pushes showed the plants were somewhat flexible. He picked only the ones that had a diameter of about a foot, then released his set of scavenger crabs from his abdomen. They both plopped down on six feet and awaited orders. Billy opened up the menus for the scavengers and selected the task *Collect Wood* from a pulldown list, highlighted the target trees, and hit *Apply*.

An assembly lowered from Billy's abdomen and turned a large brass key on the backs of each of the scavengers, and once wound up, the two began to take down trees and break them into useful logs about three feet long.

Billy watched in fascination as the scavengers went to the trees and applied the cutting edges of their large claws. There were teeth on the inside that moved back and forth in a sawing motion while the claw was grabbing the base. Every 15 minutes or so, one of them would return to Billy to get its springs rewound, but then it would return to its task with gusto.

Tree after tree toppled and was slowly delimbed and turned into logs and stacked. In only a couple of hours, Billy had enough lumber to put a pretty good dent in someone's wallet.

Getting the logs onto his back turned out to require a pit to be dug so he could lower his upper body in so the scavengers could load him up. That only took them a few minutes as their feet were especially shaped for digging through soft ground. A few minutes after being loaded up with almost 30 logs, Billy pushed himself up and out of the hole, and the two scavengers returned to their positions on his abdomen. Feeling good about his haul, Billy began the short journey back to the Lair of the Fey.

Two hours later, Billy had removed the last of the logs from his back. He had made quite a scene arriving with so much wood all at once, but the dwarves took no offense and happily helped him take the load off and stack it on the scales. Orgar had come to him at the end of this, and handed him a small bag of coins, shaking his head. He hadn't said anything before walking off, but Billy did catch the sound of him chuckling to himself.

You have submitted 300 weight of wood for a repeatable quest.

+30 silver coins.

Billy went back outside while stashing his coins. He would need to make several trips of the same amount or more if he were to get the amount of alcohol he required. Thus, Billy tossed his tarp back over himself and carefully made his way back through the rain and out into the woods again.

It was very early in the morning when Billy noticed a low-level fog developing. It was sparse at first but eventually became a thick layer of eerie fog clinging to the land. Curious about something, Billy opened up his Status to see if he could find anything involving the measure of time this world used. To his delight, he learned this particular world had very long days which lasted almost 35 hours. This explained why he felt he had been above ground for well over half a day and yet it was still fairly dark out. Now, knowing that nights usually last around 14 hours, the weather started to make sense.

Billy had also not been paying attention to the temperature. The day time had been quite warm for the majority of it. This would have the effect of allowing more time for water to evaporate, leading to quite large rain storms at night. He was unsure as to his latitude on this world, or anything else about this world really, so he had no real idea how the seasons worked here either. Or even if there were seasons. He remembered watching some videos talking about alien worlds not necessarily having seasons for any number of reasons, one being no planetary tilt, another being more than one star, and even the habitable planet being a moon around a larger gas giant.

Either way, Billy was rather enjoying the dense fog. It made it more difficult for anyone to follow him through the woods. The offset to this would be that Billy would have a difficult time spotting anything or anyone stalking him if they stumbled across him in the darkness.

While Billy had his scavengers work on the trees, he spent his time reviewing his Status, and studying what schemas he had that he could make any use of. Most of the things the schemas provided were weapons and cogworks, but Billy already had many more ideas for weapons, and had a better grasp on more useful simple tools. He felt that he could get things done without being overly reliant on old designs, but he wasn't averse to using his own knowledge from Earth. So far he found no need to apply it here. The schemas he had were enough to maintain himself, and he would have to design better in the future if he wanted to build more complex upgrades.

He had yet to even see much in the form of magic, either. Sure, the Lair of the Fey had plenty of strange things there, but Billy had not noticed anything he could point at and say for sure it was magical except, maybe, himself. As Billy reviewed his available schema, he realized that he was unsure exactly what he would need in the future. He was sure that, at some point, he would need to establish some form of base for himself. He would need to build his own repair shop, among other things.

"Charlotte, do you have any suggestions on what I should do first?" Billy hoped Charlotte would manifest her holo form so she could interact on his Status screens, and after a moment, she did just that. Her little blue holo popped into life for his eyes only, and she climbed over the screens and reviewed what he had pulled up.

"I'm not sure, Billy. I am not really designed to give such opinions. My primary concern is to ensure your structural care needs and overall maintenance are completed regularly." Her little granny voice came across as a little annoyed at being asked what he should be doing as if he should already know this. Even as she had said this, she had raised her little legs in a show of strength, which Billy knew was one of aggression.

"Okay, Charlotte. You're right." Billy had already dug a small trench and settled into it for his scavengers to load him up as they harvested the trees. He had several logs stacked up, and Charlotte was busy running small wires over them to tie them down. "I'll tell you this, then. Once we get done with this load and get the alcohol, we can take a break. I think I'm running low on power or something. I feel a little tired. When these logs are loaded, task the crew to prepare a camp right here while we go deliver them. The lighter load will hopefully make the trip faster, too."

Charlotte's little holo reorganized the agenda for Billy, placing specific tasks on top.

"If I may, Billy. Perhaps we should choose a different location. This place has plenty of organic matter to harvest, but there is a lack of other resources. I have not seen so much as a large rock sticking from the ground," She said, tapping the dirt.

Charlotte then moved to his map and resized it. She moved over it for a moment and managed to get the map to zoom out quite far. Apart from the path he had taken yesterday through the woods and subsequent maze, much of the map was undetailed. Eventually, she located the place where Billy had escaped the underground facility and she tapped it.

"Perhaps we can clean this up and set something up here. It has many resources we can delve for. Water is nearby. It is open, flat land and would be difficult to approach from any direction. And it would take little to secure." Charlotte's holo circled the spot on the ground and had been dancing while she spoke. Billy found the little dance quite funny.

"Okay, but that means eight to 10 more hours of work before we can rest." Billy was really feeling a little sluggish. He hoped, however, that this delivery would net him some much-needed alcohol and this problem could be solved.

"Yes, well, we should be done here within the hour. No need to rush things and plop down in just any old hole in the ground." She sounded pleased to have convinced Billy to plant his base elsewhere. And she was right. This location was good, but miles too close to the Lair of the Fey and the people there for his liking.

Suddenly, Billy caught the sound of cracking sticks off in the distance. He froze, and when he did, his scavengers did as well. The crabs, however, did not pause longer than a blink, as they immediately dropped their loads and rushed to attach themselves to Billy's abdominal bays. Carefully Billy brought out the tarp he had snatched earlier that night, and carefully dragged it over himself. He then buried his legs in the dirt and wiggled down as best he could.

All the while, the sounds of crunching leaves could be heard getting louder and closer. Bars of white light were also lighting up the fog. Shadows of trees were thrown everywhere as whoever held the lights moved. The lights gave the fog a strange glow. Parts of it were blue; others were red. They did not alternate or anything. It was as if the light sources were just different colors.

The crunching and cracking of wood continued to increase, and eventually, Billy could feel the ground rumble, magnified now that he was buried in it. Strange creaking sounds were also traveling out to Billy, and he got the feeling he was hearing the tread of many feet.

Billy listened hard for the sounds of people talking but could not detect anything. Nor did he hear any kind of communication. Whoever was making the noise was also doing so quietly and moving directly towards Billy.

"Charlotte, cut the logs free. Quick." Billy lifted himself and rolled to his side to help the logs slide off as Charlotte cut them loose. Out in the fog, lights were moving in his direction and he was beginning to hear voices. The rumbling in the ground was growing deeper when suddenly, it all stopped. The last of the logs slid off Billy and he quickly stood and moved to his right.

To his surprise, several of the lights out there in the fog followed him.

"Crap, I think they can track me," he said to himself. Internally, Billy felt his magical boiler heating up as he prepared to flee. He did not stand still while this happened, though, so he began to move.

With a hissing whoosh, Billy shot toward the source of the lights. He did not move straight at it, but off to the side. He was fairly certain his rear was already blocked. Panicked voices began calling out as he started to move and the lights started to move all over the place, bars of light slashing through the fog, trying to find him.

Billy tried his best to listen to anything in case he understood it, but all of it was gibberish to him, so he decided it was likely they were not dwarves or elves. Or Earthlings from America. Or other machines like himself. Those were the only languages he knew, as far as he was aware.

Out of the fog, a shape appeared in front of Billy, and it looked like it was holding up a hand and a beam of light was being emitted from nowhere. As gently as possible, Billy rushed the figure and used one of his feet to shove the figure away. His intention was not to harm but to knock down the individual.

As he reached the figure, it shouted something out, and a strange multicolored bubble surrounded it. Billy's foot shot out to "kick" when he felt it slam into the bubble with absolutely no give. The bubble burst, and something shoved Billy's foot off to the side. The figure stumbled and fell down, but Billy did not stop as he dashed past.

His foot felt almost numb, but Billy pushed past this feeling and continued to run. Dozens of voices began calling out to one another when, suddenly, an explosion burned through the fog right in front of Billy.

He raised his manipulators and his front feet to protect his eyes in the blinding light, and he felt dirt and debris spray over his frame. There didn't seem to be any damage, but his hesitation already cost him the initiative. Fearful, something happened inside Billy. He had not consciously decided to activate his defenses; however, in only a moment, his limbs rearranged and plates rolled over and reconnected in a different orientation. In seconds, Billy had transformed from a nondescript mechanoid to a vicious-looking spider with spiked plates and razor-edged legs.

A pressure built in Billy's abdomen for a moment, then released. To his eyes, there was a brilliant flash that burned through all the fog nearby, and he saw nearly three dozen figures with various weapons drawn, moving in on him. As the light illuminated the individuals, something happened and the lights they carried winked out.

In less than an instant, the forest was dark again, and Billy moved.

"Crap, how are they tracking me?" Billy said to himself as he lunged in a gap he caught sight of during the blink of light. He could feel a series of something plinking off of his body armor. The objects were probably arrows, but...

Something incredibly heavy smashed into Billy's side and knocked him off of all of his feet. Instinctively, Billy lashed out with his feet to right himself, and he felt his legs strike something several times. He tumbled across the dark ground, and he pushed hard at the thing to give himself some space, causing him to spin.

The world spun a few times before he managed to stop himself, and he felt several more arrows strike his body. This time, they seemed to carry more weight and a few stuck through the hardened plates.

Voices continued to call out to each other, and Billy did his best to locate what was probably the tracker or leader calling out directions. Decision made, Billy hunkered down, charged his systems, and then launched himself into the darkness.

Someone cried out as he flew through the air, but instead of landing near the voice, something had slammed into him again, knocking him sideways. This time, Billy was prepared, and internally rotating gyros kept him upright and specialized flywheels slammed to a stop at just the right instant, and Billy's trajectory instantly changed. He was flying back on course, almost magically.

A gruff snort of shock wooshed behind Billy as he landed in front of an individual who was holding up a hand in fear. Billy froze indecision in his mind. He did not want to kill, but he was already looking at all of his limbs, and everyone was bladed.

Cursing to himself, Billy lunged forward and smashed his giant eyes into the figure. His thick acrylic lenses flexed a little, but the figure's face did not. A *bongggg* sounded out as his curved eye bounced off the person's head, and that person crumbled to the ground. Billy turned and charged past the collapsed body into the darkness as voices moved on his position.

Nobody followed, and seconds after he made it through the circle of enemies, lights began to appear in the fog once more. None of them were pointing in his direction, however, but Billy did not take any more chances. He ran toward the Lair of the Fey zone. He needed help. And hopefully that help would come in the form of Orgar.

Billy stumbled through the poles, marking the zone for the Lair of the Fey. He was sure there would be someone guarding the zone entrance, but when he returned to the location, there was no sign of anyone particularly paying any attention to those who came or went. Crossing back into the rain was when Billy realized how badly he was damaged. Some of the arrows had punched holes or cut steam lines. He was leaking heat in several places and he needed a place where he could make repairs.

In only a few minutes Billy had made it to the dwarven forges, and he did not wait long to find Orgar at one of the furnaces. Desperate to contact the dwarf, Billy decided the best way was to simply approach him.

Stepping into the forge brought all the sounds of several working crews of dozens focused on the task of producing metal products. Dwarves were calling out to one another, pulling on chain pulleys to lift and move heavy, glowing crucibles. Billy carefully moved around working crews and walked up to Orgar.

The gruff dwarf turned and looked up at Billy as he approached. He turned back to his crew and told them something. Billy could not tell what that was over the noise of the place. The pounding of hammers in cadence and the roar of blast furnaces underground opening and closing easily drown out the words. Orgar turned back to Billy and shook his head, then waved Billy to follow.

Off to one side of the massive forging area, Orgar led Billy to one of the housing units. Orgar opened the door of one of these units and went inside. Billy poked his head in and saw there was little in the way of comforting seats. There were instead several work benches with specialized tools for fine detail work.

The dwarf moved to the back of the unit, which was nearly 50 feet long, eight feet tall, and 10 feet wide. He waved Billy in. Shrugging to himself, Billy carefully worked his way through the doorway and closed the door once he was inside. If nothing were in here, Billy could almost stretch out with room to spare. It was not, however, so he had to keep his legs close to himself and very carefully move forward so as not to disturb the dwarf's home.

The closed-door cut off the noise of the forge. The shock of the silence was almost deafening to Billy.

"So, I see yer got into a scuffle. Yer knowin' yer have some arrows stickin' from yer hide?" Orgar asked, returning from a pile of tools to bring a large pair of pliers and a crowbar.

"Yeah, I was getting the last load of the night ready when I was approached." Billy lowered himself to the floor in a mostly open space. "They seemed to be able to track me, though I don't know how."

"Auch, they prolly had some casters trackin' yer trail. Bastards are hard up fer fightin' beasts fer their pit fighting." Orgar clambered up onto Billy's back and ruthlessly ripped out an arrow from his abdomen. It did not hurt, but Billy could feel that the arrow had torn an oil line on its way in and again on its way out. He saw that his reserves were getting low, but he was doing his best to manage the flow through that particular line.

"Wat's this, eh?" Orgar asked, seeing the flow of oil coming from the wound. "Looks like it cut somethin' inside. Are yer needin' a healer?"

Billy was touched that this gruff dwarf was actually concerned with his well-being. He had no reason to treat Billy this way, but he seemed to be a genuinely kind person.

"I can take care of this myself, Orgar. I have a companion who can perform first aid of a sort and get me right as rain. I just need some things to help the process, which was why I agreed to haul in the wood." Billy watched as Orgar continued to examine Billy for more arrows, and on occasion, Billy felt his own weight shifting as the dwarf climbed around and pulled another arrow out of some nook or cranny.

"Must be nice, eh? Heh heh, I don't see many folks out here with companions that can heal. Enough of that, though. Wat are yer needin' ter help fix yerself up? I might be able ter get somethin' at a discount." After finding no more arrows to pluck, Orgar hopped down to the floor and moved to face Billy.

Billy thought for a moment. He hoped this dwarf was being honest, and truly wanted to help.

"I need pure alcohol, if you can find it. The more pure, the better." Billy's manipulator hands were moving nervously, and Orgar took notice of this movement.

He looked hard at Billy and scratched at his thick, curly beard. "I can get yer some spirits if that's what yer lookin' fer. What's it fer?" Orgar asked, turning to the back of his room. Several cloth sheets and blankets covered piles of things, probably to protect the stuff from the soot of the forge. Billy watched for a moment as he tossed one particular blanket off of a pile of wooden barrels, each with their own brass plates.

"I need it to stay alive, I guess. There is little I need in regard to food. I can consume almost anything and process it. But I do need alcohol to keep active. And right, now, I am running a little low." Looking at his Status, Billy saw again the warning light that soon he would be moving into a lower power mode, whatever that was.

"I know how much coin yer've made ternight, and I can say yer ain't got enough fer this. I can let yer have this one barrel of dwarven ale fer what yer got minus a gold coin. In return, I need yer to do somethin' fer me. What do yer say to that?" Orgar hefted a small three-gallon barrel and waddled over to Billy. With a plunk he dropped it to the floor where Billy could just make out the swishing sound of liquids inside.

Scratching his chin, Billy decided that he needed the alcohol now before he shut down, so he did not wait to think about it before reaching into a compartment on the side of his abdomen and taking out all but one of the gold coins he had and handed them over to Orgar with his manipulator hand.

Orgar grunted and pocketed the coin.

"Do yer need me ter tap it?"

Chapter 5

Instead of answering directly, Billy picked up the small wooden barrel and brought it up to his mouth. A metal pipe thrust into the barrel where the bung was, and Billy began refueling by drawing the alcohol out directly.

Immediately, Billy realized he was in luck, as the stuff in the barrel was indeed very potent alcohol. It was already processed to the highest purity he could measure, and in under a minute, he had drained the barrel into his tank.

Deciding it would be appropriate, Billy provided the equivalent of a hearty belch as he placed the barrel back on the ground. Orgar guffawed as the now hollow barrel sounded in its absence of happy sauce.

"By my beard, yer sure yer'll be a'right drinkin' it all at once?" Orgar stood stunned, looking down at the barrel.

"I think I could use another barrel, actually," Billy said. "But first, do you mind if I sit down here for my companion to take care of my injuries?" For some reason, Billy was beginning to see the dimensions of this little home start to flex in strange ways.

Looking up, Orgar began to chuckle to himself. This turned into a guffaw, then continued into a full-blown belly laugh. Tears were coming from the little fellow and he was bent over from laughing so hard.

Billy didn't understand why at first because the room kept changing pitch, and he was busy trying to stay level.

Billy's legs gave out and he banged onto the floor as the room spun around him. Orgar walked over to him and, tapped him on the back behind his eyes and shook his head, still laughing to himself.

"Tell yer what, yer can stay here an' sleep off the drink. Try not ter make a mess if yer companion works on yer wounds. I'll come back later an' check on yer," he said as he continued to chuckle. He walked behind Billy and left the unit.

Billy, however, had already blacked out. Charlotte, in disgust, popped off her place and turned to look at Billy. His eyes had already shut off, but that didn't matter to her. She already knew the dwarven spirits had already rendered her master unconscious. He had already pre-approved her maintenance schedule, so she sent orders to Billy's Assembler to make the things she would need to patch the holes her foolish master had taken earlier in his flight from the forest.

She ran a hand gently over Billy's face as she watched him sleeping. "Poor thing. So much going on at once, and the first chance you get to relax, you pass right out, drunk." She shook her spider head in consternation while waving two of her rear legs;

then she moved to the Assembler to collect the parts it produced so she could perform repairs.

Billy awoke many hours later to a splitting headache. He wasn't sure how that could be as he was not exactly biological, but once he wobbled to his feet, he "opened" his eyes and took a look at a couple of notifications that had been there for a while.

You have consumed Dwarven Ale.

Intellect check Failed. You will find poor decisions easier to make for up to 3 hours.

You have consumed Dwarven Ale.

Intellect check Failed. You will find it much easier to make poor decisions for the next 5 hours.

You have consumed copious amounts of Dwarven Ale.

Intellect check Failed. You're drunk. You will do pretty much anything that sounds fun at a mere suggestion for the next 8 hours. Vision is also affected.

You have consumed a lethal amount of Dwarven Ale.

Intellect check Failed.

Structural Integrity check Passed.

You will pass out soon and remember little of the last couple of hours. When you wake up, you will be subject to the Hangover debuff for 2 hours. This will lower your ability to deal with loud noises give you the sensation of dry mouth, and sources of bright light shall be the bane of your existence until you recover.

Maintenance repairs successful. Your Durability has been restored.

Your Hangover debuff has expired.

"Charlotte, what happened?" Billy grumbled groggily, as he looked around. He saw he was in one of the housing units, and there were small working stations along the sides of the walls. He even noticed that above him was a second story that also had stuff piled all over the place. He didn't remember seeing that when he had first come in here. Now that he thought about it, the dwarves were only about two or three feet tall, and the interior of these units meant there was enough space to split it into two floors, which would be more than enough headroom for the short folk.

Billy had been lying between two large work tables and had to carefully extricate himself from between them. Charlotte was at her station on the front of his face, but she did not seem awake. She did not respond to Billy's inquiry.

Trying to shake off the last of the effects of the dwarven ale, Billy turned himself around to find the door. To his relief, it was right where he thought it was. Walking around the workspaces, Billy made it to the door and slowly pushed it open. Immediately, the sound of pounding hammers and the clang and pop of molten metals being shaped by meat and sweat assaulted Billy's hearing.

"Gah!" He declared and pulled the door closed to keep the sounds of the end of the world out. "Where's Orgar? Hey Orgar, are you in here?" Billy looked around the unit and couldn't find anything that looked like a bed. Putting some feet up to the second floor, which was open mostly in the middle, Billy poked his head up and looked around.

"Nothing but furniture and old things." Not wanting to dig around his newfound friend's possessions, Billy returned to the ground level and looked around. To his eyes, this little home looked very similar in layout to the hardware store his uncle had owned. There was a counter space by the front door, and behind it was a little stool and a heavy metal chest with a thick lock on it. A curtain had been pulled back to let Billy inside last night, but if it were pulled closed, it would sequester the rest of the house from this front desk. It looked like there was a thick leather book with pages and pages of things Orgar could make or had for sale. It was like a little catalog, but he wasn't sure as he could not read any of the strange lexicon.

Billy was still turning pages in the catalog when he heard the door open, and Orgar stomped inside. The sudden sound caused Billy to look over. Orgar had a broad smile on his face as he saw Billy looking at his catalog.

"I see yer finally up! Good, good," Orgar wiped his face clean with a rag he grabbed from behind his counter. The soot-covered Orgar head to toe, but the little fellow didn't seem bothered by it at all. "I need yer ter make me somethin' if yer can."

He reached for his catalog, which Billy slid to him, and Orgar flipped the pages to near the back. He tapped a finger on the page he'd located and set the book down, turning it to face Billy.

"Can yer make this fer me? I have this drawing I acquired years ago fer a new press, but I could never figure out how to fashion this part here," his short, stubby finger tapped the particular part he was talking about.

Billy picked up the book and took a close look at the drawings, mildly curious as to how Orgar knew Billy could make anything at all.

The part Orgar needed was a complex set of gears necessary to perform a particular motion. It also required some other means to augment the gear ratio manually to increase torque or to increase rotation speed. Billy looked over to the dwarf, who stood by watching Billy examine the drawings.

"I, uh, I can maybe make something like this. I need to know what kind of materials it has to be made from, and the dimensions. I can't read any of that written down here." Billy tapped the page with notations sans dimensions. "And how did you know I can make things?"

Smiling, Orgar tapped one particular piece and said, "I needs this ter be about yay wide," Holding a finger and thumb an inch apart. "As fer how I knew, yer little friend there told me hours ago ye make things yerself."

Shrugging to himself, Billy took a long, hard look at the drawings again in an effort to memorize them.

Intellect check Successful. You have learned a new schema: Orgar's Torqued Transmission. You may now send this schema to your Assembler to create this product.

Billy mentally shooed the prompt away and immediately sent the request to his Assembler. He got a warning about low metal reserves, which he ignored as he adjusted the volume of the product relative to the specific gear.

Estimated time to completion: 18 minutes, 24 seconds. Hit Apply to begin.

"Okay, I should have this done in a few minutes once I begin. Do you happen to have some metal ingots I can use?" Billy looked over to Orgar, who nodded his head.

Walking around Billy, Orgar went to the back room and pulled a rope, which dropped a metal ladder leading to the second floor. He quickly climbed up and grabbed a couple of small metal bars of different materials. Each one he grabbed he tossed down to Billy, who deftly caught them before they hit the ground.

"Make sure I c'n take it apart," Orgar called down. "I will need ter be able ter copy it later."

"Sure thing, Orgar," Billy replied while chewing on the small ingots. His reserves for this project replenished, Billy set about making minor alterations to the design to include lubrication points, and adding simple cylinder bearings, which could also be removed and repacked with grease. He marked each part to be made of the proper materials and selected *Apply* to begin assembling the part.

Instantly Billy's backside began to make soft humming sounds as it painstakingly crafted the part. Billy felt the furnace he had for a heart crank up the heat and feed that to his Assembler to help mold the metals into shape. Billy wasn't exactly sure how his Assembler functioned, as it was primarily magical in nature, but he knew it had physically mechanical and magical parts that somehow moved around inside him. He had to be careful in redesigning himself for his first Status upgrade so as not to cramp this device. It was incredibly utilitarian, and if it were in a position to be damaged, he would be unable to make parts to fix himself.

Orgar rode the ladder to the ground, and walked around to sit on his stool to watch Billy. "Well, aren't yer gonna go to the back an' use one of me benches?"

"What? No, I don't need that. I can produce this magically. I have an organ that makes things, not unlike other spiders that can produce silk for their webs."

"I'm sorry, wut? I thought yer could craft things, yer friend said so. Said yer can make what yer need fer yer first aid, whatever that be."

Billy looked over to Orgar who just stared at him. "What?"

"What's a spider? And why would they make webs?" Orgar looked totally confused.

"It's an insect where I come from. It fashions a web from an organ at their rear, which they use to catch other bugs and things to eat." Billy scratched his chin while he thought about his answer. "Are there no spiders in these lands?"

Orgar shook his head in the negative. "Nay, we have silken worms which make silk, But we use it fer makin fine clothes." Orgar sat there looking Billy over again as his abdomen made strange humming sounds. "Can yer make silk yerself?"

"I can, but it uses my internal reserves far more than I'd like at the moment. But I can make tools and things like that without using those vital reserves. Not large tools, but I can make them with incredible precision, and all I need is the ore." Billy had not wanted to necessarily give that information away, but he thought he could probably trust Orgar. After all, the dwarf seemed to know what he was, if not exactly, then he had an idea and he did not seem afraid.

"That sounds like it'd be a powerful Ability. Any way you can share that with others?" Orgar shifted on his stool as he watched Billy work.

Orgar said this as if it were indeed a possibility, but Billy wasn't sure what that would mean. He opened up his Status and found the section which housed his Assembler and Dissembler, only to discover it wasn't a normal ability. It was a subsection of Special Ability categorized as Racial Ability.

He mentally tapped the little help icon beside this classification and learned he could not share this Ability with any but those of his kind: Mechanoid. Perhaps his bots could learn this?

Shaking himself in the negative, Billy said, "It isn't a normal Ability. It falls under the Racial Ability classification.

Orgar grunted. "Shame. It'd be useful ter be able ter make things like that." Reaching into a pocket, Orgar brought out one of his little cigarettes and put it in his mouth. He went to one of the lamps that lit his little home and, with a taper, lit his smoke and began puffing away on it.

Billy watched Orgar inhale and saw the dwarf seem to relax. He puffed out the smoke, and tapped the ashes on the floor while they waited fro the parts to finish.

Chapter 6

Billy spent the next few minutes flipping through the catalog, looking at the things in it. There were nicknacks, gizmos, and doodads. He wasn't exactly sure what most of the stuff did, but it all looked quite interesting. He did not, however, take the time to learn any of the drawings. He was only allowed to learn a few more, and as it was, he had already used up most of his available slots for schema.

Eventually, a small hatch on Billy's abdomen opened up, and he reached back with one of his feet-hands and pulled it free. He looked over the thing and then sat it on the counter for Orgar to take.

Sitting forward, Orgar picked up the device and gave it a critical look over. He turned the gears and spun the screw parts. Everything operated perfectly.

"What are these things fer?" He tapped a finger on one of the grease points.

"That is for inserting grease. As the bearings operate, if they pick up any contamination, the grease will keep it away from the metal. The fitting there will allow a grease gun to push more grease in there, forcing the contaminated stuff out. It makes it easy to maintain and helps the gears to run smoothly." Billy gave the thing a once over himself to make sure he didn't leave anything out of the design.

"What's a grease gun?" Orgar asked, scratching a spot on his head.

"Can I use this piece of paper to draw what I mean?" Billy asked, holding up the book.

"Aye, just don't yer be messin' up any of me own work," Orgar said while looking at the device.

In a few moments, Billy had taken a writing pen Orgar handed him and scribbled down several drawings at different angles of a common grease gun that was used back on Earth. Thinking about it for a moment, Billy reached into one of his personal maintenance compartments and brought one of his out. He had several, so giving one away would not cost him much.

"This is the tool I'm talking about," Billy said, unscrewing the back of the canister and pulling the spring-loaded piston back. The thing made a slurping sound as it separated. "Grease goes in here, and the cap screws back on. Push this tab, and it will release the spring to push the piston down and place some pressure on the grease. The tip," Billy tapped the tip of the gun, "Snaps onto that fitting there. Opening and closing this handle here," he tapped the handle, "Makes it force grease into the fitting. A quick tug and it will pop right off."

Billy performed the task as he described it with the grease gun on the device from Orgar. He showed how the grease went in and how it separated once completed.

"You can have that if you want. When it comes to putting lubrication on moving parts stuck in sealed compartments, nothing works better than a good grease gun."

Orgar, looking more and more confused during the entire demonstration, put his hands on the table and shook his head. "Yer can take that thing off, Billy. We, dwarves, don't be needin' grease fittin's when we use our magic. We spell our work, yer see, so it ne'er needs lubrication."

Reaching under his counter, he took out a tool and examined the fitting. "Can this be removed?"

Billy did his best to nod as he picked up the device. There was only the one fitting on it, but he used his manipulators to deftly unscrew it to show how it came apart. He reached back to his abdomen and withdrew a short threaded stud and screwed it down tight on the place the fitting was, making the surface look as if it had never had a hole there at all.

Orgar saw this and chuckled. "That there's a neat trick. Makin' it so yer could replace all the parts is wise, assumin' yer don't be havin' magic ter maintain it. This would be handy in places where magic was restricted or blocked." Orgar pulled out a magnifying glass and looked hard at the spot the fitting was and could find no evidence there was so much as a hole there.

"I come from a place where magic was severely restricted. It's why I know so many ways to make things that don't use it." Billy looked kind of nervous admitting this much, but once again, he felt he could trust this dwarf. He truly seemed more curious than anything else. And he hadn't tried to kill Billy yet, which was also a plus.

Orgar played with the device for a little while as Billy watched. It seemed Billy had either passed some sort of test or impressed the dwarf because Billy saw a big smile on the little fellow's lips as he played with the thing.

"Can I ask you something, Orgar?" Billy inquired. He had been on this world for well over a day, and had zero idea of what the status of things was. He desperately needed to know what was going on in the world so he could formulate some kind of approach. The Quest he had received did not provide much information and had not been updated at all since he awoke here. He had neither a timeline nor a destination for the first leg of his adventure.

Orgar, sensing the seriousness of Billy's question, set the device down and got up from the stool he was on. He went to the front door and opened it to stick his head out. He yelled something out the door, then turned and slammed it shut and threw a bar to lock it closed.

"That'll keep the boys from bustin' in here while we're talkin'," Orgar then went past the sheet into the back room and threw the sheet off a small couch to plop himself down on. Dust puffed up, but Orgar ignored it.

Billy turned and followed him in and picked a spot on the opposite side of the small room beside a desk to sit down at.

"Can you tell me what is going on here?" Billy asked.

Orgar looked hard at Billy as he lit another cigarette and took a puff. "Are yer one of 'em?"

"One of what?"

"One of the weapons the humes make?"

"No. I have never met a hume and have no idea where they live or what they want."

"Do yer plan on killin' my kin?"

"No," Billy said, waving both of his manipulator hands to emphasize this. "I don't want to fight anyone, Orgar. I'm not from here. I have no ill will towards anyone."

"Where yer be from, then?" Orgar took another long pull from his smoke and blew out a couple of smoke circles.

"I awoke from a long sleep yesterday when I discovered I was in some sort of facility deep underground. It took me nearly half of this world's day to climb out of it."

Orgar leaned forward at this. "This world?"

Billy paused, forgetting he had not wanted to mention this. Instead of explaining, he said, "It's complicated."

"Course it is, Billy. Course it is," Orgar chuckled as he ashed onto the floor. "Yer know, I've seen yer kind afore. Yer be killin' machines, makin' traps ter kill anythin' not hume. When I saw yer comin' inter the city, and folk weren't dyin', I knew somethin'd be different with yer. That's…"

"That's why you sent the Friend Request?" Billy finished.

"Yes. I wanted ter see if ye were like 'em. And yer not. Furthermore, yer be far smarter than them things. And yer lookin' slightly different, too. I can't be sayin' how, but yer seem to be shaped different than them others, move different as well."

"Yeah. I came across some Experience points as soon as I woke up. They were in a box hidden in a wall. I used them to make some minor changes because I got the feeling that, this body being made here, I could be mistaken for others that look like how I was when I awoke."

"Are yer sure yer should be tellin' me this?" Orgar asked seriously.

Billy looked at Orgar. He looked like he was sitting casually, but any number of things could be going on Billy did not know about. This whole room could be a trap designed to destroy him.

"I'm not from this world, Orgar."

Orgar blinked.

"I come from a world called Earth. That world did not have."

"Now I know yer full of it. Earth be a myth. No one alive in any corner o' this world 'as e'er seen Earth, despite the legends. It's said it be a place the gods themselves reside at, eatin' from trees thick with fruits, surrounded by mountains full o' gold an' silver." Orgar looked like he was getting angry as he said this.

Taken aback, Billy remained silent as he did not know what to say. He knew he was from Earth; he did not realize Earth would be known anywhere else.

"Are yer tellin' me Earth be havin' weapons such as yerself? Are ye all lookin' such?" Red-faced, Orgar took a moment to calm down by taking out yet another of his cigarettes, lighting this one with the spent one.

Hoping he wasn't signing his own death certificate, Billy said, "No, Orgar. Earth is inhabited solely by humans. Not humes, I don't know what those are. They are humans; tall, long-limbed, two arms and legs, five fingers on each hand, five toes on each foot, different colored hair from one another, different colored eyes, and skin, accents. I can go on."

Before he could, however, Orgar leapt off the couch to his feet and stomped over to Billy. "Yer lyin'," he said.

"Orgar, I am not from this world. I am not some machine programmed to say this or anything else. I am not a machine. I found a Quest Prompt on Earth, and it brought me here. I could not come as a human, so what of me was allowed to come was put into this thing. I did not pick this body that I arrived in. But it is what I have to work with." Billy steadily looked eye to eye with Orgar, even though he was getting an ugly look of anger from him.

Once he had mentioned the Quest Prompt, however, Orgar's features immediately changed, and he paled, staggering back until he flopped back onto his couch.

"Yer not lyin' be ye?" Orgar whispered.

"I am telling you the truth, Orgar. I am not from this world."

"Show me the quest, then," Orgar demanded.

Billy looked inward to his Status and pulled up the page that held his active quests. On it, he found, top of the list, the quest to save the world. He opened it up, and located the *Share Quest Information* button, and selected Orgar from the pulldown, then *Send*.

Orgar gasped as he received the quest information and then cursed. He ran his hands over his face and went to the back of his unit. He searched through several cases and pulled out a couple of cups. He paused, shrugged, then came back and set them on the desk beside Billy before going to retrieve one of his barrels of drink.

Grunting, Orgar lifted the barrel and tapped the bung to pour two mugs of what looked like wine.

Handing one to Billy, Orgar took his and sat back down, sipping his. "Elven wine. Sip it," Is all he said.

Billy tried the wine with one of his hoses. He only drew a little in. His systems registered it as potent alcohol, not unlike the dwarven ale, but with a different flavor.

After a while of sitting and watching Orgar, Billy got the feeling the reaction from the quest was going to be an issue soon. Deciding he wanted to get around this, Billy decided to poke and see what other information he could shake loose.

"Do you know what mithril is?" If Billy hadn't been specifically looking for it, he would have missed the dwarf's eyes go from some far-away unfocused appearance to one of laser focus. The solid black nature of the eyes only gave itself away when Orgar went from looking into his wine to looking directly at Billy's eyes.

"What do yer know of it?" Orgar grunted out.

Carefully, Billy used his manipulator arm to access one of his upper body compartments and pulled free a short, round rod of very silvery metal. The dwarf gasped when his eyes lit on it, and he shot to his feet. To forestall any argument, Billy handed the metal rod out to Orgar without complaint. The dwarf immediately snatched the rod out of Billy's hand.

"Where did yer get this?" Orgar's demand was not something unexpected. Billy had been playing around with the idea of handing this over as soon as he got in here last night. The dwarven ale sidetracked him then.

"Deep underground. More than a dozen miles by my estimation." Billy cautiously reached out a manipulator to Orgar. With what looked like infinite sorrow, Orgar handed the shining metallic rod back to Billy and turned to refill his spilled wine before lighting up yet another cigarette.

"I need ter know, Billy. I need ter know the method used ter process ore inter this. Do you know it?" Orgar looked so almost-angry he was asking this, but Billy was pretty sure the surly little guy was just proud. If what he thought was happening here was indeed happening, he needed to be forthright in his information and straightforward in his own requests.

"I have the formulas for the processing of this metal, Orgar. I will share this for nothing if you wish. I do, however, need to know what is going on in this world between the peoples of this city, its rulers, if there are any, and the humes. I need to know as much as possible about what caused the contention, why it is escalating things, and why the humes are doing what they're doing. When it began would be helpful as well." Billy wasn't sure Orgar had this information. He was pretty sure whatever was going on here now had been ongoing for a very long time.

"Yer not gonna like where yer have ter go ter get that information, Billy," Orgar said with a deep sigh. "Yer gonna have ter talk with 'Rora. And rumor has it yer wanted by her slags fer damagin' her gate."

"What's a slag?" Billy asked, sipping his wine.

"They're the local elves who've decided ter work fer her here in ther city. This itself has caused plenty of skirmishes are here, I can tell yer that much."

"Will they not talk with me and tell me what is going on here? Would showing them this quest help?"

"First off, Billy, they would likely as soon blast yer ter pieces as ter talk with ye. They hate the humes, and the weapons they've sent out to hunt us. Second, yer quest is quite vague on the details. The information I get from it be only a vague notion of savin' the world. I don't be havin' access ter the System, see."

"Yeah, I still don't know what all of it means myself. That's why I am doing some research first before I go about trying to prevent something I don't understand. You don't have access to the System?" Billy fidgeted with his manipulator while he thought about how to continue.

"What about the formula fer this mithril?" Orgar seemed laser-focused on getting this information and ignored Billy's last question. He seemed not to really care about giving away any information at all so long as he could get this recipe from Billy.

Billy spent the next couple of hours laying out the steps of processing the metal, from special chemical baths, to the right amount of time to wait between heating the ore it was extracted from. He even provided the vital steps where, things like, "expose the solution to the light of the fullest moon for not less than four hours, but less than seven hours, or until the solution turns the shade of blue that matches the sky at midday." There were over 100 distinct steps necessary to take some dusty old rocks with the stuff in them to a usable bar of purified mithril.

As Billy gave the instructions, Orgar had written them down carefully in a new book he had grabbed from under yet another cloth. The dwarf seemed to have any number of things under those. As the last instruction was provided, a pale silvery-gray light surrounded Orgar, and he gave out a hoot of joy.

"I did it, I did it, by all the gods above an' below, I finally did it!" The happy dwarf was dancing around the room, hugging the book to himself as if it were a newborn baby. "Billy, I not be knowin' if yer fer or against us fey, but yer have just helped me finish a Family Quest passed down from father ter son for over 2,000 years. We finally have our Legacy! Oh, this will change the political field fer sure, Billy, yer just wait an' see. We will finally have a voice in the Council, equal ter the Elf Queen herself!"

Billy was not sure exactly what that would mean for his own quest, but he was happy to have helped Orgar with this quest, even if he had not known he was doing any such thing. If he had known, he probably would have bargained for something more useful than a vague understanding of the political landscape of an entire planet.

It was only moments after the glow faded from Orgar when the doors to the unit were being pounded on by what seemed like dozens of hammers.

"What is that?" Billy shouted over the sudden noise. "Are we being attacked?" Billy moved to the back of the room to check the door there, which would lead to the outside of the pyramid structure and the streets, but Orgar guffawed and just went to his inner door and threw the latch.

"Boys! We finally got the recipe! Our Legacy is restored!" A great cheer went up as all of the dwarves surrounding the entrance to Orgar's little house sang out their delight.

Billy carefully opened the rear door just in case things turned violent, but in his current state, Orgar seemed to have totally forgotten Billy existed as he walked through a hole in the crowd out into the forge, and the swarm of dwarves closed around him and followed.

The pounding of hammers on anvils and the rattling of chains was absent, but in their place, Billy started to pick up what reminded him of flutes, guitars, and drums, with the occasional horn calling out in celebration.

"Charlotte, I don't know what just happened, but I think we may have made a little mistake in giving out that formula without finding out how important it was to the dwarves. It looks like they are stopping whatever production they were doing, and," he trailed off as he watched through the door, the hundreds, perhaps thousands of dwarves, begin to open barrels of drink, light up cigarettes, and lay out food for a feast of some sort.

"They're throwing a party, it looks like," Billy finished as he took it all in from the back of the square tunnel shape of the unit. Slowly, he crept forward to the inner door, closing the one he had opened to the outside and throwing its latch to secure it and the party he thought would be going on was looking like it was spilling into the streets to some of the neighboring blocks.

Chapter 7

"Okay, Charlotte, hop off and take a look around here. Try and keep out of the way of everyone and stay nearby. I am going to stay in here and make some minor modifications to my armor" Charlotte obediently popped off her port and moved outside the door, climbed it, and found a spot to sit unobtrusively to watch the dwarves.

Billy left the door open as Orgar had and moved back inside. He looked around and located the mithril rod Orgar had dropped in his haste to record the information Billy had given him. And once completed, he had managed to totally forget about the object which sparked the conversation to begin with. He now had the means to make as much of the stuff as he could ever need.

Billy stowed the rod back in his compartment, then carefully went about removing the majority of the thick plastic plates that acted as armor, from his legs, sides, all of his joints, and the removable ones that snapped off from his back, stomach, and abdomen. At some point his combat form's blades had retracted, so he hadn't had to manage those. Once he had them all organized into several piles, Billy spent the next few hours making slight modifications to each of them.

The night before, when Billy had been going back and forth delivering wood, he had seen a few actual giant spiders moving around town. There were a few varieties, but all of them, from the small two-foot wide ones to the ones as large as he himself, were very colorful. They not only had their own colorful patterns, they also seemed to share a particular set of markings, which Billy figured might be a show of their allegiance.

Keeping a mild link with Charlotte's view in the corner of his mind, Billy had noticed the dwarves had a banner of a sort, they used to announce to the people on the street who they were. So, while applying some surface carvings on the plastic plates and applying a simple indelible ink to the inlay, Billy also worked in small patterns that used the primary symbol from Orgar's family banner: a tiny silver hammer tapping on a faceted jewel.

While doing this to his plates, Billy hoped that Orgar wouldn't be upset about the sudden choice. He was not 100% sure what having such markings meant. It was only a guess at this point, but he figured that if this turned into anything controversial, he would simply wash off the paints with mineral spirits and apply something else. Either way, he hoped Orgar enjoyed the show of support.

Just in case, though, Billy had altered the whole image by arranging a series of ovals, eight of them, along the top of the banner pattern in imitation of his own eyes. Two large eyes, with three other smaller eyes on the left and right of those.

On and off throughout the day, Billy caught glimpses of dwarves playing games, eating, and generally having a fantastic time. Other groups of dwarves would come in every once in a while, in groups of 50 or more at a time, and the party would pause, then burst into revelry all over again as the news of the formula's discovery was learned.

Eventually, Billy finalized the last touches on his body armor, and painstakingly installed each and everyone back in their place. He had to be careful because some of the resin was still wet, and he wanted to make sure nothing would run or get smeared. When he was finally done, he managed to get a good look at himself in a mirror he had located on a wall over a sink, which had a cloth covering them both.

The mirror was small, but it provided Billy with enough surface area to get a good view of the different parts while they were in place. He looked quite fierce, with the engraved lines and ink making his dimensions difficult to nail down. The blues, golds, and silvers sparkled but were not too ostentatious. He liked the look of this, and since he could not wear clothing, exactly, he figured the use of these plates could fill in for the absence.

Now he thought about it. Billy probably could make clothing for himself. It would make him look very strange, with bits and pieces hanging off in odd locations. Scratching his chin, he put that plan aside for another time, though he did put together a materials list just in case he had the time later to produce some cloth.

Since Billy had finished the armor augmentation, he finally decided to turn to his prompts and notifications, which he had postponed earlier. There were several, letting him know he had helped Orgar finish a Legacy quest, whatever that was. It said he had earned a share of Experience, too.

Apparently, every generation increased the amount of Experience this quest would grant if it was ever completed. At this point, there were a couple thousand Experience points given to him. Billy was kind of put off by the meager amount, though. Looking at his Status, he saw he could apply some of those points to his Attributes again, but he wasn't sure he wanted to be unconscious in this city for however many days he would be out for, with no guarantee of safety. He liked Orgar, so far. But he did not exactly trust his people. Or any of the other people in this city.

Instead of spending any of this Experience, Billy pulled up a note program and left some notes on things he would use this on the next time he found a safe enough place to do so. He tried not to alter the path he had chosen the first time, but he had learned he would need some form of offensive capability if he were to protect himself from random attackers. Also, he was aware of other things out in the overworld that could attack at random. He could take things like that down, but he was personally averse to making weapons specifically to deal with sentient beings just yet. He still held out some hope he would be able to avoid or run from any that tried to do him harm.

It was getting late, and the party was getting ready to carry on to its tenth hour when a contingent of elves arrived in full armor with banners and everything.

"Billy, we may have a problem, dear. Elves have appeared and seem to be bringing a show of force here and the dwarves look like they might start taking offense." Charlotte's words snapped Billy out of reviewing his Status.

"I'm coming to have a look, just in case things get crazy," Billy responded.

Hopping up and making very little noise doing so, Billy scooped up a barrel of water and drained half of it before heading to the door and opening it slowly. He could feel the water moving from his collection tube to the various places inside himself where the water was purified and stored. The occasional hiss of steam lately had been mitigated due to very little motion, however, he did have to keep his boiler going and pressure built just in case. This was the cause of his lowered water level. It wasn't much, but the more Billy did things, the more he came to understand his new body.

Outside, the contingent of elves was already forming up a sort of wall past which several officious-looking elves made their way to the dwarven entrance. The dwarves had clearly taken note of the guests and led the way to this particular block. Out of the entire crowd of thousands of three-foot-tall folk, Billy had not at first located Orgar. He was, however, the center of attention for this party and was surrounded by important-looking dwarves from all over the place.

Upon counting, Billy noticed that there were at least 11 dwarf leaders talking with Orgar at a table near the central column. There were some shouts from the crowd, and the dwarves made a clear path for the elves to take.

The elves, however, had what Billy thought were looks of disgust clear on their faces. It seemed to him they saw the floors were covered in filth, and they were being asked to slosh their way through nastiness. One particular elf wearing a deep blue robe with gold trim and carrying what Billy took as a "Wizard Staff" spoke into the ear of one of the more regally dressed elf women. She looked like she would rather be anywhere in the city other than here, but she nodded to whatever words were spoken and began the short walk to the table of dwarves.

Billy tried to listen to what was being said by the other elves and the dwarves, but for some reason he could not make out anything specific anyone was saying. Then he had the feeling of someone walking on his grave, and he closed the door further, barely able to peak out. Instinctively, Billy tried to squint, and doing so changed the way he perceived his world.

As Billy imagined squinting, something about the way his two large eyes worked changed slightly, and he stopped seeing things in what he thought was normal light. Instead, strange wisps of sparkling gray dust-like trailers of stuff were being observed, making dancing patterns beyond where the door previously existed. He could see a vague outline of where everything around him existed, but this strange gray stuff did not seem to be stopped by any of it. It passed through dwarf, elf, forge, floor and wall with equal ease.

Billy backed into the room as the sphere of strange dust increased in volume until he was near the front door. The stuff suddenly paused there, then simply vanished as if none of it ever existed. Once it was gone completely, its passing happening in a fraction of a second, Billy's eyes clicked back to normal sight.

"What was that?" He asked himself. He used his manipulators to carefully wipe his large eyes, thinking something had to have covered them for a moment, but his lenses were free and clear of so much as a speck of dust.

Carefully, Billy creeped back to the interior door and looked through again. The elves, for whatever reason, had said their peace, and he could see they were already on their way out of the dwarve's block. Many of the dwarves were in groups of five or six, quietly talking with one another, but the figures at the tables were ignoring all of them while having their own conversation.

Figuring he had somehow managed to avert some disaster by not letting that strange gray light touch him, Billy decided it would be better to stay inside until later in the night. If Orgar did not return before it got too late, Billy would head outside and see about finding more information about this world. He had many questions about this world, his new home, but he seemed not to have the time to get much more than a short conversation here or there before something weird happened.

Instead of spending his time going over his Status for no purpose other than to annoy himself with his inability to spend his Experience points, Billy sat about examining all of the things Orgar had in his place. He did not poke into anything that was covered up by sheets. He figured if it was left out after all these hours of him being here, then Orgar would be fine with him seeing things.

The meeting outside carried on for some time, but during that period, Billy had discovered a plain leather-bound book with writing in it he could not decipher. With care, Billy had held the book close to his face in order to best view what was going on with the page. Every time he tried to memorize the images, however, something in his mind would unwind what he was looking at and erase itself from his memory. It was as if the last half an hour of flipping through page after page had never happened; he could remember nothing of what was on a single page.

"Charlotte, do you have any idea why I can't read this book?" She had been there front and center while he tried to understand the tome, but Charlotte seemed not to be able to comprehend such things.

"No, I cannot read what is written there. I am not familiar with the language, nor do I recognize or remember any of the writings." Her little holo appeared for Billy, and she tried to climb over the pages of the open tome, but whenever she tried walking over the pages, her image would flicker and reestablish itself off the tome entirely, as if she were teleporting.

"Do you think it could be a magic tome?" Charlotte's holo circled the open tome, trying to poke it with a foot, but each time she did, she would flicker out and reappear randomly at another point near it, but not on it.

"I'm not sure. I can tell you any number of things related to your carriage, but when it comes to magical knowledge, I am afraid I will have to let you decide," She said as she tried a few more times to cross onto the page and failed.

Billy examined the first page of the tome once more. He had seen a video talking about a gibberish book known as the Voynich Manuscript that contained nonsense language with bizarre images. This book was very similar, except for this first page. It seemed to have some form of direction, and as Billy continued to mull over the best way to decipher the words, it all suddenly clicked the instant after he received a notification.

Intellect check Successful. You are trying to comprehend an arcane tome. You can now decipher the text on this page of the tome.

And just like that, the letters rearranged themselves into proper instructions for exactly how to interpret the next few pages. Billy reviewed the instructions but quickly discovered that in order to follow them, he would have to disassemble the book and remove the individual pages. Other than this being necessary to follow the instructions, it became evident that the rest of the instructions would be encoded using the other pages, and each step would provide one more step into decoding the next set.

Unfortunately, this was not his book, and nothing he managed to try would allow him to memorize the pages or copy images of it for him to examine mentally as he did with his status. Then, a thought hit him. He was supposed to have been given the use of every function of the smartphone he'd had with him before being transplanted into this robot. His phone had an application for analyzing images and converting them to a different file type so he could use it with the bluetooth projector he'd bought to do this back on Earth.

Billy froze as he opened his Status and looked around the edges of the screen and eventually found the minimize button. Mentally tapping that, his Status page shrunk down to a smaller square and he now had access to a number of other apps that were on his phone. Looking at the top right, he saw he had full signal strength. Quickly opening up his camera app, Billy swapped its settings over to create a different formatted video file and he tapped the record button and imagined holding it just right to record what he was seeing. Then he slowly and carefully flipped through each page of the book while making sure to record each side with the highest resolution his phone, or his eyes, could.

Once Billy recorded the last page, he imagined crossing his fingers and hitting stop, which should have then performed the autosave function. Strangely, instead of instantly saving, which is what his old phone would have done, there was some icon that basically showed that the application was processing the image. There was no other indicator apart from the icon. Suddenly, a prompt began flashing behind the camera app, so he flipped over to it.

Congratulations! You have discovered a magic tome.

Billy tried to blink a few times as he read. He had somehow transcribed a magical tome without actually learning anything from it.

Billy looked around the rest of the room to see if there were any other magical tomes lying about, but to his dismay, there were not. He only hoped that if he decided to actually try and learn something from the video file he had captured, the tome here wouldn't suffer any damage. Billy had always wanted to experience magic, not just the lord of the rings kind, where it was far less flashy, but the true gamer type of magic with fireballs and lightning bolts. He just wouldn't destroy someone else's chance to learn them, especially because the tome wasn't his, to begin with.

Scooping up the tome, Billy went to the inner door area and plopped it on the counter there. After a moment's thought, he picked it up and tossed it under the counter just in case someone came in and decided to abscond with it. Who knows, it could be criminal to have the thing. There were just so many things Billy didn't know about this place, much less this world. He really needed some quality information-gathering time with someone knowledgeable.

Whatever was going on with the dwarves seemed to finally begin winding down. Several times, Billy thought for sure the celebration was finished. Unless it wasn't a celebration, patiently as he could, Billy waited. At long last, Orgar opened the door and stepped inside. Voices tried to follow him in, but he said something to them and pulled closed the door and threw the latch on it.

Earlier in the night Billy had pulled the sheet to cover the interior of the small unit, and he watched now as Orgar pulled it aside before stepping in. He looked around and paused as he watched Billy get up from between the work benches he had been sitting between when Orgar had completed his quest.

"I don't know who yer are, Billy, or why yer here." He scratched his beard, and for the first time, Billy could see the lines of age etched deep in the dwarf's face. He seemed to have aged decades in the last few hours. "I don't know what yer want from us, but tonight yer've made a lifelong friend of mine clan."

"That's great, Orgar. I appreciate the sentiment. I really do, but I have no idea what I have done, so whatever has been going on was not out of any real altruism. I simply did not know what would happen." Billy wrung his manipulators in a combination of anxiety and annoyance. "I need a great many things explained if you have the time."

"Aye, I would. But it's been a long day, Billy, an' I be needin' some rest. Is there any way yer could talk about this with me tomorrow?"

Upon closer examination of Orgar, he did seem drained. It must be the craggy lines are the equivalent of bloodshot eyes but for dwarves.

"One thing, Orgar," Billy said, sliding past Orgar to get the tome he had stashed under the counter. He returned to find the dwarf hooking up a hammock on the second floor. Clambering up there was as simple as walking, so Billy had no trouble doing so to show it to Orgar.

"Can you tell me what this is?" Holding the tome forward for the dwarf to look at, he tiredly waved a hand at it.

"It's a tome that has some form o' magic knowledge in it. It's yers if yer want, I ne'er had a mind fer the stuff." He grunted as he pulled his shirt off and tossed it into a pile. Billy figured it was all dirty. Not wanting to get a show, Billy shrugged in the way of spiders and went back downstairs.

Deciding not to waste any time, Billy opened the book to have a look. Instead of using the interface, he decided to work this out with the real thing. Billy took the time to carefully remove the binding of the tome and separate out the pages for the requisite spells, chants, and such. However, while doing this, Billy realized that some of the pages seemed to be shared with other spells in the tome. It was as if each of the spells, or whatever they would be, all shared some aspect of knowledge with one another.

The only problem Billy had now was he did not know what kind of magic was contained in the book. He reviewed his Status to see if it could provide any help. Unfortunately, it did and did not. He learned that he required a specific level in several Knowledge tabs, which he did not currently have. He thought to try and purchase the requisite levels, but then he discovered he needed other information about such topics from this world before he could allocate the points.

After more than an hour of reading through his Status, it appeared that his Abilities were quite nuanced in breaking down the different things he could possibly know. Due to his education on Earth, he was able to carry over some of the informative Knowledge he had, but not all of it. Billy figured that any understanding of physics he had from youtube videos and do-it-yourself experiments only applied to Earth because that information did not translate exactly to this particular world. Basically, the Knowledge of Physics he had was grayed out.

His understanding of many things seemed useless here. Fortunately, Language was something that carried over, as knowing how to communicate with sound or the written word was applicable here. Counting rolled over as well, but Billy was not very advanced in that particular field. One important takeaway from his time reading about his abilities was the requirements for establishing the first points in them.

Talents were things he could do without any tools and without the need to do any studying. Running, Leadership, and Jumping are examples of this. Skills are Abilities where he required tools to use in order to activate them, all Crafting fell here, along with his combat Skills. Knowledge required extensive study, which could come in the form of images, words, or symbols, or orally. Each of those also had some sort of sublevel requirements. A requirement to learn anything from books was for the reader to at least know the language it was written in. One exclusion to this was that the reader was being taught the language within, translating the oral word into the written one for the reader. Thus, reading and writing were separate from the spoken word as Knowledge and required education separately in both.

Forging things from metal requires some Knowledge of Chemistry, and Running requires one to have legs. Things like that were what limited individuals when it came to acquiring a new Ability, or so Billy had figured. The lesson Billy took from all of his reading was that he could not purchase a level in anything that would help him learn magic, for now, because he required a teacher. Instead, he poked Charlotte awake and had her perform some minor maintenance while he rested his eyes.

The boiler in Billy made some odd sounds as it vented some of the heat he had kept stored for so long. He could feel his insides moving in the mechanical way clocks do, or so he'd imagined. Carefully arranged springs, coils and parts came online or offline as he settled down for maintenance. The requisite lubrication and filter cleaning was equal to using the bathroom for Billy; it felt good to be cleaned and let go of the pressure build-up to carefully power down his internal systems.

The lubrication was like a balm on his joints, and cleaning up the burned oils and lubricants was almost as enjoyable as shaving his face each morning back on Earth.

Billy thought occasionally of Earth. He had lived a quiet kind of life up in the mountains, having a stable job and being able to enjoy his hobbies without the driving need for other human interaction. Some people needed to be around other people. Billy was one of those who could do without but had no problem with, either.

About the only thing Billy really missed was his morning coffee. He liked the feel of the drink tingling on his lips as it worked on his brain to wake him up in the early mornings. He'd had no particular preference, and whenever anyone came by the hardware store talking about this brand or that flavor, he would venture out and give it a try.

The maintenance was really the only thing here in the last couple of days that had managed to bring him any real comfort. Most of the time, he had a heart of fire and veins of copper and steel pumping boiling steam and compressed air through his metallic body. Just before he finally entered his rest mode, Billy recalled he wanted to ask Orgar what he thought about the body armor he had altered earlier that day.

"Oh well," he thought. He would just have to ask him about it tomorrow morning.

As it turned out, Billy could not sleep. He had thought that by activating his maintenance cycle, he would return to that strange park until it was done, but the more he waited, the more bored he became. Finally, after he had listened to Charlotte quietly apply oil to every joint on only one of his legs, he decided to open up his phone application from his Status.

Charlotte noticed he was once again doing something as certain components of Billy's body became more active as power was routed to his Clockwork Cerebrum and processor core. It wasn't much of a change, but the low hum increased and Charlotte had paused to see if he would be moving. He did not and she continued with her work while humming a tinny tune.

Successfully opening up an app he'd had on his old phone from Earth, Billy had noticed that his voicemail had a message waiting for him, and he had missed a call. He also saw that he had several text messages. Curious, Billy opened up his call log and rang up his voicemail. There, he entered his pin and waited to listen.

What met Billy's sonic detectors, his ears, couldn't be considered sound as much as the resulting noise of a train full of railroad tracks spilling onto a concrete highway, then the very heavy steel bars would roll downhill overtop and across one another. Flinching, Billy mentally pushed his phone away from his ears, even though he had neither a phone nor ears until the sound abated. There were some crackling noises, very disquieting popping sounds, and more metal-on-metal sounds. After 29 seconds of this, the call had ended.

Shuddering at this, Billy opened up his text app and instead of seeing words there, he observed wiggling lines, strange whirls and shapes popping in and out of existence. It almost looked like a moving background for a screen lock or something. Quickly checking the other texts he found all of them were similarly bizarre and indecipherable.

Shrugging to himself, Billy tapped the reply button with a thought and thought-typed a response.

Sorry I missed your call if the voicemail was yours. I am currently out of town working on a project for a friend. It was on short notice, and I didn't have time to let anyone know because it was somewhat time-sensitive. I'll try and get back as soon as possible. In the meantime, take care of my dog, Clemmens? Thanks, bro. - Bill

Hoping he'd guessed right, Billy mentally tapped *Send*.

He closed the messaging app and looked through his other applications and thought back on his conversation with the strange old man at the park. He'd said he would let him take his phone by incorporating it into his matrix or something. He also said it would allow him access to the internet and a store. Curious, Billy looked for a new icon or something that would indicate access to a store.

It didn't take him long to locate the icon, and he quickly tapped on it. He waited only a moment before a login prompt appeared. Billy mentally tapped his lip, which he had somehow felt, and tapped the *New Account* button at the bottom of the page. Here Billy had spent the better part of 20 minutes carefully filling out item after item that was necessary to identify him specifically, where he was from, the year, what world, the proper universe, his current location, level if applicable, specific random-seeming listings from his Status to determine which System he was currently using, and so on.

Half of the questions Billy did not know how to answer, and others seemed quite nonsensical, like picking the blocks that looked blue, or yellow, or were straight lines. Those were easy, but he got the feeling that in some universes, those lines would appear different due to the different physics the world operated with. He wasn't sure, but he answered everything as best he could and carried on with the questionnaire.

Eventually, he answered the last question, and finally hit the last *Submit* button.

Billy waited. Nothing happened.

Then, a search bar appeared with a blinking cursor in it.

"What am I supposed to do now?" He thought to himself. "Do I just put anything in here and search the store or something?" He wasn't sure what he was supposed to do now. He wanted to do something like window shop, not look for a precise item.

Instead of putting some object in the search bar, Billy decided to type *Help* and *Send*. A moment later, a little ringing phone icon popped up on his screen, and he twitched in surprise.

"Billy, if you want me to finish calibrating your isomorphic balancers, I need you to stay still. Otherwise, I will have to shut off your Ambulation Chronometer. If I do this, you will be paralyzed until I am done," Charlotte buzzed at him as her blue holo manifested.

"Do what you gotta do, Charlotte. I am looking at my Status for now, anyways." Billy felt a series of clicks and felt something in his chest pop, and then he was numb to everything except his eyes, which he was not paying attention to.

"It will only take me another half an hour; then I will have you right as rain again, dear," her old lady voice sounded cheery now that he would no longer surprise her with some twitch or jostling.

Billy did not hear her response as he had already mentally tapped the jingling phone icon and picked up the line.

"Hello. My. Name. Is. Mark. How. Can. I. Help. You. Today?" The voice paused while saying each word, much like the early artificial intelligence voice machines that could be programmed to say a limited number of things.

"Yes, I was wondering what sorts of things are available in the store. There doesn't seem to be any listings, only a search bar."

There were some soft clicking and buzzing sounds after Billy replied, and after a few seconds, he got a reply in a less robotic voice.

"I am sorry. Delivery service to your district is unavailable. Listings are unavailable. Trade is unavailable." The voice was very succinct.

"I was told by the old man at the park that I would have access to the store. I had picked up a Quest Prompt and he said I would have this opportunity while on my quest to this world I'm at." Billy didn't know what else to say. He felt like he was being mistreated by having been lied to. Perhaps he would have to speak to a manager or something and get this straightened out.

"What is the quest ranking?" The voice sounded bored.

Billy swapped over to his Status and looked at the only active quest he had. According to this, his quest was only Rare. "It's a Rare quest to save the world."

Nearly a minute passed as Billy heard clicks and buzzing, almost like static but with more of a pattern to it, before a reply finally came in.

"A ticket has been generated to address this issue. This issue has been passed on to my team leader, and it has been a very busy day. I have two options for you. One, you can wait on the line, but it may be a few days or weeks before the line is answered. Two, I can have my team leader give you a call back when your name comes up." The voice seemed as interested in one option as another, and both of them were less interesting than watching paint dry.

"Can you have them give me a callback? I have other things.."

"Thank you. You have been placed on the call-back list. Have a nice day." The line went dead.

"I can make do in the meantime," Billy finished as the call ended.

Billy spent the next few minutes going over some particulars with his Status, double checking his notes about what to apply his

Experience points to in the future. He wanted to make sure that when he got the opportunity, he got the right tools for the right job. And as this particular job required him to save the world, he felt the tools he would need would probably be pretty specific.

There were plenty of Skills he could get to increase his combat capabilities, and these ultimately would unlock access to Special Attacks. Most of this, however, was currently locked behind an initial training montage as he would have to find someone willing to teach him enough to acquire the first point. After training, Billy assumed he would merely need to apply the points and it would increase further this way.

Special Attacks, Billy learned, were linked to specific kinds of weapons. Unfortunately, Billy was a giant metal spider, and he wasn't very sure what weapons would be appropriate for himself. Checking the various combat Skills, he did notice there were a couple of "him" specific attack methods that weren't grayed out. One was the spider equivalent of kicking, and another was a sort of grappling Skill. Both were subcategories of the Hand-to-Hand Skill which linked to the Weapon Mastery section under the Discipline section of his Status, and were specializations of the 'use your body to smack things' techniques. To his surprise, he even had a bite option there.

Deciding it would be alright to move some Experience around, Billy slid a few into the Weapon Masteries for his feet and bite on the off chance he needed to do some form of damage in the future. To further increase his chance to strike successfully, Billy had to put a few Experience into Hand-to-Hand, which was a Skill. Once the points were put in he saw he also had access to some of the Special Attacks matching his level of mastery. This included a pounce attack and a few kinds of bites. He saw that if he put one more point into his combat Skill he would even be able to make use of some grapple attack that had a chance to render the target unconscious.

Upon the second inspection, all of his masteries had the chance, though small, to K.O. his targets. The overall damage, a combination of his strength and speed Attributes, was limited to his own Natural Armor. He could do far more damage to opponents if he was not limited to his own physical Durability, but that can be said about anyone. He could punch and do damage to his target and not himself by holding back a little. Should he forgo any restrictions, he could do far more damage to his opponent, but he would suffer damage as well.

Deciding only small changes have been made, most of them technical knowhow improvements, Billy hit the *Apply* button and immediately heard Charlotte sigh.

"This is going to take a few hours longer than I had planned, but..."

Billy didn't hear the rest as his world went black.

Chapter 8

A tapping on his head woke Billy a few hours later. With whirring and popping bursts of steam, Billy jolted up from his sitting position on the floor. His eyes began functioning immediately, and he saw Orgar backing up with a large smile on his face.

"Marnin' Billy. Do yer eat?"

Billy tried to blink what could be considered sleep from his eyes, but he didn't blink, and there was nothing in his eyes. Slightly confused from waking so quickly, Billy felt his boiler and mechanical systems fluctuate for a moment. He calmed down and took stock of himself.

"I, uh, I could use some water, actually," Billy said, making a sound not too dissimilar to one licking their lips thirstily.

Billy's confusion stemmed from the visual aids being present that were not there before. He had a more tactical view of the world, which was absent before he had allocated points to a combat-related Skill. Now that he had some actual skills, he also had access to targeting, highlighting things he was looking at and providing a percentage chance to successfully strike and damage whatever it was. He also saw he could not disable this. It seemed this would be a permanent change to his worldview.

"I got a few barrels over here if yer wanton' water. Myself needs more 'en that," Orgar said, rubbing his belly. "We have a cafeteria outside where we all get breakfast. I'll come ter get yer later after I make sure things are clear fer yer to pop out."

"Alright. I'm looking forward to getting out. I've been in here for well over a day already, and I want to look around again." Billy moved over to the barrels Orgar had uncovered and tapped one while Orgar went outside.

He didn't have to wait long before Orgar pulled open the door to his unit and yelled in to Billy, "Come on out, the boys are ready ter meet yer!"

Only mildly terrified of meeting so many at once, Billy checked himself to make sure the markings on his armor were clear, clean, and well-colored. He looked clean and quite tough. He would have been more intimidating, perhaps, if he didn't know his armor was nothing more than fancy plastic strips strapped onto a metal frame.

Boiling steam pulsed through Billy's body and limbs as he moved through the portal to the dwarf forge. He saw hundreds, possibly thousands, of the little people all over the place. Some construction had been done while he was inside, and the dwarves were celebrating. Almost nothing was recognizable after even a few hours of sleep. Unconsciousness. Whatever it was, he wasn't sure what went on while he wasn't aware.

Bridges, ladders, and platforms had been built throughout the facility. The furnace for the forge was mostly underground, but it seemed the dwarves had retrofitted the place to make something they had been unable to in the past. Probably the mithril.

The small folk stood around in large groups, and for the first time, Billy could see distinct differences among the dwarves. Hair color, nose shape, brow size, and skin color were now all separated into what Billy suspected were families or clans. It was likely some specific Ability was the cause of the distinct changes, and what he was seeing were groups of specialized jobs. He did see changes in himself that only happened because of his choices in Ability or Attribute. He could, however, accouter himself to obfuscate his own upgrades, unlike the dwarves.

The dwarves, upon seeing Billy exit the house, held rocks they smacked with bare hands. The rocks were round and smooth, and Billy had no idea what they were doing. In no time flat, all of the dwarves had somehow pounded their rocks into pebbles, then into powder, which they dumped onto the floor. Then, all the dwarves said something in one voice.

A wave of physical force smashed into Billy and rolled through him before he could react.

You have been given the blessing of the Water Warden, who expresses their eternal gratitude for your services. This blessing increases your Durability by 10% and decreases your Mass by 5%, permanently. The reduction of Mass only counts when determining weight for purposes of climbing, jumping, and buoyancy.

Billy staggered for a moment as he had to instantly readjust to being 5% lighter than he was, which was several dozen pounds spread evenly over his entire body. The dwarves all chuckled at this. Apparently, this was great fun for them, disorienting people just as they woke up.

Billy saw Orgar waving at him with a small flag, which held the same markings Billy had on himself, and shouted, "Billy, come. We need ter have words with yer before yer head out."

Working out his new gait, Billy managed to retain control of his feet enough to walk toward his friend. The other dwarves had begun mingling again as Billy moved among them, and some even reached out to touch him. None sent him a Friend Request, which was strange to Billy, but he suspected they did not want to bombard him with them, so they held off.

"Billy, I welcome yer ter the Cavern Clan of dwarves, made official just last night thanks to yer helpin' me finish my quest." Orgar's voice carried out from where he stood, and Billy was quite sure he could even be heard out in the street. "Without yer help, this clan'd ne'er been restored. Yer gave us a gift more grand 'an anythin' we could've possibly imagined. Yer not only gave us our future, Billy, yer've unlocked our past. We now know who we were and who we are."

Billy fidgeted nervously as Orgar began explaining the history of the dwarf people. He told their story from the beginning when the world was made. When Billy first met the dwarves, he thought they were more earth-element oriented, and so did the dwarves. Sometime in the recent past, the humes had done something to the world that erased the memory and history of all the fey beings of the world. As it turned out, dwarves are closely related to water elementals, even though they look like they are carved from stone.

Part of their history was defined by the way they bore into the ground, ever in search of the strange and mysterious. Most water spirits were born upon a tall mountain in winter and cast down come summer. Some would make it deep into the mountains and surrounding lands, while others would make it to the rivers. Deep in the past, all fey were fundamental elementals. The fey that managed to dig through the land became dwarves. The fey that made it to the rivers became fairies. Those that spread through forests and swamps became elves.

In a way, elves and dwarves are related in spirit, but as the ages passed, the spirits became more aware, eventually taking forms. The dwarves became small humanoids that could navigate the infinite complexity of the caves that permeated the lands from mountain top to ocean bottom. Elves were the life-givers of the woodlands, plains, and swamps, evolving several times into more complex beings. Spirits of the ground itself became silent guardians and protectors to all cast in their shadows, spelling doom for the unwary. Fire was brought by wild lightning, bringing its own spirits to the world.

Ages and ages passed with little change until animals populated the world. Animals were the most evolved forms of the spirits of the world. They were composed of many parts of the oldest spirits, and none of them were pure at all. Some were so diluted they moved to the point where none could interact with their spirit ancestors.

Then, humes came to the world. One year, there were animals across the land, sky, and seas. The next year, humes walked the land; with them, they brought something the spirits of the world had never known: order.

The humes sought to control the world, fashioning it to their will and desire. They were the first to unlock the System of the World, and with that, they began to meticulously manage the growth of their species, one individual at a time. Then, humes discovered ancient clues as to their ancestry and found the means to interact with the spirits of the world using magic supplied by the System.

This interaction granted access to the System to all the spirits at that time, unbeknownst to the humes.

Several more ages rolled by, and the world grew with the advantages given by the System. Then suddenly, the humes discovered something else, and they turned against the spirits of the world. They gathered in one place, forged a mighty magic, and cast it against the spirits of the world. This magic stripped access to the System from all the fey, the evolved spirits. Some of the most powerful fey burned out their lives holding off the wave of power, allowing some of the fey to retain their access to the System.

However, they could not use it, even though they could see its pages and information. The spell the humes cast changed how the fey could turn off this function by tagging onto it a cost of Experience. However, since they could no longer actively or passively use the System, nobody could use Experience.

The humes, now with unlimited access to the System, began covering the lands and seas with their houses, factories, and fires. The fey could do nothing to protect the lands that gave birth to them for ages unknown.

What Billy had done provided Orgar with enough Experience to pay to turn on his access to the System, granting him full use of it. He could now grow in character and power and learn new things by using the Experience collected from doing life activities none of the other fey could do, with the exception of a very select ancient few.

What Billy took away from this tale was that the fey beings were once equivalent to Players, and then they were turned into NPC's, non-player characters. As NPCs, they could not grow to match the growth of Players and could not fight against them on an equal footing. What Billy had done was restore Orgar's access to this System, which put him in a seat at the High Table of Flowers, the supreme council of System users in the Lair of the Fey. The elves were not happy about this and came to find out how it had happened.

Orgar had told them he had located information leading to the completion of a quest that gave him so much Experience that it granted him access to the System. The little Experience Billy had acquired was a tiny percentage of what Orgar had received; most of it had been used to regain access. Orgar still possessed thousands of Experience, however, and he was soon going to be using it to strengthen his position in the clan.

Billy had sat spider-style on the floor while he had listened to the history of the dwarves and, in many ways, the history of life as it had evolved on this world. He was a little curious about how the spirits of the world had evolved into what Orgar described as higher beings, but all of the fey creatures Billy had seen were supposedly just that, more evolved spirits of advanced elementals.

Orgar had sat with his family as Billy absorbed the information he'd been given and ate his breakfast. A few of the dwarves were responsible for cooking, and Billy observed several kinds of fish sautéed in some kind of mushroom broth, a favorite of the dwarves. They also seemed to have a penchant for cheeses, for there were many kinds of cheeses, from bland-looking bitter to colorful sweet varieties, that were treated like candies. Billy found it quite interesting, even though he no longer needed to eat to survive.

Billy had many questions about the dwarves, their culture, and their political situation. He instead reminded himself he was not here just for them, so he chose to ask questions that provided him details on the interactions between fey in general and the humes, where the humes were located, and any other information available about them. He hoped he would not come across as dismissive of the dwarf's newfound access to the System, but his Quest here meant he needed to know more about both sides if he were to have any chance to bring peace back to this world.

As it was, some of the murmuring he had been hearing leaned more to the dwarves arming themselves to fight the humes now they could grow stronger. Billy knew some of these beings wanted revenge for losing their ancestral homes, but he did not wish to either promote or convince them of other means. He was not a dwarf and felt he should not intervene in their personal destinies.

"So, what are the elves going to do about your clan gaining so much power overnight?"

"They threatened us, of course. Those flighty folk think that because they're above ground folk and have had ter fight the humes most of'en that they've a right ter tell us how we can fight, and even if we can." Orgar had a disgusted look on his face as he said this. "They think it's their right ter determine who c'n use the System, and we have somehow usurped their authority."

"They feel unbalanced?" Billy rubbed his spidery chin, thinking he had the elves figured out.

"No. They are afraid. They think we will push back against the humes, and bring more war. The elves want ter hole up and hope the problem passes us by. Cowards." Other dwarves echoed Orgar's sentiment.

"They prefer to sit and do nothing?" Billy was perplexed by this but not surprised.

"No. They want to hide. It's in their nature ter do so. We dwarves have always been explorers and delvers of the deep, fearless in our search fer the treasures of the world. The elves only cover the surface of the land and prefer the sunlight and moonlight, lounging in their hammocks and singing their songs." A few of the nearby dwarves chuckled and called them fairies as if this were a derogatory term.

"What about the other fey? The other creatures and intelligent folk? Do they wish to fight?" Billy heard some dwarves chuckle at the thought of elves being 'intelligent.'

Orgar grunted as he thought of his response. "The beasts here ne'er wanted ter hide in a city such as this. They're wild and cantankerous. Forcing predator and prey in ter peace has e'er been a delicate balancing game." Orgar slurped some of his mushroom broth, then wiped his beard on his shirt and stood up, waving Billy to follow him.

The two went up a series of stairs to a split in the housing units that led to the roof. Up top, there were more stairs leading up and down, probably for general maintenance. Orgar continued upward. Billy watched him climb and then followed. Up on the highest unit was a redoubt where a couple of dwarves were using spy glasses to watch the blocks around them, both on land and in the sky.

"We have ter keep an eye on our neighbors, see. If trouble comes, we need ter be ready ter protect ourselves." Orgar waved at a couple of dwarves, and they went down to the forge for breakfast. "Here, take a look," Orgar turned one of the larger glasses to point at a particular block.

Carefully, Billy squatted down and looked through the spyglass to the particular building. Then he lifted his head and used his enhanced vision to get a better zoomed-in look. "What am I seeing here?"

"That's one of the elves' palaces. It is where they sometimes hold meetings ter manage the city." Orgar's tone showed his contempt for the elves.

Billy's primary pair of eyes were telescopic internally, allowing him to get a far better zoomed-in view of the palace. Not only could he make out individual units through all of the decorations, but he could also make out individual elves.

"Do they always have so many out patrolling their block?" Billy had counted more than fifty on the sides he could see. The guards were moving in odd patterns in and out of designated units, as if those were stations placed seemingly at random. This would also allow them to change guards and reach the interior.

"They have ter. Many of the beasts stuck here blame the elves for losin' their lands." Orgar had grabbed the spyglass when he saw Billy did not need it. "See there, on the southern corner, in the street there. Those beasts are there ter petition the elves for the rights ter hunt. The elves protect all beasts cause they're not very smart yer see, and have ter send patrols out with 'em when they go. Thing is, the elves don't want ter leave the city safety, so they of'en make excuses not ter go out."

Billy saw the beasts Orgar mentioned. These particular beasts looked like large otters with flat heads, wide cheeks, rich dark brown fur, and hands with sharp black claws. Their eyes were much like the dwarf's were, solid-looking black. These did not wear clothes, however, but did have very large bodies. Standing upright, they were almost four feet tall, not including their two-foot-long tail. The cluster of beasts numbered almost twenty, and they were moving over and around each other, barely under the control of a pair of larger otters. Billy couldn't pick it up clearly, but he imagined the growly barks these large beasts would be making to control the pups.

Curious, Billy asked, "What stops them from just going out on their own?"

"The elves won't stop 'em. Most of'en those that go out on their own come back fewer in number… if they come back at all."

"I see," Billy said as he watched the argument between the elf guard and the otter beast. The beasts apparently received good news, for they soon headed off with two elf guards in tow. Behind that group, another cluster of beasts waited for approval.

"The elves determine who comes and goes, why exactly?" Billy turned away from watching the distant commotions to watch Orgar.

Orgar watched the otters leave, then said, "They have shared access ter the System to a limited number of themselves. Not all of them are willin' ter go out and put their necks on the line fer the likes of simple beasts as they see 'em."

"They grant access to those they wish to, huh?" Billy scratched his spider chin in thought. "Sounds like they will have met their match now that you can do the same for the clan, am I right?"

Orgar chuckled at Billy's insightfulness. "Right y'ar, friend. I can now grant access ter others of me clan with the right number of Experience points. I have become, if yer not aware, a legitimized merchant. I can sell goods and services fer Experience and use it. Others can trade, see, but they can only accept it or trade it; they cannot use it. Some do this in the hopes that one day they'll be given the gift of the System."

Billy, his internal mechanisms giving away his sudden surprise at this revelation by emitting strange whirring sounds and clicking noises, along with a few puffs of steam, "I made you something like the king, didn't I?"

Orgar beamed broadly. "Yer did, Billy. The heads of the houses in the clan spent all day yesterday talkin' about it. The ceremony will be later this mornin' if yer wantin' ter show yerself."

Billy was already doing his best to shake his head like a spider.

"Sorry, I need to go out myself. I need to get some more coins to purchase a few more materials. Will you still pay for wood? Or will you need something else?" Billy was willing to help Orgar and the clan, but he did not want to be indebted by accepting any form of gifts. He had not made Orgar a leader with any intention and would not pretend he had done so.

"Yer don't have ter, Billy. Yer can stay here and get whatever yer needin' jus' fer the askin'." Orgar reached over and put a meaty little hand on one of Billy's legs.

"I can't do that, Orgar. I am glad to have helped you overcome the limitations imposed by the humes upon all fey, but I did not do so intentionally. I will not impose upon your hospitality. I am more than sure you will have far more things to manage without having to deal with my own precocious needs. I am not even aware of all I need to do, anyways." Billy reached over with a manipulator and patted Orgar's hand in a friendly manner. "Thank you for saying so, though. I am really happy I was helpful."

"Right, well. I think I will return ter the clan downstairs then. I will let the other Scarls, those would be the heads of houses in the clan, know they can give requests ter yer fer some coin. We have already stopped production with the iron now we know how to produce the mithril. It'll take us a few months ter retrofit the forge ter be able ter begin production of the stuff." Orgar looked up at the bright sky above and ran a hand through his long, thick beard.

"Alright, Orgar. I will have a look around the city, then, and I should be back in a couple of days to look for any requests for work." Billy reached out a manipulator, and Orgar took it to shake. "Good luck, King Orgar."

"Good luck, Billy."

With that, Orgar climbed down to the interior of the block, and a couple of other dwarves scrambled up to maintain the watch. Billy skipped the stairs, walked to the edge of the upper unit, and began to walk down the walls, careful not to damage any doors or frighten any dwarf on the way down to the streets.

Down on the ground, outside from the dwarf block, almost a dwarf hold, Billy was again plunged into a morass of many kinds of peoples and cultures all jammed together. The beasts were as varied in type and size as the more intelligent beings, such as the dwarves, elves, centaurs, and the like. Beetles and bugs, bears and snails, centipedes, and more – all were housed in the Lair of the Fey. The one thing Billy was unsure about was the scale of the place. The blocks were organized by height and spacing but not in straight lines. This made it impossible to see too far down one street before a block of housing units was in the way.

As Billy walked through the crowds, he did his best not to touch anyone. He did not wish to bother or be bothered while he scouted the area. He still saw groups of similar beings standing guard in clusters of blocks at the roads and intersections, which made it a little easier to determine which species were where. He also caught snippets of conversations in dwarven and elven, mostly complaining about being denied permission to go outside today.

Hundreds of ramshackle stalls lined the streets, with groups assessing the legality of the setups. Everywhere, there were beasts and other fey trading goods for coin or coin for goods. Clothing and food, tools, or other materials were carried in rough packs on the backs of beasts of burden – animals really. There were horses, oxen, donkeys, and even giant tortoises. The spaces between units and people were packed with trash piles, and Billy imagined the smells while observing the masses, avoiding the piles as much as possible.

Taking in as much of the place as possible, Billy thought about what he could do to make some coin. He saw much of the problem in the area was the trash. It was everywhere, in piles on the streets and stuffed in corners at the housing units. Going over to a pile that was well over six feet tall, Billy saw there were some folk scavenging through them for anything useful. Often, this was rotten food, which small children seemed to be gathering in dirty baskets. The remainder was mostly broken stuff.

Food seemed to be quite an issue here. "So, there is an abundance of garbage and a deficit of foodstuffs. If I took some time to take this rotting stuff and process it, I could probably make some fertilizer and start a farming project." Billy talked to himself while he stood beside several small mouse folk who were rummaging as well. One looked up to him, and its ear twitched before it went back to scavenging.

After another hour of wandering the streets near the dwarf block, Billy had a solid route mapped on his HUD. He began to refer to this naturally as he looked at it and placed markers every few minutes. It reminded him of his gaming days back in high school. Back then, Billy had enjoyed FPS games, first-person shooters, and he was one of those tactical players who used the HUD minimap to coordinate rather than rush ahead and get ambushed.

So it was that sometime around midday, Billy returned to find Orgar to ask him a question or three, perhaps for that favor. It didn't take Billy long to locate the busy dwarf, who was neck-deep in meetings with his clan.

"Orgar, do you have a moment? I have a couple of questions, if you don't mind," Billy's manipulators were making their usual nervous motions by playing with one another or cleaning one of his many feet when Orgar excused himself from the other dwarves.

Orgar looked worn but smiled at seeing his friend. "Of course, I can spare a few minutes. What do yer need, Billy?"

Billy squatted down where he was to be closer to Orgar and spoke to him as quietly as the forge ambiance would allow.

"I need a couple of units to set up for myself, Orgar. I have a plan to make some spare coin, and I need a place to operate out of. Are there particular steps I need to take in order to arrange my own housing? Or, if possible, to establish my own block?"

Orgar scratched at his beard for a moment, thinking. "Normally, yer would have ter talk with the elves ter get yer own block fer housin'. However, I have access ter the System now, and so do yer. First, spend some Experience points and get the Ability Real Estate Management. Then, open up yer Status, and pull up yer Map."

Billy spent the Experience points on the Ability and maximized his map. "Done and done," he said.

"Good, on the top left is a pulldown menu. Select that, and access the Lair of the Fey. On this map, off ter the right side, is a button ter start yer own block, or ter start a block fer someone yer select. Choose this, and find a space somewhere ter set it up on yer map. It'll take about 10 minutes er so ter appear, then all yer have ter do is enter the administrator's office and assign a unit ter yerself. This will establish both yer as the Administrator of yer block, and give yer authority ter modify the units, or ter house folk."

Billy carefully followed Orgar's instructions. When he used his map to locate a place to set it, he found he could only drop the red-outlined building on the edge of the city, where it would then turn green. He did his best to remain close to the areas he had mapped a short time ago but figured the longer route would give him access to more materials for his endeavors. After another minute of mulling over the decision, Billy dropped the application for the building on the edge closest to Orgar's clan and hit *Apply*.

"Alright, Orgar. Thanks again. I have a few ideas to help out the folk of this city, and with any luck, it won't take me very long to get things rolling."

Orgar smiled up at Billy, "Glad ter help yer, Billy. If yer needin' anythin' in the future, feel free ter visit."

Billy gave Orgar quick directions to his new block so he could visit as well, and with a quick handshake, he left Orgar to manage his clan as their new King.

By the time Billy arrived at the edge of town, only a couple of miles walk through the streets of the city, the block had already appeared. Several people were walking around the place, but as no administrator had activated it officially, none could make it past a few feet from the street toward it until Billy arrived. Some sort of static barrier rebuffed any trespasser.

Billy calmly walked through the small crowd examining the building, and he had to ignore them as he received a few notifications. He continued into the building while he pulled them up. They were only alerts letting him know the building he had requested was completed and that he had only a couple more minutes to claim the administrator position before it became public. He found the pedestal near the central column and placed a manipulator on it.

A new screen appeared in Billy's mind.

Welcome. This new facility does not have a name. Do you wish to establish the name of this facility and become its administrator? Yes. No.

Billy chose *Yes*, named the facility 'Billy's Recycling,' and selected *Apply*. A slight ripple of grayish light washed through and around the facility, and suddenly, lights came on, brightening the area inside.

He took a moment to highlight several units and assigned them to himself. Billy then spent the next hour meticulously combing through the menus for his new block, selecting several security features, changing the colors of the exterior of the individual units, and making other decorations available. All of these minor changes required Billy to expend Experience points, and now he realized how much power and authority he had granted Orgar. With access to the System, Orgar and his clan could now spend Experience points and make their home more adapted to them and their needs. It also explained how so many changes had occurred in such a short time while Billy had been closeted away in Orgar's unit.

"Alright, Charlotte, I have activated a magical protection for the place, which should prevent low-level scrying, and we also have a screen active so that those outside of this place cannot see what is going on inside past a certain point." Billy poked at his little assistant, and she disconnected herself from her port and jumped to the floor to have her own look around. Her metallic feet clicked as she landed.

Looking around the place, she said, "It is quite large, Billy. Are you sure you need something so large just for yourself?" She scuttled here and there on her own little spider feet to examine the cleanliness of the place. "At least we don't have to clean up before we occupy."

"Yes, it is large, Charlotte. And we will need it to be much larger at some point. I plan to open a recycling plant here. I will go out and collect the refuse from the streets, bring it back here, process it, and produce raw materials. Some of those materials I will sell at the cheapest rates I can set, and others I will use to fabricate a farming center. I have tentative plans to set up some hydroponics if that technology won't get me banished by the fey here. That's why I need all of the rooms. And for a while, I will need every scrap of time and wood I can get my mechanoid hands on to build things up and try some things out."

Billy slowly spun around, looking at the vast open space he now had total access to and was complete owner of. Squatting down, Billy let loose his small, armored bots and had them stand by in a corner while he went out to collect some stuff. There were dozens of piles right outside, and he wanted to get things rolling immediately.

After the first load of rubbish was dragged inside, Billy personally processed it all to produce a makeshift backpack for himself. He then used this to load up more trash to haul back inside. Back and forth he went, choosing his garbage with care to be as efficient as possible. By the time it became dark, Billy had moved several tons of trash from around his block to its interior. He, along with his two bots, disassembled everything and made piles of various raw materials.

Throughout the long night, Billy and his bots separated out all the useful material and processed the old decaying food to produce a chemical-rich fertilizer. He would have to go outside of the city to get dirt later to mix it all together, but for now, the rich nitrogen and other organic matter would need to remain in piles. He had a lot of wood materials to process and used some of this to produce a few bins in which his raw minerals could be placed. He was set up near the junk pile, shoving things into his face hole hour after hour, while his bots remained near his abdomen, collecting the materials and separating everything into their own stacks. Every few minutes, Billy automatically scooped up a bot to rewind its springs and then let it loose to keep working.

Rock and stone were also consumed and reformed into loose bricks, which he planned to use for his composting piles. He found some metals and made simple ingots out of them. These were kept secured in one of his units. When morning came, Billy had finally gone through all of the junk he had brought in and had earned some Experience. Some of the metals were then used to make a few more bots to help with the fabrication processes after he increased his Leadership Talent by a point to allow him to manage them all.

These bots were smaller than his two scavenger bots and could be folded flat when not in use.

More than a week went by as Billy traveled outward from his block to collect rubbish and process it. After the first day, Billy had to make rain barrels to collect water at night. It rained regularly for many hours, and he needed this to power his systems as he spent enormous amounts of energy performing the processing tasks. He also continued to slowly build up his own bot force, producing the small, wind-up machines a few at a time as he located and processed the material for them.

Once his water issue was handled, Billy had no real problems spending hours and days going through all of the rubbish he had collected and processing it into useful material. He found the time spent walking around his block refreshing. Many of the nearby residents noticed Billy taking in the trash from the streets and would stand around watching him. Occasionally, the beasts and other fey would stop and ask him some questions. He would be polite to them but was vague in his replies when he could understand them. He did not want to let them know he was trying to do what the humes had done to the world, but in a different manner.

The humes had used magic to create their own form of control over their world, including the climate. Billy was working in this messed up world to create a more harmonious method of having the things people wanted to have a better life while dealing with material waste.

Some of the things, such as the small mountain of slag the dwarves had produced over uncountable years, would soon be repurposed. As it stood outside one of the gates that led out of the city, there were huge piles of slag poisoning the land. The dwarves could not use the stuff, as they were the impurities for the metals they were producing, but they had no means to do anything with it. Billy, however, could break down the crusty metal trash and create pure element ingots of the stuff they were composed of. He planned to make regular trips out to this wasteland the dwarves had inadvertently created, but for now, he only made a few trips to get a few tons for its metal-rich usefulness.

After the first week, Billy had filled many of the lower-level units with wooden bins full of raw element ingots. Some, such as the phosphorus and magnesium, had to be kept very dry. For this, Billy had managed to locate a schema for silica balls on his Store app when it finally came online. It cost him a two-hour phone call and almost half of his current Experience, but he decided that the need outweighed the cost. He had to make sure moisture did not make contact with some of the raw elements until he could figure out how to make a useful fertilizer.

"Charlotte, I think it is time to begin making our first hydroponic garden. Bring in all the bots and get them ready to bring me the materials as I request them. I have selected one of the units up top to use as our first testing area. While we are doing this, I need you to manage a few of the bots there to modify the ceiling and run some piping there for water distribution."

Charlotte bobbed her little spider head, and with a few clicks, her little cogwork body scampered off with two of the bots in tow.

Over the next couple of days Billy built the pots, pipes, and lighting access for his soon-to-be garden. It would be more like a greenhouse than a garden, but he was more focused on the technical issues like fertilizer content than naming conventions. It didn't take very long to build the layout for the pots each plant would eventually grow in. Some of the vine plants would require a lattice for them to grow on, and others, such as potatoes, would need large amounts of dirt to grow in, while the leafy part was also given access to the right amount of sunlight and water.

As each plant required different things, Billy had to figure out those things through experimentation. Before he could do any of that, he needed some seed to plant. And for that, Billy had to go out and explore.

Near the end of his second week of construction, Billy had at one point tried to go out and purchase seed, only to discover nobody kept any. All of the food was found out in the wilderness by countless hands daily. This would be brought in and bought or sold to those who either ate it, or cooked it to then sell, no one farmed.

The beasts did not require cooking in order to consume their meals, but the more evolved beings preferred cooked meals over raw. Their palette was more nuanced, and this showed in their dietary preference. And they did not go out of their way to have farms, either. They simply used coins, or Experience points, to exchange for large quantities of raw food they would then prepare themselves.

Chapter 9

While things were rolling right along as planned, Billy bid Charlotte farewell. He had communicated to her he would only follow others out into the wild to collect a variety of seeds. He carefully secured a crate onto his back with Charlotte's help. This would be used to hold his haul. He also had her prepare a few stacked units to house trees, time permitting. This would require some of his bots to carefully disassemble floors and ceilings to make room for the tall trees, but if he found fruit trees aplenty, he planned to see if he could grow some indoors. He left most of his bots but brought with him the large scavengers and a few of the smaller ones, which all attached to his abdomen in various places.

Billy had dozens of people each day asking what he was doing with all of the trash, to which he would reply he was making things that soon others could use. One such individual, a large gray female mouse who had followed him around for the last few days on his outings, had told him she knew of a place where many plants grew in the wild. It was where she would go on occasion to get food for her family. Her name was Sharea, and she was quite lively. Sometimes, Billy would let her ride on his back while he walked around collecting trash. She would pretend he was her mount, and she would help spot piles of useful things to collect with her sensitive nose and sharp eyesight.

"Shar, I need you to take me to the place outside where you collect food so I can collect some things. Can you guide me?" Billy, his hands always moving in a nervous motion despite the solidity of the rest of himself, asked of the mousy beast.

"Sure!" She squeaked out. "I can take you. I'll ride and point, you go!" She deftly climbed Billy's legs and sat behind his big eyes. He could still see her, though, so her directing was made simple by her pointing and he walking. "That way!" Off they went.

Sharea had navigated Billy to a gate a few miles west of where his place was, and he now understood why the little mouse didn't make the trip very often. It was through several neighborhoods with cat-like people who looked at all of the smaller beasts with hunger. This made them very fierce-looking, but Billy, being quite a bit larger than them, was not impressed.

The catfolk were more intimidated of Billy than they were willing to pounce the mousefolk on his back, so they kept their distance and kept a wary eye on Billy as he quietly walked by.

"Usually, I have to sneak around these," Sharea waved back to where they came. "They find it a game to chase us around the city if they catch us alone." Sharea hid behind Billy's eyes as they passed through.

Maneuvering around a group of jackal folk, he said, "It will be fine, Shar. These kitties won't mess with us." Billy's confidence helped calm the little beast while they walked on.

Once through the gate, Sharea guided Billy to a place a few miles out, and Billy had to go carefully. The land around them had trees lit by a brilliant sun, but they also had bushes and shrubs all over, hiding in the shade. The critters would occasionally flee as the two snuck by them, startling them into a panic. Billy did his best to ignore the smaller animals, though he did snap pictures when he could. He was not there for them.

As he walked, Billy paid close attention as Sharea pointed out plants and whether or not they were edible, how juicy they were, and how long it had been since she had any. For Billy's part, he would carefully pick the fruit or vegetable and place them in the wooden crate tied to his back behind Sharea. She would help sometimes by collecting berries or by digging for the root plants, like carrots or the occasional potato.

At one point, they had spotted a cluster of wild tomatoes, and Billy plucked a few of the more ripe ones with the hope he could get a few to take back to his block. The breeze kept Sharea cool despite the warm day, and once or twice, they had to find a stream to get their fill of water. Billy had topped up before they had left, so he did not partake. He did, however, manage to scoop up a couple of large fish he had spotted in the water while the little mouse was drinking. She even managed to take a quick bath, and for a little while, as they walked, she spent some time cleaning her fur while riding on his back.

"If I don't clean it well enough, I could get sick, you see. I have to make sure it's as dry as possible, or I can get sick and get the rest of the family sick as well." Sharea was very strict in her regimen. She didn't stop brushing and licking until all of the water had dried to her satisfaction.

"Shar, do the humes ever come out to places like this? Have you ever seen one before?" Billy asked this while he was collecting some cucumbers, and Sharea was sitting on his back looking around.

"Humes? No, I have never seen one before. But I have heard of them. They come around during the day, sometimes, and kill any animals they find. My momma used to tell us stories of how the humes used to let us run around cleaning their homes, but then they made friends with cats and would have them chase us away or catch us and eat us." Her little mouse whiskers twitched as she smelled the air while telling him this.

"Your people used to live amongst the humes? How long ago was this, do you know?" Billy placed the cucumbers carefully in his crate and moved on to a large pumpkin he had spotted a little ways off.

"A very long time ago, Billy. Long ago. My people only have stories of living around them. None in recent memory have." She continued to sniff the air while Billy worked.

Coming around a large tree, Billy spotted a small rock outcrop a few yards across. A large plate of rock had pushed up from the ground and a small stream had managed to find its way to it. Water trickled into the hole in the ground there, and as Billy approached, he got an alert.

Congratulations! You have discovered a new Lair, the Crab's Hut! What secrets are hidden within? What treasures await? Only the brave may find out!

Rank: F

Status: Fresh

Threat: Minimal

Experience for Discovery: +2,000

Do you wish to challenge Crab's Hut? Yes. No.

Billy paused as he read this, and Sharea spoke up. "Is there danger nearby?" Her whiskers twitched wildly as she both smelled the air and looked around.

Billy scratched at his chin as he replied, "I don't know, Shar. I think this hole in the ground may be a Lair of some sort. Do you know anything about them?"

Billy heard her gasp in surprise as he said, "Lair," And he did his best to watch her as she reacted.

"Yes! Those are rare, Billy. If we can go in and get rid of the monsters, we can get Experience and treasures!" Her excitement was felt by Billy as she spun around on his back. She moved to the top of his head and leaned over to look into one of his large eyes, upside down, when she said, "Do you think we can clear it? I have never been inside a Lair before."

Billy paused for a moment as he nearly went mentally cross-eyed, watching the little mouse before he looked back to the hole in the ground. "I don't think we can fit inside, Shar. It looks a bit too small for us to make it in."

A strange squeaking sound erupted from Sharea as she did the mouse equivalent of laughing. "Oh, Billy. You don't go in through the hole in the ground, silly Billy. You go up to the hole, and if you have access to the System, it will tell you how to enter."

"Oh, so you need to have access to the System, then?" He asked, surprised.

"No, of course not. But to challenge it, you need to have access. Do you have access to the System? I think you do; you own the block you live in by yourself. You must have access. Can we go in, do you think?"

Her rapid-fire questions would have put a smile on Billy's face if he'd had lips to smile with. Instead he gave a little chuckle and said, "I do have access. Do you, Shar?"

She paused at this, and he saw her little mouse whiskers droop. "No, I don't. Do you think it won't let me challenge it if I don't?"

"I don't know, Shar, but do you want to try?" Billy walked nearer the hole in the ground until he saw the prompt asking if he wanted to challenge the Crab's Hut Lair. He ignored it and backed up a few steps while looking around.

"Yes, please! Oh yes. If I can get enough Experience points, I can get access to the System! I would be the first in my family in so long to do so. Oh, can we please go, Billy?"

The little mouse girl ran all over Billy in excitement while he did his best to carefully examine the area. He found a depression near the small cave and carefully removed the crate from his back and placed it in the hole. He then spent a few minutes doing his best to cover the goods so that if anyone came by, they might miss seeing it while they went to challenge the Lair.

"I think we can try, Shar. Let's hope it's nothing too crazy; else, we may have to run away and let others know where this is and bring them back to clear it out."

Shar squeaked in excitement and even helped Billy conceal the food before hopping back onto his back. She jumped back down and, snatched up a rather large-for-her-size stick and returned.

Mentally preparing himself for the first real adventure in this life, Billy looked to the prompt in front of him and chose *Yes*.

Instead of entering, he received another prompt.

Please invite Sharea Skitterswift to your Party before entering.

He paused here, trying to figure out how to do that, when a second prompt appeared.

Sharea Skitterswift has invited you to form a Party. Would you like to join? Yes. No.

"How did you do that, Shar?"

"Do what?" She asked quizzically.

"You just invited me to form a Party. How did you do that?"

"We fey don't have access to our System, but we are told that our desire to do certain things will push the System to fulfill some desires. It is how we can earn Experience even though we can't spend it."

Billy thought about this, then focused on Sharea and thought about forming a Party with her.

Would you like to invite Sharea Skitterswift to join your Party? Yes. No.

Billy selected *Yes* and waited a moment. Almost instantly, Sharea accepted.

Leadership check successful. You have formed a Party in the role of Party Leader. Please set Loot and Experience Distribution.

Billy decided to split the loot and experience 50/50. At last, he pulled up the prompt asking to enter the Lair once again and chose *Yes*.

Subconsciously, Billy stepped forward, and the world rippled around him as they both entered the Lair. It looked similar to a large cave system, with detritus and animal litter. The entrance smelled like urine, probably from whatever was inside, marking their territory here.

Billy felt Sharea moving when she said, "Ew, gross." Realizing she was being too loud, she continued to complain silently.

"Careful, Shar. Anything could be in here and on us at any moment. I will do what I can to take them out. Be sure to get your smacks in with your stick when you can. Otherwise, you might not get the Experience."

"I know how this is supposed to work, silly Billy." She tittered as she spoke, and Billy couldn't help but chuckle to himself.

Billy took stock of what he had for combat and recalled he had a few special attacks at his disposal. He could grapple opponents and "kick" them as well. He could produce spiderweb silk since his last upgrade, and he could climb. He was not looking forward to biting things to death, but he would do what he could to get Experience.

The cave itself, as he looked backwards, was lit from outside. It was not, however, lit further in the cave. He did not require much light to see by, but hopefully, whatever was down here did. He could ambush things if this were the case.

As carefully as he could, Billy moved through the cave. His combat interface highlighted whatever he was looking at, and having disabled normal matter targets helped him pick out shapes. It was hopeful this would help him find treasure, too. Once around the first sharp bend, the cave became very dark. His shadow was cast in front of him, but this would not be a problem for long. He focused on his eyes and they switched to a combination of the low-light and the dark vision he had used climbing out of the underground facility he'd arrived here in.

The walls of the cave were mostly even and were wide apart and tall as well. This gave Billy and Sharea plenty of room to fight if they needed to. Billy could also feel Sharea's tiny claws digging into his armored back as she remained almost frozen in place, sniffing the air.

As Billy moved, he thought he heard something ahead. Sharea did as well, as he felt her tense momentarily.

"Shar, something is ahead. Be quiet and be careful." Billy whispered as quietly as he could, but Sharea heard him, and he saw her nod.

Doing as spiders do, Billy carefully climbed the walls of the cave and worked his way onto the ceiling. Sharea carefully moved around him to eventually rest on his stomach. It would have been his stomach if he'd had one of those. Billy easily gripped the rocks of the cave and had no problem seeing this way. The floor had several bones on it in key locations, probably for intruders to disturb. Bypassing this primitive alarm system, Billy managed to sneak up on a creature digging at the cave wall.

At first glance, Billy thought it was some kind of turtle. It had a wide, flat back that reflected the little light to be had uniformly.

What it also had were pincers, like a giant crab. It also had several spikey crab feet. Its pincers were busy digging at the wall, occasionally bringing a scrap of something to its mouth for it to try and nibble on. It would spit whatever it was out, only to go at the wall again.

Wondering how he was supposed to attack a giant crab thing, Billy sat silently for a minute and watched. Sharea leaned over to see below as well, waiting on Billy's decision to act. He saw the giant crab move around a large rock lying on the ground beside it to scratch at another part of the wall. Then Billy had an idea.

He had the schema for producing a spider silk substance. It was cheap to make, fast to produce, and sticky. "Shar, hold still while I make some webbing. I'm going to grab that big rock and see what happens when it drops onto the crab."

He barely heard her hushed "Okay" before he moved over the crab and began making a silken string. As he made the stuff, his rear legs grabbed it and guided it to the large rock directly under them. On contact, the webbing stuck to the rock, and Billy made sure he put enough onto it to hold the weight.

Billy then guided the webbing to his second set of rear legs, and together with the back pair, they slowly and silently lifted the large rock from the cave floor. The giant crab did not even twitch as the quarter-ton rock floated up and over its back. Billy watched its eye stalks to make sure it was focused on the wall. It was. He then released the silken rope, and the rock fell the half dozen feet downward to squish the crab with a quick *CRUNCH*.

Immediately, both he and Sharea received a prompt telling them they had received a small amount of Experience. Sharea did not have access to the System, so she did not react. Billy quickly read the prompt, then moved it aside as he studied the body of the dead giant crab.

It didn't move or twitch. It simply lay there with a large rock having broken open its back.

"It's dead, Shar. We got it in one shot,"

Sharea gave a tiny squeak of happiness, then, without warning, dropped off Billy to scramble down the wall to the corpse. She reached a tiny paw out and touched it, and Billy saw the body vanish in a haze of pale gray light that did not illuminate the area as Sharea deftly hopped up the rock wall and back onto Billy. As the body vanished, he received yet another prompt.

Congratulations, you have successfully looted the Giant Crab. Rewards will be sent to your Mailbox upon completion of the Lair.

"Shar, do you have access to a Mailbox?"

"No, what's that?"

"This prompt I just got says the rewards for looting the giant crab will be sent to the Mailbox." He said this as quietly as he could while also navigating the ceiling of the cave and looking for more monsters.

Riding along on Billy's belly, Sharea cleaned at her whiskers while she thought for a moment. "I didn't know that, Billy. I only remember my mamma used to tell us that if we ever find a dead monster, we could touch it while thinking the words, "Loot Monster" and we could get Experience. I did get the Experience, I think. But I don't know how much."

"How many Experience points do you need to unlock your System, Shar?" Billy had not thought to ask anyone this question before. He did not want to sound like he was some sort of outsider.

"Didn't your momma tell you when you were little? Well, some don't have mommas that stay around. I think my mamma said it was something like 1,000 Experience points to unlock the System. But you can't just trade for it; you have to earn it, somehow. I think if we can clear this Lair and I can get more than 1,000 Experience points, the 1,000 will be taken automatically, and I will have access to the System. The rest I can spend to get stronger and bigger!" She sounded excited at this prospect, and Billy could sympathize. He'd love to have this access back on Earth, and even here, it was an unimaginable boon to those who had it.

"Going into a trade blind must be terrifying for these people," Billy thought to himself. Not knowing if you had what you needed to get things for your own survival. He shuddered a little inside.

"We just got a little over 120 Experience points from that giant crab, Shar. If we find something larger or can take out a whole bunch all at once, you could be leaving here with your System active."

Billy's words stilled Sharea as he spoke them. He wasn't sure she hadn't already thought about this.

"You really think so, Billy? I might get to use the System?" Her tiny voice was barely audible.

"I think so, but we need to make it through here first. So let's get to it, shall we?"

The next few openings also had the giant crabs crawling around and scratching at the rocks. Billy ended up having to go back to the first room and bring the large rock with him, as he needed it to take out each of the giant crabs with it. He had not found another such rock yet but hoped more would be around somewhere so he could use multiple attacks at the same time.

After dropping the heavy rock on the eighth giant crab, Billy let Sharea hop down and loot it. That was when he heard something large scraping on rock in the next room. He even felt the rock of the ceiling tremble a little. It wasn't enough to break him loose, but it was enough that he could sense it.

Concerned, Billy said, "Shar, I want you to sit tight on me for a little while. I want to wait around and see if something happens, alright?"

She patted his stomach in the affirmative, and he could feel her start to quietly groom herself once again. The evidence of the monsters being killed was long gone, so there was nothing that would let any other monster know something was hunting them. It was Billy's hope that like in games back from home, monsters in places like Dungeons and Lairs would respawn. This was a game's way of repopulating the place and forcing the players to move forward lest they get trapped by reappearing monsters.

Billy knew that there was a way to get large quantities of Experience in one go if the monsters respawned. However, it would require more rocks. For now, he just wanted to see if they came back at all or if they were one-shot mobs. Some games had instance Dungeons where the monsters, often referred to as mobs, roamed and, once killed, stayed dead. It was Billy's hope this was that kind and not the other. He did not want a line of giant crabs sneaking up on him as he crept around.

After a few minutes of waiting, Billy had seen no sign of any other giant crabs respawning. It was then he decided to let Sharea know they were going to keep moving forward and that he thought the room up ahead might have a boss or mini-boss monster. He was hoping for the latter, but it was likely to be the former. A low-level Dungeon would not have many fast or dangerous monsters, and the boss would not be strong enough to need sub-bosses to protect it.

Cautiously Billy moved to the mouth of the next cave room, and there he saw one of the largest animals ever. It was a crab, of course, but it was absolutely gigantic. It had a back plate that had to be 15 feet wide. Its giant claws were almost five feet long and three feet wide. There were the typical crab bumps along the claw, which would be the pinch points it would use to crack open things like clams with ease. It was busy using its claws to dig at the wall and pulling away what looked like damp algae to eat. Behind it, in a shallow pool of water, Billy could make out dozens of crab eggs the size of basketballs. They were very pale in color, and he could just make out the dark spots in them moving around as the baby crabs inside grew.

Looking around his floor, the ceiling, Billy tried to locate stalactites to break off and drop. He saw there were several, but they were not evenly distributed. He also tried to see if there was anything on the ground which could be useful, and to his delight, he saw there was a large rectangular slab of stone. It was near where the eggs floated in the water. Billy, if he'd had a face to make one, imagined he wore an evil grin as he formulated a plan to take out the giant crab and its spawn all in one trap.

It took nearly 20 minutes for Billy and Sharea to lift and place the giant slab of rock over the bed of eggs and to very carefully snap off the largest stalactites and suspend them in key locations. He had to be careful and time snapping the large rocks with the giant crab boss scraping at the wall. The sounds were very similar, so they both hoped the eye stalks of the monstrosity wouldn't turn their way while they were mid-setup. Fortunately, Billy's camouflage was well done with its shape and coloring, as it was almost impossible for the crab to spot him due to the very low lighting. Only a single tiny crack in the roof let any light in, and it only illuminated the area directly in front of the crab.

Lastly, Billy had to leave Sharea on the flat rock being suspended while he went down to the ground to set the trap necessary to kick off the show. As silent as a ghost, Billy went around the edges of the small pond and lay down his super sticky webbing. He had to carefully lay it out so that as the boss moved around, it would become more and more immobilized by the web. He put down what he thought was too much, but then he remembered the old saying, "Overkill is underrated," And this eased his mind.

He paused at the pond for one quick sip of water to top himself off once he was ready, and then he gave a soft tapping signal for Sharea to be warned that he was about to begin and to hold on to the walls. When he saw Sharea was in position, he turned to the boss monster and readied himself. Then, without waiting further, he started to smack the ground with his metal feet.

The boss monster turned far faster than Billy had thought it possible for something so large, but he was not unprepared for this. The large rock he had carried from the first room was already spinning above him, connected by a thin silken strand which he held the other end of. With a quick whipping motion, Billy let go of the silken line, and the heavy rock crashed into the mouth of the boss crab.

The giant crab's massive claws immediately moved to prevent another such attack while it spit gobs of blood from its frothing mouth. Bubbly hisses could be heard through the darkness as it sought to find and crush whatever caused it pain. Billy carefully backed up and put his foot into the water, and splashed it around aggressively. The boss once again did not hesitate and it rushed forward on its crab legs, massive claws up in the air, showing its aggression.

Quick as a spider Billy reached up with his other feet and rapidly pulled himself up to the ceiling using the suspended silken rope he'd set there, being careful not to let any of the silk hang under him as he climbed. The boss had not heard Billy leave the water, so assumed he was still there. In its rush to defend its nest, the crab did not notice the webbing sticking to its exoskeleton.

The webbing was laid haphazardly, but all of it was carefully attached to the walls. Once the boss traveled a few giant crab steps, it found it had problems moving its feet. It spun to find what was holding it, and this caused other strands to become entangled with its feet. The dumb monster tried to use its big claws to cut the sticky threads holding it, but the claws were far too big to do any good against such small sticky ropes. It spun in place several times, trying to free itself before it became so entangled it could no longer walk.

While it was spinning, Billy carefully produced several fixed lengths of sticky threads and just dropped them onto the top of the boss. This caught its eye stalks and its big claws, further restricting its movements and vision. Finally, once it was in the right place, only a foot or so off from where Billy had centered his trap, Billy moved over to Sharea and handed her a special tool he had been making while setting his traps. It was designed to slice through the sticky threads without getting stuck, and she took it.

Then, Billy carefully guided Sharea's paw to the thread holding the netting of rocks and the rocks hanging right over the giant boss until she cut the one thread holding it all together. It took a fraction of a second for all the rocks to drop the two dozen feet to splatter the giant boss and every single egg in the pool. Blood, goop, and stinking liquids leapt up to splash both Billy and Sharea, covering them.

Sharea made a loud squeak in fear, as she could not see as easily in the very low light as Billy, and he had to quickly reach out and catch her before she landed on the rubble below.

As all this was happening, Billy had received a number of alerts vying for his attention at the same time, little Sharea began to glow that strange non-light, gray light. She went immediately limp as the light took hold of her. He held her gently with his two manipulator arms, hoping she would be alright, while he looked at the ground above.

He watched for a few moments to be sure the boss had indeed died, at which point he carefully climbed down to the floor to loot the boss. He reached for one of the feet sticking out from under large rocks and initiated the prompt to loot it.

A cascade of alerts bombarded Billy, and he had to take a moment to look at them. He had cleared the Lair and defeated all of the monsters within. He even received bonus Experience for taking out the spawning pool. He also got an additional bonus for clearing the Lair without taking any damage, being spotted, being detected, or even touched by an opponent. He had accomplished many achievements all at once. On top of all of this, he also got bonuses for clearing his first Lair while having fewer than the number of recommended party members.

Congratulations! You have defeated the Giant Crab Boss in the Crab's Hut.

+7,000 Experience points.

You slew 9 of the Giant Crabs along the way to the boss.

+4,500 Experience points.

You took out the Spawning Pool, preventing additional monsters from spawning during this adventure.

+500 Experience points.

You were as stealthy as a ghost, and none of the monsters detected your presence until it was too late.

+1,000 Experience points.

You have cleared the Crab's Hut without taking any damage!

+700 Experience points.

You have cleared Crab's Hut with fewer party members than was recommended.

+100 Experience points.

+100 gold coins, +250 silver coins, +300 copper coins.

All in all, this one Lair netted Billy just over 15,000 Experience points. This was a monstrous amount. If Sharea received the same amount, minus the cost of unlocking the System, they both could become very powerful individuals. Thinking about what had happened with Orgar and his clan, Billy grew concerned that by providing a route for Sharea to access the System, she would then pass this down to her family or clan if she had a clan. What he just did could begin destabilizing the hierarchy of the city. This would then further anger the elves, people he did not yet wish to confront.

Once Billy had gone through all of his alerts and prompts, a portion of the ceiling of the cave crumbled away, revealing a stairway leading out of the place. It also cast light in the room, the first real light the place had probably ever had. Cascades of blinking rainbow refractions lit the place as the shaft of sunlight struck a wall of quartz crystals. They were tiny, not much longer than half an inch in length, but there were hundreds of such crystals.

Billy carefully removed several handfuls of the crystals and bundled them up temporarily with a wad of sticky thread. The thread would not last long and would dissolve after about 20 minutes, but that would be long enough to make it topside and place them in with the vegetables. Hopefully these were some form of commodity he could trade back in the city.

On his way up, he noticed that Sharea was snoozing away, no longer unconscious, just asleep. He gently shook her awake, and she came to just as they broke through to the surface.

"EEP!" She eeped as they were once again blasted in the eyes with alerts telling them about the loot that had magically appeared right in front of them on the ground.

Billy had been prepared for this and so minimized the alerts as they appeared, but Sharea was just coming to, and she had access to a System her people had not seen in probably millennia. It would take her a little while to get used to it.

"Shar, don't do anything to your Attributes or Abilities until we get back. You can stay at my place when you apply them because you are likely to be out cold for a while as your body adjusts to your new strength." Billy hoped she would listen to his words, but he also knew she would not wait to at least read what she had never been able to read before.

"I will ride on your back if that's okay, Billy. I have so much to read all of a sudden." She sounded very distracted.

"Okay, but only this once will I load up everything myself; you have quite the haul there on the ground if I say so. I will be careful to keep your stuff separated for you." Billy shook his head in the way of spiders, a slight rolling of his body. He began to construct a second crate to put Sharea's things in. It took nearly an hour to get everything tied back onto his back because he had to fashion a cover to hide the loot. Then, he was following his map back to the gate to the city, and home.

The area around Billy's block was typically packed with the many citizens going about their business. Billy had not noticed any particular elf cadre moving through the area during his days of trash collecting, but now he spotted a patrol here and there, checking the street vendors licensing and handing out fines to those trying to sell goods without the proper tax documents and licenses. Most of the locals had their paperworks in order, but there was the occasional shady street vendor who was shooed off.

Billy took this all in as he walked into his block, making sure he was not being paid any particular attention to. Passing inside his gate a few feet meant the haze field hid him from the exterior, and he was glad to see Charlotte managing the assembly of the pipes leading to the various makeshift greenhouses in preparation for the hydroponics. The pipes led to tanks of water that had been filtered after it was collected from rain barrels. The pipes were capped with special heads that would cause the water to mist the plants so long as there was sufficient water pressure.

Billy had run some calculations early on to determine how large the metal watering cans had to be for optimal mist and built them just so. The heads of the sprayers were slightly spring-loaded, so once the pressure dropped below a certain threshold it would shut off the water flow. This did two things by giving the whole water system time to clean the water and for it to build up at the right intervals throughout the long days and nights. He had a variety of springs prepared and simple bladder bags inside the containers to change the rate and amount of water flow as needed per plant. Some needed more water than others, and more or less frequently. He had made sure that he had an adaptable delivery system.

Now that he had seeds, and a rather large pile of dirt he had scooped up while getting ready to leave the Lair entrance; Billy could begin his experiments with the soil content and the seeds. He already had stacks of biodegradable pots and some ceramic ones he had purchased with the little coin he'd had while out collecting trash.

Chapter 10

"Shar, why don't you hop down and take the room over there? I will have some furniture moved in for you. Take your time to go through your Status. If you have made your decisions on your dispensation, let me know, and I will be sure to have some things ready for you after you are done, alright?"

Billy lifted Sharea off his back and sat her down, but she seemed not to be paying any attention. For the next few minutes, Billy removed the crates from his back, careful to separate his loot from the little bit Sharea had earned. Sharea had started wandering off when Billy decided to guide her to her new home if she wanted it. He opened the door for her, and she blindly walked in and hunched down inside. He grabbed one of the chairs he had made, one with a nice cushion on it, and popped the legs off. He sat it on the floor beside her and she scooted over to lie down to continue reading.

"She'll be at that for a while, I think. Charlotte, have one of the smaller bots keep an eye on her, will you? If she needs anything or comes looking for me, show her the way." While he gave Charlotte more instructions, Billy went through the fruits and vegetables to separate them out. He then spent some time carefully taking the various foods and digging out the seeds. He had to pause for a little while so he could produce some thin paper squares to pile the different seeds, but this took very little time and effort and soon he was back at the piles of fruits looking for seeds.

The System was not very useful in determining if or whether the different seeds were viable, but then he figured that if the reality here were anything like video games at all, the plants wouldn't produce seeds at all if they wouldn't grow. This was proven as, while he took apart each plant for seeds, he did not always find seeds inside the plants. He also did not find as many as he thought he would from each individual plant. Most of the time, he only located a single seed; sometimes, he would find two, and only on a few occasions did he discover 3 seeds in one plant. By the time he had taken apart the very last vegetable, he'd discovered just over 200 seeds in total. There were two dozen varieties, but he only got a few seeds of each, even if he had more than 20 fruits or vegetables to dig through.

The only plant he knew he did not need to dig into was the potatoes. Each of those need only be cut into chunks around the eyes. The downside was that most of the potatoes had only one eye, so he could only get one plant to grow from it. He wouldn't plant the whole tuber, but he could only get one to grow from such cutting.

The one fortunate thing that came from all of this was that he was sure each seed would grow into a plant if not every fruit or vegetable gave out seed. Billy finally got up from the floor he had been lying on while he organized the seed when Charlotte's little glowing holo appeared in front of him.

"Ms. Sharea would like to speak with you, Billy." She said quietly.

Moving the seeds away from him, he said, "I'm on my way now, Charlotte."

Billy rose and left the seeds in their piles to take care of later and went to the unit he had already registered to Sharea. As of that moment, he could not simply walk into her home without approval, so he approached the door and knocked. She answered immediately with a big smile on her whiskery face.

"Oh, Billy. Thank you for coming so quickly. Come in, please. I need to ask you something, yes, yes." The words gushed out of little Sharea in seconds, but Billy caught the jist of them and entered the empty home.

Looking around, he said, "I'll have some furniture brought in here as soon as you want it; all you have to do is ask my assistant Charlotte here." Billy waved a manipulator at the tiny mechanical spider. She rattled away quietly.

"Oh, that's fine, Billy. See, I have decided on how to spend some of my Experience, not all of it, mind you, but some of it, and the notification here says I will need to hibernate for a few days and that I will need to wash well afterwards and eat plenty of food and get lots of fluids as quickly as possible. Oh, Billy, can you please make sure I can have a bath and get some food and something to drink when I wake up from my hibernation? Please?" Her tiny little black eyes were big and wide as she spoke all of this in one breath, and Billy had to pause for a moment to parse it all.

"Sure, Shar. I can do that for you. Do you want a pillow or blanket or something? I can put something together real fast if you want?" Billy was already looking through some of the schemas he knew to see if he could make anything useful.

"Oh, I was just about to go outside to get some clean straw to make a nest. You don't have to make anything, really. You've done so much for me already, Billy." She was playing with her hands nervously, and even her tail was showing how anxious she was about hibernating.

"I'll go get some for you. If you want, go ahead and lie down, and when I get back, I'll make you a comfortable nest and place you in it, alright?"

Sharea looked down at her tiny little feet for a moment, then back up. "Okay!" Within moments, she had laid down where she was, and Billy saw that soft, non-light, gray light surround Sharea as she initiated her Status upgrade.

Shrugging to himself in the way of spiders, a strange lean forward and then back, Billy quietly left the room, leaving the door open so he could get back in.

"Charlotte, I'll be back in a few minutes. Go ahead and begin placing the fertilizers in the pots. Be sure to mark the pots with which mix is inside like I have already shown you. And make sure this door stays open. If you have to, put a bot here to hold it open." Billy went to one of the crates he had from his trip earlier, strapped it to his back, and went outside.

It didn't take Billy long to find someone who had brought in wild straw to market. Billy traded a few coins for a basket full of new straw and even managed to find a simple blanket made of coarse wool. It was just barely the right size for Sharea, and it had a simple color pattern on it. "I hope she likes this. It isn't much, but it's what I can get right now." Happy with his shopping, Billy turned to head back home.

"Hold, there, bug!" An elf called out to Billy. The elf was clad in full plate armor but it was not made of metal. It was crafted with what looked like veneered flower petals, a process requiring multiple layers of flowers of similar size glued to one another on top of a piece of wood, which gives it stiffness and flexibility. It also looked lacquered, as it was quite shiny in the daylight.

Billy took in the colorful elf in an instant and, without missing a beat, he crouched and jumped right over the elf and his compatriots to land right outside his block with a soft thump. He kept on walking, but with a wave of one of his legs, he shouted back, "I'll have to get back to you later, fellas. I'm very busy at the moment." The rest of what Billy was saying to the trio of elves rushing to follow after him cut off as Billy entered his block. A couple steps in and the elves could no longer make out anything of him or what he was saying.

Billy called to his little assistant as he made his way to Sharea's unit, "Charlotte, please keep an eye out for anyone trying to sneak in here. Lace the place with webbing if you must. I do not want anyone in here who isn't invited." He was untying the crate from his back as he moved inside. It only took him a few moments to fashion a suitable nest for the sleeping mouse beasty, and he gently scooped her up to place her on it. She did not so much as twitch. Before leaving, he placed the little cloth blanket over her and tucked her in, then closed the door most of the way.

"Alright, Charlotte, it's time we spend some Experience points and do some upgrades. The elves are already poking around outside, and I want to make sure that nothing here sparks their suspicion." Heading to the central column, where his Administrator's access was easiest, Billy started the laborious process of trading hard-earned Experience points for necessary facility upgrades.

During his days of trash collecting, Billy had set aside quite a lot of materials. He even had to Assemble some things from others, such as boards of wood, from trashed furniture. To do that, he needed plenty of glue. Fortunately, he could fabricate this himself because he was, after all, a spider. Most of the wood Billy had found was turned into wood chips of a certain size and then were carefully pressed into boards with the glue, and heated as it was all extruded from his Assembler.

He had found no shortage of old wood. Most of the people outside would make new things to replace the old. As there were probably millions of people living in this place, there was no end to the piles of things Billy could choose to pick from.

The wood was necessary to build specific room upgrades and facility requirements, and collecting it from the wild would take time, so he recycled it. He had several plans rolling all together, but none of them could be completed any time soon. What he wanted to do was deal with the very local food issues. To do that, he needed a huge number of things to kickstart it all. First and foremost, he had to be able to build downward, and this required lots of different kinds of metals, and a large amount of wood.

Welcome to your Administrator's Tools. What do you wish to do today?

Upgrade Units from Modified Container to Apartment.

Upgrade Interior to house shopping stalls.

Expand Upward.

Expand Downward.

The list of things to do went on and on, but being able to prioritize manually, Billy arranged his tasks beforehand and chose to upgrade the units from modified containers to full-blown apartments. Billy had not seen any outside the elf district of the city, but even so not all of the units had been upgraded there. As for his own place, Billy opted to upgrade all of them. He absolutely needed the extra interior space for his greenhouses and storage.

As he mentally selected for this to *Apply*, almost all of the raw materials Billy had collected so far vanished in a puff of faint gray dust and the whole block took on the strange unlit glow of that gray light. Then he saw the notification and that it had a timer indicating completion. It would take just over a day for things to finish.

Time to completion of habitat upgrades: 28 hours.

The small army of bots Billy had was still running around preparing the pots and pipes for full installation once the rooms were completed. Others were on standby in case they were needed. The small bots also had to be wound up to work, and only the large crab scavengers could do this, but they also required their own recharge. Billy occasionally spent a few minutes charging up the large crab bots, which would then quickly turn the shiny brass keys on the little ones until they were buzzing away and carrying on tasks once again. He let the little bots return to work while he left to get more materials.

"What about our visitors, Billy? The scouts report the elves have not left the entrance and seem to be waiting for you to return to them." Charlotte's voice caused Billy to almost stumble. He had managed to forget about them in his rush to begin the upgrade process of his block. "I will need to take some time soon to clean you off as well. You are starting to look ragged from all of the dumpster diving. And you stink," She waved her little spider manipulator in front of her face as if she could smell him.

Come to think of it, he probably did smell bad. He had returned from a giant crab boss hunt covered in goo he never cleaned off, which had dried on his way back. Then he stood around inside while doing nothing but messing with what looked like a stone column. He probably reeked. Likely, it was the lack of his sense of smell, as well as not being physically bothered by being dirty, that let him continue working as if nothing were wrong. Thinking on this, Billy realized that the undead from stories back on Earth likely smelled horrible because they had no physical tells that let them know they were getting ripe. He shrugged to himself, deciding it would be good to clean up before approaching the elves outside.

Setting down a box of materials, he said, "Alright, Charlotte. I need a full scrub down, top to bottom. The elves can wait." He moved into position below several tanks of water, which were stored in the upper units. Each held several hundred gallons of water yet to be purified, and all of them had piping going to a number of units. One, in particular, went to a space with a drain cut into the floor and had several shower heads on it for washing off the garbage in bulk.

Charlotte orchestrated the cleaning dance she and her minions always did as they meticulously removed all of his thick plastic plates, cleaned them, and him, dried all the parts, and then lubricated all the lube points. She was getting very efficient at doing this while she waved her legs to direct her personal cleaning orchestra. In less than 20 minutes, every surface and crack had been brushed, scrubbed, and cleaned free of any goop, goo, or nastiness collected from the Lair.

To Billy's surprise, he had been unaware of how dim his vision had become until squeegees wiped clean the lenses over each of his eyes. Thankfully, Charlotte had waited last to clean out his filtration system, which had been slightly clogged, as well as some of his air testing sensors. As soon as those filters had been cleaned out, he could immediately smell the water running off of him, carrying away quite a rancid stench.

Waving a manipulator in front of his face, he faked coughing out, "Wow, that's gross. No wonder those people outside, and the cats, gave us plenty of space to walk by. We reeked of week-dead crab meat."

Charlotte just shook herself in the way of spiders, indicating disgust at having to witness the smell. Her spindly legs were doing their best to touch as little of the nasty runoff as possible while still doing her job. She wasn't very happy about it, but she performed wonderfully.

"If I may ask, Charlotte, how is my cloak coming along? Will it be ready any time soon?"

Charlotte had taken it upon herself to collect various fabrics to fashion a large cloak for Billy to cover his back and abdomen without hindering his legs. It would, by necessity, be quite large, but she had been at it for nearly a week now. She wanted Billy to do his best to impress upon the elves his stature, whatever they thought of it and wanted him to at least dress nicely.

"I completed the last of the stitching while you were away, of course. I decided to use a few of your coins to spin out the silver thread and used that to apply the markings which cover your armor plates on the part which covers your abdomen. It will cover your whole back and abdomen, but the main symbol would shine on your abdomen for all to see." Charlotte was already doing her spider dance to communicate to the other bots and several were already bringing it over to drape over Billy. He held still while they fastened belts and buttons, and soon, he had a cowl covering his eyes just a little bit, but he quickly moved it out of the way as it hampered most of his visual range.

"This looks fantastic, Charlotte. I can't wait to see how the elves react." Billy would be smiling, but he had no lips to smile. He did so inwardly, though, and this was enough for him and hopefully enough for Charlotte.

Now that he was cleaned, Billy was about to turn around when a thought struck him. "Hey Charlotte, can you see about cleaning Sharea while she's asleep? I don't think she realized she was also covered in that nasty stuff, and she will be out for quite a while. Also, replace the straw after she's cleaned? I want her to be surprised at how fluffy and clean she is when she wakes up."

Charlotte did another of her cute spider dances, and little spider and crab bots began assembling for the new instructions. "I will have her cleaned and brushed in short order, Billy. Now, you go take care of your business. And don't forget to go speak with Orgar." She then returned to organizing the bots to clean a sleeping Sharea.

Billy grunted his agreement on the task list and went to leave his facility. Before he left, he turned slowly to take it all in. The interior was still bare and lifeless. Only one room was occupied at the moment. Most of the place had pipes and cables going all over the place in a seemingly haphazard manner. He knew when it was all done, it would look almost nothing like it does now. But he did not want others to see what he was doing just yet. Not even Orgar.

Billy had a vision for this place. It was grand beyond reasoning and slightly borrowed from utopian architecture artwork. But he'd also had quite a load of gaming experience from his youth and a wellspring of knowledge to pull from when it came to tools and craftsmanship. He was very well trained in how simple and complex machines worked, not computers, but analog machines he could handle. His grand hope was that the fey here could be convinced what he was doing here was better than whatever the humes had done. And that he would not be found out as being similar to the humes in what he was doing.

Exiting the block, Billy was confronted by the trio of elves who had waited patiently by the entrance. The one who had called out to him had removed his feathery helmet, only for Billy to see the helm was open on the back to let the elf's own feathery hair loose.

"Are you the Administrator of this block here?" The elf waved a hand at the stack of containers everyone could clearly see was going through some sort of change.

"Yes, is there a problem?" Billy turned and waved a manipulator hand vaguely at the block. "I chose an out-of-the-way location, and the System expanded with no issues to accommodate."

Running a hand through their feathery hair, they asked, "Did you acquire proper permitting to expand here?" The elf had a stern look on their face. Billy couldn't decipher if they were male or female by their voice or looks alone.

"The System did not alert me there was any need for permits or permission." Billy stood tall to look the elf full in the stomach. He was not intimidated, mostly because he probably had almost half a ton more mass than the slight elf.

The elf snorted, "Nevertheless, you were required to notify the city council before establishing this structure. I'm afraid I will have to block access to the streets until you have submitted the applications to receive permits." The elf waved a hand, and from the streets, several more groups of elves walked forward to begin cordoning off the block surrounding Billy's facility.

"We shall see, kind elf. I have no intention of begging permission for doing what is clearly allowed already. If you wish to stand around, then by all means, do so. I, however, will go in and out of my facility. I hope you are not foolish enough to prevent me from doing so." Billy stepped up closely to the elf, giant spider eyes glaring up into the elves. "And you best not try to stop those I invite to abide here from going about their business, either."

Intimidation check successful. The target is Intimidated. Fearing harm, the target will subconsciously follow your directives for the rest of the day.

Mentally shooing aside the notification, Billy continued forward to the streets, forcing the trio of elves to step aside else he walk right over them.

"And elf, I will not tolerate any antagonizing of the people here. If you force them to vacate the area, we will have a problem." With that said Billy continued on his way to see his friend Orgar.

Several of the fey beings, and none too few of the beasts, watched as Billy bullied the elves and left them with mouths agape in fear. As he moved, Billy did his best to conceal the sound of his pressure tanks releasing as the tension lowered due to his departure. Billy had been prepared to fight if need be, and his mechanisms had reacted subconsciously. Now that he was cooling down, he needed to release some of the pressures built up, which he did in long, quiet gushes. His cloak was very useful in covering the releases by billowing all over the place. He went further by ensuring his legs would often brush his cloak to obfuscate his inorganic functions.

The people around him, however, only saw a giant spider with a decorated cloak stomp away from a group of elves after telling them off. His strangely harmonic movements could, therefore, be misconstrued as the natural movement of a giant spider walking away from a social encounter as the winner of the argument.

The next few minutes brought Billy closer to Orgar's block and further from his own, and he saw almost immediately where the lines were drawn from where he had come out to collect refuse. He would need to put together some machines to help process the variety of rubbish soon, and perhaps he could even post job listings to hire helpers to collect it all for him. If he was here to save the world, learning how to recycle would be a good start for the people here.

Finally, Billy came to the block housing the dwarves. He looked it over and saw how organized everything was on the outside. Even now, there were lines of citizens bringing various things the dwarves needed or wanted for their works and crafts, while other lines were those citizens who had already been paid for their labors and were off to spend their coin.

Several of the dwarves outside the facility managing the incoming and outgoing folk recognized Billy and waved at him with wide smiles. Billy returned the waves with gusto and carried on into the block. The lines of citizenry made way for Billy at the behest of the dwarves, and he had no issues entering the clan's holdings.

The noise and smells of construction on the inside had been muffled through the same magic that Billy used at his own place from carrying to the streets. Once Billy crossed that threshold, the sounds of diligent working dwarves washed over him, and he couldn't help but smile inwardly. These people were certainly far more cheery than they had been a couple weeks ago.

Billy called out to a couple of dwarves he recognized from his last visit here, and they happily waved back to him with soot and dust-covered faces. After a quick inquiry, Billy was directed to where Orgar was last seen, and he carefully made his way through the masses of small folk to find his friend.

It didn't take Billy long to locate Orgar. He was surrounded by a cadre of other dwarves reporting on this or requesting that. They waited in lines while reviewing papers with stuff written on them, and when their turn came, they would give what information was relevant, receive instruction, and then move off to do them. Billy mosied up and got in line behind a dwarf carrying a small quartz crystal in one hand and a scrap of paper in the other.

Unable to help himself, Billy had read that the number of crystals available was very low. Once the dwarf got up to Orgar, who saw Billy in line waiting patiently, he handed Orgar the paper with the numbers, and Orgar scratched his beard.

"You'll need ter send out parties ter look fer more of em. We bought all we could find in this part of the city. Take volunteers and send em out ternight." The dwarf grumbled at this, but turned and walked away, calling out names to a nearby group. Billy mentally shrugged as he waited for Orgar to address him.

Finally, Orgar called out that he was taking a short break and to come back in a few minutes. The nearby dwarves mostly just plopped down on the floor, unwilling to leave the line they were waiting in to wait out the few minutes for his return.

"Come, Billy. Let's talk over here while I get me somethin' ter drink." Orgar ushered Billy to follow and he did so. They went over to a table laden with small and large casks and several stacks of wooden mugs. Orgar grabbed one at random and filled it from one of the smaller casks. The rich amber color pooled into the cup quickly, and then the plug was replaced.

Taking a large gulp, Orgar looked at Billy. "What can I do fer yer today, Billy?"

"Good day, Orgar. I hope all is well?" The two friends shook hands.

"Yes, yes. We are well on our way to retrofitting the place to begin production of mithril. We have many other contracts we must still accommodate, but we are more than capable now that I can access the System." His large smile assured Billy all was well with his friend.

"That's good to hear, then. Look, I set up my block near the edge of the city, and some elves blockaded it a few minutes ago. Anything I need to do to get them to go away?"

Orgar took another swallow of his alcohol before scratching at his beard. "Have yer tried ter bribe 'em?"

Billy paused for a moment, then chuckled to himself. "No, I did not. I think I frightened them, actually. I should probably take care of that when I get back there. But first," Billy reached under his cloaked body and, pulled out a small wooden box and handed it to Orgar. "A gift. I had just cleared a Lair this morning and these were some of the treasures we got."

Orgar took the box and popped off the lid. Giving out a low whistle he then looked past Billy and shouted to the dwarf who had just requested more of them that he needn't worry. The dwarf in question wobbled through a small crowd and came up to Orgar for clarification.

"What, boss?" the surly dwarf intoned.

"Here. Take these and restock. Don't yer worry about headin' out ternight. Our brother here just dropped these off fer us." Orgar patted Billy on the leg as he spoke.

The dwarf took the rather large box for his size and gave Billy a sour look. "Couldn't've given me this while we were in line, could ye?" Before Billy could reply, the dwarf huffed and walked off with the box in hand.

"That all yer needin', Billy?" Orgar slapped Billy's leg again and took another swig of his drink.

"Not exactly. I need some of the metals you have been producing, if you have any to spare. I can exchange coins or Experience. I would prefer to use the coin, but I am willing to let go of some of the Experience points I've accumulated."

Eyeing Billy curiously, he asked, "What 'er ye needin'?"

"I need tin and copper. And aluminum, if you have any of that." Billy was looking around at all the activity while he spoke to Orgar. To his credit, Orgar did have some of what Billy needed.

"I have a few bricks of copper ter sell. I'll take coin fer that. The tin I have more than enough ter be gettin along with. Yer can take what yer want from the piles we have o'er there." He waved a hand to a corner that was covered in tarps.

Billy noticed Orgar had not mentioned the aluminum but nodded in thanks anyway. "I do have another question, though. Is there a particular food dwarves enjoy that is plant-related? I am trying to start growing things in the empty apartments I have to see if I can provide food for the people here without having to go out and shuffle around for it."

Billy's words had an effect on Orgar he wasn't sure he understood right away. The short fellow with the curly beard set down his mug and looked up at Billy with what he thought was a stern expression.

"Billy, I know yer've told me yer not from here, but one thing that separates the fey of the land from the humes is their role in tryin' ter control the world. It be dangerous ter do this thing. It be bending the natural order ter yer desire. Makin' this, this," he waved his hand while trying to find the right words, "Planting of foods inside the city not be natural, see."

Taken somewhat aback Billy said carefully, "I know how it seems, Orgar. But everywhere I look are people doing things to the foods they bring in and changing it from one thing to another before eating it. What I am doing is only adding a single step to make the foods themselves more convenient. I am not clearing land to make what are called farms, but I am working on transforming the unnatural block of housing units we all live into a more harmonic state with the world outside this city. And," Billy peered carefully at Orgar, "If I had to venture a guess, the humes are the ones who created the cityscape in the first place."

Orgar did not look pleased at Billy's logic. He was not unaware of the parallels either. "Yer may be right, Billy, but yer pushin' boundaries that aught naught be pushed. Some folk might not like what yer doin'."

"You didn't answer my question, however. Is there a type of food you would like to see more of that is not fish?" Billy nervously moved his manipulator arms, as was the way of spiders, while Orgar thought for a moment.

"Well, we do love a particular kind o' mushroom. They're rare ter find, though. I have a few spores yer can use ter try an' grow some. But you will need ter find some proper dung fer it ter grow in. Can't be just any dung either, has ter be underground giant crab dung." Orgar reached into his pocket and pulled a tiny paper packet. He opened it and showed Billy the few spores within.

"I think I have that covered as well, Orgar. Are there lighting or water requirements?" He gently took the packet and stored it in a side compartment underneath his cloak.

"Nah. Just place the dung in a place where its soakin' in warter an' toss the spores on 'em. They should grow in a couple of days. After a week or two, they should be ripe fer the pickin. We do this ourselves whenever we find their nests, so many of us hold on ter these packets in case." Orgar seemed happy he was asked about the conditions for which the fungus preferred. It gave him some confidence he would soon be able to rake in a small profit from selling the rare foodstuffs, even if they were grown in an unnatural way.

"I will probably use the first few seasons of growth to harvest more spores and use those to kickstart other crops. Crops are the different sets of growth periods for plants and such. I don't think fungus needs any care beyond having something to grow on, so I should be able to get a couple of my empty units to provide plenty of these soon enough." Billy looked around at the dwarves nearby as they began to grumble more. "I better let you at it, Orgar. I will go and grab some of the tin, and purchase a few ingots of the copper. When I get a reasonable harvest in, I will bring them over for you as a gift. I won't charge for this first batch in exchange for the spore."

Billy held out his manipulator hand, which Orgar shook firmly, before moving over to the stalls to purchase the copper. He bought a few dozen copper ingots and took nearly double that of the tin. He managed to get ahold of several buckets of very nice clay as well, which would come in handy for the plants. He also ordered more to be delivered to his block, which he also paid for in coin. Lastly, before leaving, Billy had left some coins to exchange for some of the slag the dwarves were unable to process. The slag was free; the coin was for having it piled on sleds and brought over to his place.

He made an arrangement then and there with one dwarf to have a fixed amount brought daily, and payment would be made upon delivery for the next shipment, thus he ended up paying in advance for that load as well. If he missed a payment, he would have to return here to begin the cycle again so as not to inconvenience anyone. The dwarves were happy to be able to clear up some space, and Billy was able to order, for nothing, as much of the bauxite as he wanted to extract aluminum from. The slag piles were filled with the stuff, and the dwarves didn't seem to know what it was.

Heavily laden with metals, Billy ramped up his internal furnace to provide the power he needed to move with ease, and began his trek home. Along the way he had to stop by a barrel along the side of the street to draw in some water, as he was using up his reserves at a prodigious pace with the weight he was carrying. Fortunately, he was not planning to carry so much more in the future. He just did not want to make more than this one trip for what he needed today.

Billy thumped his way past the elves trying to prevent the people in the streets from getting closer to the new upgrading block and went through his gates. Inside he unloaded his goods and instantly felt relieved to not be carrying nearly a quarter ton of stuff. Charlotte tutted at him, he knew she would want to go over his joints and limbs to make sure he didn't damage himself while carrying so much. He ignored her for now, and turned to go confront the elves.

Stepping out of the shadows of his block, Billy quickly scanned the faces of the elves to find the one he had spoken to earlier, and approached him. The fellow was still cowed by Billy from earlier, but Billy did his best to reassure the poor fella by holding out a manipulator hand to greet them.

"I am sorry about earlier, but you came at a poor moment. I did, however, want to thank you for your fine work out here."

Leadership check successful. The target is gladdened by your praise.

-50 silver coins.

"Here, take this as an apology." Billy reached under his cloak and brought out a small sack.

The elf smiled as he felt the weight and heard the clinking of coins inside. "Ah, well friend spider, it is of no concern. We had ambushed you on your way out, and should have taken a moment to better explain our situation." He turned to his comrades, shaking the bag full of coins. "If you would, please send a letter to the capitol building explaining the structure here. They would like to make sure that residents are well taken care of by their block Administrators and are not being taken advantage of." The oily smile the elf gave told Billy many things, none of which he addressed at the moment.

"I will do so at my earliest convenience. For now, enjoy the gift, and I will have sent the letter before end of day." Billy watched the elf smile again, then he waved to the others around the streets and they all moved to return to the more central parts of the city. Billy could only shake his head in the way of the spider in disgust.

Billy looked around at the condition of the other nearby blocks, and began to feel mild disgust for those who would take advantage of the people they supposedly housed. Even as he watched, he saw an elf roughly dressed and clearly drunk throw a bundle of fur onto the street. The furball barked out a cry of pain as it landed.

"You're out now, filth. Don't come back without the rent. If you don't have it by the end of day I'm letting out your place and you'll have nothing to return to." He kicked the thing on the ground and it let out another barking cry, not dissimilar from a dog's yelp.

Billy watched as the dog-like creature hung its head in shame as the others around watched it get tossed into the streets. This pulled at something in Billy, and without thinking he went over to the person who looked like it was a mix between a basset hound and a humanoid. It stood upright and was only about four feet tall, but had big, long floppy ears, dog-like legs, and strange fingers themselves a mix between paws and hands, but with only four fingers. He went over to the poor thing and helped it up.

Quietly, he asked, "Are you alright?"

Billy thought of this as a beastkin, as it was similar to a beast, but evolved along the path of bipedal humans. He understood this was not actually the case, but he had yet to learn how these few referred to one another without names.

"Fine. I'm fine," The voice barked out, making the same whining sound dogs would when they were hurt or scared.

Chapter 11

"It's alright, I won't hurt you." Billy tried to sound reassuring as he helped the beastkin up.

The poor thing had not seen Billy approach due to its very long ears covering its disheveled face. It wore very rough looking pants tied with a rope around its waist, and was covered head to toes in short, matted fur. The coloring was uneven, much like many dogs from Earth would be, in no pattern at all. There were splotches of white rolling around with tans, browns and blacks.

As it flopped one of its ears out of the way, the beastkin let out a baying bark and tried to back away, but Billy had a hold of its hand and did his best to be reassuring. He crouched down onto the ground. The beastkin tried once or twice to break free of Billy's grasp, but after the second attempt went limp and hung its head. It stood there for a moment, shaking, then Billy saw it had urinated on itself. The yellow puddle slowly pooled on the ground.

"It's alright. I am not going to hurt you. I just saw from across the street you were kicked out of here. I just so happen to be an Administrator myself, and I have some vacancies. Would you like to have a place to stay there, at least for the night? No charge, of course.” Billy slowly released the beastkin as he spoke, and the more he said, the more the head slowly raised.

Big puppy dog eyes looked back at Billy with hope, and he already knew he had found another guest for his new home.

“I’ll take that as a yes. Come, we will get you cleaned up and get some food in you. You look hungry. We will pick out one of the units for you to nap in afterward. When you wake up rested, we can talk. How does that sound?” Billy ushered the now wet dog across the street while trying to ignore the onlookers. He could not help everyone right now. But he could help those who could not help themselves, at least until they were up on their own feet again.

“Alright,” The beastkin replied, finally pushing down the fear long enough to speak. “I would like that, thank you.”

“My name is Billy. What is yours, if I may ask?” Billy walked the beastkin through the gates, and when he was prompted immediately granted permissions to this fellow in hand.

“Elsie. My name is Elsie.” Her voice wavered a little as she spoke.

“And, are you male or female, Elsie? I have a hard time telling sometimes.”

“I am a girl. Can’t you tell?” Elsie said, sounding both defensive and rebuked at the same time.

“No, actually. I have never met someone like you. I have met dwarves and elves, and a giant crab boss monster in a Lair just this morning. I do not know how to address any of the other fey, or how they are presented.” Billy walked Elsie to the place he had showered off only an hour ago inside his block.

For her part, Elsie was looking all over the place. Billy had dozens of little bots running around the place adjusting this, moving that, installing these and those, all very efficient-like. The mostly empty space under the apartment pyramid was filled with the buzz and whirring of gears spinning and tiny feet tapping. Piles of goods and trash were arranged neatly, and most of the units not slated for housing were open to the interior, with things being constructed or moved to particular apartments even as the whole place was undergoing its upgrade.

"What is this place?" Elsie's voice was faint as her head spun and she subconsciously sniffed the air. "It smells strange. I've never smelled anything like this before."

"I only just took over as the Administrator here a couple weeks ago. I plan to use it to make things people need, and to make use of the things people throw away."

"I thought so. You speak dwarf passably, but it was a dead giveaway you were going to be making things if that's the language you use to talk to strangers with." Elsie's words caused Billy to pause. Thinking back, he had spoken to almost everyone in Dwarven, but it seemed that many of the folk here had also learned to speak it.

Curious, Billy reached out and poked Elsie in the shoulder, and she flinched as she felt her trying to exchange Experience for something. "What are you asking me for? I'm not rich like you, I don't have access to the System."

"I was going to trade some Experience for the language you speak. I do not know the proper way to do this, but both of the languages I speak were learned this way.

"How much Experience?" she asked, looking hesitant.

"I was going to give you 10 Experience points in exchange for you teaching me your language," Billy said, still walking Elsie around to the showers.

"12, or we can just keep speaking dwarf," She quickly rebutted.

"I can do 12 Experience," Billy said while sending a request again. She had to focus hard on what she wanted to do, and after a moment she had accepted the exchange and her eyes lit up with delight. Billy, in exchange, learned the Basset language, a dialect of the Hound language.

"Well, now that we have that taken care of, it's time for you to take a shower, You stink," Billy said in her native language, and he pretended to give her a sniff and flinched back from the bad smells.

Elsie giggled, and stood where Billy had indicated. "Sorry, it's something my people do when we are frightened. I didn't mean to do that in public."

Billy communicated to his drones with a series of leg motions, a simple sign language he was working out with Charlotte, and in short order there was a stream of warm water raining down on Elsie.

She looked up in amazement as the warm water quickly soaked her. Billy brought out a bar of soap and tossed it to Elsie, who dropped it immediately. She picked it up, sniffed it, and gave a little shrug. Elsie lathered herself up with the soap and quickly she was covered in tiny little bubbles. At some point she had removed her ragged pants and was washing them too, but Billy had a hard time telling what was going on because the poor Basset was both covered and surrounded by a slowly growing mound of bubbles.

The beastkin simply delighted in popping all the bubbles as she did her best to rinse off. Eventually Billy had to have his bots increase the water flow or they would be there for an hour trying to get it all washed away. The deluge quickly flushed off the soapy bubbles and washed them down the drain.

Once done, Elsie plopped right down and began licking herself. Her long doggy tongue started with her arms, then her belly, she did her best to get her back, and eventually one leg and another. Billy watched, fascinated, as this beastkin meticulously licked every bit of her fur. It was like watching a cat clean itself, she was so flexible.

Once clean to her satisfaction, Elsie carefully stepped off the wet floor and looked around.

"So, where's the food?" Her tongue was lolling out slightly as she looked around, sniffing loudly.

"What would you like, and I can see about getting it for you," Billy asked.

"Meat?" She looked to Billy with hopeful eyes and he watched her.

"I have recently come into several pounds of fresh crab meat, would that be alright?" Billy asked, moving to a storage crate nearby. It was being kept cold inside by some ice, which Billy had to make himself every few hours. It was a simple process of freezing water within himself, so he did not spend long on the task. He lifted the top of the crate, and stacks upon stacks of fresh crab meat steaks were lying in a bath of ice. He had several such crates nearby, which he was planning to sell here soon.

Elsie's eyes grew large as she barked out, "Oh that smells fantastic!" She rushed over and put her hands on the side of the crate so she could lean over and sniff a few of the large steaks. "How many can I have?" She asked, her very large, deep brown puppy dog eyes glowing.

"As much as you can eat, for now," Billy said, nudging the crate closer to her.

Instantly Elsie reached in and grabbed at the raw meat and began to take surprisingly large bites from it. She barely chewed as she practically swallowed the bites whole.

"Slow down, Elsie, I don't want you to get sick from eating too fast," Billy tried to hold his hands out placatingly, but as soon as he moved towards her she turned with a feral look in her eyes and growled at him.

Freezing in place, Billy looked deeply into Elsie's animalistic eyes, full of hate at being stopped. She was desperately hungry and would fight to the death for the feast in front of her.

Sternly Billy said, "Elsie. Eat slower or I will not let you have any more."

Her hackles rose as he said this, but he did not relent in his will pushing against hers.

"Elsie," Billy said again. "Stop growling at me, or I will throw you out."

His simple words seemed to stab right into her fearful mind, and she blinked dazedly at him.

"Billy? Did, did I do something wrong?" She looked at Billy with a deep sorrow, almost as deep as the rage had been a moment ago.

"No, Elsie. You haven't done anything wrong. I just want you to
eat slower so you don't become ill." Billy sat down on the floor to
watch her. She seemed to have almost forgotten the food in her
hand until Billy motioned to it. She looked at the large slab of meat
and licked her lips again before looking back to Billy.

"I.. I didn't want you to take the food from me. I haven't eaten in
days. Please," her eyes begged him to let her continue eating.

"Eat, Elsie. But eat slower. And drink some water as well," he said,
as he slid over a small barrel of clean water. He grabbed some of
the ice from the crate and dropped them in the water, hoping the
scent will entice her to drink more of it.

"Okay," she said, as she took a large bite from the steak. She
chewed the meat this time, and Billy saw she was tasting the
delicious food for the first time. He heard her making a sound in
her throat that was well beyond his old human ears ability to pick
up, and he figured she was enjoying the feast.

"I have some things I need to do for now," he waved at all the
crates nearby. "There is plenty for you to eat, but don't make
yourself sick by stuffing yourself. Eat your fill, and go rest. I will
be doing some work here in the meantime. Once you pick a unit, I
will receive an alert at which point I will assign that space to you
for the next month. The units with no doors are for a project I am
working on, so choose any of the ones with a door and it's yours."

Elsie nodded her head and her long floppy ears did a little dance
as she did so. She kept chewing her food, though. She was far too
hungry to speak any more. Billy got up then and went to a stack of
the copper ingots. The space the ingots took up was very small, the
dense metal bricks making it simple to stack them orderly. Billy
grabbed a few of these ingots and went to one of the units being

fitted to house the potatoes and he started chewing on the bars of metal, one after the other.

In minutes his Assembler was extruding lengths of pipe for him to continue constructing the sprinkler system for his hydroponics. Several of his bots were arranging wood and fastening them together with screws. Occasionally Billy would subconsciously wind one the bots as its springs unwound and it began to slow. Then it would hop back up fully charged and carry on with its work.

At some point during construction, Billy received an alert for a request by a potential resident, which he addressed. Elsie had apparently finished eating, finally, and chose a unit to stay in. He heard the door creak open, but didn't hear it close.

"Charlotte, what is she doing?" He asked, using the language of spiders, to pass the message from himself to a bot to her, as she was in another unit. The game of telephone was played to perfection, and in moments he learned Elsie had actually not gone into her unit, instead she had crawled in with Sharea and snuggled around her while she was asleep.

The fun spider language Billy had worked out with Charlotte was a combination of leg movements and swaying. Different leg positions and sway patterns meant different things, but they'd had weeks now to work out many of the kinks in communications. It was thanks to increasing his own Intelligence he could use this new form of silent communication, and he practiced it as often as he could.

Billy smiled to himself as he continued to work away at his project. He hoped it would be successful, but wasn't sure. This world was in many ways identical to Earth in that plants grew and produced seeds. Some seeds would not grow on Earth, and that was probably why the System did not waste resources on having them make those failed seeds here. His hope was that he could accommodate the seeds and coax them to grow in pots. He had seen nothing of farming, or greenhouses here, so he was unsure the world would even allow indoor plants to be grown in pots.

Eventually Billy completed the greenhouse for the potatoes. The block eventually finished going through its upgrade period, and as soon as it was complete he cut away sections of the ceilings and replaced them with hinges he would use later to open and close to air out the rooms and let in sunlight. Once the room was completed, Billy had received a prompt.

Congratulations! You have completed the construction of a Hydroponics Greenhouse. The Schema for this unit has been added to your lists of available units to automatically construct through your Administrator menu for your block. All of the required components must be available before construction can begin, or costs may increase accordingly.

Note: Hydroponics Greenhouses can grow a number of different fruits and vegetables, and even other smaller plants such as flowers or fungus. To select the setup for a particular crop, use the pulldown menu from this schema in your Administrator menu for your block and choose the appropriate selection.

"Do you see this Charlotte? We won't have to manually construct these units anymore. Run the pipes to the units from now on. Don't do any interior work, I will start producing the components for the rooms and use the Administrator menus for this from now on." Billy was ecstatic that he could produce his own schema for his units. He was not sure this would happen, but was more than happy enough to take the win.

For the next few minutes Billy went about rerouting his bots out of the rooms with all of the stuff they were moving in, instead having them pile the stuff in a room he had designated for storage. After a moment of thought, Billy went to the central column and opened up his Administrator menu and reviewed the schema he had there; he had missed viewing this menu earlier somehow.

To his delight, he could designate any of the units as storage for the facility. All he needed was a number of crates to be placed in the units once he allocated its designation. He did this now as he had more than enough crates to be going on with, and a couple dozen vanished from the stacks he had and he assumed they were placed into the unit he had chosen.

A quick walk to one of the lower level units and Billy opened the door to peak in. He saw the boxes had been lined along the sides so he could pile things in them in some basic form of organization. The System was even accommodating enough to make shelving for him to place more boxes or material on.

"Well, I think at some point I will need to upgrade this to something more useful. We are going to be producing a large variety of things that will need to be stored," he said to himself as he scratched his chin.

Billy propped open the door and had his free bots begin moving things into the crates. He returned to the column and designated several more rooms to be storage and watched as the remainder of the crates he had vanished. While his bots were busy reorganizing, Billy sat next to the piles of raw materials and began utilizing his Dissembler by consuming the ingots and materials to produce the things his greenhouses would need. As he made parts, a bot would come by and take it to the appropriate room. Occasionally Billy would scoop up a bot and wind it up again to keep it in top form.

While he was making simple things, Billy also queued up a couple more helper bots. He could do this rather quickly as he had so much copper and tin available. He also had some of the slag from the dwarves which he happily consumed to provide additional minerals to produce a rather high quality brass which he would in turn use for his bots. He found he could queue up to three different tasks at the same time, but only one if it were very complex. The bots were simple, wind up movers that were designed only to carry things, and these only took him about 20 minutes to make. He alternated between making pipes, shelving, screws and other smaller things with his bots.

The very small stuff, like fasteners, came out in a very steady stream which landed in a small bowl held by a bot. When the bowl was full enough, it would wander off and another would move right into place without missing a beat. The pipes slid from his extruder and two bots would take those once they were done. He kept up this pace until he had gone down the list of components for a greenhouse three times, before he finally stopped.

The night had passed slowly as Billy sat in his nest of stuff, converting it from its useless state to its useful. He kept an eye on the door leading to Sharea's unit to make sure the two beastkin in there didn't walk in seeing him doing what he was doing. After he had finished making the greenhouse components, Billy began to work on some simple furniture for them. He was not exactly sure what they would need, or even want, so he kept it simple. From what he had seen in Orgar's room, there was very little in the form of comfortable furniture. There were desks, chairs, and hammocks, casks and sheets, ladders and windows, but nothing fancy.

After making a set of simple chairs, and a simple bed frame, Billy figured he would need to go out to get more trash before he could finish. He wasn't sure what he would need to make a mattress, but he had ideas. He knew he could not create organic matter, but he wanted to see about getting some feathers for a pillow for the two beastkin. Maybe he could make large cushions for them to sit on if they did not want chairs.

Pausing, he said, "Charlotte, have the bots move the rest of this stuff into storage. I have the other three greenhouses under construction now, and in a little while I want you to check on them personally when they're complete. Each should be seeded automatically, but I want eyes on them just in case anything funny comes up." Billy looked around his facility. It had gotten bigger since its upgrade, nearly doubling the floor space. He wasn't sure how much taller it got, but was unconcerned about this. Other units he had seen were of varying heights, his would not stick out as strange.

"Alright, Billy. I'll have the bots line up in the storage units and shut down once they're done, then. No need to waste energy rewinding them when they won't be useful." The cute little dance Charlotte did as she spoke made Billy chuckle. She did not use her little holo often as it drained her power faster, and did not actually talk. The spider language was the waving of manipulators, feet and stance, and it was deadly silent, even if it was fun to watch.

Billy, however, spoke in return, "That's fine, Charlotte. When that's done, keep an eye on the beastkin. I'm going out to find some food for them, to trade some things, and am going to get," he grunted as he situated a couple crates onto his back and carefully strapped them down, "More stuff to Dissemble later. I think I'll have a couple more hours, and I can get several more piles of stuff in that time."

Once the crates were secure, Billy did a double check over everything. His cloak was under the crates, and his form was made obscure by it. The crates were stable on his back as he swayed and walked in a small circle. "I should be back in an hour or so," he said, as he went to a large barrel of water to drain several gallons. "When I get done tonight, I want you to do some work on me, so rest while you can, alright?"

Charlotte communicated her joy at knowing she would be able to do some of her favorite work soon, and the little dance she did caused Billy to chuckle again as he turned and went out through the gates.

Billy hadn't gone more than a dozen steps before he realized he was being watched, if not followed. His eyes, being positioned as they were, were not his only means of accessing information about his surroundings. He could feel the air, taste it, and smell it very clearly. He also had a sense most small creatures had. He had a sense of danger.

This sense wasn't obtuse, it was a Special Ability unique to his nature as a Mechanoid. It allowed Billy to randomly make Perception checks if danger was around. It was not something he actively controlled. It just happened, and if the check was successful he would receive an alert about it. If he failed, he would remain unaware the check was ever made. In this case, however, he had succeeded in making this Perception check, and he simply knew he was being targeted by others whom he could not see directly.

Special Ability, Danger Sense activated. Perception check successful. Your Danger Sense has determined you are being watched, and possibly being followed by a predator.

Billy read this alert as he walked away from his block. He had made plans to look around the local area and pick through some of the rubbish. He did not need everything, as he had when he began, but now he was in the neighborhood for some specific things, such as cloth, feathers and wood. It seemed this time out he would also have to deal with an old friend as well. Or perhaps a new one. Either way, Billy kept an eye out as he went about his chores.

He was digging through a pile of old furniture when he was approached by a cloaked figure. It was light out and the figure that approached him was pulling back a tan hood when Billy turned to the figure.

"Insect. You will hand over your equipment and purse, or we will end you here and now." The elf, for sure that was what this was with the feathery hair and bark-like skin, pulled free a long dirk from their belt. The blade was in rough shape with a slight curve to what should have been a straight one, and Billy saw at a glance it had spots of rust on it.

Without saying a word Billy did the spider equivalent of a shrug and turned back to his pile of trash to continue picking through it, totally unconcerned.

Without paying attention, Billy reacted to three simultaneous attacks from all around himself. Three armored legs raised to block three thrusts of rusty dagger and dirk. Thanks to the plastic plates he'd covered his body with, the sound the weapons made striking his legs sounded like they struck chiton.

In retaliation, Billy kicked out with his three blocking legs, turning his defense into offense. One of the elves evaded the kick, but the other two weren't fast enough and were knocked off of their feet to smack the street.

"I'm sorry, I am a little busy here," Billy said, turning to face the only standing elf. "If you want to talk or something, feel free to stop by my place over there," he waved a manipulator down the street, "And knock on the gates later. My assistant.."

The elf attacked again, but this time he was alone. The blade stabbed at Billy's cephalothorax, what he referred to as his chest, but two of Billy's legs swung in to block the thrust. Bone crunched as the elf's arm was trapped. The blade dropped to the ground, and Billy tossed the elf aside, then he turned to look down at the fella.

"As I was saying," Billy lowered himself to put his large eyes directly in front of the elf, who was cradling his arm and hissing in pain. "Stop by my block later. I am busy." And with that, Billy turned back to the pile of garbage. He heard other elves gather around their comrade and then heard them hurry down the street.

There were plenty who watched what Billy had done to the elves, he could see some looking out of windows and through cracked open doors. He pretended to not notice them as he continued to collect the wood he needed, along with the occasional scrap of cloth. He was even lucky enough to find someone selling rough sacks stuffed full of bird feathers not unlike those from ducks.

The wood was carefully piled into a crate to maximize the load, while the cloth was folded and stacked. The sacks of feathers were only tied onto the crates. The wood would be processed later, and the cloth cleaned. Anything not in halfway decent condition would be processed and reproduced. It was easier to clean and repair old stuff than it was to Assemble it.

An hour later Billy entered the gates to his block, loaded with his goods. While he was out he also stopped by a vendor and purchased a barrel of whiskey. They said it was whiskey. So long as it was alcoholic he was fine with it. He wasn't going to be drinking any of it. He needed it so he could purify it and use it for fuel and disinfecting. It also helped when cleaning certain parts of his.

"Alright, Charlotte, I got the stuff and it's your turn to do your thing," Billy called out as he entered his block. The interior was quiet, but well organized. Stopping by the room Sharea slept in, he saw her and Elsie still cuddled together. He dropped off the crates in one of the storage units, leaving them for the bots to organize later, and placed the barrel in another room. He carefully marked the barrel so he knew it was alcoholic, then closed the storage units. He could just make out Charlotte making her way out of one of the greenhouses as he sought out his own unit. A quick menu check and he assigned himself several adjacent units, modified them by expending Experience points, and waited. It only took a few minutes for the block to adjust the units to his needs, then he went in the only door left for the extra big unit.

Sitting down just right, Charlotte began her maintenance. She had several smaller bots bring in extra tools and materials that would now be kept in this room.

"You have damage on the legs, here," She tapped, "Here, and here. And is this blood?" She tapped again as a speckle of blood on the inside of two legs.

"Yeah, sorry about that, I was jumped by some hoodlums right after I left. I gave them what for, and they took off." Billy watched as Charlotte removed all of the armor plates for inspection and repair. He then watched her meticulously inspect every joint, piston and gear, all the cabling and pulleys, and even the pipe and framework. She carefully scrubbed every surface, lubricated every joint. She would climb and complain in her quaint granny way as she saw parts with small scuffs, or scratches from simple use.

One by one the limbs were checked and cleaned. After she finished all of his limbs, including his manipulators, she went to check his chest and abdomen, 'tsking' at rope marks and debris caught in cracks. She also topped off his water levels, cleaned bolt heads, and replaced anything that looked too worn for her liking with new parts Billy Assembled. All of the old grease, bolts and such were Dissembled and reconstructed as new.

Billy thought about the entire process going on as he watched and aided Charlotte in fixing himself up. He liked looking at things and taking them apart to understand them better. He was curious about how things worked and was fascinated at his own construction. He had detailed diagrams, schema, of himself. But seeing the lines on screen and seeing the thing in reality were a little different. He saw how his parts were wearing, and how they were repaired. He took mental notes of the procedures as it was all done.

Charlotte did not complain about the complex or simple methods required to perform her work, but Billy wanted to make things as easy on her as possible without sacrificing his own Durability. This was why he was pondering the best ways to make use of the small bit of mithril he'd collected from the first day he was underground. Part of his inner construction was composed of the stuff. The small pencil rods he had were not enough to reinforce his entire structure, but were enough to make a couple very minor alterations. He just did not know where he wanted to make the changes. More importantly, he had to predict how this would impact Charlotte's ability to do the maintenance he required almost daily.

Then it struck him, why didn't he just upgrade Charlotte? If she were more capable, she would more easily be able to do her work. Before making any decisions, he thought he'd just ask her about it.

"Charlotte, what say we upgrade you a little bit. Are there any external or internal changes you would like made so your work would be done easier?" Billy watched her as she torqued down a bolt.

"It doesn't matter to me, dear Billy. I will use whatever you have made available as best I can." Her cheery response was a red flag to Billy. Women never said what they meant to say, and he got the feeling Charlotte was much the same in this regard.

"Charlotte. What upgrades do you need to do your job better?" He figured being direct would be the best way to go.

"Are you saying, my dear, dear Billy, I am not capable of doing my job?"

Yep, he'd done it alright. Running a manipulator over what he had for a face in exasperation, "Charlotte. You know what I mean. I am not, repeat not, demeaning you. I only want to know if you want any upgrades to make your life easier."

"I'm making life harder, is what you're saying?" Her little spider dance said far more than the translation alone. Billy knew she was teasing, but he also knew she was being serious. That one little leg wave told him so.

Without saying another word, Billy began using some of the mithril to produce some replacement parts for Charlotte. He even put a few designs on it to make her look prettier, such as some very fine, colorful hairs.

An hour later Billy watched as Charlotte was prancing around, far more colorful than she had been. Her new limbs were finely crafted to help both clean himself, and be aesthetically appealing. Her new limbs were covered in very fine hairs to make her prettier than just bare metal. He also installed a component which, when wound, would alter the color patterns of the hair, which now covered all of the new paneling wrapping her tiny framework. She was now a very real looking peacock jumping spider, with iridescent hairs and all.

She was also given a few brushes designed to specifically clean and care for the hair. Most importantly, she was made happier. And nothing was better than a happy employee.

Armed with her new set of personal care products, Charlotte skittered off to put her new things away. Billy got the feeling he would be making plenty of the haircare products for her in the future. Fortunately, the degreaser was easy to make. Lemons and oranges existed in this world.

Day became night, and night inevitably became morning. Elsie finally woke up to discover the tiny puff pillow she had found was still snoozing, so she got up and left to see if she could find some food. To her absolute delight she smelled something mind-bogglingly delicious once she opened the door to the unit she had slept in. It smelled sweet, burnt, salty and meaty all wrapped up in one smell. She practically floated outside, her powerful sniffer leading the way forward. It took her directly through the open area of the block and straight to the unit at the ground floor opposite hers.

Inside she saw Billy, the strange giant spider she had met the day before. She had been kicked out of her unit because she didn't have the rent, and he had taken her to his block, cleaned her up, fed her and gave her a unit of her own. He hadn't even set up rent payments. It was hers as long as she stayed in it, for a month anyways. She was so happy thinking about that fact while smelling the supremely wonderful smells ahead. Billy was working over a fire with a flat piece of metal. On that metal were thin slices of meat sizzling away.

"What is that wonderful smell?" She asked, going closer to breathe in the smells.

"It's called bacon. I purchased several animal carcasses a few days ago, and figured you would enjoy some of this one." Billy looked over to see how close Elsie was getting to the cooking bacon and chuckled to himself. Reaching over he grabbed a plate from the table he was stacking the stuff on and swung it around to Elsie.

Blinking, Elsie took the plate in her paws and Billy watched as she basically rubbed her muzzle in the meat. It wasn't burning hot, but it was fresh. She didn't seem to mind, however, as she snuffled it, then began gobbling the crispy meat slices as fast as she could put them in her mouth.

"Slow down, there's plenty for you to eat, Elsie," Billy said, chuckling at the little beastkin.

Elsie had not eaten so many delicious things in her life. Admittedly she was not that old, but she had never had bacon. She could barely afford to eat the tubers she got every couple of days. She had never found steady work, and she was too afraid to go outside the city zone to gain Experience. Sure, she did not have access to the System, but who did? If she had points to trade, she could have been able to get nicer things. As it was, it was all she could do to make enough to eat every couple of days.

Billy went to place a few more freshly cooked slices when he heard Elsie growling. Her lips were pulled back and her eyes were locked onto his manipulator holding the bacon on a fork. Ignoring her reaction, Billy kept moving his manipulator and shook off the bacon onto the plate Elsie held. She kept growling louder and louder until his manipulator was removed. That was when she saw he had placed more on the plate, and she paused. Her eyes, which had been focused in anger at his hand one second, were wide in the next second as she realized what she had just done.

"It's fine, Elsie. Eat your fill. I won't take any from you," Billy said, practically reading her mind. He went back to placing more slices of meat on the flat piece of metal while she continued to eat.

Chapter 12

Another thing Elsie hadn't seen was the other pan frying potato chunks in the grease made by the bacon, which was only brought to her attention when a second plate appeared out of nowhere piled with the strange stuff. A quick snuffle of the pile and she understood the tubers were fried in the oil from the meat. It smelled amazing, but she could see the tubers were still steaming with heat. She kept stuffing the salty, but sweet, crispy meat into her mouth while the tubers cooled more.

Before she started in on the tubers, Elsie looked over to see the giant spiderkin watching her eat. She had a question she wanted to ask, and tried on several occasions, but she was too hungry, and all the food in her mouth made her unintelligible. Between her second and third helping of the meat slices she paused to ask Billy, "So who's the puffy one I slept with last night? Was it a cat or something? A squirrelkin? It was very fluffy, but it didn't wake up the whole time."

Billy waited for her to start on the fourth helping of bacon before responding.

"That was Sharea. She is a mousekin, I think. She unlocked the System the other day, and will be out for the count a few days while her new Attributes are upgraded. She had quite a bit of Experience points spent all at once." Billy waved a manipulator to show his minor exasperation. "She did not want to wait and spend them in bits here and there, instead opting to use it all."

"She unlocked the System?!" Elsie asked, surprised enough that the bacon she was eating fell from her open mouth. She quickly scooped it up and stuffed it back into her mouth, not wanting to waste any part of this buffet.

Chuckling he saw Elsie scrambling to stuff the food into her mouth, he said, "Yes, she helped me clear a Lair and got enough Experience to unlock the System, and have enough left over to raise some of her stats." Billy turned from the beastkin and began to wipe the plates and pans left over from Elsie's breakfast. He did not need to eat, but wanted to make sure she got a good meal before starting the day.

"Enough about her, though. I want to discuss some things with you when you're done eating. I'll let you finish up here and wait outside. Inside, whatever. I may have a proposition for you, if you're willing." Placing the pan on a shelf after wiping it off, Billy carefully maneuvered around Elsie while she began on the potatoes, and went into his facility to open the roofs to let the sunlight in, and to check on the plants to see if anything happened yet. Nothing had, yet, but everything was prepared.

Elsie thought about what the giant spiderkin had said, and a shiver ran down her spine as she did so. She did not want to do anything weird with the giant spiderkin, but if he threatened her she would bear it in step. She didn't know what he wanted from her, and hoped beyond hope he wasn't fattening her up to eat later. She had heard giant spiders preferred their food alive.

Her senses weren't telling her he was dangerous, though. She trusted her senses, but she had been tricked by other kin before. She thought for a moment to run out the front door, circle around and enter her own unit and hide, but she got the feeling there was no need to. This Billy the Spider bloke seemed alright, as far as she could tell. She set this train of thought aside for the moment, though, and tried the tubers. To her delight, they were almost as good as the meat. Almost. She gobbled the whole plate and even licked it clean. Not knowing what to do with it, she just left it on the floor where she had been sitting, and went inside the block's interior.

The interior space was strangely quiet. Normally the inner block was full of fey talking, doing laundry, or cooking meals of one sort or another. This block looked practically empty, but it wasn't at the same time.

She could see that several of the units were open to the inside. Instead of having doors, there were portal arches anyone could walk into from a catwalk that linked all of the units. She saw sunlight in them, telling her that either those units had far too many windows, or the units were retrofitted to be something new. She watched Billy climb out of one and walk along the wall of several units to another, he didn't use the walkways or steps, he just walked along the walls like it was a floor.

She waved up at him, and he waved back. He went into one of the lit units for a minute, then came out and climbed down to the floor level. Elsie felt a little squeamish as she saw him move the way he did. She couldn't identify why she thought he moved strangely, but something in her told her it was not quite right.

Billy had a cloth in his manipulator and was using it to wipe his "hands" free of the dirt he had run his digits through. He had a moisture measuring sensor in those digits for some reason, and this came in handy for checking soil water saturation levels. They were good for now.

"Well, Elsie, now that you have eaten, I have a question for you, if you don't mind," Billy said, walking towards the central column of the block. He looked over to the beastkin - she looked well despite the rags for clothes she had on.

"I hope it's nothin' gross, mister spider," Elsie stated upfront. There were no conditions set for her to stay in her own unit, but neither were there any conditions for her leaving. If Billy asked her to do anything immoral, she would leave and let what happens, happen.

"I have only just begun to experiment with a few ideas I have here. I will need to unlock the gates soon, to make some money back for the coin I have already invested. As it so happens, you are here already, and I find I need someone to watch the place," Billy waved a manipulator around to indicate the whole interior of the block.

Elsie shuffled side to side as she waited for the shoe to drop.

"To do the job properly, the individual I require must have access to the System so they can use it to manage the administrative privileges for this facility." Billy turned to see if Elsie would react, but as he turned to her, he saw her tail dropping.

"I don't have access; you know that already," She said, looking down at her feet with a sad expression on her puppy dog face.

"That's alright, Elsie, because this particular position comes with a sign-on bonus." He waited again, but she seemed not to put two and two together.

Shrugging to himself, Billy turned and approached the beastkin and held out a manipulator. She looked at it, confusion clear in her eyes.

"Enough to unlock the System and a bit extra to purchase a couple of points of Attributes," Billy said, still holding out his hand with the offer.

She didn't hesitate one moment and had the strange spider's feeler in her hands. It felt cold at first, but she could feel a line of heat there as well. She focused all her will into accepting this offer, unable to let it pass one single second longer than necessary, hoping beyond all reasoning this wasn't some kind of nasty trick.

Billy chuckled as he saw Elsie's reaction to the exchange. He knew she just saw the trade window closing as the System absorbed the Experience to unlock itself for her, the gray not-light glowing, then fading around her. He also knew she had a little more than whatever she'd had a moment before. Her tail went from limp and sad to stiff and straight to wagging all over the place as the System became available for her.

Gasping, she cried, "How is this possible? I thought you couldn't trade Experience points to unlock the System? I have access to the System!" Elsie was practically wiggling her entire body as Billy watched her.

"If you would, please, purchase at least one point for your Intelligence and your Wisdom. It will help you keep track of things. If you can get more than one in each, please do so.

Everything left over is yours. And, I will give you a fixed amount each month, er.. every 28 days. It will be more than enough to get whatever you need. Also," Billy said, pulling out a bag that jingled with the sound of coins from a compartment Elsie couldn't see. "This is also part of your pay, but the coin will be given every seven days to ensure you get food and other things you might need. As to why this worked? Well, let's just say it has something to do with work and not with actually trading. I paid you Experience. I did not give it to you, which is how I hoped this would go."

Elsie stood, shocked to see so much being given to her. She wanted to reach out and take it, but she didn't, not immediately. "Why? What do you want me to do for so much?" Her voice was trepidacious, but Billy thought he understood.

Calmly, he said, "I need you to manage this place while I am away. To do that, I need you to dress nicely and have Attributes high enough not to be swindled by customers. You also need to be tough enough to defend yourself from anyone who gets out of hand, so putting points into Strength and Dexterity is something you can now do as well."

"You expect me to fight to protect this place?" She didn't sound very sure of herself. After all, she was just a pup and all alone; she couldn't be expected to do much.

"Of course not, Elsie. I expect you to manage this place when it opens. I will be selling fruits and vegetables grown here. You will need to gather what is collected, stock the baskets, collect payments, and make deposits. To do the depositing, you need to access the System, and the Administrator column here. This way, you can't be robbed, as all the coins will be stored here or in your unit." As he spoke, Elsie saw she had a notification box, something she had only ever heard about, appear in front of her. It asked if she would accept the position of Manager and showed her the pay in both Experience and coins.

Billy would like to promote you to the position of Manager at Billy's Recycling. You will have access to all of the unoccupied units in the facility, can manage the stalls to sell products and collect payment, and have access to the block Bank for deposits and for accessing change. You will be given 30 Experience points every 28 days and 10 silver coins every 7 days. You will also accrue a percentage of all Experience and coins collected through trading on all sales, deposited monthly. Do you accept the position? Yes. No.

Elsie read the notification over twice, unwilling to believe how lucky she was for being kicked out of her unit yesterday in front of some random stranger. She mentally acknowledged the position, and the screen vanished. In her mind, she saw new options that allowed her to examine the current contents of the block.

Billy watched her as she read and knew he had made the right decision. He saw her eyes glaze over for a moment, and her hands going to her head as if she had a headache, as she spent some of the Experience she had to upgrade her Attributes. Noticing something, a small image with Elsie's profile pic on it suddenly appearing; he looked back at her as her eyes came into focus.

"You have your information set for anyone employed here to see. I have not looked at it, but I just noticed it was set. If you want, you may change it to private. This way, other employees cannot see your stats."

Blinking away the slight confusion, Elsie accessed her Status, went to the block status, and set her profile information to *Semi-Private*. This would let Billy see her Primary Attributes, her Life and

Armor values, but nothing else. Billy's was set to *Secure*, so nobody but he could see his stats.

"Where do I start? When do I start? I don't see anything set up just yet," Elsie said, wiping her now-sweating paws on her torn pants.

"First thing's first. I have a list of things I can make for you and your unit. I have set the information in the Administration menu using a note appended to you. Go have a look, select what you want, and I will make it," Billy indicated for her to approach the column as he stepped aside. "I will go up to my workroom and make whatever you want. It won't take me long, either. But I will need you to not complain about the little buddies I will have running around getting things for me. They're resting right now, but when they get moving, they can be noisy."

Billy wasn't sure how Elsie would react to seeing his bots buzzing and clinking all over the place, but he figured if she didn't ask questions, he wouldn't have to explain.

"S-sure," She said, moving over to the column and placing a paw on it.

Billy went to his personal unit and closed the door while Elsie did her shopping. While she was looking, he wound up his bots one by one to have them on standby.

Billy watched as Elsie chose new clothing for herself. She had selected and deselected items several times and Billy got the feeling she was unsure what she was allowed to choose for herself. After a few minutes, though, she had chosen a number of items which would serve different needs.

She had chosen a variety of dresses, skirts, and pants, as well as shirts and shoes. She even chose a few hats, and other accouterments. He made each item, one after another, while his bots went back and forth to get raw materials. He hummed to himself as his Assembler made each article of clothing, and when it was done, he carefully folded them and set them in an empty crate for delivery.

After the shopping spree was done, she ordered a few simple things for her unit. She requested a pallet, then a bed, then another pallet, and a bigger bed, canceled all of that, and ordered three dozen pillows of various sizes. Then, she requested a mattress. Shaking his head as best he could, he built her bed and made her pillows. He even put the color in the thread and made the patterns she wanted on them. The simple items did not take Billy long to make, and almost as soon as she was done making her selections he was finished with the last component.

Billy waited a few minutes to make sure everything was as she'd wanted before gathering up the crates, stacking them on his back, and then he left his unit. He used the stairs so as not to spill his load, and he watched her watch him descend to the ground level.

Sounding cheery, Billy called down, "Alright, I have everything here. Let's put this stuff in your room so you can get everything situated and change out of those rags."

Elsie's tail was well out of her control. She was far too happy to want to stop swinging it all over the place. She was so happy she was almost waddling as she followed Billy to her unit. She had to let him in, and inside, he carefully set everything down. He assembled the dresser in a minute, piled the feather pillows, unrolled the mattress and set it on the assembled frame to keep it a few inches off the ground, and laid out her clothes. He put together a pole on some legs and showed her how to put the clothing on the clothes hangers to hang them to keep them wrinkle-free.

It wasn't until Billy turned and looked at Elsie that he saw tears in her eyes. Her little paws were clasped at her chest as she took in her new home. It was by far the nicest place she had ever seen, much less lived in. Running forward, she hugged one of Billy's legs as she sniffled.

"Oh, hey there. It's alright. You're in good hands here." Billy continued to give comforting words to the beastkin and waited for her to pull herself together. It wasn't until now Billy realized just how bad things probably were for her. He wasn't sure how this was going to turn out, though, but figured by putting forward his best foot, he couldn't go wrong. He liked being nice and helpful, and as this mechanoid, he could make almost anything from anything. He was walking usefulness now, and he was willing to be so.

"I-I'm sorry. I j-ust d-don't know w-why anyone would, would be so generous to m-me," She sniffled, wiping her nose with one of her long ears.

"It's alright, Elsie. I'm doing this to help you as much as to help me." Billy wanted to pet her head but fought that urge down hard. She was not a pet, and he was not her owner.

So, he let her get her feelings in order and just stood there, not knowing what else to do. After a few minutes, she wiped her eyes and nose, dropped her old shorts there on the floor, and went to get into one of the new dresses.

Billy turned away in embarrassment; not wanting to peep on her, he scooped up the rags and went outside while she got dressed. He closed the door and went to wait at the gate as he Dissembled the ragged cloth.

Billy needed to go out again, this time out to the overworld, to gather some more things. He wanted to do some exploring but had to make sure Elsie calmed down some, first. A thought struck Billy, and he quickly processed a request with his Assembler and produced a short dagger, sheath, and belt. He held the items in his manipulator while Elsie got ready. It was only another few minutes when she came out.

Billy saw she had taken a moment to brush some of her fur and had cleaned off her ears. The fur around her eyes was also dry, and her eyes looked wide and aware. She saw Billy standing by the gates and came over, her tiny paws running over the fresh dress.

"I have one more thing for you, Elsie. To protect yourself when you go outside." Billy handed her the belt and dagger. She took the items with wide eyes and a puppy dog smile. She then whipped the belt around her waist and hooked on the sheath for the dagger. Last, she slid the sharp blade into its sheath.

"I don't know how to use this," She said, looking sheepish.

"You put the pointy end into the troublemaker until they run away or stop moving," Billy said. "You can spend a little Experience and purchase a point or two in Melee and get a point or two in the Proficiency for daggers."

She nodded as she took this in, as if she never held a weapon before.

"Alright, Elsie, I have a companion who will look after the place while we go out. Today, I need to get out and be shown places. I hope you can show me the places you know. Afterward, if you're hungry, we will get some food," Billy said while placing the travel crates onto his back and carefully tying them around his chest.

They had been beside the gates, just inside, as he prepared to leave. He invited Elsie to his Party before heading out, and she eagerly accepted the invitation.

"Okay. I can show you around a little. I haven't been far, though, but I'll show you the places I know about if you don't mind seeing some rather bad-smelling blocks." Billy could see she did not want to go to such places, but he needed to get the lay of the land, and he would not let a little thing such as bad smells deter him.

The next couple of hours were spent roving around the area near his block where Billy had initially found Elsie. She had given him information about the various people she had encountered, where they lived, and the places where smells were bad enough to avoid. Billy noted each place on his map, leaving markers with notes attached.

Elsie had been to dozens of different blocks, moving from place to place, trying to find work or food or both. To his surprise, Billy learned Elsie was only in her teens. To him, she was a child, yet here she was, roaming the streets all alone. She had made a living cleaning blocks and moving trash outside. She would carry burdens for some people and perform other chores where she could find them.

Several times, Billy caught her looking at a particular place, and she would close up, unwilling to speak until they were around the corner. He saw her shuddering as they passed these places, and Billy would quietly mark the place for future visits. This city did not seem to be capable of maintaining a police force, and the elves only roamed the streets to make sure the paths weren't blocked by drunkards or layabouts. And it would seem there was no place for justice to be served.

"So, what do you do if there is a crime happening?" Billy asked at one point.

"What is a crime?" Elsie asked, not really sure of the word.

Billy thought for a moment before responding. "Are there no laws here in the city?"

"Laws? You mean the law of might? Sure, the strong do what they want. The weak do their best to survive, or they die. Is that what you mean?"

Billy, taken aback by the law of the jungle being a thing in a place so full of different peoples, paused when she said that. Elsie turned to face him as he stopped.

"If someone stole something from someone, there is no recourse the victim could take to get justice?"

"If they were fast enough, they could catch and beat the thief. Or, if they have other people on hand, they would do it for them. But, no, there is no other way to handle these things." Elsie did not look upset by this. It seemed to be the way of the world.

As Billy looked around at the milling masses, he saw exactly that going on everywhere. Some beasts would try and sneak food, beastkin would react. Other fey would shout and chase, while others did nothing. It was almost complete anarchy everywhere. And yet it all somehow never seemed to spread beyond thief and mark. Then again, nobody wanted to get involved in other people's business because they were busy managing their own business. Though people had total freedom here, there seemed not to be any form of justice.

"What if someone kills someone else? Does anything happen to the killer?"

Elsie scratched her muzzle and thought for a moment. "I guess if a relative or friend were there and caught the killer, they could kill them back. Or take their stuff. But nobody else would do that. The strong survive, and the weak die. It is the way of things."

Billy thought about this as Elsie continued to point out places or businesses around the area. He remained attentive while she talked and continued to make notes of the places around his home that she pointed out. Occasionally, she would enter a block to show him particular points of interest, but for the most part, they only walked around the blocks while she talked about the different occupants of the units she knew of.

Several hours later they had stopped at a place Elsie said had some particularly good meat, and Billy found himself digging out a couple coins and handing it to her. She took the coins and then argued for five minutes with the vendor to wrangle the price down for select cuts. In the end, she managed to get the price down almost 20% and was happily chewing on her success.

"Elsie," Billy said while they were walking back to their block.

"Mmm?" She said, chewing on her hank of meat.

Casually he said, "In a moment, several folk are going to stop us and try to rob us, I think. I want you to stay close to me, get under me if you can. Do you understand?" Billy was tracking four individuals who had been trailing them for the last few minutes and caught part of the signals passing between them. He knew that when they went to walk between the large mounds of trash ahead they would be stopped by two of the folk in front while the other two came up behind them.

He could feel Elsie tense up but bumped her with one of his legs carefully to keep her walking normally.

"Are they going to hurt us, Billy?" She was whispering now and he could hear her voice tremble a little.

"No, but they will probably try. I won't let them, however." Billy quietly increased his boiler heat in preparation for the ambush.

They continued forward until they were passing between the trash piles Billy spoke of. He stopped and, with one foot, pulled Elsie under his bulky cloak. The cloak did not rest on the ground, but it was wide enough for her to easily fit. She immediately went on all fours and hurried under. One of the sensors on Billy's chest indicated something hot was under him, and he knew she was safe for the moment.

Two individuals walked out in front of Billy just as his cloak settled. One of the elves looked around for Elsie and didn't see her. Both of these elves looked bedraggled, their clothing well worn, with holes in places. Nothing the duo had looked new except the weapons each held. One had a large club; the other had a worn hammer.

"Drop your coins, and we'll let you go," The closest elf demanded.

Billy just stood there, waiting. He could feel the furnace in himself fire up further, and he could feel the springs tightening and preparing to act. He slowly let the steam pressure build up as he waited.

"You heard me, bug. Drop your coin purse, or we'll stick ya," The second elf called out. Both were looking around casually. None of the nearby folk would approach now. Billy also knew nobody would help.

Billy still said nothing. He didn't move.

"Fine. Take 'em, Brag," The first elf said, and he swung out with his hammer as his partner swung his club.

Billy acted instantly, thrusting one foot at one elf, then another foot at the other. He repeated this for the two elves lunging in from behind. Four impacts and four weapons dropped to the ground. Almost at the same time, four bodies crumpled to the ground, unmoving.

"Elsie, pick them clean and put whatever they have in the crate on my back," he said as he ushered her out from under him with a leg. As she exited from beneath him, he released some of the pressure he had built up. The whoosh it made was drowned out by the hundreds of onlookers talking to each other about what had just happened.

Elsie went forward and scooped up each of the weapons from the elves in front and checked their pockets for anything useful. She pulled at what she could and used her new dagger to cut what wouldn't come loose. She tossed everything in the crate on Billy's back as she went behind him and did the same to the two back there. While she checked those guys, Billy carefully lifted each elf and moved them off of the road to lie against the garbage pile. Neither was breathing, but he didn't want anyone else to think otherwise for now.

He felt more things landing in the crate on his back and turned to move the other two elves beside their compatriots. They were also not breathing. Billy set this information aside for now and made sure to keep the elves off the street. He wasn't sure who these guys were, but all of them were dead now. If he was right, nobody would stop him. Might makes right, he supposed. He was stronger, and that meant he had the right to do what he did.

Elsie continued eating as they left the elves behind. The crowds continued to mingle as before, but Billy noticed he and Elsie were given a little leeway after the incident, at least for a little while. Billy put the violence out of his mind so he could deal with it later. He hadn't intended to kill those elves. He had only wanted to take them out of action. Reviewing his logs, the list of information about the things he was doing, he realized he had dished out some pretty decent numbers to those four.

You have slain an elf bandit. Attack made with foot. Roll to hit is successful.

Chance to hit Determined by Skill: Hand-to-Hand, and Proficiency: Weapon Mastery: Feet.

Damage for Hand-to-Hand calculated using Strength and Stamina.

Damage modified by Surprise attack, an Initiative modifier granted by Perception.

Damage modified by target's Armor Value and Natural Armor.

Total damage reduction: 0.

Damage dealt: 128.

Part Durability reduced by 1.

Elf bandit expires.

+14 Experience points.

A similar log block repeated for the other three elf bandits, all with similar Experience point gains. It wasn't much, but he'd been attacked, and he'd defended Elsie. She wasn't hurt, and neither was he, and that was all he was concerned about at the moment.

Twenty minutes saw the pair entering their block. Passing through the gates shut out all the noise from the streets, and only the sound of their feet striking paving stones was heard echoing around them.

Billy went to one of his storage rooms and unloaded his burdens to sort through later. He saw Elsie go to her unit with the few things she had purchased for herself. Using the language of the spiders, Billy waved a couple of his feet about, and in a moment, he saw Charlotte crawling out of their unit to see him as his message was passed from his bots to her.

"How was the exploration, Billy? Did you find everything you need? How," She trailed off as she noted the lowered Durability on four of his eight feet. "Already? I just repaired you this morning and you go off breaking things again? Dear, oh dear."

Her indignity was revealed in the leg waving and bobbing she produced as she continued to silently berate Billy as she approached. She examined each of his feet while he stacked the things from the crates. She made some minor adjustments here and there, then moved to the other feet to repeat the process. She continued to complain, but he let her vent as he focused on Elsie's door in case she returned while he was undergoing this unscheduled maintenance. Fortunately, he only needed some quick mechanical adjustments and no part replacements. In less than five minutes, Charlotte was done and back to checking out the new things he'd brought back with him.

Durability has been restored to foot #1. Durability is now 20 out of 20.

Durability has been restored to foot #2. Durability is now 20 out of 20.

Durability has been restored to foot #7. Durability is now 20 out of 20.

Durability has been restored to foot #8. Durability is now 20 out of 20.

"I will come back later and process this into raw materials. I need to check in on Elsie and see what she wants to do. I may," he paused as he looked down at Charlotte, "Have to explain what and who I am to her at some point. She will eventually find out, and I must know sooner rather than later if she will keep our secrets."

"If she runs, you will need to kill her and dispose of her body, Billy. We can't let this secret out. It's bad enough Orgar knows what you are, but he won't tell anyone." Charlotte finished giving Billy her piece and left to go to her unit. He had a queue a mile long she had sent to him while she examined his feet, and he would need to make the stuff eventually. First, he would need to take care of Elsie.

Elsie could not believe her luck. Not only had this random spiderkin taken her in and unlocked the System for her, but he was also strong enough not to be robbed in the street. He didn't even flinch when those elves ambushed them. She didn't want to say anything, but she checked on the elves while taking their stuff and discovered Billy had killed all four of them. All four! He kicked out to each one once, and they dropped like sacks of moldy melons. Her tail was wagging as she thought of how brave and strong Billy was. He even protected her. She had never seen another fey protect a beastkin like her from anyone before.

She had even been in his Party and gotten Experience points. Over 50 Experience points! That was amazing! She could get some Abilities now, or even bump her Attributes. She had never had so much free Experience before unlocking the System, and now she had that AND enough points to make herself stronger than she'd ever been.

She was growling happily to herself as she removed the dress and hung it back on the hanger the way she'd been shown and tried on another of the beautiful ones Billy had made for her. He was even able to make slits for her tail! Oh, he was so wonderful to her!

She heard a tapping on the door and rushed to open it. Billy was there, with his giant spider eyes looking at her.

"Come in! I was just changing to get the smell of the streets off of me," She said as she returned to her room. She grabbed a brush from her, what had Billy called it, a dresser, and began running it through her short hair.

"If you place the dirty clothes in that basket over here by the door, I can get those cleaned for you. Just fill it up and place it outside before you go to bed, and I'll have it taken care of," Billy said as he saw Elsie had changed already.

"Oh. Okay!" She said as she pulled the dress off the hanger and tossed it into the basket.

"Also, I think I will sit out here and talk with you for a few minutes. There are some things about myself I need to tell you. Important things that you might not like. I don't know, really. I've only told one other who I am. More importantly, only one other knows what I am." Billy hunkered down outside the door, close enough to be present for the conversation, far enough away to not pressure Elsie in case she got scared.

"Is it that you're a Mechanoid?"

Her blatant statement would have made the hairs rise on the back of his neck if he'd had hair or a neck.

"How do you know that?"

Elsie turned to him with a confused look on her face. "When I unlocked the System, it told me who gave me the Experience points. It said your name was Billy and that you were a Mechanoid. I don't know what that is, but it sounds like a spiderkin kind. Is it?"

"No, it is not a spiderkin kind, Elsie. I am not alive, not in the way you or anyone else is." Billy pulled off one of the coverings from a front leg to reveal the steel and brass below. Giving the metal a tap with a finger, the two heard the clear response of metal on metal ringing out. "My body is a machine used to hold my soul. I interface with the machine using magic and science. I do not need to eat food, per se, but I do require fuels and water, lubricants, and such."

Elsie approached not one hint of fear in her features. She reached out and felt the metal that was Billy's leg. He could feel the contact somehow, a slight warmth at the point of contact. The polished framework was incredibly intricate, and the mechanical parts which were now exposed showed how his leg moved. She waggled his leg, which he let her do, and she saw how some of it worked. He had tiny cables and wheels, cogs and springs, pistons and valves all over himself, and she wanted to see them all.

Billy removed the plates covering himself but had trouble with some. "Charlotte, come on out. You might as well say hello to Elsie," he called out loud.

Chapter 13

"Charlotte?" Elsie asked, one of her ears trying to perk up. It didn't because it was so long, but she was sniffing the air anyways. Faint clicking noises could be heard as Charlotte walked across the mostly empty block interior as Elsie watched.

Waving a colorful front limb, Charlotte called out, "Hello Elsie. It is a pleasure to finally meet you, officially. I am Charlotte, personal assistant for Billy, here." She spoke out this time, and her old granny voice was bright and cheerful.

"Oh, so pretty!" Elsie almost cried out as the palm-sized, colorful spider approached.

"She is also a machine, Elsie. She will be helping run things for me," Before he could continue Charlotte interrupted him.

"I can speak for myself, Billy." Turning she said, "Hello Elsie, I am Charlotte. I maintain Billy's frame. I also manage the bots that perform other tasks for him at his command." She spun around in a little circle to show off her new frame and colorful hair. She was quite proud of her new do.

Elsie got down on all fours as she looked at Charlotte and watched in glee as she spun around, showing off her magnificent frame. Billy chuckled to himself as Charlotte got some much needed attention and affection from someone other than him. He took a moment to reattach his plates as Elsie watched Charlotte.

"I have several projects going on here, Elsie. I have converted several units into storage for some of the things I make, and others are now greenhouses, which is where the fruits and vegetables I am trying to grow will be. Those we will collect and sell to the neighborhood. However, to make things run much smoother, I need to go out and find something specific. I would take you with me, but the things I am looking for carry a stinger on them, and I am immune to those as I am." Billy pointed to the units as he called them out and, when he noticed Elsie wasn't paying any attention, continued to talk.

"I need to go out today and get those things, to give them time to settle in first. Before I do that, though, I need to know if there are any insects in the city." Billy waited for Elsie to look up at him.

"Bugs? Aren't you a bug?" She asked, an ear perking up as she tilted her head to one side.

Sighing, he said, "No, I am not a bug, Elsie. I mean things like crickets, butterflies, beatles. You know, bugs. Are those in the city anywhere?" Billy tried to not sound insane. He had seen each of these things in the city, but all of them were kin of some sort or another. What he wanted to know is if the animals were present.

"You mean animals? Sure, they're all over. Why?"

"I need to go out and collect a beehive, with the bees. I will need a hive nearby to pollinate the flowers of the plants I am growing. I could do that manually, but the insect is by far the best. I can also use the honey they produce, and the wax." Billy scratched at his spider chin as he explained.

"Bees need big open spaces, don't they? They need lots and lots of flowers to get the pollen to make honey." Elsie scratched one of her ears.

"Are there any parks in the city? Places where trees and grass grow for folk to walk in?"

"Parks? No, if anyone wants to walk in the grass, all they need to do is go to the overworld." She still didn't look at Billy, so engrossed in watching Charlotte pose.

Billy thought for a minute, then moved past Charlotte and Elsie to check the Administrator menu at the column. After he couldn't find what he was looking for, he went outside. Pulling up another menu through his Status, Billy found the selections he had used when acquiring his own block. He found the selection for opening up a new section of land and looked for options. He mentally poked all over the place to find the pull down button and after a few minutes he succeeded.

Perception check successful. You now better understand how the City Interface functions in the Lair of the Fey, and are able to make more nuanced searches.

His menu flickered for a second and the new menu option was now easier to find. He chose a new plot of land right next to his, and designated it to be a park. He chose the proper trees, type of grass, and selected the restrictions for visitors. He decided to place a booth at one of the two entrances. This would require visitors to transact one coin per hour of visit, or one Experience point per day.

This would in turn be used to maintain the place, clean up trash, and such. The cost of activating this plot of land was substantial. Oddly, it went down as he selected a wide variety of plants to fill the area. He even included a little pond that held small fish.

Billy set all the parameters for this section of land and mentally selected *Apply*. He could feel his Experience pool empty as it fed the creation of the place within the city. As this was not a housing unit, the System pushed out the boundary magically, and within five minutes there was a new plot of land surrounded by shabby looking apartment blocks. There was another benefit of this not being strictly used for housing, that being its extended width. The floor space of the entire park was at least four times his apartment's footprint. Hundreds of trees sprouted up to grow to around 10 feet tall. A gentle rain fell for a few minutes to moisten the grass, fill the pond, and provide nutrients for all the flowers that were rapidly blooming.

"Wow, what is that," Billy heard several nearby fey say as the park appeared. He said nothing as a large crowd formed around the place. As they all watched, a short bushy wall rose around the boundary of the park, leaving two breaks. Each had a booth and a sign board stating the price of entrance.

Before people tried packing into the place, Billy quickly checked and found he could place a limit on visitors, and did so. He would limit the place to a few dozen at a time. He also checked the box allowing people to schedule appointments to use the park in advance.

People began grumbling as the System updated the information on the board, and many walked away. Some, however, dropped a coin in the bowl, which vanished as it hit bottom, and the individuals were let in. There was no physical barrier here, just a field that prevented any from entering without paying first.

Smiling inwardly to himself, Billy returned to his facility to have a quick chat with Elsie before going to collect some honey bees.

Stepping into the block, he noticed Charlotte was already showing Elsie the ins and outs of the place. He hoped she was having fun watching over the beastkin. He was within eyesight of Charlotte, so he used spider language to let Charlotte know he was going to the overworld to see about some bees. She didn't seem to slow down at all as she waved a couple legs in response. Billy quietly equipped his cloak and strapped on the crates which had already been placed by the gate. He was getting pretty good at strapping the things on himself, and in a couple of minutes he was exiting the block once more.

Billy walked by the park, now with fewer people checking it due to the price of entry, and made his way to the zone exit. He checked his inner clock, noting that he had just over five hours before dark set in, and stepped past the poles into the woods.

As usual, only a few people were moving in and out of the city to hunt during the day; the fey typically preferred coming out at night when it was safer. Billy moved to a nearby tree and snapped off a limb. In seconds he cleaned the branch and trimmed it down to size. He had himself a fine club in no time. As he traveled in a direction he had not gone last time, Billy looked for choice pieces of wood he could collect from the trees he walked past. He had been walking for almost an hour when he finally felt safe enough to use his drone to scout. He leaned back a little and launched it through a large break in the trees. The little thing went high into the air and then performed a long sweep of the surrounding area.

The drone couldn't go far, and it could only communicate what it had seen once it returned, but it was faster than mindlessly wondering about. The flight, more a glide, only took a few minutes. The images it had captured expanded Billy's map only about half a mile in every direction. It was all trees, so he continued onward.

Every mile or so Billy would wind up his powerful launching springs and let the drone loose. It would scan while he waited, and return to update his map. Occasionally it would provide a rock outcrop, or a small stream. Mostly, all Billy saw were trees. He wasn't put off by this, however, and carried on. Walk a mile, launch the drone, check the map, repeat. All the while he would collect choice cuts of wood, berries, or other edible plants as he came across them.

Some plants Billy transplanted into pots he produced on the spot. Most went into smaller baskets in the crate for sale or use later. Sometimes he found a flower and would scoop it up for himself. Wild flowers, their bright orange petals visible from quite a distance, were some of his favorites to pick. He didn't know if these were similar to ones from Earth but he collected them anyway.

At the eighth mile from where he'd begun launching his drone Billy finally lucked out. He'd found a small open clearing and it had some kind of grass. His drone had circled to it once it saw the clearing and took some very high definition images. Billy zoomed in on those and saw, clear as day, tiny bugs flying all over the place. He turned in the direction his map indicated, and hurried ahead.

Once he reached the field Billy slowed to a walk, then cautiously moved into the open and listened carefully. He watched the bees, to try and piece together their flight patterns. He tried to determine which direction they were coming from, and which they were going, in an attempt to locate the nest. He finally saw most of the bees were coming from one side of the clearing, so he circled around and began checking tree limbs and watching the ground. His keen vision took in every detail as he searched for the tell tale signs of bee activity. After a few minutes, and only a dozen yards inward, Billy spotted the hive hanging from a tree branch.

Now that he'd spotted the hive, Billy hunkered down and began Dissembling some of the wood he had been carefully collecting. He would insert the limbs into his mouth, and it would process through his body. One of the hatches on his abdomen opened to extrude the clean wood cut to size, length, and sterilized. He stacked the slats in a small pile until he was done making them all, then swiftly assembled the parts. His Assembler also dumped out the remnant wood chips into a pile.

He'd opted to use half-dovetail joints to assemble everything, and he produced a glue-like substance to fasten it together firmly. He had an extruder near his abdomen's web mechanism which also secreted just the glue. In a few minutes he had built both the box and the frames for his portable beehive. He also made some edible strings to support the layers of hive. He would have to cut it up in stages and store it all even as he looked for the queen. Fortunately he was totally immune to bee stings and didn't have to fear them flying into his eyes for real.

Carefully, so as not to frighten the bees, Billy produced a smoking wick from some of the grasses nearby. He wafted the smoke around the bees to try and calm them, or disrupt their pheromones, as he lifted the whole of the nest by removing the branch that held it from the tree.

Lowering the branch with the beehive, Billy kept an eye out for the fat little queen. He would need to trap her and place her in the hive so the other bees would follow her. He carefully separated the hive, placing each section in the order he had cut them away into the new hive box. He did not want to disrupt the hive structure, as this would only cause the bees to waste time and energy to repair it. As he took each layer off, he would look for the fat queen. He would then place the section in a rack and tie it into place with the edible strings. He continued this a few more times before he finally found the little monarch.

A quick motion and Billy had the little lady in a special kind of clip which would allow her caretakers to enter and exit, but would keep her inside and safe. He looked over her and saw her pretty orangey-red coloring, then placed her into the new home for her hive. After the queen was made safe, Billy quickly disassembled the remainder of the hive and placed the sections into the box. It only took a few more minutes, and in that time the other ladies of the hive were already all over the new hive box. The queen was already doing her job well, it seemed.

Billy waited around for an hour, and during that time the rest of the collectors had returned to find their home moved. They had no problem following the pheromones to their queen, and in no time at all they were all inside. Billy positioned the hive in a spot on his back that would be the absolute most stable during his return home. Fortunately, bees on this world were very similar to ones from Earth, but different as well. Once the nest was secure, Billy had received an alert.

Kenning check successful.

Congratulations! You have successfully acquired an intact beehive without harming the bees!

Feeling good about the success, Billy opened his map and turned in the direction of home. He moved quickly and quietly through the still woods. He was not out here to hunt, nor was he meandering this time, or with anyone to slow him down. He was free to travel at the fastest pace possible without disturbing the beehive on his back. About two miles from the city zone poles was where Billy chose to slow his movement, not wanting to run into or over anyone coming through the same area. It was a good thing, too, as he had almost immediately spotted several beastkin heading in the same direction as he.

Billy didn't want to bother anyone at this point, but he did want to try out some things. He'd seen he had some Proficiencies at some point, and one of those would give him an opportunity to sneak around. He focused his intent to move around quietly without being noticed and could feel his Proficiency activating. It was something akin to a channeled spell from his gaming days; as long as it was active he would have to continue spending to keep it going. Stealth was like that, he could actively try to be stealthy, and some random roll somewhere would determine if he was. Then he would have to make random checks every so often to determine if anyone noticed him. If anyone were around, they would also be making their own rolls, but would not be aware of them unless they were successful.

There was too much back and forth in his logs for Billy to worry about, so he just focused on being a stealthy ninja as he moved like an eight-legged ghost with the rest of the city folk. To his surprise, not one person became aware of him. Well, if they were aware of him he had not noticed any reaction from them. He was practically invisible to everyone around him up until he walked through into the new zone of the city.

Several beastkin jumped when he practically materialized right amidst them, but otherwise carried on with their own affairs. For Billy's part, he did his best to imitate whistling while he went to his block. The streets were full of fey going about their business, but as it was not yet night, many were still either asleep or just wandering the vendors along the streets between the blocks looking for food to eat.

Deciding it would be better to be free, for them at least, Billy went to the park he had installed. At the booth he placed a coin in the bowl and the field around the place let him in. Billy saw a few couples out today, walking around and talking. He ignored them and went to a location near the pond. There he found a spot where he unloaded the beehive and placed it on a raised stand for it. Then he carefully lifted the lid of the hive and opened the clip the queen was in to let her out. Her little caretakers immediately ushered her deeper into the hive, and Billy closed the lid to keep the heat inside.

When the lid closed, the entire hive vanished and he received an alert.

Quest complete! You have found a beehive and transplanted it to the park! From now on, the flowering plants will produce more seeds, nuts, pods, and other edible fruits and vegetables. The hive's location is now hidden from visitors to protect them. To access your hive, open the park's menu from your City Management menu and select your beehive to make any adjustments as needed.

+100 Experience.

Billy blinked as he read the notification about his hive. He had hoped the System would work to protect the little ladies while they did their thing, and it seems it had done just that. He closed the notification and left the park to return to his apartments.

Outside the gates to the inner block he saw a few dwarves standing around unloading some stuff. Billy watched as the packages were placed in a particular spot at the gate to vanish there and reappear inside one of the storage units. The dwarves were then immediately paid for the stuff they'd delivered, the System transferring coin or Experience as was agreed for the particular goods. Billy watched the dwarves drop off the packs they used to carry the stuff from Orgar, deciding not to interfere. He did not wish to speak with them yet, he was in the mood to relax after the business of the last couple of days, but had something to do.

Once the dwarves left with their payment, Billy slipped inside. He dropped off the wood and other things he'd picked up during his walk, and looked around. Elsie was asleep in her own unit this time, and Sharea was asleep in her unit, which still had the door cracked open so Charlotte could check in on her.

Before heading out to some locations he'd previously marked on his map, Billy had to mentally prepare himself for what may come. He also needed to wait for it to get dark, which wouldn't take long now. He was silently meditating when he noticed the light outside go from full daylight to middle of the night dark, and the lights he had preset in his block flickered on with magical fires lighting the lanterns in the place. Billy quietly stood, sent Charlotte a message he would be back in the morning, and slipped out the gates.

Billy returned to his block a couple of hours before dawn. He'd watched a particular unit long enough to get an idea of what was going on inside, but had done nothing. He needed more information, so he'd gone around the area and searched for it. He had been following a shady character around as they made their rounds and spotted a few more places he would need to investigate further. Ultimately, he knew the first place he'd stopped by was only a waystation for the depravity that was going on, and any action taken there would ripple outward and alert the others involved in what was going on. So he'd decided to watch and wait until he could locate the head of this terrible snake. Then he would act.

Coming back home, Billy removed his cloak and carried it to his unit. He scooped up the laundry outside Elsie's unit and took them to clean. Inside his unit he went about the task of carefully washing, then drying the clothing. He'd used steam to clean out any stains, a deodorizer to blast away any odors, and he released hot air to help dry the fabrics. While he did this he looked at the timer he'd set up for Sharea. She would be waking up some time tomorrow, and he wanted to make sure she had a meal. He also wanted to be prepared to make any clothing she might want.

Sending orders to Charlotte, who had sat and watched him clean the clothes himself, she brought over the bots for Billy to wind up and perform the tasks she then gave them. The bots went to the storage unit and began bringing pieces of wood and bits of old clothing and shreds of leather for Billy to process anew. The clothing came out in wide swathes which he would carefully roll up. He'd chosen a variety of colors, but the limiting factor was the volume of cloth available. He did not need much, fortunately, as Sharea was quite small and compact, so he'd only made a couple of yards of each color. The leather was printed out similarly, but he'd made only one roll of this to work on later.

The wood was reconstructed into boards and stacked against the wall. He'd had some variety to choose from, though he was unsure what they were specifically. There were strange names of the different wood, but he'd had to lay it out in piles by its color and hardness instead of by type. He didn't want to take the time to figure out all of the names for the stuff he was using, at least not right now.

Eventually the sun appeared in the sky, and the new day began officially. The couple of hours he'd spent producing raw materials gave him quite the inventory to use when he needed it. He had the stuff moved to an empty storage unit by his bots once he was done with the cloth and leather, to make room for the piles of lumber. As this was made, he'd had that taken to the unit where it was all stacked. Once the sun had risen, he decided to do the last few pieces then went to his oven to cook breakfast for Elsie.

The day went smoothly once Elsie awoke and breakfasted. Billy had gone through the inventory with Elsie and got ideas from her on some of the things he should make to sell at reasonable prices for the local area residents. He left her at the block to dig through the menus there to pick out those things while he had donned his cloak and crates to bring in more trash to repurpose.

Billy mingled with the thick crowds of fey as he went about collecting the things he was looking for. Others also dug through the piles of trash for similar reasons, but he was pretty sure what he was doing was far better than just wiping something off and listing a thing as used. He was optimistic that what he was doing could be scaled up, but the sheer amount of garbage that had built up around just this part of the city was staggering. He was still uncertain as to how large the city was. It had to be much more than 10 miles across. It could be 20, he wasn't sure. What he did know was that he had a near endless supply of material he could process into new things. For his part all he really needed, and which he could not produce himself, was water and fuel. He could purify either, but not make it. It was a limitation of the alchemy pot device inside him that prevented the creation of these things.

Billy went back and forth from the streets to his block to drop off the crates full of stuff, swapping out for empty crates, then heading out to fill them up again. Half way through the day one of his personal timers went off in his head, and he worked his way back to the block. He'd barely made a dent on the trash around the area today, but he would worry about that later. For now, he wanted to check in on Sharea. She would wake in a few minutes.

Just as he'd walked through the gates he saw Sharea stirring. Elsie was with her already, and so was Charlotte. Mentally shaking his head, mostly because he had no neck, Billy took the loaded crates to the storage unit and unloaded it himself while the ladies took care of introductions. When he was done he went to his unit and grabbed the platters he'd covered with food. He'd let Elsie take some coin to get as much bread as she wanted, some jams and butter, meat and fruit. She had set it all up at his unit for the time Sharea awoke, and now it was time for Billy to serve it all up.

Scooping the large platters with his manipulators, and somehow managing a cask of cold water and one of a cider the dwarves had brought on his back, Billy worked his way down to the floor level and to Sharea's room. He laid out the platters of food, and set the casks down. Charlotte had a pair of bots bring in mugs, and Billy filled them for the two beastkin while they ate.

"Welcome back, Shar. It's good to see you finally awake. Eat your fill. Take your time. I'll be out there making some things for Elsie to put up for sale later." Billy looked at the two and smiled to himself. His manipulators moved in their nervous motion, the way spiders do when they're happy. The two wouldn't know that, but he was fine not telling them. He handed the mugs out, and turned to leave.

"Thanks, Billy, for watching over me while I was asleep." Shar's cute voice called out as he moved into the facility proper.

"No problem, Shar," he said, waving a leg at her. "Take your time. Enjoy yourself a little. Charlotte will give you some information. I'll be out here getting things prepared." With that Billy went to the unit and began processing the piles of things he'd collected earlier.

Over the background hum from his abdomen and the chittering of his bots, Billy listened to the ladies talking. Elsie and Sharea were swapping stories about how they'd met Billy, and then they talked a little about themselves. He listened as they talked, and watched Charlotte doing her spider dance to manage the bots while speaking with the beastkin.

When asked about the dance, Charlotte turned to Billy using the dance to ask if she should explain. Billy gave his ascent, and then he listened as she explained the complex and nuanced spider language she and Billy had worked out. The ladies fell over in fits of giggling as Charlotte explained how each limb motion at the right time meant different things. The beastkin tried a few times to use the spider language, but when one of the bots walked up a wall and fell flat on its back the two laughing beastkin gave up. If they'd kept going the bots in the area would be doing all manner of crazy things.

Fortunately, Charlotte was there to right the bot, and get it going about its tasks. Eventually the conversation rolled around to clothing, which had the ladies going to Elsie's unit where she showed off her new outfits. In no time flat, Billy found a long list of requests piling up in his queue for a wide variety of clothing which mousekin could wear, most of which were belts, mitts. And 20 or so skirts.

A few leg waggles had bots bringing in the bolts of cloth, which Billy fed back into his Assembler to put together the requests. Any scraps were immediately recycled. As each item was crafted, Billy folded it and had a bot deliver the item. He also set about making the mile long list of furniture for not just Sharea, but for both Elsie and Charlotte, who was also queueing up not just her own little furniture, but full sized stuff for the beastkin to use when they visit Charlotte in her own unit. He was even getting requests for outfits, for Charlotte no less.

"How does that even work?" Billy said to himself as he made the things to scale for Charlotte. He'd not needed to modify the schema he had for the outfits, she had done that herself. He just needed to produce the stuff, so he did. For some reason, she'd ordered sets of very tiny skirt things, in batches of eight. Billy had no idea how they would be used, but he'd made dozens of sets nonetheless.

The one article he figured out were little scarfs he knew were for wrapping around the abdomen. She even requested little hats. Hats! "Women," Billy mumbled to himself when, as soon as he got requests for hats from Charlotte he also received requests from the other two.

Once the very, very long list of clothing was at long last completed, Billy made three matching items for each of the ladies. He printed out little cloth necklaces for each of them, and on each he put a tiny silver bell as the centerpiece. Those only took moments to produce, and when they came out he chuckled to himself again.

"I'm so going to hell for this," he said to himself as he ordered three bots to deliver the items separately.

He thought he was going to get an ear full from Charlotte, but as it turned out, she thought the bells were quite novel, and requested enough for each and every bot, except the large scavengers. Sighing to himself, Billy made the bells and necklaces, and then went back to processing all of the garbage into raw materials.

Elsie, Sharea and Charlotte all enjoyed their new apparel, and spent hours trying everything Billy had crafted for them. They especially enjoyed wearing their little bells. So much so, in fact, they went to ask Billy to make more of them with different kinds of necklaces to go with them.

Exasperated, Billy had consumed his already limited supply of silver to fashion as many bells as possible, going so far as to eat into his coin supply. He gave up keeping any of the coins he had on hand, and even made a number of gold bells. All of these would go up for sale when the facility opened up in a couple of days, and the ladies were already working on the best manner in which to show off their wares.

Eventually, all the precious metals Billy had available were consumed, and he had to start in on the slag piles. There was a mix of metals in every pile, as the dwarves had been studiously removing as much iron as they could for their own use. This left a mix of randomly dispersed metals, most of which were oxidized, but posed no issue for Billy and his inner magical matrix. He chewed and chewed the crusty chunks of stuff from the dwarves until it was all gone. This took him the rest of the day and most of the night.

Charlotte had taken care of the beastkin's need for food by providing dinner. The trio then spent the evening arranging Sharea's room, Charlotte's room, and Elsie's room until they all ended up falling asleep in Elsie's room on a pile of pillows. Charlotte didn't require sleep, but she did need some down time to recharge every once in a while. She was partially battery powered, and once Billy noticed she was asleep he went and scooped her up and placed her in the port on the front of his face to recharge. Once plugged in she immediately settled in place, and remained there while Billy processed more trash into treasure.

While Billy worked, he read his logs, learning more about the System. He checked a few things relevant to his plight with the humes and fey, trying to figure out what the differences were between the two parties. He also spent some time looking at Sharea's information, which was still shared with him. Comparing some of her information with what he had himself, he noticed very little difference in the way things worked. From what he could tell, she had almost as much access to Abilities as he, except in the instances where his particular species was relevant, or hers. She could increase her species' Ability to smell things from a distance by purchasing points in it. Billy had a sensor that could do something similar, but it had a larger range of things it could detect. He could not directly put points into this either, as this was not a normal Ability, it was a particular type of Special Ability under the classification of Acquired Ability. This basically meant an item he owned granted him this power. To make it better he would need to either get a new item and replace the one he had, or he needed to upgrade the item he was using.

This was a revelation to Billy. He was concerned some of the Attributes, which were fundamentally different from the beastkin's, would not improve himself as he added points to them.

However, as the Attributes applied to his body and mind, and not his individual components, he could improve himself some. To do more, he would need to upgrade some of the things that were added to his body, such as his Alchemy Pot, his Dissembler, Assembler, Clockwork Cerebrum, Cogsprings and so on. These could be altered to specialize, but he preferred to optimize variety rather than specialize in a particular thing. Increasing his Attributes did not increase the effectiveness of these devices, it allowed him to utilize newer versions of those devices and replace them during his upgrade cycle.

Billy also learned, by going through his logs with care, that almost everything he produced or consumed with his devices gave him a little bit of Experience. It was not much, but every little bit added up. Today, for example, he'd earned almost 30 Experience points for all of the things he'd crafted. That was enough to increase a couple of his Attributes, or he could increase any Ability or even affect some of his Proficiencies. Instead of doing any of this, however, Billy had opted to hold on to his Experience for when he wanted to process a larger upgrade in the future.

That decided, Billy then went on to collect something he'd been expecting. At midnight he received an alert. He opened the notification, and was delighted to see he had earned a portion of the Experience and coins collected from his new park already. It was not much Experience, but there were plenty of coins there now, and after applying some of it to the maintenance of the park itself, he placed the rest in the block's bank for safekeeping. Billy only charged a single coin per hour for entry to the park, but he'd pocketed several hundred after paying the upkeep for it. This would probably turn into a windfall if he played his cards right. This would also be a boon as much of the stuff he bought from the dwarves was exchanged with coins, and now he had more than enough to last him for a while. It also refilled some of his silver and gold cache, as there were individuals who had already paid for weekly and monthly access ahead of time. Then another idea struck him, and he went back to work so he could make it happen.

Breakfast came and went, but Billy kept working. He had gone out several times during the night to collect more trash, opting to clean the streets around his block entirely of trash instead of roaming around while the ladies rested. The people out at night did not interfere with Billy, and some children even helped a few times by pulling stuff from the piles, or climbing the piles and throwing stuff onto Billy's back where his crates were secured. He paid each child a coin when they did this, but the children were not always out when he was.

During the day he had continued to go out and collect, but this time nobody would help him. The people had their own problems and chores, and so it took him a little longer to get the streets in order around his place. Over the next couple of days Billy continued this routine, including producing clothing for the ladies to try on, and remaining focused on his new goal. Finally, after nearly a week had gone by, Billy emerged from his personal unit.

"Charlotte, have the bots prepare the facility. Have them lay out everything the way I've outlined for you. I will be outside setting this up," he said, placing the components for a vendor's booth on his back, along with some various goods to sell. "Elsie, Sharea, do either of you want to help me today? I'm going into the park to set up one of our new businesses."

Sharea and Elsie had been spending more time with one another. They whispered to each other quietly outside Elsie's unit, then Elsie herself came over to Billy. Before speaking to Elsie, Billy had sent Sharea a notification letting her know she has the options to help Billy manage the business as a manager, just like Elsie was, and she accepted the terms of employment in moments.

"I'll manage the park business, Shar will manage in here," Elsie waved at the interior of the block. "What exactly will you have me doing?" She was wearing a full length skirt of pale blue with a green belt that had blue patterns, and a matching blue hat. She also had on her little bell with its blue ribbon choker holding it around her neck.

"You will be selling these," Billy said, showing Elsie a box full of different colored ribbons with bells on them.

Elsie's eyes lit up at the sight of so many sparkly things, and her tail began wagging immediately.

She cried in surprise, "Oh, I get to sell these?!"

"Yep, and I have already set the price for each, all you need to do is lay them out and keep an eye out for thieves." Placing the box of ribbon chokers in the crate on his back, he moved several other boxes from his unit, brought to him by a line of bots, placing them in the crate with the first.

"I will set up a booth in the park for you to work. You keep a portion of what you sell, and the rest will come to the bank here, at the end of the day." Billy loaded everything up, including a comfortable chair and umbrella he'd fashioned through experimentation. It was bright green and large enough to keep the bright sun off Elsie as she sat out there. He also placed a basket with some food in it for her to nibble on throughout the day.

"Also, if you need a break, I will send a bot with you. Just wind it up and let it go. It will come straight here and I will come out myself while you rest a little."

Elsie was more excited now than ever. She had never been offered work where she could have food with her, and she could take a break whenever she needed one. It was so amazing how thoughtful her new spider friend was being toward her needs.

Elsie half cried, half barked, "Oh, I can't wait!" She was very happy to begin her new job.

Holding up his manipulators to calm her he said, "Alright, alright. I'm going. Come on, Elsie, let's get you set up." Billy walked around his block into the park, Elsie hot on his heels. He'd already set up himself and Sharea, Elsie and his bots to have free access so long as they were there for business. Taxes were taken out automatically from all sales, be they Experience or coins. All he'd needed to do was buy a permit from himself, and he was given a collection plate for his sales at his booth. Last, he needed to find a good spot.

Looking around he asked Elsie, "Where would you like to set this thing up at, Elsie? I'll leave that decision to you." He paused inside the park as Elsie came through.

She looked around for a minute before pointing to a spot under the bow of a large tree. "Over there, in the shade," She said happily. "It's the perfect spot. Everyone who comes in will pass by it." Her tail was wagging back and forth the whole time Billy installed his booth.

Chapter 14

Setting up the stand was a simple affair. A large box which was open walled at the back was where Elsie would sit. Inside the box was a set of shelves where extra stock was kept, along with Elsie's snacks. He placed out a few stands which displayed the tiny bells suspended on colorful ribbon. The slight breeze caused a few to tinkle, and already there were fey and beastkin coming over to look.

After a few minutes, Billy had placed the chair for Elsie to sit in, set the collection plate, dropped the bot behind the display on the ground, and bid her good luck, before leaving. He heard her calling out her wares before clearing the entrance.

Returning to his block, Billy went about helping the bots set up more stalls of goods he'd produced throughout the week. The ladies had selected all of the goods they were going to sell, and it coincided with some of the vegetables which had been growing rapidly in their nutrient rich planters. He busied himself with picking the veggies while Sharea and Charlotte organized the layout down below. He was more than happy to also note that when he picked the plants, more began growing almost immediately. It would take time for them to be ready to pick, but he was happy to see the results of his minor labors.

He gathered what was ready, and placed them in simple wooden bowls for people to choose from, and set those on a separate counter he'd constructed. One thing he'd worked hard on for his block was having proper ventilation. He'd had to expend Experience points to adjust various units to provide access to the outside so air would blow through and keep the place cool, while also keeping the nightly rain from puddling in unnecessarily. This provided clean, fresh air moving through the entire interior, which would help keep the vegetables from spoiling too fast.

In front of each bowl of particular foodstuff, Billy had placed a collection plate. People could drop coin or trade Experience for whatever they selected, and carry on with their business without needing to wait for Sharea. He had also procured enough collection plates for every stall he had set up, so that Sharea did not have to collect anything directly.

Sharea's job was to answer any questions her customers would have, and to replace goods sold on the counters. She could also adjust prices as needed. She would get a cut of all sales, the rest being deposited directly into the block's bank account. Normally the block would collect taxes on all sales, but as he owned the block, he could opt out of taxing anything. He did, however, place the smallest tax possible for minor upkeep expenses.

In this world, all goods would degrade at a fixed rate. This included the booths and stalls all the goods sat at. Instead of replacing the stuff, an Administrator only needed to pay a daily upkeep to keep things looking new. Billy chose to do this for now, but planned on bypassing this issue in the future if he could. In the meantime, he would simply use the tax to augment the time required to maintain the stalls and booths instead of rebuilding everything every few days.

Once everything was in its place, Billy closed all of his storage unit's doors and all the greenhouse doorways had curtains covering them. He had lit dozens of lanterns and lamps to illuminate the interior, and at long last turned to Sharea.

"Are you ready to open the block for business, Shar?"

The adorable little mousekin, nearly a foot taller since the day they'd met, had her whiskers twitching all over the place as her big, dark eyes took in every detail of the stalls and booths. She smoothed her own little skirt, and adjusted her belts. Lastly, she donned her own floppy pink hat, and moved to a stool behind the booth showcasing some fine garments.

In a clear voice, "Yes! Open open open!" She cried in excitement.

Billy pulled up his Administration menu at the column, and selected Open For Business, and hit *Apply*.

The haze that had blocked out the noise of the world vanished, and sound wafted in from the streets. Many of the people outside saw the block's gates swing open, and tentatively moved inside to look around. Billy turned to collect one covered basket of specialty items, and left to pay Orgar a visit. The dwarf was incredibly happy Billy had remembered the delicacy, and Billy arranged with his friend to have a dwarf come by every two weeks to collect what he had grown. They haggled a little on prices, but in the end Billy was practically giving the stuff away. He only managed to force the little he did because Orgar refused to take the rare fungus for free.

Billy then purchased a few barrels of alcohol, bid his friend farewell, and returned home.

Around half way into the day the little bot he'd left with Elsie trotted into his apartment, and he scooped it up automatically and wound its spring. Getting up, he checked the time and blinked, inwardly, at how much time had passed. Elsie had been out there for quite a while, and she finally wanted to take a break. Peeking inside the facility, Billy saw there weren't many people there but he saw Sharea was still up and about, taking care of the customers who were there. He then turned to leave using his own door to the outside, closing it shut as he exited.

This was the first time he'd used this doorway, and only now did he realize it was situated to have a full view of the park. Climbing down the units, Billy made it to the streets with no issues. Once he entered the crowds mingling and traveling about their business, Billy made his way to the gates of the park, which somehow managed to have a line form. People seemed to be waiting to gain entrance, and as those inside exited, others gained entrance and went inside.

Billy watched as he saw other people with their own stalls also selling goods. Scratching his spider chin, he made his way to Elsie to relieve her. When he approached, he saw the line of people waiting. Elsie caught sight of him, and waved at him through the crowd.

"Hey, Billy! I need more stock! I'm almost out and there is a line a block long waiting to buy a bell!" She shouted at him before he could get there.

Without missing a beat, Billy spun and left while the fey looked around at who Elsie was yelling at. He did not give them a chance to pin him down, but then again he was not hard to spot during the day, being a giant black and brown spider with sigils lacquered on his exoskeleton.

He casually dropped the bot with instructions to return to Elsie, and went back to his place. There he spent half an hour making more bells, and laces for them. He hurried back to Elsie as soon as he was done.

Once he'd returned she said, "It took you long enough."

Shrugging he replied, "Yeah, I had to put them together, and they were all over the place." He handed her several boxes full of new stuff. The tinkling of the bells could be heard as Elsie took them and opened first one, then another box.

The people waiting were all beginning to talk about the giant spider who had made the pretty bells. If Billy could blush he would have, with so many people talking about him. He could not understand everyone who spoke however, they were not all using any of the languages he knew at the moment. He did his best to ignore them as he unloaded all his goods.

"Do you need me to watch over the place for a little while for you to take a break, Elsie?" Billy asked while placing inventory on the shelves behind the stall.

"No thanks! I'm having too much fun talking to all these kind people. If I do need a rest period, I will be sure to let you know," She said, already turning to her waiting customers with one of the new bells in hand.

Doing his best to shake his head, Billy turned to head back out of the park. He took note of the spaces where others had set up their own booths, and paused by a shade tree to check his park's interface. He saw there were a limited number of spots available for booths, and also saw people had actually moved to bid on those. He had not set that function up, but it appeared some of the vendors in the city had enough authority to enable this on his behalf. Prices for spots skyrocketed quickly, then leveled off as time had passed and spaces became limited.

Billy was not unhappy about the results of the bidding, but was a little concerned his own booth would necessitate he bid to keep its location. A moment later he learned he did not need to worry. One spot was always available for him to use, so he would not have to bid. He need only pay the minimal fee and his spot would be reserved, and none would be the wiser unless there was some cabal out there checking everyone. He didn't think this would be the case, however, so let the matter drop. Billy closed his screens and stood, preparing to leave. The little birds that had rested on his legs flew away as soon as he stood. He watched a moment, then left the park to return to his apartment.

This time he went around the front, and followed the few people who were curious inside. He wandered around, checking the various stalls, and worked his way to the column at the center. He casually touched it and did a quick check of the resources in the bank. He withdrew several bags worth of silver coins, and casually went back to his rooms to make more bells. If he'd known those simple things would've sold so quickly and in such quantity he'd have made much more to sell. Now, he would take the silver he'd earned and convert each coin into several tiny bells. The ribbon was simple enough to make that he could make yards of it in practically no time.

The next few hours flew by as Billy converted coins into little silver bells. After he ran out of silver, he took a few gold coins and made several other items. He didn't recall anyone wearing jewelry, but he figured he would give it a try. If anything, he could take these elsewhere to sell to those who wanted them further into the city. He still needed to have a better look around, though, so he planned to take time tonight to stockpile things for Elsie and Sharea to sell tomorrow. He also arranged break times for them by having them switch places every other day. He only hoped they would be alright with the arrangement as he'd not asked them.

"Charlotte, come here for a moment," Billy called out when he cracked open his door to the interior. She responded immediately and skittered up the steps and into the unit.

"Yes, dear?" She asked once in.

"I am going for a walkabout, I need to see what is going on in this city. I will be going out tomorrow morning, but tonight I plan to craft. I need you to do some alterations to my armored plating while I'm doing that, if you don't mind," he said to his little assistant.

"Of course, Billy, whatever you need. I can even perform your daily maintenance while you work. In return, I need you to print out more bots to help around the place." She rebutted.

"I will make four more of them, but no more than that. I don't want to flood the place with bots. They're only going to be used here, aside from the one Elsie has in the park. But I can't manage more than that. My Ability is not high enough to manage anything other than that." He double checked his Leadership Ability to make sure he was right. To his surprise, he found he could manage far more than the thirty-odd bots he had, with his Leadership at 3. Thinking back, he probably read the Ability wrong, because he could actually manage well over a hundred bots, way more than he could make now, even if he wanted to. He said nothing, however, and so only made the four additional bots for now.

Unconvinced, she said, "That's fine, dear. I just wanted to make sure there were enough to watch the place for you while you're gone."

"Alright then. I'll be in here for a little while. Take these items and give them to Shar so she can set them out as needed. I want the rest to go into storage for the park booth." Billy handed Charlotte one of the little boxes with the bells in them, the silken ribbon lying beside the little bells. She plopped it onto her back and made her way to Sharea, following his orders.

Billy quickly sent out commands to have some of his bots surreptitiously bring in some raw materials for him, taking the little tunnels running from the various storage units to his. He'd had those installed today while the people were shopping, and nobody seemed to pay any attention to the additional noise.

As the wood, slag and other metal ingots came in one or two loads at a time, Billy processed them into things to sell. The remainder of the day went by without a hitch. Just before dark there was an influx of customers looking to buy some of the food he had up for sale, but most of what he'd had available was already cleared out. Ever vigilant, Sharea did her best to assure the people more would be brought out tomorrow, and if they still wanted the fresh produce to come first thing in the morning. A few grumbled about not having anything now, but agreed to return on the following day. Billy made another mental note to open up another greenhouse for more vegetables.

Elsie eventually returned to the block just before the sun set, a bright smile on her little beastkin face. Her tail wagged underneath her skirt as she came in through the gate practically skipping. Sharea hurried to greet Elsie, and together they both went to Elsie's unit to gossip and talk about their day and eat the dinner several bots were bringing in.

Charlotte made her way to her unit and put some things away, changing into a different outfit before reporting for duty with Billy. The gates to the block had closed on their own, and the lights were put out until only a few lanterns were lit to cast some light into the large open space.

Charlotte performed her maintenance, and also took the time to modify the armored plating that covered the many places of Billy's frame. She did this while Billy consumed raw materials and garbage that was brought to him, and kept extruding parts he would then assemble into useful things. He had to get the greenhouses together tonight and up and running in the morning. He also received payments from both the sales in the block and park, and his mind staggered at the amount he'd made.

Then he checked the Experience he, Sharea and Elsie had earned throughout the day, and he almost fainted. He couldn't, but that didn't matter right now. They had made almost 200 Experience each from their cut of the profits. In the bank there were hundreds of Experience points, and double that in coins.

"Charlotte, we earned far too much Experience today. Do these logs make any sense to you?" He said, sending her a copy of today's sales logs.

She paused in her work and looked at the spreadsheet with all of the information, and rubbed her spider legs together, her way of showing confusion. "No, I can't see why we made so much. Do you have any ideas?"

"I do, but I need to experiment a little before drawing any conclusions. I think it has something to do with how the things were recycled, but I'm not sure. I mean, it would make sense if I'd taken something valuable and refurbished it and sold it at a higher price, but the prices were fixed, and we managed to pull in more than they were sold for. It's almost as if," And then it hit him. "Ah, I see. We got compound Experience from the totality of the work I'd been doing here. I was wondering why I wasn't getting any real Experience from most of the stuff I was doing. Now, seeing people purchasing the stuff, the System backlogged the Experience I'd earned and added it to the sales. That would explain why we got so much more Experience when almost everyone bought stuff with coins."

Charlotte paused again at this revelation, then continued as she asked, "Does that mean the park will do the same?"

Billy almost choked on the bar of copper he was Disembling. "What? No, I don't think so. That would be crazy. I didn't make the park, only manifested it. The taxes from sales come out of each sale, not from nowhere."

"Yes, but the park is also a product people are investing in. I believe the Ability is called Real Estate Management?" She said, flicking out a leg.

"Oh, riiight, I forgot about that. I created a secondary business that leeches some of the profits in a place I control the rates of. And as I do have that point in Real Estate Management, necessary to purchase this block in the first place, I earn Experience points every time the land makes income." Billy thought about this for a minute while chewing on the metal bars. "That seems like a broken Ability. If any one individual owned property in the city, they would be rolling in a ridiculous amount of Experience points every time anyone earned or spent coin or Experience on the property," Billy trailed off as he voiced this conclusion.

He let his mind rove around the concept for a while as he worked. There was something to this, and he needed to figure it out if he was to confront the humes. He needed some kind of power base to work from, and if the System let him use the land itself to stockpile Experience, he would need to figure out how to start his own city.

"I need to go explore the city, now more than ever, Charlotte. There's something going on in this place, and it's making me itch." He subconsciously scratched at his chin with a manipulator as he chewed a bar of tin.

"Well dear, once we finish here tonight you can run around all you like. Now stop wiggling, I need to finish lubricating your joints and wiping down these pistons."

Charlotte continued to talk to herself as she worked, her cute little spider legs waving around in the spider language. He let her as he continued processing trash into treasures. If he was right about his hunch, he was about to tip the scales in this world like no other. That is, of course, unless someone else were in on it.

Throughout the night Billy activated several more greenhouses, and had seeds planted and fertilized and watered a little. He took a significant bite into his Experience reserves and fast tracked the growth so that all of the plants could be harvested twice daily. By morning the first could be picked, and around dinner time picked again. This should keep a steady supply of food on the counters for sale.

He then did as much work as he could to make the other items on his list. The bots could assemble everything later, with Charlotte's guidance, for the beastkin to vend. Hopefully he had enough stock for the whole day.

As his body mechanically did its work, Billy was intent on researching new schemas. He knew designs from Earth he wanted to introduce here, which would make other steps simpler, but he had to spend time making the schema here for his Assembler to use. It was a simple process, much like a game really, but he'd needed to formulate every part individually which he did not already have a schema for. The last couple of weeks he had spent time designing clothing, which was far simpler, even in the short term. He would cut out the shape in the cloth, and note where the edges needed to be sewn together. Then he'd have to make notations for size adjustments. This was so easy even Charlotte could do this, which she had when designing her strange looking leg skirts. She had even designed tiny boots for her feet, of all things.

"Women, what can ya do," he thought to himself.

An hour before the morning sun spawned into being, Billy at long last completed his list of things to make. The last of it was being hauled off by his small army of bots to storage. He selected two of the bots to bring with him, and they obediently clamped themselves into place onto his chest. The two much larger scavenger bots attached themselves to his abdomen, on either side. Those would be useless here without something to do, and he might need them to get him out of a pinch if things get messy in town.

Charlotte also had a couple of the other bots assist her in reattaching the modified armor plates onto Billy's body and frame. She had gone through and painstakingly added tiny hairs all over the plates, to make Billy seem more alive than before. If anyone saw him now, he would look much like any other giant spider. She even modified the large, wide plates which covered compartments and most of his abdomen to look similar. She had also gone across his back, chest and face and added countless tiny hairs. He looked at himself through her eyes for a moment and he was positively terrifying now.

She had made every hair solid black. Meanwhile, she was a veritable peacock with the iridescent colors she had for herself. And Billy, well, he looked like a gigantic jumping spider with no coloring. Well, there was nothing for it now. He would make other changes later tonight when he got home. Or, whenever he made it back. He intended to explore the whole of the city, even if it meant climbing to the tops of the blocks and looking around to map the place.

Lastly, Charlotte had the bots help her drape a new custom cloak across Billy's back and abdomen. It had several pockets he could reach into at various points, and also had several belts to hold it all in place. It was made of some tough leather, but was thinner and softer than actual armor-quality leather. His plastic plating would protect him far more than the leather. The cloak was just camouflage.

Billy topped up on water, and guzzled down a whole barrel of purified alcohol, double checked his oil levels, and triple-checked his grease fittings. All was as it should be. The very last thing Billy equipped himself with was a simple wooden club. It was a short, slightly curved stick with a round knob on one end. If anyone got handsy, he would knock em on the nugget and shoo them away. Before walking out of his own door, he flicked his information to private, and slipped into the night.

Billy moved through the streets quickly, avoiding contact with anyone as best he could. He moved rapidly past the places he had been to before, following a path that traced around the boundary of the city. All he needed to do to determine the area was trace out the outline, and that was what he planned to do. Block after block Billy quickly walked. He passed dozens, then hundreds, and thousands of blocks, all looking variously run down, worn and with streets lined with trash, all the while his map continually updating.

He was appalled by all the waste lining the streets. There were tons and tons of garbage in huge piles, all just rotting away where everyone was born, lived and died. As the day wore on, Billy finally noticed a curve of the city on his map. He kept going, though, determined to circle the entire thing.

By the fourth day, Billy had traveled well over 100 miles. If this city was round, it would be absolutely gigantic. If it was square, it would be even bigger. That meant there were probably millions, if not billions, of fey living in this one place. Disgruntled by how long this was taking him, Billy decided to turn and head back to his own block. He would need to rethink his plans.

Eight days after leaving, Billy walked back into his block. His legs were doing their best not to fall off. The last of the emergency oil he'd had was a day gone, and he'd had to fabricate some short term grease to maintain his joints. He was in rough shape. Billy had had no problem locating water or alcohol, there was plenty to be had from the masses. He just did not have access to fresh grease or other gear oils he required. He was feeling like a well used excavator after that walk.

"About time!" Charlotte said to him as soon as he walked in. "We were getting very worried you'd been killed or something," She went on to say. She continued to complain as Billy went to his unit while avoiding the beastkin. He walked in, shut the door, plopped down on the floor, and let Charlotte do her job. He was too mentally exhausted to say much.

In an attempt to sideline the complaints he asked Charlotte, "Are the ladies doing alright?" She then spent the next couple of hours explaining all that had been done while he was away. He listened with half an ear while she removed the cloak and plates, and took care of his body's needs. 20 minutes into her rant Billy had zoned out as his mind finally shut down in what he thought of as sleep. At some point Charlotte has plugged herself in and slept while she recharged.

The next day, nine days after he'd set out to circumnavigate the city boundary, Billy left his rooms to check on things in his facility. As it turned out, everything was going alright. Charlotte had convinced the girls to put out requests for old clothing or broken furniture, which they would pay for. Then they would store it in the various storage units. Sharea had full access to the facility, or maybe it was Elsie, Billy could not recall exactly, but they had used some of the Experience the facility was earning to expand the units on his behalf.

The greenhouses were doing great, and now there were regular customers coming by each day to select their choice vegetables. More greenhouses could not be opened as Billy was the one who constructed the parts, but more pots were added to the existing ones, pushing the individual greenhouses to their limits. With the added planters and pots in the four greenhouses they had, along with the production increase Billy had purchased, the plants were producing a solid quantity of delicious food twice a day.

Billy inspected the storage units and found more than a dozen of them packed floor to ceiling, with a small aisle leading from the front to the back. Several were filled with wood, others packed with old clothing. Billy sighed to himself, then began the long task of simultaneously making new clothing, and working on a new schema to take this task over for him. He eventually designed a device that could recycle old cloth and produce bolts of undyed cloth, a second for taking in old wood and extruding new boards. He also threw together a machine that required some powders to be dumped into it with water, and he made a fourth machine for making the powders to add into the third one. The fourth machine would produce the powder for the glue-making machine; then the machine mixed the powders with water to make the glue for the board making machine.

Creating all of the schemas was very frustrating, but the System had turned it all into a long series of games that got progressively more difficult but not impossible. He had to complete the schemas to make the machines, so he worked until he had them all while he processed the materials.

Through the day and into the night he worked, tirelessly converting the useless into the useful. He made the machines others could feed things into, and so on, until the line was done. He could, at this point, sell individual bolts of cloth fairly cheap and lumber at a fair price, too. All he needed to arrange was for water and the powder machines to work in concert. And old food products to stuff into the powder-making machine. It would do all the work of converting waste food into the proper powders.

The next morning dawned, and it was only then the ladies realized Billy had returned. He had sequestered himself in his own units as soon as he'd come home, unhappy with the realization of how absolutely gigantic the city was. Its scale was far beyond what he'd imagined. The depravity was worse. He'd seen things happening out there in the streets around the blocks he'd passed, and it had affected him. He could get behind animals living by jungle rules. But these people here, and they were thinking, expressive beings, had to have something else. Being caged in this city was destroying them. And it didn't look like they had much longer to go before they all went crazy.

But what was forcing them to live in the city? If it were a person, he'd seen nothing of who they were, or why would they want the fey concentrated here? What did they get out of millions of beings being cooped up in one place, when their place should be scattered all over the world, free? A few ideas came to mind, and he spoke often with Charlotte about his conclusions.

Waving his legs in the spider language while he worked Billy asked, "Are you sure there is no ruler of this city? There has to be someone who initially found or founded this place. Things like this could have been around naturally, but something began the process of determining the city rules and layout. That same something..," he went on and on to his little assistant as he worked.

Charlotte did her best to compile the information and the, well, she considered it nonsense, ideas that Billy spoke to her of. There were some points he'd made here and there, but she mostly listened to him vent to her while she studiously went around his entire body and brought everything back up to snuff. The whole time Billy worked out his thoughts and concerns verbally as he also worked on his projects.

At one point, Billy aggressively waved his legs, saying, "I mean, this is a fantasy world, right? The fey and magical creatures are all living in one place while the humes, whatever those are, dominate the rest of the world. Why are the humes letting the fey stay here?

273

It makes no sense." He rubbed at his chin as he felt Charlotte tugging on a stuck piston so she could polish it and drain the fluids to clean and replace them. He held that leg still as he Dissembled another ingot.

Casually waving her legs, "What if it isn't the humes deciding this? What if it is not the fey either, but some monster or another?" Charlotte posited.

Thinking for a moment, Billy replied, "Monster? Like the gigantic crab from that Lair?"

"Yes and no. What if it was a monster, but one not stuck in its Lair? Or, what if the city," Charlotte began.

"Was the Lair!" Billy finished her sentence. "That would mean this entire place, whatever it is, isn't a city at all; after all, its name is the 'Lair of the Fey.' But, what could devise such a scheme that it would trap every fey in the world? Why here?" Billy pondered more as he tried to look at all of the angles.

According to Orgar and the girls, the humes hunted the fey, hell-bent on dominating everything in this world. Meanwhile, something opened up its Lair and lured or brought in the fey. If these fey were lured, to what end? If they were escaping extinction and the monster let them in, does it get something from this action? Monsters aren't good or evil, from what he had learned of them. They just kill and give out Experience and loot when killed. Is there a monster in this world strong enough to keep the humes away and keep the fey trapped at the same time?

Billy worried over this issue until Charlotte finally completed her care of him. He had some ideas about possible monsters, none of which were appealing to him. Billy did not want to figure out how to fight something that could alter its own Dungeon or something that could let others alter its own Dungeon by spending coins or Experience points.

"Charlotte, I need to find Aurora."

Cautiously raising a pair of legs in surprise, "The elf that tried to capture you?"

"Yeah, I think she may be able to give me some clues about what's going on. If anything, I need to know how this city functions. Orgar only recently gained access to the System, but I think Aurora already had access." Billy walked around his room while thinking. He did not let the walls deter him from his pacing, as he just walked up them and kept going.

Waving her limbs, she asked, "What do you think she can tell you about this place that Orgar or the girls can't?" Charlotte watched as Billy walked around his unit, content to wait for him to make some sort of decision.

"I think she can explain how the units are rented, how she acquired the Experience she needed to unlock the System, and why she wanted me in the first place." Billy paused upside down on the ceiling. "It may be slavery here is a thing, but it could be something else. I never asked when I had the chance, and I haven't wanted to go back until now, but she knew what I was and acted as soon as Ageel brought us in. Perhaps she knows more." Billy walked back down the wall to the floor and scooped up Charlotte to plug her into her port.

"You don't want me to help around here?" She asked as he placed her in her port.

Speaking through their internal relay, he said, "No, I think the beastkin can take care of things around here now that I have things rolling for them. I do not want to leave them alone for very long, just in case something happens, but I will need them to stay here and be able to run things for a while."

Peeking out of his door again, Billy saw there were plenty of people still in the block, shopping and selling stuff. Elsie and Sharea were busy restocking foods and showing off the bell necklaces he'd replenished while placing old clothing into crates to place into the storage units later. Thanks to Charlotte, they knew how to command the bots Billy had, and those were running in the background by helping process materials in the new machines Billy had produced. Occasionally, one or the other would pick up and wind a bot before going back to their business.

"When will we head out?" Charlotte asked.

"Tonight, right after sunset."

Billy did his best to utilize his Proficiencies to stealth his way to one of his storage units. As far as he could tell, no one saw him. Either that, or they saw him but weren't concerned. Or they weren't paying attention. What sold it for Billy was the little bit of Experience he received once he closed the door to the unit. It wasn't much, but it was something. He'd maneuvered through a well-lit area, actively trying to be stealthy, and was successful. The System rewarded him for that act.

Rogue Proficiency check successful. You move through the shadows undetected.

+3 Experience.

Inside the unit, Billy did a quick check to see if this one had the metal. It did; he was sure the unit he'd moved towards was the one with all the metal in it. He sat down near a shelf of stacked copper and iron ingots and several crates of broken slag.

Settling in place, he said, "I need a few upgrades, Charlotte. Pull some more bots in here to help."

Billy began stuffing ingots into his Dissembler and pulled up his Status page while Charlotte wrangled the bots. He looked at the Experience points he had accrued over the last couple of weeks, and started on upgrading himself. He had to be careful; he couldn't make big changes, or he would be shut down for too long. He could spread out some points to his Attributes without a complete rebuild, but he could not do very much with his Abilities. Those changes would require outright replacing whole sections of his body, and he wanted to avoid this for now.

Fortunately, the System kept track of how the changes to his Status would translate to downtime. It also gave him a list of tasks which he handed off to his assistant for the detail work with an *Apply*.

Several hours later, the sun finally set on the day, and Billy heard the gates close. He opened the door to the storage unit and moved to the interior of the block. Thinking about it, he realized it was much like a lobby. Putting that random thought aside, Billy moved into the lobby and saw the beastkin hard at work placing crates onto shelves while talking to one another.

"Hey, can I talk with you two for a few minutes? I'll have the bots put those away if you want while we do that." Billy called out.

The ladies both looked up, and Billy thought he caught a strange glint in their eyes as he'd interrupted them, and that gave him pause. When he looked again, he saw them both smiling and making their way over to him.

"Sure, what do you need?" Sharea asked, her fluffy fur making a swooshing sound as her skirt brushed against it.

When they got close enough so he didn't need to shout, Billy said, "I need you two to take a couple of days off if that's alright."

Immediately both of the beastkin spoke out together.

"What about Grazelle and her morning vegetables," Sharea said on top of Elsie's, "I have several people returning tomorrow for some new ribbon!"

"Okay, alright, hold on a minute," Billy said, holding up both of his manipulators. "I will be closing the block for the next two days and putting all booth rentals in the park on pause. Nothing gets bought or sold here or there for the next couple of days," he said, not giving them an opportunity to comment. "I need to go somewhere again, but this time I want you two here and relaxing and not stressing out about me or work."

Billy waited while both beastkin gave very good reasons why that "Just won't do" or how it's "Necessary for a good business." Once they both said their piece, Billy moved to the Administration column and made the necessary changes. He also restricted access to all functions for the two days. He then took out the pay for both of them and sent it to them directly.

"I have just paid you in full for what's been done up until today, just in case you go out and do some shopping of your own," Billy said, trying to calm things down at least a little. "I have also paid up until the end of the next week, per your contracts, and placed those contracts on hold for now."

He then went on to explain some of the things he was piecing together about the city on the off chance either of them had any ideas of their own. Neither had and so Billy set about preparing the place for his departure.

"I plan on two days this time, but just in case, I made sure you have enough coins to your names and enough Experience points to get by until the second day from today. The rooms are yours either way, so don't worry about that. There is more than enough in the block account to take care of this place and the park for the next six months at the very least, but I don't plan to be gone nearly that long."

<h1 style="text-align: center;">Chapter 15</h1>

Billy bid them both good night as they went to their units. He turned down the lights and collected all of his bots, Threw his cloak on, and then placed a small packed crate of supplies on his back. He activated his stealth Proficiency and slipped out into the streets from the door to his unit. The front gates were currently locked.

It did not take very long for Billy to backtrack to the very first place he was taken to when he'd arrived in this city.

Switching to his internal relay, Billy asked, "Charlotte, do you see anything unusual here?"

"I do not have the same ability to make such observations, dear. I aid you through care. I am not some," She began to say.

"Yes, I know what you do regularly, Charlotte. I mean, look around here. Do you see anything strange going on, anything out of the ordinary?"

"I am not sure, Billy. I see people moving around all over the place alone or in groups. Most are carrying items for trade or are looking for something."

Moving through the streets carefully he said, "Correct. And what's missing?"

Cautiously Charlotte said, "I am not following, Billy. I see what is here. I can't see what isn't here."

Billy thought for a minute about how best to explain what he was seeing. The beasts, beastkin, and other fey were here. They instinctively separate themselves from one another. Fey closely related to a beastkin cluster together as they move, and a beastkin closely related to a beast also cluster together if the fey was absent.

Highlighting a group he said, "Look at how the groups divide themselves. See them side by side." He highlighted another nearby group for her to compare.

Charlotte observed as Billy commanded, but all she saw were biological beings doing biological being things. Charlotte never really understood the needs of biological things, as she was both very old and quite young. She had knowledge from centuries ago, but she was only activated this year.

Exasperated he said, "Okay, first, the elves that tried to take us aren't here any more. Second, the people seem to be aware of this; they aren't visiting this block the way they had the last time we were here." Billy pointed to the places the elves had been stationed when last he was here, and the typical places were indeed vacant.

"What does this mean, dear? Did they move? I think criminals would likely move around rather than stay in one place very long," Charlotte said, making all of the logical connections.

"Or they could not stay because they would otherwise be affected, or they were affected, by whatever is running this place." Billy put forth one of his hypotheses.

"So what are we going to do from here on?" Charlotte asked, curious to see where this was all going.

"I am looking for any indications of where they went. Some groups will leave marks others recognize. I am looking for those marks, if they exist." And he was looking for any graffiti on the walls of the units, or perhaps a particular arrangement of things. The markings would be the most obvious though, with all the trash any totem would be lost in the crowd.

"Or, you could always ask," A voice spoke right next to Billy.

"Holy sh..." He began.

"Yes, hello again, great spider. I see you have unlocked the System," The cloaked figure said to Billy quietly.

As Billy moved to get a better look at the person, it moved with him.

"I don't want to be seen, if you don't mind," They said before Billy began being aggressive in his turn.

Pausing, Billy stopped trying to catch a glimpse of the figure and said, "Where can I find Aurora. I have questions about this city and what's going on here."

The figure placed a palm on the plating of one of Billy's legs, and he received an alert.

A mysterious elf is requesting to update your map. Will you allow this? Yes. No.

Billy selected *Yes*, and accepted the trade. A moment later his map was updated. It took a moment for him to locate the updated place, and it took a moment to realize the map was of the overworld, and the location was several days, perhaps a week, to the east of here.

"Hey, how," Looking over as best he could, Billy stopped talking as he realized the mysterious elf had vanished. Sighing to himself, he spoke on his internal relay, "Alright, then. Looks like we go to the overworld, Charlotte. It's a good thing we stocked up on things before leaving."

"Yes, dear, you are quite clever. Are we going, or are we staying to watch the mobs?" Billy recognized Charlotte had already conceptualized the residents of the city as possible enemies, and used the term he would have in games from Earth.

"We're going, Charlotte. We're going." Billy, cloaked in shadows, moved across the units of the blocks. His Experience added up every few seconds as he avoided contact with the fey in the area successfully. It was not much, but every little bit counted. It didn't take him long to make it to the poles which lead out of this zone, and he slipped through without pausing as other groups crossed.

Outside, in the dark woods, Billy looked about and whipped around to go behind the poles to start the trip to the east. This area was densely populated by the fey exiting the city to scavenge for food to take back. Several fantasy story scenarios came to Billy's mind as he left this time, recognizing the actions here for what they possibly were, but was unaware of before because he was a part of the movements. He did not want to jump to any conclusions, however, so he held off judgment of the situation until he could speak with the elves again.

The night wore on as Billy made his way through the woods. Checking his map, Billy saw he was heading deep into unknown territory. He'd arrived at the city from the opposite direction before, and this was going to be all new territory for him to cover. Being sure to maintain his stealth, Billy spent several hours avoiding contact with anyone who'd exited the city, or who were returning through that particular set of poles. Several times he'd come close to being spotted, but the abundant brush and the rather large trees helped to hide him in the dark, even should the fey be able to see well enough in the dark to spot him.

After a while he said, "Charlotte, how are we on time?"

"At this rate, Billy, we should be able to make it more than a dozen miles from this location before daylight is set to occur. That should put us far enough out that there would be little to no chance of contact with the city dwellers or scavengers." Charlotte was using her little holo to walk ahead of Billy as they traveled. Though she could not actually see beyond his sightline, she was able to appear to do so whenever she would maneuver her holo around trees or duck under bushes which she could not see around or through.

The light from her holo, projected in Billy's mind directly, did not affect his ability to see in the dark either. She did not emit a glow, or cast illumination anywhere she went.

It was many hours after they had left the city when Billy noticed the sky lightning for some reason.

Concerned he spoke on the internal relay, "Charlotte, where is this light coming from? Is it some kind of hume weapon?"

Popping out of her port, she quickly scrambled up a tree. Billy stood silent, but alert, beside it as she ascended, and in a couple of minutes she returned.

"It appears that dawn is soon approaching," She said to him as she resettled into her port.

"What? I thought the sun just appeared in the sky here at dawn, and vanished at night. Are you saying that isn't the case outside of the city?" BIlly scratched at his chin a moment, before beginning to walk again.

"It seems that whatever is going on in that Dungeon is all artificial. As I had never been up in the overworld prior to you bringing me, I was unaware this was out of the ordinary."

"What about all your records of the history of this world?" He asked back.

It took her a moment to respond. "I do have records, but it mostly consists of facts and raw data, not anything as simple as 'water is wet', or 'the sun rises and sets each day'. I think these things were so basically understood that our creators felt it unnecessary to add them to the database."

"That seems like a gaping hole, in my opinion. If someone was to build some sort of database of life on this world, it would need to begin with the basics and go from there." Billy thought about this as he walked, thinking perhaps the information was there, but was dismissed as corrupted or something when evidence conflicted with it. He'd have done the same thing in her shoes, if all he knew was what he saw, and not of his past life on Earth.

"Well, that's just one more mystery about that city we need to figure out, I suppose," Billy said to Charlotte after a few minutes of walking. During the trip, he'd begun using their internal communication relay since she was plugged directly into it. It meant undetectable communications between the two, and it let his sensors work easier at listening to their surroundings.

The further from the city zone poles they went, the more life around the area came into being. Bugs were soon heard calling out to one another as the sun began to rise. Small critters could be seen now all over the place looking for food, or returning from their own hunts. Billy also saw flying things every once in a while. He thought there would not be any out here, but as it turns out, whatever is going on with the city seems to have pushed nature back quite a few miles.

Finally the sun rose, and Billy could make out the wonders of the forest he was trekking through in the full glory of dawn. The tree's were very tall, and now there was a large variety of them. The leaves looked similar to leaves from Earth, but many here had long hairs which hung down to capture water from the air. It wasn't until Billy touched one of these bundles of hairs did he realize it wasn't water, but it was sticky threads and there were tiny little bugs trapped in the goo.

Fascinated, Billy wanted to stop until Charlotte tapped him on his nose with a dainty leg and he snapped out of it.

"Sorry, I've just never seen anything like this before. I wonder what the sticky stuff is for? Why did the tree produce it? Are they carnivorous trees?" He went on for a few minutes, talking to Charlotte about what the sticky fluid could be used for without using his System interface to cheat. He liked learning about the plant life around his mountain home on Earth, and this was a new world of wonder to explore.

"You have a reason for coming out here, dear, and it isn't to examine the trees," Charlotte reminded him on several occasions.

"Yeah, yeah. I know. Save the world," he said back, then continued walking onward. Charlotte did not deign to reply.

Long, rolling hills began to manifest as they walked into the morning. What started off as a gentle rise gave way to a gentle drop in elevation. This began repeating over and over as the hours passed, until the hills became quite significant. Some of the hills reminded him of the areas approaching the Appalachian mountains from the east coast on Earth. When he'd driven the roads traversing those hills, they seemed gargantuan to him, but now walking them they were almost their own little mountains. The change in elevation could be 300 feet, over a mile, or 1,000 feet.

Most of the trees began to thin out as well. They went from what could be considered rugged hardwood trees to more softwoods, capable of surviving in the cracks of large rocks and handling strong winds. The brush changed in composition as well, going from bushes to many smaller trees tangled in vines which he'd have to cut his way through.

All of this hid large, irregularly shaped rocks, boulders and gravel patches. Billy's weight, as one large metallic machine with eight points of contact, helped him spread out his weight, but the ground had many soft spots where he'd almost slipped on any number of occasions. He was having to pick his way more carefully through the rocky areas so as not to get stuck, or he risked falling back down the way he'd climbed.

"Charlotte, remind me to get better directions next time we go anywhere," Billy said, unnecessarily grunting as he pulled himself to the top of the hill he'd been climbing for the last half hour. He did not feel exhaustion in the conventional sense, being a machine, but he was becoming mentally exhausted. The focus to maintain footing in such a dynamic landscape was beginning to takes its toll on him.

The top of this hill was not long in the direction he was traveling, but it was very wide. It was also quite steep, but fortunately not loaded up with trees like the base of the hills were. Pulling up his internal map, Billy checked it as he also looked out in front. The long, rolling hills went well over the horizon. Some had patches of fog still moving through them as the sun heated the moisture trapped there. He was not very high up in elevation compared to some of the hills, but he was much higher than he'd been last night.

Looking north and south, Billy saw the land carry on much the same as it was going forward. The long hills going northwest faded into what he could just make out were distant mountains. And further southeast the same was happening, although those mountains were somewhat closer. He could just make out snow capped peaks on some of the taller mountains, and was glad his map wasn't taking him in their direction. He wasn't sure how well he would fare traversing those as he was now.

Moving forward, Billy saw this part of the hill dropped straight down into a ravine. The cliff face was bare rock, and almost perfectly smooth. Testing his footing, he found he had no problem holding on to it, and so he tilted forward and began his walk down the cliff.

"People would pay to ride a giant robot spider straight down cliffs like this back on Earth, Charlotte." Billy saw Charlotte sitting primly in her port, totally unconcerned with the 100 foot drop in front of them.

"I can't see why they would, it's only walking. Do people from your world not know how to walk up walls?" Her little holo ran around in circles along the cliff.

Pausing in his descent to think for a moment, Billy tried to recall if he'd told Charlotte about being a spider from another world or not. He couldn't remember, so figured he'd kept it a secret for some reason, but forgot.

"No, not all can. Like, some spiders can produce silken thread to make a web, and others cannot. Or, some spiders have offspring that use silk to fly to other locations so they can spread out, and others cannot do that either. Some spiders can dig holes and make burrows, other spiders only hunt other spiders. It's all very diverse back home."

"That sounds very interesting, Billy. One day you will have to tell me more about your world." Her little holo was also climbing down the wall, but with far less effort than Billy had to make.

"One day, perhaps," he told her as he continued the climb down.

The next few hills came and went, and on this last one Billy could just make out the sound of running water nearby. The fog had already begun to burn away as the sun rose ever higher, and it was now several hundred feet off the valley floor making the sky look like a bright white river. Approaching the little creek, Billy saw there were other animal signs in the area. He spotted scat in several places, the largest bit of evidence he'd seen of an animal yet. Moving to the water, large river rocks sat on the edges which he carefully maneuvered over. A short drop of about a foot cut right through the bedrock here, and this is where the water gurgled past.

Looking around to make sure he was more or less safe, Billy leaned forward and used a hose to draw in some fresh water for his boiler system. It felt like ice as he drew it into his reservoirs, and he had to fight off an instinctual shiver. Once he'd topped off his tank, he withdrew his hose and looked up. That was when he saw the rock begin to topple over.

Quick as thought, Billy skittered sideways and activated his stealth as hundreds of pounds of rock came crashing down around him. Dust flew up and out as the first rock displaced others. They all came down in a shower right on the spot Billy had been a moment before.

Billy tried to hunker down near some other large rocks, but that was when more rocks came flying at him from the other side of the creak.

Perception check successful. You have spotted enemies!

Billy saw the message flash at the same moment he saw something in the rocks above him. He saw something dark and skinny stand and throw a handful of rocks down at him, then duck back down behind another large boulder.

"Looks like we encroached on some animal's territory, Charlotte," he said to her as he ducked behind a rock to avoid being hit.

"Yes, it seems we have," Charlotte said as she updated his local area map with red markers. "There are more and it looks like they are trying to surround us."

"Right, we need to move," Billy said as he slipped out between thrown rocks, his tactical overlay keeping track of targets moving to intercept. Without looking back Billy hopped right over the creak and began to climb the steep side of the hill he had planned to walk. His feet settled and held onto each point he placed them as he did his best to climb the rock face quickly. He watched the red dots on his map move to cut him off, but none of them were directly above his location as of yet, so he focused on climbing and avoiding the sticks they were now being thrown at him.

"Charlotte, when we get away from this place you'll need to look me over. I think one of those sticks has wedged itself into one of my legs," he sent to her on the internal relay as the aforementioned leg refused to bend properly. Fighting with a frozen limb to climb the rocks, Billy struggled to maintain his other feet while doing his best to keep the busted one out of the way.

The grinding sound coming from his hip joint was not a pleasant one as he finally crested the top of the cliff. He spun quickly to look down and saw a dozen of the strange dark figures below looking up at him, aggressively waving pointy sticks in his general direction. Reaching back, Billy yanked the piece of wood from his hip, which seemed to have ruptured a line, and it began to spray out a thin but high pressure stream of steam.

Thinking quickly, Billy mentally accessed his Status and tried to shut off the pressure going to that limb. All he got back was an error.

"Charlotte, I need you to fix that leak, now. I can't shut it off. If it keeps spraying I will run out of pressure in under three minutes," Billy said to Charlotte, who immediately popped out of her port to assess the damage.

"Drop me some of the bots, quickly. I need their leverage," She sent to him using her spider language of leg-waving and swaying now that she was disconnected from the internal relay.

He did so, and in under a minute she had twisted a shut off valve somewhere, cutting off the loss of vital steam. While Charlotte took care of securing the leg against his side, Billy was carefully watching the critters below. Concernedly, he saw they were beginning to climb up the rocky side of the hill. When they saw him looking down at them, they made some kind of barking noises which all of them picked up together. This seemed to have motivated them even more and they were all moving to find ways to scale the cliff.

"We have seconds before they get up here to us, Charlotte. Hurry," Billy said as he did his best to prepare for the assault. Twisting carefully he saw there were piles of rocks here and there. He used his feet to shimmy them over the edge of the cliff in hopes to slow the things down.

He heard several cries of pain as the small rocks pelted heads and shoulders. He took a second to look back over the edge and jerked back almost immediately as a sharpened stick, practically a spear, flew past his eyes.

Dodge check successful. You have dodged an attack.

He dismissed the prompt as soon as it had appeared, not wanting to get distracted. He heard the stick strike rock behind him, and as he turned away from the drop he saw another spear flying towards him. He grabbed it with his manipulator and flipped it to point down.

"Any day now, Charlotte," Billy grunted out as the first of the strange animals reached a hand to grip the edge of the ledge.

Stabbing down, Billy heard something cry out in pain, and then the hand disappeared as it fell away. He heard the thump of a body striking ground, but was too distracted by two other sets of hands coming up from two different locations.

"I'm doing my best, dear. I almost have this tied up," Charlotte signaled to him in their spider language. He knew she was behind and below him, yet he still caught sight of the message from the corner of one of his eyes. He was crouched down a little, and he did have eyes in the back of his head, but it was still a little bewildering to him when he saw her waving legs while he was looking almost 180 degrees in another direction.

Billy worked hard to ensure he had good footing as he swept the spear, now makeshift club, side to side in an attempt to dislodge the climbers. He had not wanted to harm the critters, but they seemed very intent on doing something to him, so he held little back. The spear cracked hands and knuckles, wrists and foreheads as he saw them. Once, he'd had to push a climber right off the cliff with a foot as it had popped over the side while he was struggling with another of the things.

Finally, just as another was getting ready to pop over the ledge, Billy saw Charlotte struggle into her port and pop into it. WIthout waiting, Billy spun and used his seven remaining legs to climb the wall behind him. He kept the spear in his manipulators, as they weren't being used to climb. In less than a minute he cleared the next wall of rock, and moved back so he couldn't be seen.

Billy pulled up his map, quickly reviewing the local area, then turned southeast and dashed ahead. He eventually came to a more open area with more dirt and hill than rock, and turned back east, up the hill again. He saw no sign of anything following him as he climbed, but he did not slow down. At the top of the hill, Billy turned southly again, and followed the hill for over an hour, steadily weaving around ancient withered trees and boulders he could not quickly climb over.

Cursing himself for not paying more attention to the area around him, Billy kept an eye on the eastern side of the hill, looking for a better place to descend. This particular hill, however, seemed more bare rock on this side than anything else. He'd make due with some gravel, even, but almost everything going east was large rocks piled on larger rocks, as if the entire hillside had been blasted away ages ago, and the wind and rain kept them clear of anything that grew.

Eventually, Billy had to slow down and re-secure his leg, which was beginning to feel funny to him. In desperation, Billy launched his aerial drone to have a quick look around. He'd avoided using this so as not to draw any attention to himself from anything capable of seeing it and tracking it back to his location. He knew animals would notice such a strange thing floating around, and he also knew that if any fantasy creature with enough intelligence saw this, they would think this odd enough to investigate as well. He didn't feel he'd much of a choice, however. He needed to find a place to stop and have Charlotte look at his leg, but it needed to be a safe spot he could easily defend, or even camouflage into if possible.

Waiting the few minutes for the drone to return was nerve wracking for Billy. He knew those creatures back there were smart enough to track his scent. He had leaking fluid that was not being pumped back into his leg's piston, but it was leaking and anything he touched would smell pretty distinct. He had little choice, though, if he wanted to find someplace safe any time soon. Everything looked different at ground level, and the trees didn't look like they could hold any kind of weight, much less his.

Listening hard, Billy thought he could make out something a few miles distant, back the way he'd come, but he wasn't sure. Dropping down, Billy released hold of one of his drones. He scooped it up with one of his feet and rubbed it in the fluid to get it covered in as much of it as he could. Then, he'd wound it up as much as he could and gave it directions to head down the opposite side of the hill and find a place to hide. It was to touch as much stuff as it could as it went to try and leave the fluid trail. He then scooped up a handful of dusty sand and tossed it on his leg, hoping the dust and granules would hold long enough for him to get a few yards down the side of this cliff undetected.

After the brave little bot was released, and the dust was applied to his wound, the drone slipped out of the sky and Billy caught it with his manipulator. The handoff to one of his feet had it back into its slot in a moment, and Billy's map updated.

"Good, it found something, Charlotte. Time to go," he said, as he immediately turned to the east and began his descent. "We only have about an hour before those things catch up to the spot we rested, and we have to make it down before then. There's another cut in the ground down there we can hide in where they won't be able to spot us from above."

The climb down was rough on Billy. He wasn't one for being afraid of heights or anything, but some of the places he'd had to leap across in order to keep going were certainly worthy of being worried over, especially with one bad leg. He kept going, though. He didn't have much of a choice there. Besides, having had points in his Talents helped tremendously. This boosted his natural ability to leap fairly good distances with accuracy. If he were too short, he'd plummet to his doom. Too far and he'd overshoot the top of the rock and fall off that side, if he were unlucky. As it turned out, he was accurate on every jump, and he slid down into the small canyon's base at long last.

Billy sat for over two hours as Charlotte did repairs on his damaged leg while they hid. In the end, she'd had to remove the leg to fix the mechanisms inside his torso, which had gotten damaged while he was moving around with the spear in his leg. Billy decided to not go offline while this operation was performed, instead doing his best to set aside the feeling of having his leg removed by deploying several of his bots to watch the top of the hill.

He watched as a large group of the strange, almost monkey-like creatures crawled over the top of the hill looking for him. He saw there were dozens of the things, and after only a few minutes of looking around, he watched them disappear from the hilltop to presumably follow his decoy drone. While that was going on, he was also producing fluid to replace the amount he'd lost. It took most of his water reserves, but this particular canyon had a small stream of water moving through the bottom of it. He'd had several bots collecting it and bringing it to him in makeshift bowls while he was somewhat paralyzed.

Billy also spent time reviewing his logs. To his surprise, there was little of note going on there. The attacks he'd made showed variations of success and failure, and even estimated damage dealt. However, as he'd moved away and there were no observers, he earned nothing despite actively trying to be stealthy. This contradicted what he had been earning in and around the city. He thought at first it was because of the nature of the zone that he was earning crazy amounts of Experience points, but out in the overworld he was earning very little. Only when he was directly accomplishing something was he earning anything. When nobody was around, he earned almost nothing at all no matter what he did.

In the city, he was earning Experience almost non-stop, even when he was alone. Even inside his own block, before anyone else showed up, who was conscious anyways, he was earning a steady stream of Experience for doing things. He thought it was, again, part of the nature of the zone, but that made very little sense. Why would anyone leave a place where they could constantly earn Experience without having to go out and put themselves in danger? It made no sense at all. And yet, outside and away from the city his gains were minimal, except when he was dealing with the local fauna.

The more he compared his recent logs to his earlier ones, the more of a pattern he began to make out. His bots did not earn him anything at all, as the little bot decoy should be earning him Experience the longer it remained actively hiding from searching enemies. Even Charlotte was not earning Experience while performing her duties. He chalked that down to all of them being autonomous machines, not really being alive. Neither were they specifically part of him. He used them, but the hammer did not gain Experience for forging the sword, as the saying went.

Ultimately, after fending off the Yogenki Monkeys, as his logs had shown him they were called, he'd only earned a few Experience points. He earned some from climbing while being attacked, and some for dodging them, but once out of immediate combat he'd stopped getting Experience. That would mean, the entire time he was in the city he was considered to be in a combat zone. This was strange considering the city was supposed to be a place of safety. He appeared to be more safe out here in the rocks than he was back in the city zone. The only thing he could think of to make that make sense, were to make the Lair of the Fey the name of the zone, and its description.

"The repairs are done, Billy. But some time soon I want you to find a place so I can run full diagnostics on your body," Charlotte said while inserting herself into her port.

"Alright, Charlotte. As soon as we find a good enough place for supplies, we will do that," he said to her distractedly. "For now we need to get away from here and out of these hills." He sent out a command to the nearby bots with a wave of his legs and they all skittered back into their places around his body, and were secured. Once all but the missing bot was in place, Billy stood on his newly repaired leg and moved it around.

It felt almost normal to move it, but there were some little resistances he could make out. This was likely what Charlotte wanted to look into later. Deciding all was as well as it was going to be, Billy hopped across the small creek to the other side, and began carefully climbing the canyon wall.

The reddish-gray rock was rough, almost like granite, but Billy could tell at a glance this was a stone which held a high ratio of iron in it. The red color was oxidized iron, the gray part was the granite. It provided a very firm grip for his feet to hold onto while he climbed, and in short order he was over the canyon and into low brush.

Without wasting more time, Billy moved straight to his destination marker, all the while launching his drone to map the area around and ahead of him. He'd covered several miles when his drone found a nice location for them to stop at for a little while. It was what looked like a series of holes leading into the side of the next hill over. Long vines hung over its entrance, and rock formations made a convenient set of steps to climb up to the half-moon shaped hole.

Billy topped off his water every chance he could at places water ran, but he never needed much. He would also keep an eye out for animal marks on the trees or for scat from possible predators. He'd spotted a flock of what looked like birds at one point, but they did not remain in the air very long before dropping between distant hills.

The journey was a lonely one, but Billy had long been used to being alone in the world, especially in mountainous areas. He often explored the range of mountains near his home during his times off. He'd collect rocks, fossils, and anything that looked interesting. He took pictures as well, to share with friends online. He was able to do the same here, thanks to the features of his cell phone being integrated into his System, but he'd noone to share his pictures with. He kept them in a folder, though, and did his best to leave little notes about each one as he took them.

At the base of the next hill, Billy could make out the shapes of an ancient civilization all around. Huge, square-cut rocks littered the area here, covered up by ages of plant growth and death. Dirt was also abundant, thanks to the cycle of plant growth and decay, and Billy thought most of what was here was likely buried; the little he could see was the tallest of the remaining structures. This valley was also wider than others he'd passed through. Looking across to the next hill with the cave system, he had to look up a little to see its entrance. The large blocks that lead up to the caves were probably intentionally placed there, now that he had a clear view from above to see them.

Billy made his way through the ancient valley, keeping an eye out for anything interesting while managing the placement of his feet. He had yet to spot any sign of animals larger than rats here, but that didn't mean something larger was not skulking around somewhere. Here and there Billy saw ancient remnants of tools, bits and pieces pushed out of the ground as plants grew around them from below.

Many of the trees growing in the area were quite squat and rotund, but their roots went far and wide in the search for nutrients and water. Billy had seen many ancient oaks back on Earth with thick roots reaching out to the surroundings, and these trees were like those, but 10 times more abundant, maybe more.

The short, squat trunks had spines for leaves, not unlike aloe plants, but much stiffer like pine needles. The leaves were also several feet long as well, stabbing out from the few branches the trunks had. Billy looked up at them as he walked past and saw the same glue substance dripping down from the leaves, incidentally catching tiny insects like the other trees he'd seen were doing. As he approached the flattest section of this valley, the trees covered more of the area and Billy had to step carefully so as not to disturb the leaves. He didn't want to be seen in the area by bumping into the trees and shaking them. He wasn't sure if that would be the only thing that would happen either. He was, after all, on an alien world where magic existed.

Chapter 16

Billy eventually made it through the strange round trees without incident, and was now on the side of the valley where the cave system was located. No grass seemed to be growing on this side of the tree line, and this gave Billy some pause. He stepped a few feet out from under the trees and looked long and hard at the surrounding area.

The ground was open, and sloped upward slightly, with some rocks larger than his smallest eye lying around. Most of the rocks were large, clearly cut, and toppled over. It was as if there were buildings here once, and they were made of this stone, and then at some point in the past they were knocked over to lie there.

He then noticed there was a clear pathway leading up to the cave system entrance. The rock surface was clean and clear of debris, sand or rocks, as if it had been swept recently. Walking to the first visible part of the path, Billy tapped a foot to it carefully, with no result. It was just windblown rock, apparently. Slowly spinning around, Billy did another scan of the area, careful to pay attention to the higher areas and the sections of ground covered by the trees.

Nothing was moving unexpectedly, and he could barely feel the air stirring either. No particular odors were detectable, and his senses were telling him he was perfectly safe for the moment.

This feeling of safety gave Billy some concern. He could see nothing dangerous to the point of it looking inviting and safe. This, if anything, was definitely a red flag. This place was dangerous, or there was something here which was dangerous. It was keeping every animal out, leaving the place quiet and undisturbed.

"Charlotte," Billy said through his internal communication relay. "Do you have any records of this place? Or any place that would look like this if some giant monster moved in and took over?"

He waited a moment while she did her best to go through her records, but then her little holo appeared in his field of view, and she looked around at what he was seeing.

"No, not as far as I can tell. There are large gaps in my knowledge base for some reason, when it comes to some topics. This place seems to be an ancient village of some sort, built after my records ended, perhaps. Whatever happened here happened a long time ago, dear. Be careful, though. Anything could be hiding around here." Her words of wisdom were unnecessary. He was already about as alert as he could be without launching his drone.

"Yeah, alright, Charlotte. Let's get up to the cave and see what's going on."

Billy moved forward carefully on the smooth stone path. He was actively using one of his Rogue Proficiencies, Move Quietly. This would actively reduce the sound his steps made as he walked or ran. He didn't have many points in this proficiency, but he'd begun with some when he'd been born into this body and he had only placed a few more in it just in case. He wanted to compound this with his Hide in Shadows proficiency, but there were no shadows nearby which he could use, so he settled with being quiet instead and moved onward.

Fortunately, this seemed to be enough, as he could barely hear himself taking a step, and his internal systems were also being muffled more than usual. Moving quickly and quietly, Billy reached the top of the path which terminated in front of a large cave opening that immediately plunged almost straight into the hillside. The cut in the hill only went in a few dozen feet before ending in solid rock, the rest resuming straight down.

The sun, still high in the sky, cast the entrance into deep shadow, though Billy had little issue seeing inside thanks to his keen vision. He looked at the ground for any indication of marks or any recent activity, and saw nothing. Looking left and right he saw nothing suspicious. Following the lip of the entrance up and around he saw nothing but vines hanging down from above which made most of the entrance's hole look dark and leafy from a distance. Nothing looked out of the ordinary at all. It seemed a perfectly normal cave some people had explored centuries past. Then abandoned after the place was leveled. Mysteriously.

Sighing to himself for what he knew was going to happen, Billy placed a foot into the cave. He immediately received the prompt he knew was coming.

Congratulations! You have discovered a new Dungeon! What secrets are hidden within? What treasures await? Only the brave may find out!

Rank: B

Status: Overflowing

Threat: Dangerous

Experience for Discovery: +2,000

Would you like to challenge the new Dungeon? Yes. No.

He also received several other prompts granting him the Experience points, and updates on his overworld map marking this location for future reference.

"It's a Dungeon?" Charlotte asked, herself surprised at seeing the prompt.

"Yep. I thought it would be, but I didn't want to jinx myself just in case it wasn't," Billy said, sounding resigned. "But, it looks like we might have a chance to sidequest a little for some lovely Experience and loot."

"Or death," Charlotte said. "That's always an option when it comes to Dungeons. They're not like Lairs, Billy. Dungeons usually take armies to clear. Dozens of trained people working together to get past the hordes of monsters and past deadly traps."

"I know, Charlotte. But lest ye forget, we have our own little army with us," Billy said with a sigh, absently tapping his abdomen where he was carrying a few dozen bots, and a couple of scavengers.

Selecting *Yes*, Billy moved from the entrance they were transported to and looked down the hole. There were steps carved into the side of the hole going down along the wall in a spiral. The steps were a few feet wide. The hole felt intimidating to Billy, and he could sense danger below somewhere. He switched his vision to low light sensitivity, and he could make out more contour etched into the rock. There were what looked like names of people, probably dates as well, now meaningless without a calendar to compare timelines. Ocres and charcoal were used to make the different marks. Only a few were actually etched into the surface. He took pictures, though, for future reference.

Billy did a quick inventory of himself and his available bots. He had some stuff carefully packed onto his back as well, under his cloak. The quick count showed him only missing the one bot he'd sacrificed earlier that day. Everything else was accounted for. He still had the stick he'd snatched from those monsters earlier as well. So there was that, he supposed.

Moving carefully, Billy began to descend into the Dungeon. The light faded quickly into darkness, and he had to adjust his vision to see in the lowering light. The hole did not go straight down. Like many natural ground holes, it went through the softest rock, which meant going all over the place. A few dozen feet down found him standing on the roof of the lower level. The steps cut into the wall as it continued around and downward through a wide crack. The most dangerous spot was where the steps doubled back on themselves as they went down and under the roof he was on. Looking carefully, he could just make out old pitons stuck in the wall, used by some group long ago to manage ropes to secure the spelunkers. He plucked those out and Dissembled them, just in case.

The first real room, a large opening about 10 feet tall and a wide irregular shape of a few dozen feet wide, was where Billy spotted bodies. They were mostly skeletal now, all the meat and muscle long gone to dust. Whatever protection and clothing was worn had also rotted, leaving only vague lumps of metal where buckles were located. He didn't spot any weapons or metal armor, or even any coin, so he left the bodies alone after he examined them. There were only six bodies, and all of them had been laid next to one another along one wall.

Looking around, Billy could see this place was used as some kind of campsite. The remnants of a campfire were easily seen, the black soot staining the rock directly above it. He saw a few remnant pieces of wood, which were probably used as kindling, but other than that and the bodies, there was nothing special here.

Billy looked around the walls, and he noticed several other holes cut into the rock by natural processes eons ago. All of the holes were narrower than Billy would have preferred, but he could get through them by climbing on the side of the wall and going forward that way. Instead of bowling headlong down them, though, he opted to set a couple of his bots up as scouts.

Dislodging three bots, one for each tunnel, Billy wound each up and gave them instructions to scout a little way down each tunnel, then return. He set each one down where he wanted them to begin their trek, then set them loose. Hunkering down, he took stock of his situation, now that there were neither people nor monsters to interfere with him.

"Charlotte, I have enough materials here to do a pretty good-sized upgrade. I have more Experience than I feel comfortable with, but also need to make myself much more durable than I am now." He went on to explain what he wanted to do, and dropped off most of his bots, the crate of stuff on his back, and Charlotte to begin things.

The versatile bots went about setting up some simple machines that Billy unloaded from his multitude of compartments. They assembled each part efficiently and quietly. Charlotte orchestrated the construction while Billy went through the stocks of raw materials he had on hand. He had a lot, but not enough for a full upgrade rotation. He spent the next hour doing some math, and double checking his Status to make sure he could get everything necessary without going over his timetable.

He carefully popped off most of his armor plating and made a stack of it, then began to Dissemble them one after another. He would need the extra matter to make the new plates and coverings. Charlotte had also helped here, guiding several bots to assist in removing the ones Billy could not easily reach. By the time he'd consumed the last of his plates, the first of his bots had returned.

"Let's see what you have here, little fella," he said, scooping it up and removing its recording device. He downloaded the information quickly, then replaced the recorder. He ran through the simple images in his mind as he traced the route the bot took down its tunnel.

That tunnel opened up a few hundred feet into the rock, then dropped down to another level. There, a large room linked to several other tunnels that led off into the dark. Water dripped down from the rocks above and formed a tiny stream, which slipped down into a crack to disappear below. The tiny bot went down one tunnel at random, found a dead end and returned. It did the same for the other tunnels, and had to return from the third it was exploring to report before its springs died.

By the time Billy had finished reviewing the memory, the other two bots returned. He repeated the process of reviewing what they had seen, and then opened up his map. It automatically updated as he'd reviewed those bots recordings, and he saw that the tunnels went every which way as they cut down into the belly of the world. Several tunnels were dead ends, and a couple of the bots had returned once the ceiling and floor got closer than they could easily squeeze through. Those were dead ends as well for Billy; there was no way he would be able to fit through those slim cracks.

Ultimately, he had several options he could choose from to descend, but he was looking to cheat. He continued to Dissemble metals from his crate while rewatching the memories, looking for the telltale signs of repeated passage. It didn't take him long to find the scuff marks in ancient dust evidencing passage by several people. He checked the other routes and found nothing of interest, beyond a couple interesting looking crystal patches. He could spend a little time collecting those and, now that he thought about it, decided he would.

"Charlotte, I'm marking a spot on the map here. Send a scavenger with some other bots to get the crystals there." Billy waved a manipulator to indicate the appropriate tunnel to send them down. "It's not far, but I want whatever they can break off of the wall. They can do that and it shouldn't slow us down here while we take care of this little upgrade period."

"Of course, dear. Glad to be of help," She said, as she waved her spidery limbs to give commands to the specified bots. Billy wound each of them up so their springs would be fully charged, and Charlotte shooed them away with instructions to hurry, but be quiet.

"Alright, I have my selections made, and all the materials listed ready, Charlotte," Billy said, turning to look at his little assistant. She was very colorful, even in the darkness of this hole. "Take good care of me while I'm asleep."

"Certainly, dear. Now hurry, the longer you wait," She began.

"The longer it will take, I know," he finished. With a mental command, Billy hit the *Apply* button, and his world went black.

Billy awoke some time later. As usual, he could feel his inner furnace firing up, and his boiler burbled to life inside him as he awoke. His new Attributes did not increase his capability all that much, as he would be down for days making the appropriate changes to his body. He did make changes, though, which required the removal of several components and hardening them.

His legs were now much stronger and stiffer, able to take hits far better than before. His joints were also more protected, to prevent debris or weapons from getting in there and making a mess of things. His bad limb was also repaired completely during the upgrade, making not a sound as he moved it around. He was much lighter as well, sacrificing the heavy plastic plating for thin layered sheets of hardened ceramics that now served as his armor. He would make noise if he bumped anything, but he could also take some hits. More importantly, he could dodge attacks easier, due to the thinner, lighter plates.

The one downside to using those kinds of plates were the bushings necessary to mount them. The small rubber rings would wear over time, and would require replacing frequently. That was well worth the loss of weight, however, so Billy was not overly concerned. He also added some sharp edges on his legs. He had no physical weapons to use, like teeth or horns, but he could adjust the structure of his limbs to be sharp or pointed without affecting maneuverability. Those extensions also acted as additional armor, as they had to be reinforced enough to hold an edge.

"Good work, Charlotte, as usual. Everything looks good. Did you have any problems with anything?" He asked as he spun around looking at the room. The floor was littered with extra pieces he would need to Dissemble, and the bots were busy piling those up for him to do just that.

"No problems, dear. Everything went as planned, of course." She said this as if there were no other option but for things to have gone as she had planned.

Chuckling, he said, "Right then, let's get this stuff consumed and stored, and be on our way." He quickly Dissembled the leftover materials, and then saw the pile of crystals. He couldn't immediately tell in the dark, but they did not look like regular crystal formations. Picking up one, Billy saw he received an alert, and pulled up his Status.

Congratulations! You have found a Gemstone! It has an unknown Uncut Value. Take this to a Gemologist to have it Appraised.

"Wow, this is a gem, Charlotte. Those are only one class down from the rarest kind of crystal, Jewels." Billy was excited to find something so valuable in a cave. He'd found quartz crystals before, but nothing like this. He couldn't see the color clearly, but it was not clear like a diamond.

"Oh, that's lovely, dear. What a find indeed. We can use those to upgrade some of your internal components if you have enough of them," Charlotte said, as she poked at the small pile of stones.

Looking down, Billy saw there were almost 20 crystal pieces of varying sizes, all also identified as Gemstones once he picked them up.

Congratulations! You have discovered 20 Gemstone quality stones with an unknown Uncut Value.

Take these to a Gemologist to have them Appraised.

"You should store those in one of your cloak's pockets wrapped in a cloth, to keep them from getting damaged," Charlotte advised.

"I have a padded compartment for stashing things like this," Billy said, slipping the handful of valuable stones into said compartment with his manipulator. The little compartment clicked open quietly, and snapped closed just as quietly once all the little rocks were inside. Air hissed momentarily to fill small gas bags that filled the rest of the compartment, then all was silent. The crystals made no sound as he moved, and they would not move around in there either thanks to the air bags.

"Right, well, that's taken care of. Come on, little bots. All aboard!" He called out, using the language of the spiders to coordinate them. In a couple of minutes all of the bots were secured in place, and Billy stood up. He was feeling excited about exploring this Dungeon, and hoped that if anything attacked, he could handle it with ease, now that he had bladed weapons.

"What are they?" Billy asked Charlotte silently.

"I'm not sure, dear. They certainly are cute, whatever they are," Charlotte replied.

"Are they dangerous?"

"I don't think so. They appear to be going about their business, is all."

"Business?" Billy asked, watching with fascination.

Charlotte's little holo appeared and she moved to a corner of the dark cave. Billy saw there were tiny little pockets in the rock, which were decorated like tiny little houses. There were even walking paths with their own itty bitty lamps.

Cute little blobs, wearing a variety of cute little clothes were busy going about their day, just like people would. As Billy carefully approached, he saw they were little blobs with tiny dots for eyes, wearing their version of dresses, robes, and some even had hair. It was by far the weirdest thing Billy had ever seen in his life.

"They're like.. little blob people. And they've built a city here," Billy said in awe. The tiny blob people, which only had little bulges where arms were, held little baskets with stuff inside them, covered by a tiny patched cloth.

"I think I have found a description in my records, dear," Charlotte said after a while. Billy was fascinated watching the little rolly blobs going here and there quite slowly, but with purpose. They would wiggle and make faint blurping sounds to one another, and brief waves of fluorescent light would flash through them as different emotions played out through their biochemistry.

"Mhmm, go ahead," Billy said distractedly to her.

"They're called Bloopos, and are usually kept by the most brilliant students of the arcane. They are friendly, and make wonderful components for certain spells. They are easily bred, and supposedly the more colorful varieties are the most valuable." She went on to describe diet and reproduction, but mentioned nothing of making cities in caves.

"Are they common in cave systems deep underground, Charlotte?"

"No, it is likely a sorcerer of some renown was down here in the past and had some of these with them. Something happened, and they got away and began living down here." Charlotte seemed equally intrigued by the little blob people, the Gloopos, and her little holo shrank down to mock play with them as they walked around.

Billy, many times larger than the little apple-size blob creatures, easily avoided contact with the tiny things. He stuck to the wall and watched from a distance with his extra sensitive new eyes.

"What are they used for?" He asked.

After a moment Charlotte said, "According to my records, they have something to do with the alchemical pot you have built inside you."

"They are used to make alchemy pots?" Billy asked. He very much wanted to scoop up some of these little creatures. He would need to upgrade his own alchemical pot soon, and it seems these little guys were the one component he required to do this.

"Yes, but the records I have aren't clear on how, precisely."

Billy thought for a few minutes, going through his Status to see if it provided any information on either the Gloopos or alchemy pot production. He found very little.

Sorry! Kenning check failed. You are unable to identify the properties of the target creature.

"I think I need to come in contact with one to learn more," Billy said, looking around the floor to see if he could spot one off by itself. He did find one, a strange red blob with a little mustache and a tiny little stone ax held over a shoulder by a little blobby protrusion.

Moving as quietly as possible, Billy positioned himself to reach out a leg to block the path of the little logger. He watched as it saw his appendage resting on the floor, it wiggled a little, then blobbed its way over the tip of his foot. On contact, he saw the prompt identifying the Gloopos as a reliable component for alchemy pot production.

Congratulations! You have discovered a Gloopo. They are an intrinsic component used in the fashioning of the glaze placed on the interior of Alchemical Pots. With proper preparation, this glaze can increase the efficiency of alchemical brewing, and occasionally increase the rarity of materials used in them.

"That wasn't helpful at all," he grumbled to Charlotte, who also read the notification. "It doesn't say anything about how to process them into a glaze, or how it's applied."

"We may as well capture a few of them, and place them in a compartment for experimentation later," She said, her holo still playing with the little blob nearest her.

Billy, not very willing to capture seemingly sentient beings, set aside this moral conundrum and scooped up the little Gloopo blob creature. It jiggled in his manipulator, and it flared red for a moment, but his hand had already moved to hide it under his cloak before stashing it in one of his watertight compartments.

"Do we know if they require anything to eat or drink to live? I don't want to keep them in there without sustenance only to find them dead in a few hours."

Charlotte's holo paused as she checked her records again, and shook a leg in the negative. "No, there is nothing here providing dietary needs. I think they will eat whatever is given to them to provide them the nutrients they need."

"Alright, let's get a few more and stash them together, then we will keep going. We've been spelunking for almost half a day now, and this is by far the most we have seen to indicate people have been here," Billy said as he stealthily went about targeting and acquiring more Gloopos.

"Five should be good, I don't want to disrupt the population too much here." Billy quietly left the squat cavern the little blobs were living in, and made his way downward after marking this spot on his map.

The last eight hours had gone by in almost total silence. The only break in the monotony of cave diving were the occasional crystal deposits near water, and once he had even passed a thin gold vein. He had spent an hour carving away at the rock to mine the gold vein, and after all the work he had added another seven ounces of gold to his stores, a veritable haul.

Sadly, he had not spotted many signs of exploration. Much of the time he was squeezing through cracks in the rock, and in many places rock had cracked and fallen to the floor, covering up any markings that may have been present. Other times he was moving through ice cold water, which would entirely fill some areas.

During those occasions, Billy would submerge himself carefully and navigate the underwater passages. Fortunately none of the sections were more than a few dozen feet separated. He doubted anyone would have come this far otherwise. The Gloopos had not ventured past the first waterlogged area, and he saw no more signs of the little blobs beyond that first dive.

Looking at his map, now, Billy saw they had traversed many miles of tunnels and passages. They had descended several miles as well, and thankfully were moving generally eastward, too. Maybe there was a way to the surface somewhere in here that would let him out near his destination. That was unlikely, but he kept it in the back of his mind just in case.

The little Gloopos settled down quietly in the compartment he'd stored them all in. They were not moving around or anything, or doing anything that he could tell. It seemed they mimicked intelligence but did not actually have any. He wondered about the clothing but put that off for later. He needed to finish this Dungeon.

It was close an hour later when Billy spotted signs of an old battle. Coming around the curve of a tunnel, Billy saw large scorch marks on the side wall he was passing. The rock itself opened up to a gigantic cavern hundreds of feet in length. It dropped down to a lower level, too, some 10 or 12 feet below. Some kind of animal was down here, all along the walls, glowing a pale greenish-blue. The thin worms were not bright, but the number of them together lit the area quite well.

Immediately, Billy spotted a skeleton clad in old metal armor lying on the floor. The armor was dented all over, and the helmet of the poor person was caved in as if a large hammer or rock had smashed the skull in. Billy turned from the body to look around the ceiling from the passage. He'd remembered his old gaming days with monsters that would drop from cavern ceilings to crush unsuspecting prey. He saw nothing that would indicate any such monster existed. There were only a few stalactites, and they were long and slender, coming close to the floor to hang over their stalagmite cousins, around which some of the glowing worms crawled.

Carefully, Billy poked his face into the room and looked around. He didn't see anything ominous and so moved to the edge of the rock slide that led down into the room. He tested it with one of his feet and stopped the instant the slope started to give way. Instead of trying this, he moved to the wall and gripped onto it to walk along the wall, down to the floor below, to examine the corpse.

The body wasn't human, that much was sure. The head, crushed and ancient though it was, had horns. The legs bent forward at the knees, meaning this was something along the lines of a satyr or a minotaur. It was difficult to tell for sure, as many of the features were crushed beyond identification. Taking a closer look, Billy saw the remains of a wooden shield and evidence it had once been wrapped in leather. Very little remained of any clothing. Only portions made from metal remained, apart from the scraps of wood.

While examining the skeletal arms, Billy caught sight of a glint of metal around one of the bones of a finger. Carefully, Billy lifted the bone hand and pulled free the band. It was a simple loop of silvery metal, and it had a few scratches along the inside. Those marks could be some form of glyph or rune, he wasn't sure. He took the ring and stored it in another of his compartments, then looked around the room again.

All around, Billy saw small broken glass pieces. The colors varied from a dark green to a clear yellow. They also differed in size as well.

"These were probably potion bottles, Charlotte. What do you think?" He toed one of the glass shards but received no prompt identifying it.

"Possibly. They are very useful in a pinch when recovering certain energies."

"And for healing, I suppose," he said, continuing his investigation.

Along some of the walls, Billy could make out scrapes likely made from blades deflecting off of them. He could just make out scuff marks made by metal studded boots on the rock floor nearby as well. In the center of the large room was where the largest evidence of a mortal combat was found. As Billy moved to the middle of the cave, he saw a huge blast pattern on the floor, scorched black and spreading outward from the center of detonation. A small pocket of rock had been ejected, leaving the edges both glassy and sharp.

"What do you make of this, Charlotte?" Billy said, tapping the small crater with a foot.

"Possibly the result of an electrical attack of some sort," She said after a moment.

Looking up, Billy saw nothing there; it was unlikely the result of a lightning bolt striking downward. It was probably produced by an arcane user of some power, and the floor here was the point of impact. Whatever had stood here would have exploded, just like the rock had.

"Well, whatever it was, the thing here was killed a long time ago. And it looks like it took down at least one other before it was taken down." He looked around the room from this central point and saw only the one body. There were fallen stalactites but no other treasures.

"This was probably a mini-boss room, right Charlotte? A sort of mid-boss here in the Dungeon?"

"I know what you mean, dear, and I agree. This looks like it held a boss monster of some power, and it was indeed taken down." She was using her holo to investigate while she remained in her port.

"Is it likely to have had some kind of treasure, then? Like a treasure pile, or chest, or anything like that?" Billy asked, looking around.

"Billy dear, I know you're new here, but the monsters are practically living treasures. Most of the monster's parts are very valuable. And if they were smart enough to pile treasure, they'd be more valuable still and more deadly. A large group did fight here, though. And as the monster is not here, it seems like the Dungeon was never fully cleared." Charlotte waved her holo's little legs around as she spoke this time, preferring not to distract Billy by actually speaking in their internal relay.

Billy looked around for the exit to the room and found a tunnel along one wall near the opposite side he'd entered from. It was cleverly hidden near a stalagmite and was just big enough for him to walk in without crouching.

"Do you think any treasure they had is down here somewhere?" He inquired.

"Unlikely. Monster hides and parts need to be preserved or used soon after they are skinned. If they aren't cured properly, they will rot just like anything else. Even powerfully magic monster hide will decay if not properly cared for."

"What about these worms?" Billy asked while closely examining a few.

Charlotte's holo walked around a few of the tiny things before answering, "I don't know, dear. They look like normal worms that can fluoresce. Perhaps the Gloopos can use them as food?"

Shrugging to himself, Billy scooped up a few of the little wriggling, glowing worms and placed them in the compartment with the little blobs. He hoped they would eat them, or at the very least, that the worms would not hurt the little things.

Billy took one last look before he turned to move down the tunnel leading further in. He caught sight of more markings on a wall, probably indicating direction or even some kind of date. In either case, he didn't need to use such crude markings to navigate, though he did take pictures of each one he came across for his records. Maybe he could identify the markings in the future to see if they meant anything.

"Billy, the temperature is dropping rapidly," Charlotte said to him some hours later.

"I know, I can feel my body reacting slower by the second," Billy said. If he had breath, he would already be able to see it if he were to breathe out.

"If this keeps up, it will be sub-zero in another two minutes."

Billy paused going forward. They had gone through a maze of tunnels and caverns, all of which led in a line with no alternate paths. Most of the last few hours were spent walking rather quickly. It wasn't a straight path, but the tunnel had widened up, and there was no real debris blocking the floor. He swiftly traveled from cavern to cavern, finding next to nothing. He was, however, a few more gemstones heavier.

It wasn't until he left the last large cavern that he felt something happening here. There seemed to be some kind of force acting to pull the heat out of the air beyond a certain distance into the tunnel. Backing up, Billy examined the floors, walls and ceiling for anything that would indicate a termination point. He only backtracked a few feet when he found something interesting.

Perception check successful. You have spotted markings, which could be the reason for the temperature change. It is possibly magical in nature.

A line of tiny, repeating symbols was carved into the rock with care, entirely circling the tunnel wall, ceiling and floor. On one side of the symbols, the air was cool but not cold. On the other side, it began to chill rapidly.

Billy took a very careful series of pictures of the symbols before removing a tool from his cloak. He held it in a manipulator and moved to rub out one of the marks.

"Perhaps," Charlotte interrupted, "You should see if you can discover why an arcanist would seal off this tunnel before removing that?"

Pausing inches away from gouging out the mark, Billy thought for a moment. "You're right, we should go and see if there is anything on the other side that is being imprisoned before we let it loose on the world." Putting the chisel back, Billy focused on his Status. He pulled up the portion which gave him information on his resistances, and saw he had rather high thermal resistances, and saw he was also well insulated. He would stiffen some as he chilled, but the grease and oils he used should not freeze until they were far colder than they were likely to get.

"Alright, we should be okay to go in for a little while. Hopefully, the Gloopos will be fine in the compartment. I'll crank up the furnace to maintain the temperature while in there without cooking them. This will put a dent in my fuel supplies, though," he said, double-checking his alcohol stores. He had almost eight gallons stored, but if he had to burn his furnace hot for too long that would deplete much sooner.

Chapter 17

Moving back into the cold tunnel, Billy began to see evidence of the water from the air collecting and freezing along the walls. Thin sheets of ice covered the walls, and a low-hanging fog covered the floor. This fog made Billy nervous, as he could not see where his feet were placed.

As he moved, the exposed metal on his body began making pinging sounds as it rapidly chilled in proximity to his internal heat. His pistons were also becoming louder as they required more pressure to move along cold bushings. He went slowly, testing each step. The low fog moved around every step with tiny wisps swirling for the first time in ages.

He only had to travel a few hundred more feet before he saw bodies. There were dozens, possibly hundreds of people, frozen solid. Most of the bodies were hidden in fog, which came to the waist of all the standing corpses. All of them seemed to have turned to ice where they stood, either too stupid or too blind to escape.

Billy moved close to one of the corpsicles and tapped it on the head. The ice there cracked, and he saw the crack move through the whole head. A chunk of the head broke and slid off to shatter in the fog on the floor. Then he looked at the remaining eye. It was solid white under the clear ice, and he could make out teeth marks on exposed, frozen flesh.

"Charlotte, do zombies exist in this world?" Billy asked as he turned to leave the room.

"You mean the animate dead? Yes, but they are terribly dangerous and near impossible to slay," she replied with her legs waving.

"Can they be killed?"

"Billy, dear, I just said they were animate dead. They are not alive, so they can't be killed. You must slay them by destroying the heart or brain. Bites and scratches pass a magical plague to the victim, so one must be extremely careful when dealing with them." She, too, was very cold, but her slow leg waving got the message to Billy loud and clear.

One by one, Billy went through and shattered the heads of the frozen zombies. None of them moved, but he could hear the ice cracking as they tried to. He paid the slightly rocking ice statues no mind as he went by each one and smacked it with an armored leg. It didn't take long, and then he was done. To be sure, he located every body and broke them apart further, and crushed every hand, broke every jawbone. Nothing that could attack was left to chance. His eight feet made the work several times faster than it would have if he'd only had two hands. Being made of reinforced metal helped as well. His old human body would have frozen stiff minutes into the task.

As he crushed the last set of hands, Billy turned to bear witness to the carnage. The red and gray chunks of corpse meat stood in broken pillars, the upper torsos having torn off to shatter on the rock in the fog under his assault.

"This should do for now, Charlotte. Let's get out of here," he said, turning to the back of the room to delve further into the dungeon. Not far down the tunnel, Billy spotted signs of the other seal carved into the walls. He knew it was there by the body just inside the seal, resting against the wall, hoarfrost encasing the corpse which had a hand covering a wound on the opposite arm. The poor victim of the zombie bite had volunteered to stay inside the freezing seal rather than hinder the party. The head shattered on the floor as Billy crushed it, breaking the upper torso off the wall and pushing it further back the way he'd just come from.

"Rest in peace, brother," Billy said, giving prayer to the poor soul. Faster than Billy could perceive, a notification appeared and vanished.

You have blessed the bravely fallen. This action has not gone unwitnessed.

Billy crossed the seal's barrier and immediately felt the metallic framework of his body warming. He waited for a few minutes while he warmed up, and while he waited, he looked around for any more evidence of the party that had come down here. He saw nothing, and after five minutes, continued onward. Several hours later, Billy stood in front of a solid wall of rock.

"Are we sure this path ends here?" Billy asked again, already aware of the answer.

"Yes, Billy. This was the only path through the Dungeon, and it seems to be a dead end here. We did not check the other paths back near the entrance. Perhaps one of those is the correct way through."

She was using her holo to crawl over the long map of the Dungeon, turning it and reexamining the multitude of pathways. They had carefully checked each one to ensure they were heading in the right direction, but now they stood at a dead end after dozens of miles of cave tunnels.

Billy looked closely at the rock at the end of the tunnel. It seemed solid and looked to be one continuous chunk of stone. But the edges seemed to meet too perfectly for his liking. It was as if the tunnel was mined up to this point, then squared off perfectly and halted. Then, everyone turned around and stopped going further.

"There's got to be a way forward, Charlotte. Paths like this, after what, 34 hours of continuous walking, don't just abruptly stop. This is a Dungeon; there has to be a way forward."

"I agree, Billy. We have yet to find the Dungeon boss, or any mobs for that matter. It's likely there is a hidden path somewhere; we just have to find it before continuing forward."

Billy reached forward and tapped the rock again, doing his best to feel how the rock reacted to sudden impacts. If the wall was thin, it would make an echoing sound. If it were solid, it would make a more solid sound.

He was looking along the edges when he spotted it, a thin piece of wood on the floor cut almost in half. He tugged at the splinter of wood, barely a toothpick, and as it broke off, he saw the remainder stuck in the rock.

"Do we have anything to move boulders, Charlotte? I think this rock here is blocking the passage," he said, tapping the wall.

"You have enough Strength to try without damaging yourself, if you want to prop yourself against the wall and push," she said, her holo crawling over the walls, marking anchor points.

Billy spun around, placing each foot in the correct locations Charlotte marked out for him. Small protrusions he barely noticed would be supports for him to leverage against as he pushed, which would prevent his feet from slipping. Feet positioned, Billy squatted down and began to push against the blockage.

He struggled to keep his legs aligned, but as Billy increased the force being applied by the pistons in his legs, he began to feel the boulder shift. It felt like it was sitting in a slight socket, but he knuckled down and pushed all the harder to dislodge it. Six feet were pushing off the wall while two feet were pressed to the boulder. Just as the forces were about to cause his legs to fail, the rock tumbled out of its socket and rolled out of the way.

Billy immediately relaxed the pressure in his limbs, and a blast of steam jetted from his exhaust ports in a sharp hiss.

"Whew, that was close. I almost maxed out the force I could apply there," Billy said, as he checked his legs for damage. All looked well, though.

"You had plenty of force you could have applied, dear. You just weren't settled properly to be pushing at the correct angles," Charlotte said, moving her holo to form the correct shape he should have taken to push.

"Good point, Charlotte. I'm just glad I could move it, then." Billy didn't remind her she had highlighted all of the spots to push from.

The large boulder was slowly rolling backward into a large open cavern while they spoke. Billy slipped in with the rock and put a couple of feet on it to stop its motion. The grinding of rock on rock was very loud, and he was worried that if anything else were still active down here, it would easily pinpoint him thanks to the ruckus.

"Billy, there are lights down that way," Charlotte waved with her legs, indicating direction.

Caught off guard, Billy had not noticed the subtle change in lighting. He looked now and could see a very faint light coming from down the tunnel to his left. He checked his map and saw this particular cavern branched off in several directions. He also saw bodies on the floor. There were many bones in this room. Billy wasn't sure how many skeletons could be assembled with them, but it was close to a dozen, maybe more.

While he was busy counting skulls, Billy felt a tremble run through the ground. He looked upward and caught sight of small motes of dust which had broken free of the ceiling to float down. A moment later, he felt another tremble. And another. Then he heard the drums. They had to have been large drums, the bass so low he could almost feel the shockwaves traveling through the air, pushing him gently.

"Alright, Charlotte, I think we've located the rest of the critters in this dungeon. Hold on tight, it's time to lay some web and set traps," Billy said, quickly moving to the tunnel where the light was steadily growing, and from where the drums could be best heard.

Billy quickly produced his webbing, available in bulk after his last upgrade, and began applying a complex pattern familiar to most trapping spiders. It was a series of spirals connected to other anchoring threads. Billy made use of his new extremely high Dexterity to manipulate the threads, using the giant boulder as another anchor, and the bones as intermediary joints. He lined them up so the light made weird shadows with them, hopefully causing confusion.

Billy made a series of web tunnels solely for the purpose of diverging the incoming enemies down the other pathways before eventually backing out of the tunnel he'd entered through. He rapidly produced what his organic cousins were best at making: sticky silken threads in vast quantities. He made sticky patches, false walls, and hanging traps using sharp hooks he made from his metal reserves. Years of dealing with drug dealers who would hang fish hooks from trees to deter explorers taught him how to set these simple but painful traps with ease. He varied the heights and spacing to not provide some pattern easily recognized. He mixed those with patches to force whatever was coming into jumping into the near-invisible hooks above.

Billy kept walking forward and laying traps, being absolutely sure the traps were spaced enough that a fire would not spread to them all in one go. The rooms he came to were similarly trapped with webbing, using whatever rocks were available. Having invested many points into trap-making, a Proficiency rogue-types would utilize, eased the ways in which he could apply it all by filling Billy's mind with many variations of traps.

It didn't take very long before he began hearing the cries and screams of pain as the monsters contacted his webs. He'd laced it all with a painful mix of potent capsaicin drawn carefully from some of the spicy plants he grew back in the city. Once the stuff hit his alchemy pot, he'd made sure to break it down to acquire the schema for it. That schema allowed him to coat anything with powerful chemicals that would cause immense pain if it contacted the face, assuming these monsters had a similar ability to feel it at all. He had an acidic mix he could use as well, but that stuff used quite a lot of his chemical reserves to create. He stuck to what he'd stocked up on instead, hoping it would work. By the intensifying screams of pain, it did.

Billy moved quickly down the tunnels, setting hooks on invisible silk, and scattering ultra-sticky threads in a fine mist along walls, floor, and ceiling at random intervals. He used rocks as weapons, activated by moving certain threads at entrances, or in the middle of rooms, and he used some designed to tangle everything that came in contact with it by being very thin and scattered over a wide area.

He was unaware of how many monsters he would have to take out in order to get through, but he was willing to keep backing down the tunnels until he reached the seals marking the zone of deadly cold. Once he'd trapped as many of the tunnels and chambers as possible on his way backtracking, he finally reached the section of broken, frozen corpses. It was at this point Billy decided it was time to see what he could do in combat because nothing but him would make it beyond this point anyways, and he was tired of running.

"Charlotte, apply the non-stick solution on my limbs. It's time to go in there and tie up any loose ends."

Charlotte dismounted and quickly applied the thin layer of special gels which would prevent the webbing from sticking to Billy, then plugged herself back into her port. A small, clear lens rose to protect her while still providing her visibility.

Billy slowly moved back into the silken maze he'd created, and it did not take long before he came upon the first of the monsters.

Undead horrors, limbs decaying and rotting, writhed in the webbing while others tried to push through. Animated corpses of animals and fey filled the tunnels, their screams of rage filling the air. Billy began fighting as best he could in the confined space. His spider body seemed purpose-built originally to fight in such close quarters, and he very quickly dispatched monster after monster. His modified legs served as both bludgeoning and slashing weapons, as all he needed to do was kick out with a leg to smash or swing vertically to slice at his foes.

This close-quarters combat made it so that no matter the situation, his attacks come swiftly and powerfully, lopping off arms and bisecting corpses in a single strike. The weakened bodies of the animate dead seemed to feel no pain, so when a limb was severed, this only changed the available attack for them, and they began to try and bite.

Billy's thick armor protected him from any damage, and his own animate form was immune to the curses and diseases transmitted by the various undead, but still, Billy found himself quickly hard-pressed moving forward. Webs held onto arms and legs, torsos, and heads, while he deftly removed them from his enemies. This didn't stop them from moving, but it did make them far less dangerous once the limbs were removed.

Billy stepped and slashed, stomped and cut, body-checked, and even had bitten down on a few of the monsters. His bite secreted a potent acid which dissolved the undead corpses, but he avoided such an attack as it ate into his reserves of the caustic stuff unless he was in a pinch. A large animate scorpion monster came at Billy, its own toxic stinger shooting forward to bounce off of Billy's armored back. This had the added effect of forcing Billy into his own webbing, but thanks to his non-stick gel he came off it immediately. The stuff would not last forever, so Billy did his best to avoid such instances by climbing the web instead. The attacker tried to tackle him, only to find Billy going over them while they were caught in the sticky web behind him.

The scorpion came at Billy several times, even as zombie after zombie fought to get to him first, with pincers and stinger. Billy dodged and slapped both aside as he continued to slash at the smaller bodies. Finally, the furious monster rushed, its claws raised and its tail preparing to strike yet again. Billy raised his own front limbs and stomped down on the claws with two feet, and with his manipulators, he caught the stinger as it lunged for his eyes. His own feet pierced the claws and pinned them to the ground as he caught the stinger. He then lunged forward and bit the scorpion's own face and dissolved it with his acid. The body twitched for a couple of seconds in spasms, then stilled. Billy held still, with dozens of grasping corpse hands and tentacles trying to hold him, as the scorpion zombie stilled.

Other monsters continued to try and pile onto Billy, but he used his spider instincts and pushed, shoved, or bumped the animate corpses into his already prepared webs, themselves already filled with still more wrathful undead. As he moved around, he casually stabbed out with his feet into heads and hearts, hoping to end the monsters' struggles quickly. This worked most of the time, but not every skull was crushed, and not all stabs were directly into hearts. When he noticed, he would lunge in again and give it one more go before being forced to either move forward or go back. He pushed forward into the horde every chance he could.

If Billy had a sense of smell, which he did in his own way, he would have lost all of the meals onto the floor and somehow it would have had spaghetti he did not remember eating, along with strange chunks of carrots he also had never eaten. He did have the ability to see what was going on though, and he was doing his best not to think of these things as corpses. Intestines looped all over everything while hands clenched at nothing, all caught in webs of fine spider silk or hanging on other undead fighting through the same web, or piled on the floor of the tunnels, put there by Billy's sharpened leg armor blades or ripped apart by sheer force if they were small enough. The underground Dungeon was a slaughterhouse of unidentifiable internal organs and coagulated fluids.

Billy was doing his best to maintain his sanity while slothing through the piles of undead monsters as he mechanically disassembled the undead that came at him in wave after endless wave. He had been frustrated somewhat by the strangeness of this world and how obfuscated his purpose seemed to be for him. He had awoken miles underground, revived in the guise of a magical, mechanical spider which could self-modify. He was in a world with very few specifics about what was happening, his assistant having plenty of access to information that was centuries out of date or missing, with some disaster happening to the supposed elemental spirits of the world happening and he knew of no reason why. He wasn't even really sure any of it was true.

Humes were fighting the fey, but he did not know why. The fey, spirits of the elements of reality itself, literally personified, were trapped inside a city that wasn't a city. Something was going on with that city zone, and he had only vague ideas. He'd been hunted in the city and frustrated by the city. And even though he had made a preposterous load of Experience points there, he had no idea why, or even why the fey there were living in such abject squalor. This Dungeon was dead and empty for hours on end, and then just past a rock there seemed to be this endless horde of undead.

"Why is it always zombies? Couldn't the bad guys be original once in a while?" he thought to himself.

On his internal relay, he said, "Charlotte, I think when we get done here I will need to take a shower. I can't feel my body quite like I used to, but I feel dirty right now, and I am a machine." Billy ducked around a stalagmite and bisected a family of animated giant earthworms, then stomped them for good measure.

"I would suggest the same as well, dear. This stuff is drying, and I think a shower will help get it out of some of the places it seems to be congealing in," she said, her tiny but colorful legs tucked behind part of the clear little shield she rolled down from in front of her port so that she could see what was going on. It wasn't helping much for visibility or protection at the moment, and she was already complaining about ruining the four pairs of skirts she had on and forgot to remove.

Exasperated, he said, "I will also make you more skirts, Charlotte. I see you making design changes mid-combat." Billy would have shaken his head at this, but he was very busy dodging several animated snakes the length of school buses, and a rather large deer-otter hybrid thing, with extra claws attached to extra arms.

"You know," Billy said between eviscerating snakes, "I think I know what the boss will be, if nothing else. And," he snipped off a snake head which flopped onto the floor, still trying to bite at him, "I was wondering if a necromancer can affect me in any meaningful way?"

Spinning webs with a speed only spiders could manage, Billy wrapped several rushing corpse monsters together and pushed them off to the side into another approaching group.

"Not unless it can affect decay, and even then you have replaced many of your exposed parts with alloy I've never heard of before you created them. Using pottery for armor or crystalline strings," she began, confused.

"Kevlar, yeah," he growled as he did some kind of spinning kick, but using all eight legs, to chop off many pairs of legs.

"Kevlar, to slow piercing damage. I have no idea how you know what you know, but I do not think a wizard of death would bother you in the least," Charlotte finished, once again doing her best to disentangle herself from the ropey intestines flying all over the place. Billy thought he heard her grunting while pushing some of it from around her. With a mental command, the clear hemisphere Charlotte had up in front was made whole when its other half rose from behind her, cutting the intestine free.

She immediately had it retracted and began complaining about the small bits that were left leaking all over her. She reached back to grab them, then tossed them away. "I hope we don't have to do this much longer, Billy. The tunnels are getting quite full of corpses."

Billy grunted his agreement as he bisected yet another zombie bear, its body spilling gore as its head continued to try and gnaw angrily in his general direction.

"Charlotte, any idea on how to, like, kill these things? They keep biting and trying to claw at me even when they're in several pieces," Billy inquired, dodging volleys of tentacles.

"Well, dear, they are much like you are; they cannot be killed. They do not have Life values, they have a Durability value. If you reduce their Durability to zero, they will cease to function, as you will have slain them."

"Slay? What kind of damage is best at reducing Durability, then? 'Cause cutting them to pieces ain't it!" he said, desperately dodging a group of ravaging rat zombies.

"That would be Blunt damage, dear."

"Of course it is," Billy said to himself, realizing he'd known that already. Switching tactics again, Billy began to smash the monsters around him. Instead of pushing his pointed foot into a monster, he widened it as much as he could and stomped on them or smacked them with his foot knuckles, as he began to think of them. He wasn't punching at them, or technically kicking, and he didn't exactly have feet, so foot knuckles would have to do. That was what he told himself as he used those metallic foot knuckles to cave in faces, break legs, and crush hands. He'd even dropped on several writhing bodies on occasion, his compact yet dense weight easily squishing the animated dead organic matter. He could feel it dripping off in stringy nastiness as he moved from zombie gopher to zombie beastkin.

Standing in the room with the boulder that had blocked the tunnel, Billy waited. He dripped copious amounts of gore, blood, and fluids. Random corpse parts were stuck in joints here and there, or stuck on pieces of his armor. The tunnel leading back was a river of gross.

"Charlotte, remember that pool we passed on the way here?"

"Yes, dear, I recall."

"Lead us there, if you please. I would like to wash this stuff off." He was doing his best not to move so he wouldn't have to feel the stuff covering him.

"Dear, you have to finish the Boss first. It should be in the next room," Charlotte said, waving a leg towards a tunnel with a faint green light visible.

"Can it wait?" Billy whined. "I can barely see."

"Of course not, Billy. If you leave it alone, it will turn all of your hard work into another horde, and we will have to do this all over again," Charlotte said as she squeegeed the lenses of Billy's eyes as best she could from her perch. The gelled blood mix covering him annoyed her and Billy, making sagging piles around his eyes, and some was already filling in her port while she was cleaning.

Billy grumbled, shaking his legs much like a cat would when its paw gets wet, trying to get some of the stuff off of himself.

"What about looting the bodies?" Billy inquired.

"I wouldn't worry, dear. They're not likely to have much on them, and we don't have the time to loot them all anyway."

"All right then, let's get this over with," Billy sighed, giving up on trying to clean himself off and stomping his way to the only room which glowed green, dragging several yards of intestine and a dead badger behind as he went.

As he moved into the room at the end of the short tunnel, Billy cranked up his Perception. He soaked in as much detail in the room as he was able to parse, some items being strange and unidentifiable. Once Billy caught sight of the tip of a glowing staff, he stopped and yanked on the intestine he was dragging, along with its badger friend, whipped it around, and hurled it straight at the necromancer as fast as he was capable.

"You," was cut off as a blood and gore-soaked lumpy bag of bloody fur and pokey bits slapped the necromancer in the face with a wet t-shirt-on-concrete sound.

Billy burst around the corner, snatched the staff from the necromancer by expediently removing its arm at the elbow with one foot and caving in the head with another foot. He reached forward and crushed the crystal on the necklace of the twitching necromancer, and its body exploded in a blast of black soot which settled slowly over Billy and the floor around him. A quick scan of his logs, and he sighed.

Congratulations! You have cleared the Dungeon. It was in an overflow state for more than 10 years.

Experience has increased by 150% for the Boss!

Additional bonuses will be sent to your mailbox after you leave the dungeon.

You have 10 minutes to loot the Boss's treasure room, then you will be transported back to the entrance. Good Luck!

Billy read the notification and asked Charlotte, "What is a boss treasure room? Is this it?" Billy shook his foot once more to disentangle the intestine still wrapped around his foot annoyingly as he pointed at a nearby doorway.

"Yes, dear. I will detach the drones to aid in looting," she said, swiftly giving action to words as drone after drone dropped off of Billy's body to begin hauling small wooden boxes forward and emptying their contents after Billy turned their keys to wind their springs.

Box after box of coins and jewels piled up in front of Billy. These were deftly stored in the appropriate compartments as quickly as possible. There were several books, weapons, and clothes brought forward as well, which were placed in the crate he had brought into the Dungeon with him.

Charlotte orchestrated the whole affair while Billy watched dispassionately. He was not really interested in the loot; he was most interested in the Experience points he'd earned. Billy had only received a few Experience points per zombie he had slain, but he had slain uncountable numbers in the last few hours. He wasn't exactly sure, but he thought it was a little over 1,000 zombies he had dismembered and crushed; perhaps it was closer to 4,000; he wasn't sure at this point. The necromancer, however, gave him well over 10 times that total in Experience points by itself. That was then increased by 150%, which made his gains nearly obscene. When he had the time, he could do another full upgrade and still have Experience points to spare.

Curious, Billy tried to place the points in his Intellect and Wisdom and tapped the button to *Apply* once, which he knew would give him an estimation of time to upgrade himself. To his shock, the time to upgrade was set to instant, and he froze.

"Charlotte, quick, when dungeons are cleared, is the timer for every being reduced to zero for applying new Attributes and stuff?"

"I believe so, Billy. Why do you ask?"

Billy did not immediately respond. He once again cranked up his Perception and crunched numbers. He had a ludicrous amount of Experience from here and the city, and he would upgrade instantly in this place. He only had another...

...to go, and limited material reserves. He thought for a moment and immediately doubled his Strength and Dexterity Attributes. He put as many points into his Hand-to-Hand Skill as he felt safe doing, spread some out in his Proficiencies, and dumped the rest evenly into his Stamina, Intellect, Wisdom, and Perception, then tapped *Apply*. Billy lit up like a nuclear explosion, and the world went fuzzy for him.

Billy looked around, only to realize it was still dark. Then he turned around and kept looking, and noticed it was dark, and he was in fact outside of the Dungeon he had just cleared. He also had notifications and alerts, which he saw as the blinking icons in his field of view. He quickly reviewed them, which told him of his reserve depletion which fed his Attribute growth.

Looking inward, Billy felt his furnace and boiler. They felt unusual before, but now he felt the silent power prepared to push pistons and fluids, turn gears, and empower cogsprings throughout his body. His vastly stronger and more mobile body. He also felt far lighter, as if his mass had somehow changed, or something.

Billy looked around for Charlotte and noticed she was not plugged into her port as was normal.

"Charlotte?" he asked aloud, and then immediately felt something unwrap itself from around his body.

"Oh dear, it appears your upgrade has augmented your shape quite a lot. And mine upgraded as well, it seems," the little old lady's voice said aloud. Charlotte disengaged from Billy and then stood beside him, now easily five times larger than she had been previously. "I will have to have you produce new skirts for me, if you don't mind, dear," she said, examining herself. Instead of having a body about the size of an apple, she now had a body a little closer to the size of a cantaloupe, with much longer legs as well.

Billy had lost much of his mass somehow and was almost three-quarters the size he had been previously. Charlotte, likewise, gained mass and her size had increased as a reflection of Billy's losses. Unlike Billy, however, Charlotte's new form was quite delicate, her very long legs suspending her compact body, which housed a much more capable memory system and more powerful optics.

Her legs were narrow and triangular along the length and formed of some kind of crystalline material that almost sparkled in the darkness. Her body was as opaque as her legs were clear, which caused Billy to try and imagine how the new leg skirts would even fit now.

Looking down at himself, Billy saw he had shrunken in volume but had also thinned out. He had been quite large before, similarly in size to the weird robots from the Appleseed anime, but now he only occupied the volume of a normal-sized man, even with his legs deployed, except that he was a mechanical spider. If he spread his legs out flat, he could still reach about ten feet, but his body was sleeker, which meant his legs had lengthened some. He moved these legs and almost could not feel their weight or any resistance. In a way, he felt strong. And fast. And he wanted to move. But first...

"Charlotte, is there a river or something nearby? I am still covered in this gunk from below," he said, peeling back his now much larger cloak, which pulled back to reveal ropes of viscera with scraps of hide attached hanging over his brand new frame.

"Yes, dear. A few hundred yards over there," she waved a leg, careful not to get the goop on her, because she somehow came out of this upgrade perfectly clean.

Billy saw the marker on his map Charlotte had placed for him and decided to run there. He turned and dashed off down the rocky steps, past the sticky trees, over rocks, and over more loose rocks, in a blur.

"Cheese and rice...," his voice trailed off as he practically flew overland, and in moments he arrived at a waterway he'd not seen on his way into the valley. The stream was surprisingly wide and deep for being so high up in the hills, and he opted to step into it and begin thrashing around.

Charlotte arrived not long after Billy, her long, lithe legs allowing her the opportunity to move almost as fast as he. She helped peel the cloak from Billy's body and began to wash it herself while Billy tumbled around in the sandy river.

While underwater, Billy flushed all of his water reserves through himself and replaced it with fresh, clean, filtered water from the river. The ice-cold water caused his internal components to ping and pop as they came close to the boiler chamber and helped cool him internally. He vented steam from his boiler as well, pushing out anything that may have built up in there during the hours of zombie bashing.

For the river's part, it carried away the bits and bobbles collected from the undead Billy had dismembered and managed to collect in his various joints. The blood stained the water downstream shades of black, green, and red, eventually diluting as it traveled.

A dozen little bots separated themselves from Billy as he commanded them to scurry over his body and pluck out reluctant passengers. The fingers, fangs, and fur were soon sent slipping downstream with the more liquid hangers-on as they diligently dug through the crusty layers of corpse parts and bile. Sheets of torn flesh, organs, and other icky bits were finally removed from Billy, and he let the sense of cleanliness literally wash over him as he sat at the bottom of the crystal-clear stream for a time.

At one point, Charlotte had joined Billy in his tumbling bath to help remove more obstinate zombie parts while Billy used his new, more advanced manipulators to clean off the skein of goo crisscrossing his sensitive eyes, the strange pads of his manipulators helping scrub the stuff away. This was when Billy realized he was covered in this ultra-fine layer of hair. They were all a solid blue color, close to royal blue, and only about a half-inch long, but his entire body was covered in the stuff. He also realized, now that he was getting cleaner by the second, that he could feel the water moving around his body. He could track the varying currents moving in and around each of his limbs, his chest and back, and especially his abdomen.

With his now clean eyes, Billy noticed all of his bots were now attired similarly in ultra-fine hairs and seemed more lifelike than the robots they had obviously been despite the shiny brass key on their backs.

Chapter 18

"Charlotte, can you show me how I look from your point of view?"

A moment later, she reached over and touched him, and he received an image in his mind on one of his many screens, a three-dimensional model of himself in very high definition. The framework of his body was shaped a little different, but still resembled that of the jumping spider he originally mimicked. Now, he was a little more compact, but also longer and slightly wider. He wasn't as round as he had been before with the bulbous abdomen. And his legs had lengthened some, but not much. And he was covered in a layer of very fine, dark blue hair.

His body looked more alive than before as well, with his joints more incorporated into his exoskeletal frame. The vents were carefully hidden in segmented folds which overlapped in very clever ways, allowing for steam pressure to vent quickly and quietly over his entire body. He also noticed that his body moved much like a real spider, as its life processes worked to allow it to breathe, and for its heart to move blood around. He very slowly pulsed at his abdomen, just like a living spider would as it breathed.

"Care to do your maintenance, Charlotte? I will be producing those skirts you keep pushing up the queue despite being at the top already, while you do that," Billy asked, moving out of the water onto the sandy beach. He located a large, flat rock that faced the open night sky and arranged himself for her. He ordered the rest of his bots to disembark, and pulled up his inventory in his Status to see how much of what materials he had remaining. He had a vast store of materials, and this gave him pause.

Pulling up his Status, Billy reviewed his combat logs from inside the Dungeon. He saw the places where he had snatched up various bits of metal, weapons and armor as he tore undead apart for hours, and he also checked the logs where he raided the treasures from the Dungeon Boss. He had, somehow, more in his storage compartments than he had volume to store it all.

This was when he saw his upgrade notifications, which provided him with some answers.

Congratulations! You have transcended your Strength and Dexterity to Rank 1, allowing you to drastically upgrade your might!.

Your Intelligence and Wisdom also reached the threshold for Tier 8. You comprehend aspects of physical reality beyond the normal levels.

Access granted to Dimension Compartments.

Alert! One of your compartments contains condensed, living magical beings. This compartment will be upgraded to facilitate living beings, but will reduce the total maximum volume of functional space for other storage purposes.

You have unlocked 2140 cubic feet of space to store materials, all accessed through your compartment doors. While stored, all the object's mass is suspended. One compartment has been augmented to facilitate lifeforms in a three cubic foot space.

Note! All objects or lifeforms stored in your personal storage occupy their exact dimension of space, but are suspended in time until removed. This includes plants, animals, fungus, and other elemental entities, whose total combined volume does not exceed three cubic feet in space.

You may access your DImensional Compartments via Status menus or by interacting directly with your Dimensional Compartments.

"Oh wow, I have my own personal bag of holding built in me now," Billy mumbled to himself. "And plenty to work with as well." Billy pulled up his construction queues and began production of Charlotte's leg skirts.

Thanks to the modifications made not just to himself, but his bots as well, the maintenance timetable was reduced considerably. Billy was quite happy with this, as he was able to get up and move around almost as soon as he finished making Charlotte's clothes. She had the bots help dress herself, while she admired the sheer, silvery cloth that now hung loosely over her long legs. She was now almost three feet tall, with a leg span of close to double that if she laid down flat and spread her legs out all the way, and the skirts only covered from the last "knee" down, making the skirts almost two feet long themselves, but very narrow. She even managed some strange dress thing which draped over her abdomen like a scarf.

"Aright, bot bois, saddle up!" Billy called out. He squatted down and each of the bots, including the two larger scavenger bots, attached themselves to the various ports on his abdomen and chest. He'd even taken the time to replace the one he'd lost yesterday, and now had an even 40, plus the two scavengers. Interestingly, most of the bots climbed into the compartments he had, and stored themselves in his inventory, leaving a few stuck to his exoskeleton for convenience.

"That's neat," he said. Charlotte looked over at him.

"What is, dear?" She asked, waving her thin legs around and watching the sheer skirts float through the air.

"Some of the bots are in my new dimensional storage space. This lightens my load considerably, and means I could probably make more and store them in there as well." He considered this a moment, and looked at his stats. "I can also control more than before. I think this says I can now easily control up to 135 spider bots at a time, now. I need to calculate this, but that's probably accurate."

"That's good, dear. I'm glad you have gotten stronger," Charlotte said, still not really paying attention to him as she waved her legs around.

"Okay, then Charlotte, let's get going. We got this particular Dungeon cleared, and we still have days of travel to go." Pulling up his map to orient himself in the right direction, he saw a blinking red dot nearby. Zooming in, Billy saw the little red dot was slowly getting closer. Rubbing some dirt from one of his feet subconsciously, Billy wondered what this red dot was as he watched it creep slowly across the broken ground on the hill back where…

"Charlotte, I think that bot we lost the other day has made it back to us somehow. It looks like it's almost dead, though. It's barely moving."

"Shall we fetch it then? I can go and collect it if you wish, dear."

Billy rubbed his manipulators together as he thought for a moment. "Sure, Charlotte. I'll wait here while you go scoop it up."

And just like that she was gone, moving so fast Billy almost hadn't seen her disappear. Billy turned to look around, but he saw her as a line moving across his map. It only took her a couple of minutes to travel to the red dot, then she and the dot were forming a line coming back to him.

The round trip only took 10 minutes, and then Charlotte was standing there with a smaller, older version bot clamped onto her back. She plucked it off and tossed it to Billy.

"It was broken like this when I got it, and I'm quite surprised it made it as far as it did," She said in approval of its design.

"Well, I'll just put this in storage and deal with it later. We need to get moving before those other things show up looking for it." Billy then stowed the old bot and had Charlotte mount up. She did this by wrapping her legs carefully around his eyes, and her body rested in a depression between his two primary eyes. She settled in, and they took off, heading east.

The night air brushed through Billy's ultra fine spider hair, and he could interpret the cool breeze with comfort. He detected variations in the temperature and humidity, and it was almost like having skin again. It wasn't pleasure or pain he was feeling, but pressure, temperature, and moisture contents. He had gotten used to feeling numb all over, unless something pushed pretty hard against him, and now that his stats were far higher he was able to process more data, now reflected with the addition of the hair.

"Charlotte, how are you liking your new body?" He asked on the internal communications relay.

She opted to spawn her holo, exactly as it had been before, riding on his nose this time, and said, "I love it, dear. My legs are long and slender, but strong and agile. I can think faster, and move faster as well. I almost feel like my old self," She said, waving her little spider legs around as Billy zipped around tree trunks and over small boulders.

Billy had no idea what she meant, but he did not feel like his old self at all. He felt like a comic book hero: fast, strong, and with abilities no person back on Earth could possibly imagine actually having. He could manage seeing from eight eyes independently, could now run at highway speeds over uneven terrain; he could probably jump over your typical house, and many other things. He wasn't sure yet.

He was also very strong, physically. And he could think clearly, far faster than he recalled being able to. His thoughts were organized like a computer, but varied as his mind on Earth was. He had almost perfect memory recall, and he was his own walking repair shop, and manufactory. Most importantly, Billy had access to a realm of information that allowed him to see his own inner workings objectively. That objectivity was itself subject to the particular universe he was in, but while in this universe his knowledge of himself was very objective. Someone with one more

Strength point than he had would be that much stronger than himself if they lifted weights side by side, regardless of how big or small they were to one another. Leverage seemed to be taken into account, along with all other local factors, when determining maximum results.

As for his existence now, Billy was very strong, tough, and fast. And that meant he could now deal with more problems that got all up in his face with much more aplomb and alacrity. This did wonders for his confidence, letting him make somewhat more rash decisions than he would have otherwise made. That was probably why he failed to notice the dark shadow high above him, tracking him through the landscape as he sped away. It followed Billy for a few hours, just before the sunrise began to tinge the night sky far to the east.

Just as the sky began to lighten, Billy reached a place to stop near another small stream. The slope to the water was lined with large rocks, dark green, rough, and round. The rocks ranged from golf balls to pumpkins in size. The stream was nearly 30 feet across but only about three feet deep. This river nestled between two long ripples in the ground, a portion of it cutting through the edge of the opposite shore a mile or more downstream. The water was warm, and Billy caught sight of hundreds of tiny gray and blue crabs crawling on the bottom. As he placed a foot in the water, he watched as several crabs came to investigate and plucked off what could be removed from his ultra-fine hair and pads. After a few minutes of this cleaning, the crabs got bored and floated away, looking for more tasty morsels hidden in the rocks.

That was when Billy looked closely at the green grass growing in the water as well. It was thin and wavy in the current but brilliant emerald green. As the water currents shifted, he could see tiny silver fish, not much more than half an inch in length, moving cautiously in the grass. He left them alone as he backed away from the water to find a place just off the rocky shoreline to sit down.

"Charlotte, have the bots scavenge the area for anything useful. These rocks look like they may have plenty of copper and other useful minerals in them. Have them collect pieces I can quickly Dissemble while you perform the general maintenance after that long run across the countryside." Billy directed most of his bots to disembark and follow Charlotte's instructions. He pulled some other things from his storage, his old cloak and the older version bot among them, and began to Dissemble them one at a time. He wanted to craft a new cloak for himself, so he set to work on this first. In a few minutes, however, he was crunching away on the rocks brought to him. He watched his inventory for the mineral reserves and was happy to find he had many of his stocks climbing, if very slowly. These rocks were rich in a variety of useful minerals.

"Charlotte, do you think I should upgrade our aerial surveillance? I think something was watching us run out this way, but I couldn't see it. I'm pretty sure it was flying." Billy grabbed one rock after another and shoved it into his Dissembler.

"I thought I heard something just before the sun began to light the sky, but I wasn't really paying attention," she said, sounding almost sheepish.

"Yeah, I saw your holo waving its little feet around like you were on a roller coaster," he said between bites of yummy stone.

"I don't know what that is, dear, but if it was like riding a wild beast, you weren't' controlling' and didn't know where it was going to go, then yes."

Billy chuckled at this. She wasn't wrong in her description.

"Right, so I have a few ideas from my old world, and I was wondering if I should attempt designing them," he said, mentally opening up the research tab from his Ability tree. Normally, someone would need a place to work and, draw out designs and make prototypes. However, Billy had all of this R&D built into his mental matrix and Assembler. This allowed him to design on the fly and build anything he could possibly need, so long as he had the appropriate mineral cache necessary to construct the stuff. The strange thing was that the required mass of all of the minerals never matched the mass of the product. Up to 10% of all of the minerals he was required to provide vanished during construction, and even that varied from identical product to identical product.

Fortunately, these particular rocks here were rich in several minerals he needed a lot of; calcium, magnesium, aluminum and iron were rich in these particular rocks. There was also a lot of sodium, but he didn't really need that, so he just stored some of it in his dimensional compartments and discarded the rest. He also built up a good supply of silica, but as he wasn't exactly in the mood to make ceramic or more fiberglass, so he kept a specific supply and discarded the rest of this as well.

Billy was lucky he had enough raw minerals to manufacture the oils and stuff necessary for his lubricants. The stuff was a pain to make and required an array of raw materials and minerals, but finding the right plants here and with the leftovers from the Dungeon run and upgrade, he had enough to produce a few pounds of the stuff, enough to last him weeks or months.

Billy had access to enough elemental bits and had enough ideas for any number of things to make for a number of problems he'd witnessed in this world, but he had yet to grasp the specifics of both the schema for construction and the political landscape. He knew he was sent here to save this world. What that meant, exactly, was up for grabs. So, as he sat and munched on rocks, he thought about what he knew while piles of sand and silica built up around him.

Supposedly, this world had access to the System at some point after it came into being. The spirits of the universe converged in this location and became things: rocks, air, water, and such. It evolved over time, and bits and pieces of these elementals became other things. These beasts were not intelligent but had more intellect than rocks or the wind. Then, they evolved again and diversified into more beasts and some beastkin. The beastkin were more intelligent than the beasts, but not as much as humans were from Earth. Other evolutions of the beasts and beastkin produced specialized fey, like the elves and dwarves. These were more humanoid, and vastly more intelligent.

And somehow, all of this occurred right alongside other life in the world, such as plants, insects, and animals. Billy wasn't sure, but these things did not seem to ever have access to the System. They just existed as a byproduct of aging matter. And so there was diversity in the plants and animals as well, if more so. Spirits were less likely to change in unpredictable ways, as their base nature was more or less fixed, but the animals in the world weren't limited in the same way.

Then there were the Dungeons and Lairs and such. These things he did not know the purpose of. He assumed it was just part of the System's design, but was unsure. He put that mystery aside for now.

The animals and fey existed in some form of stable harmony for however long they had existed before, according to Orgar, some few thousand years or so ago humes came along. The humes seemed to have similar traits that humans did from Earth: bipedal, two arms and legs, upright walking, two eyes and ears, et cetera. He had yet to see what a hume looked like, however, so he was only guessing at the details. But the humes had done something, had managed to strip access of the System from the fey of the world. And around that time, the fey fled to the Lair of the Fey, hiding from the humes.

Billy had no idea what the humes were doing now or why they'd never found the Lair of the Fey. They had centuries but never took the place down. And then there was the city itself. Billy knew there were issues there; the Experience gains were far too high compared to just outside the zone, and the constant draining of individuals' Experience pools for nearly everything they did there was strange. A preference for Experience trade was more than the coins exchanged were worth. Ten coins to one Experience made it an easier decision when coins were so difficult to find or earn and Experience was so easy to earn. And there were the weirdos there manipulating the prices of the blocks and the unit rental prices, fluctuating almost daily for no conceivable reason.

Billy did not earn Experience outside the city or a Dungeon or Lair like he did when inside those places. He was beginning to wonder what made that city so special, but he still couldn't put his finger on it. And, one more thing, why was this Dungeon he'd run across in its overflow state? Is nobody clearing them? Wouldn't this just cause the monsters in them to flow out into the world, wreaking havoc? Is that what the humes want? If the monsters got out, they would deplete the resources around the area, then slowly spread as more monsters spawned in the Dungeon or Lair and pushed out.

He didn't know. But hopefully, when he caught up with the elves in their stronghold, they would be able to answer some of these questions. Maybe they would even show him what a hume looked like. Someone, somewhere, ought to have an image, drawing, or painting of one somewhere. It seemed so unlikely they'd talk about humes and how dangerous they were but not have any image or description of what they looked like to put a face on the danger.

"Charlotte, were your records restored after this last upgrade?" He would have turned to see her, but she was busy with two of his rear legs.

"No, dear. I have cognitive upgrades, and other physical changes, but the memory itself was not something upgradeable. The information I have in me is very old, dear. And I sat for all that time without power. Not having that power prevented my other systems from maintaining integrity, and so it likely became corrupted to beyond useless. I.. I purged it." Her hesitation was apparent to Billy.

Placatingly, he said, "It's fine, Charlotte. You did what needed doing. It would be easy to misinterpret partial data. Getting rid of the temptation to do so was wise." He relaxed as he opened up his own Status to look at the universal System's network to see if he could learn anything about this world. The only thing he seemed to have access to was the Store. Thinking a moment, he mentally put in his selection to search for, and to his utter amazement, he got a hit.

You have selected to purchase one book, The Entire History of the World, as told by the right hand of the Frugal Milgwimp, Grandmaster Frithel XXIII. The cost is 12,500 Experience points, plus Taxes, Licensing and Sending fees, bringing the total to 985,000,000,025 Experience points.

"Well, that's absurd," Billy said to himself. "I wonder why it costs so much more than the base cost." He pondered this for a few minutes, not finding anything in the store to help with the cost breakdown, and canceled the order. He hit *Apply* on the cancel button, and the screen blanked down to just the search bar again. Then Billy got curious, and put in the search for Sell.

Immediately, his own inventory opened up, listing all of the things he had on his person. He had fixed weights of metal, wood, dirt, rock, his bots, and so on. He scrolled way down to the bottom of his list and saw the Gloopos. The ones he had with him were worth a gargantuan amount of Experience. If he chose to exchange one, he could get that book. It made no sense, and so he scratched at his chin with his manipulator.

Shrugging, Billy tapped to select one of the Gloopos to sell and saw there was an auction option. He tapped that and hit *Apply*. As soon as he did so, he felt something wiggling inside himself and reached back to the compartment which held the little buggers. As soon as he had one exposed to the air, it floated right in front of Billy's face and waved. Then, it folded into itself several times until it simply vanished.

In Billy's Status screen, he saw a timer counting down until the auction began, which was less than 15 minutes. So he waited while Charlotte continued to do her chores. He would lift one leg and hold it up, then another. Then, he would articulate each while she inspected. Soon, she was opening each and every compartment, crawling inside to inspect things from in there, which felt a little strange as all of them were extradimensional spaces now.

After the timer ran out, Billy watched as strange symbols, shapes, and other things that could be considered names, listing bids on the thing he'd discovered. The numbers fluctuated tremendously from a few Experiences, to trillions. It made no sense to him. If he had that much to use, he could be a god here in this world. The auction went on as Charlotte finished her work, and soon Billy was in tip-top shape once again. His joints moved silently, and he could articulate them all with next to no effort. His boiler was freshly scrubbed internally, and he felt more stable mentally and physically. He rather enjoyed this feeling.

The auction kept going as Billy thought about things and scrolled through the many pictures he'd taken in the Dungeon. The morning came into being, finally, as the sun fully crested the horizon. The sun itself was slightly bluer than the one he was used to, but then again, he was on a different planet somewhere else in the universe or perhaps in another universe. He finished the production of his last bot, having consumed the older style to make the newer one. His Leadership Ability lets him control a large number of things, but he could only carry so many before he became a walking storage unit.

The interesting thing about that Ability was that it allowed him to have exponentially more followers for every point he placed in it. The first point let him have three followers, and each point after that increased it by an order of magnitude, if that magnitude were translated from a base 12 system. The second point put him up to 15 followers; the third gave him access to up to 135. He had three points in this at the moment, as he had absolutely no need for over 100 bots, but this also allowed him to add Friends to his Friends List, upon which were several names.

Sharea, Elsie, Orgar, and Charlotte had their own listings on his Friend List. This list was under the Leadership tab, which described the Friend List as providing a list of people whom he could call on to form Parties with and who would follow him. Likewise, if they had enough points in Leadership, they could do the same with him. They had to have enough points in it to account for not just him but his bots. He wasn't near anyone to invite, so the option was grayed out to form a Party. This Ability basically meant he could treat all of his bots and all of his Friends as potential Party members. In his special instance, all of his bots were automatically in his Party.

Finally feeling like doing something, Billy pushed away all of the materials, mostly sand, that he did not want or need from the Disembling process. He acquired a number of rich minerals, though not in large quantities. With all the bots in place, either attached or stowed, Billy stood, and Charlotte climbed up onto him and wrapped herself around his head again like a strange crystalline tiara. A subtle rotation of joints and her limbs no longer refracted the sunlight in every direction. With another jiggle, they ceased to be reflective and started absorbing sunlight in small amounts.

Internally, Billy cranked up his boiler in preparation to leave; when he turned back to the valley, they had left and started going back a thought struck him.

"Where are we going, Billy?

"I want to collect more of those little critters we found. I figure we can spend a few hours, even this whole day, going down there to collect them. Hopefully, we can do that before the Dungeon resets, and they're all killed off."

"I see," Charlotte said contemplatively.

At the Dungeon entrance, Billy received a prompt telling him the place had been cleared and that it would reset in a few days. He chose *Yes* when prompted to enter and continued inside. This news made Billy happy, and several hours later, he had climbed down the entrance of the Dungeon and into the area where the Gloopos were congregated. He saw their little city undisturbed, and the little colorful blob creatures were going about their business.

Without any hesitation, Billy began scooping up each one and placing them into the compartment designed just for them. He was careful not to frighten the little things too much, but as he was so overtly abducting them, the others were doing their best to blob themselves away from him and his endeavors. It didn't take him long to find all of the little blob creatures and scoop them up. Once he was sure he got them all, Billy carefully began disassembling their little city and storing all of the different buildings in other compartments to rebuild later. He was very careful not to break anything, and with his much higher Dexterity he had little problems there.

You have acquired 31 Gloopos of varying quality. Seek a Kenning Specialist to have them identified.

There were only a few buildings he recognized as structures, but Billy did what he could to detach everything from the cave walls and store them. In little less than an hour, he was moving to leave the Dungeon from the way he'd come down, and a few hours later, he was back outside in the sun, heading back on course for the rendezvous with the elves.

On the way out of the valley, Billy finally received an alert letting him know his auction was completed and that he had to approve the sale of the Gloopos. The original bid was some absurd number, but the cost of mailing the thing, which was both alive and highly magical, from his location to the recipient was deducted from the bidding price. Billy rubbed his spider chin as he read the notification of the bid results. The others had bid more or less than each other, but their relative locations altered shipping costs, which they would have to add to the bid, and this was what had thrown Billy off.

When he'd tried to purchase a book, the cost was extraordinarily high, and now he knew it was because, as the buyer, he would be the one paying to have the article shipped to him from wherever the provider was located, just like if he were to purchase from a store. But as the seller in an auction, he would not have to pay the cost of shipping because this cost came directly out of the bid itself. For a moment he wondered who got the payments for the shipping. A few of the bidders had opted to trade other things, but none of it was of any use to Billy. He could not use magic that he was aware of. Nor could he wield swords, or hammers, or bows. He had other options. Thus, he chose to trade for the Experience and, with a few mental taps, selected *Accept* and *Complete Auction Trade*. A moment later, as he was walking over a large boulder, a bar of gray non-light splashed over him, and he received his Experience points.

Congratulations! The Auction is complete. Here is the offer you have chosen to accept:

+190,295 Experience points.

"What is it, dear?" Charlotte asked as she felt Billy pause mid-step.

"You didn't see that light?"

"What light? I didn't see anything but the reptile over there slipping into the trunk of that tree," She responded.

"It was nothing," Billy said. "I thought I saw something, is all."

Billy had received more Experience with that one trade than he'd made from the Dungeon, which made him begin to wonder what he would need it for, but he decided to postpone using it. He should probably stockpile some and, if necessary, use it to improve himself later.

Up one side of the hill and down the other. This went on for hours and hours and then into the night, with only an occasional stop to look around at the world. Billy loved walking through the mountains back home, and now that he was in much better condition, he was taking the time to look at the life of this world for what it was: unique. He thought about this strange world and compared it to his life back on Earth and discovered both had their own unique aspects.

The flora here was very sterile of variation despite the history he'd been told. There were the large trunked trees with the sticky ropes of goo hanging from them, there were grasses covering the ground, and there were some flowering plants here and there. For the most part, everything looked the same, which he supposed was possible even if each valley was almost its own ecosystem. Still, this bothered Billy, as it was in direct contrast to what he was expecting to find.

All of the streams seemed to have the same small, shiny fish in them and the brilliant green grass that grew from the bed that the tiny, shiny fish lived in. The grass didn't get long, and the fish didn't get big, no matter where the water was coming from or going to. The tiny little crabs were also present in the streams, grabbing at any stray thing floating in the water with their tiny claws to nibble away at it.

Billy's map showed both Charlotte and him traveling for dozens of miles each hour, and after the day turned to evening again, the hills were finally fading out to a large, flat grassland with sparse trees clustering here and there on the horizon. It wasn't until dusk he noticed the horns of large herd animals poking up from the grass in great clusters, and then he saw the large beasts themselves.

The tall, sharp-edged grass was a dull greenish-brown. This matched perfectly the long, sleek bodies of the giant reptile creatures he saw. On his approach, several of the larger animals took notice of him and turned to watch him as he trespassed near them. While they made loud hissing sounds, their skin changed from a dull green to a shade of orange. Billy watched them as he walked, doing his best to show his lack of interest in them in the hopes of easing their fears. Some animals, if they were herd animals, would ignore you if you ignored them long enough, accepting you as not hostile. If he had tried to lurk by, they would likely have been on high alert or perhaps even aggressive towards him. But Billy had places to go, and he was not interested in either the meat from them or the Experience points. He had enough of that going on for now.

As darkness came in on full, Billy could hear the wind blowing gently through the tall grasses. It made soft, swishing sounds as the blades of grass rubbed one another and made slightly more as they rubbed against his limbs. Needing no real creature comforts, Billy reached a spot in the grass with a very slight depression and simply sat down. He watched the skies above, the stars' brilliant dots in the dark sky. He saw no recognizable constellations to identify, and thanks to his improved vision, he caught sight of something no human could ever perceive with their own eyes. He saw, slowly coming over the horizon, the galactic arm of the galaxy he was in. The distant clouds of gas, practically dots, were visible to him, and the array of billions of stars was obvious to him. He had no idea where this solar system, or galaxy, was in regards to him, but he was privy to a light show he had not previously caught sight of since he'd arrived on this world, nor had he been capable of witnessing back on Earth.

Bright red dots moved near pale white and glaring blue dots. He was lucky enough to just perceive a nebula not far from this world, and its rainbow of hues filled his mind with awe and wonder. He watched these stars turn across the night sky as the hours slipped by, so captivated was he. He barely made out the local stars, moving faster than the more distant ones. He thought he even recognised what could be nearby planets, pale-colored dots that weren't pinpricks of light so much as round smudges. There was no way for him to know for sure without observing the night sky for months or perhaps years.

Charlotte watched the night with Billy, quietly waiting to fulfill any needs he may have. She said nothing as he observed, and neither did he. She was content to wait to be of service, alert but calm. Off in the distance, she could just make the sounds of the animals moving around. There were many of them, and they all seemed intent on eating the grasses here. Eventually, the herd moved on, and Charlotte listened and watched them go, her own eyes resting slightly higher than Billy's were at the moment.

The sky began changing colors, and the dull greenish-gray of the night began to lose its gray color. The stars in the sky, still visible, became less clear as the atmosphere up above was lit by the first rays of the day. In another hour, the sun had risen, and with it, so had Billy. He was about to move when he noticed something.

"Charlotte, do you see that hill over there? It's a few miles out, but do you see it?" He asked on the internal relay.

"I do, dear." She said after a moment.

"Does it look like it's moving to you?"

"Yes. Quite magnificent, isn't it?"

"What do you mean? Do you know what that is?" Billy turned to look directly at the massive, distant hill as it inexplicably moved across the land.

"It is the Great Shaper, an ancient turtle that moves about the world. It leaves devastation in its wake, but with that destruction comes change. It is what forces the lands to never remain stagnant for too long. It can create mountains or knock them over. It can dig out a lake or pull up land and fill one."

"It's alive?" Billy asked in amazement.

"Oh yes, it's alive. It is one of the oldest beings in this world." She said nothing more as they both watched the hill moving. Billy tried to feel the ground to detect its passing, but he felt no vibrations from something so large moving.

"I can't feel it moving. Is that normal?"

Charlotte thought a moment before answering, probably pulling up ancient documents from her archives.

"It is the ground itself, alive and with will, moving around. It isn't separate from the world, you see. It is the world itself, manifesting as the Great Shaper. Some records I have say it can move as much as halfway around the world in an instant, others say it crawls along at a barely perceptible pace, shaping the ground it covers into something new. Nobody then knew why it does this, or if they did, I have no records of the results."

Billy, ever curious, checked his map to see how far off course the elf rendezvous was from this hill. While he was looking at his map, the thing had simply folded into the land and vanished. When Billy noticed this, he said, "Where'd it go?"

"It has moved on, dear. Probably to do other important work elsewhere."

Billy, a bit nervous that something so massive could vanish so completely in moments, moved his manipulators to show this nervousness. It wasn't a conscious decision but something of a reaction.

"Do you think we have time to go look and see what it did over there?"

"I don't think we would be able to tell, dear. From what little I have on record, it leaves no marks of its presence once it moves. It's just not there any longer and is somewhere else." Charlotte rubbed one of her legs along the side of Billy's head in an attempt to calm his nerves. "It is only part of nature, dear, much like a rainstorm or a hurricane."

"I see," He said before turning back on course to the elves. Then he turned to look again. "It's not that far; I wanna see what happened over there." And with that said, he dashed forward through the tall grass. The whisking sound of the grass scratching at his legs and chest followed him to the site of the turtle.

Chapter 19

The ground looked like freshly turned soil, with the occasional stone jutting out. Testing the ground, Billy pushed a foot into the soil to test its resistance, seeing how far his foot would sink down with a steady push. His foot sank easily, and he retracted it.

Looking around, he saw the area here was occupied by a vast hill according to his survey map from a few hours ago, and the results of the Great Shaper's passing left new, smaller hills in its place in a matter of hours. He looked left and right and saw no path the thing had taken. Deciding to do his due diligence, Billy quickly launched a drone to image the area for his historical records and to update his aerial survey. He waited for the few minutes the drone spent gliding around, taking pictures, and then stowed it upon its return to incorporate the images for later review.

Scooping up some fresh dirt, Billy stuffed it into his Dissembler to get a taste of its composition. It was just dirt, no organics, a bit of clay in the mix. Nothing special. What was strange was that as he watched the area, he saw grass poking up through the fresh dirt.

He had found no seeds in the sample he'd taken, but apparently, there were some in the mix out there.

"Charlotte, it looks like that great turtle tilled the soil here and left some seeds to spread more grassland. No idea what was here before, though, other than a big hill." Billy meticulously cleaned the foot that he'd dipped into the soil, getting the dirt off of it. Backing up, he looked around the area, seeing nothing else but this giant patch of fresh dirt surrounded by grasslands. Way off in the distance, there was a cluster of trees, but other than that, the land was flat, and the sky was strangely pale blue with green highlights.

Billy mentally shrugged at the strangeness of this world, turned back toward the rendezvous, and began walking at a semi-swift pace. It took less than half an hour to leave the fresh dirt patch behind him. He hadn't gone far when he noticed something out of place.

It wasn't a direct spotting. Billy, at first, noticed a strange breeze moving through the grass far to his right. It seemed to be parallelling him, but after a minute watching, he realized it was not caused by the wind at all. He watched only a moment longer, counting the different ghosts moving through the grasses. He stopped counting at 30.

"Charlotte, we have enemies incoming. At least 30. They're about a mile out and closing fast. Ideas?"

Charlotte carefully turned to look in the direction Billy's manipulator indicated as he picked up his pace from a quick walk to a run.

"They're likely Lowland Caiman, reptile monsters that rove in packs. They are semi-intelligent, nomadic hunters that operate in areas such as this," She said. "We can probably take them head-on and scare them off. Most pack monsters prefer to surround and take down prey weaker than them, but if they lose enough of the pack, they will likely run."

Billy thought for a minute as he ran on, looking for a good place to engage on his terms. Far ahead, there was a cluster of trees, somewhat different from the ones with sticky goo hanging from them. He adjusted his course to pass to its left side and sped up, hoping to put the large copse of trees between himself and the caiman. If they lost sight of him, perhaps he could avoid killing any of them.

Billy felt his internal boiler heating up, his pistons pushing hard, and his new gear springs twisting harder to reset his limbs and keep him balanced. His legs blurred as they slashed through the grass, carrying him forward at a blistering pace the caiman seemed able to manage. Billy moved directly towards the trees, the caiman moving swiftly a couple hundred yards to his right and behind. Just before he breached the trees, Billy saw something that made him slide to a dead stop.

"Crap, Charlotte, there are people in there. We have to," Before he could finish, the caiman broke from the grass, forming a hissing horseshoe around him. Dozens of the large monstrosities had their long snouts open towards him, powerful hissing sounds erupting from their throats in unison that morphed into deep growls.

Without warning, half a dozen caiman moved in towards Billy and snapped at his legs. Billy lashed out with several of his legs, raising them and then dropping them down in devastating stomps with reinforced metal feet. One-two-three caiman heads staved in with his extra durable feet. Billy performed a short hop sideways, leaving the thrashing, dying caiman rolling around in the grass as other monsters moved to bite.

Instead of reacting, Billy lunged forward and grabbed one of the monsters with his manipulator and bit into it, his Dissembler injecting potent acid into the caiman before dropping it, then he spun and snapped out a few strands of very sticky silken threads to tie it to the ground where is tumbled around.

Billy kicked out as several other caimans tried to grapple him from behind, but he used the move to dash to another large lizard monster. He grabbed this one as well, biting into the spot just behind the head and injecting acid there as well.

Then, Billy was busy dancing aside and kicking caiman in the snouts as he spun through them, purposefully stomping on tails and snouts. Blood splattered across his torso and abdomen as the giant lizards thrashed from their wounds. None of them attacked each other, which was a shame. He had hoped they'd fall on their weak and injured, but it seemed they would not.

Billy used his webs to entangle the caiman as much as possible, his rear legs pulling the threads from his extruders and tagging the low-sitting lizards. The web would stick to snouts, tails and torsos, grabbing onto the nearby grass and other caiman. The struggling lizards would snap at each other when they got too close to one another in their frenzy to break free. While his rear legs took care of the rear with webs, Billy was busy spinning around and pouncing on unsuspecting targets to deliver devastating acidic bites or to stab body parts with his powerful feet.

Billy was quite surprised that, after losing more than a dozen of their number and him not being much larger than any one of them, the caiman did not relent in attacking him. This didn't stop Billy from lashing out and killing them, however. These things were very aggressive, their hissing and growling filling the air as mouths snapped closed and tails smacked at his legs with decent strength.

Billy moved into the high grass, drawing the caiman away from the trees, and found he had far more leverage here with his webs than with the shorter grass near where he'd started this fight. The tall, sharp blades were stronger, with deeper roots that allowed his webbing to grasp at the giant lizards as they got caught up in the stuff Billy trailed. He would spin and toss out ropes and sprays of the super sticky silken strands by the bucket load, and the caiman obliged by dashing blindly through it, only to get snagged.

The hissing soon became the only thing Billy could make out after a few more minutes. The caiman was shorter than the grass they stood in, so they never saw the blanket of webs he'd lain over it as he ran through the grass. In less than five minutes, the entire area was laced with the stuff, and during that time, he managed to entangle most of this pack.

Heat came off of Billy's abdomen in waves as his boiler struggled to vent, and Billy felt like he should be panting. This was quite like the deluge of undead he'd faced in the Dungeon as far as exertion was concerned. Down in the ground, he'd trapped everything and only had to cave in skulls and smash apart rotting, animated corpses. Above ground, the caiman sought to surround him and bite at his legs to bring him down, and he'd had to avoid this. He was strong, but he was strong because he managed his footing with care. Now that the engagement was over, he had a moment to cool himself down. The steam blasted from all of his vents in a deep whoosh, quiet but obvious. The high-temperature steam cooked the nearby plants and scorched some of the caiman upon release, which further enraged the tangled reptiles.

Just as Billy was about to start finishing off the caiman, he heard some yelling coming from the copse of trees. He could not identify any words in the yelling, which was likened to loud bellows, grunts, and strange clicking sounds. Several whistles burst from somewhere further in the copse of trees, and the bellowing halted. Billy made his way out of the tall grass, leaving the caiman trapped to deal with later.

As he approached, Billy heard the sounds of large sticks smacking hollow-sounding tree trunks. It was rhythmic and wild, and as he got closer to the trees, the banging and bonking grew more fervent and cacophonous. Suddenly, Billy's vision began to see strange gray bubbles forming and moving around the trees. The pale gray stuff changed shape subtly as it moved, morphing to the odd beat of the makeshift drumming. Then he heard some form of chanting, deep and primal. He focused and almost burst out laughing.

Trying to contain his mirth he asked, "Charlotte, are they saying, 'ooga chaka ooga ooga oogachaka'?"

"I have no idea, dear. If they are saying anything, it is not in any language I am aware of."

Billy continued to watch the strange gray bubbles forming and moving around the tree line, then vanishing into large, furry bodies that stood near trees. He stopped just short of crossing into the shade of the trees, the growling and hissing of the caiman behind growing less in volume every moment.

Still, Billy waited, unwilling to interfere with the strange, hairy people. As he waited, he watched one particularly tall fellow, nearly eight feet tall, step behind a tree and suddenly walk out from behind the tree right in front of Billy. Startled by the sudden appearance of such a large fellow from behind such a small tree,

Billy took a half step back, but continued to watch as the large, hairy humanoid reached over its shoulder and brought forward a giant, six foot long bone. There was a small knob on the narrow end, and a large double knot on the wide end. It was like a giant bone club.

"Charlotte?"

"Yes, dear?"

"That thing looks familiar to me, for some reason."

"How so, if I might ask?"

"There is a legend I know of, speaking of a forest dweller. This dweller is very reclusive, leaving little evidence of its existence except for the occasional witness. Recordings were always low resolution and in poor lighting despite the technology being readily available for far better images. It would be seen in remote places, sometimes harassing trail climbers, or crossing an open place far in the distance. Sometimes, they would be spotted very close to the observers, and still the video evidence is poorly done, or containing only a single blurry frame with a vague outline. This dweller was known as a squatch. Is there anything like this in your records?" Billy continued to watch the large hairy being as it approached within a few yards and let its gigantic bone club drag the ground.

"No, dear, nothing like that is in my memory records."

"Okay, Charlotte. Any ideas on how to deal with it, then?" Billy rubbed at his chin nervously as he waited. It was another minute when the drumming stopped, and the giant squatch bellowed. Its large, toothy mouth opened wide as it let out a bestial roar right in

Billy's face. Spittle flew all over Billy's eyes, which Charlotte immediately wiped away with a small rag in hand.

When Charlotte did this, the tall being paused in its shout, and tilted its head in curiosity.

"HrrRR?" It grunted, pointing with one large sausage finger at Billy.

"Uh..," Billy responded in earnest.

"MmmHRrrRRR?" It growled with its toothy mouth, pointing again at Billy.

Scratching his chin, Billy pointed up to his eyes, which Charlotte nestled around, and tapped her leg. "This?" he asked.

"HhhAAhhhh" It said, thumping its large bone club into the dirt.

"I think it wants to see you, Charlotte," Billy said, tapping her leg again.

Carefully, Charlotte unwrapped herself from around Billy's head. Her long, thin legs sparkled in the light, sending rainbows scattering around on the grasses. She moved off of Billy's back and stood beside him, far smaller but with a much greater body-to-leg size ratio. She looked like a dainty daddy longlegs, made of metals and crystalline legs, each nearly four feet long, glittering in a quiet, alien forest.

The large, solid black eyes of the giant squatch were as wide as its mouth was in surprise. The large bone club thumped to the ground as it squatted down to have a closer look at her. It moved its hand out carefully, and passed it over and around Charlotte, not touching, but admiring. Out of nowhere Billy noticed he had an item in queue for production. These mineral costs were low, so he hit *Apply* and his body began doing the work Charlotte had sent his way. In a few minutes, while the squatch was admiring Charlotte, the task was done and a small box was extruded from his Assembler. He took it, using a rear leg, and brought it forward to examine the thing.

Charlotte noticed the device was completed, and turned to Billy, holding forward two of her legs along with her own manipulators. He handed the heavy metal box to her, and she took it, handing it to the squatch, who was still squatting and looking at her as she moved.

She held it forward to the giant squatch and it carefully took the heavy metal box in hand. Charlotte reached forward and tapped the large red diamond shape on the top of the box, and it suddenly began unfolding itself. The squatch nearly dropped the box in surprise, but managed not to. They all watched as the box unfolded slowly to take the shape of a smaller version of Charlotte herself, little crystalline legs included. It was only about a foot tall as it stood there, but it was otherwise the spitting image of her.

The squatch marveled at the tiny Charlotte model, and it held it up to carefully examine all of its shiny parts. Meanwhile, Charlotte herself walked back to Billy, climbed onto his back, and wrapped herself around his eyes and face again, this time turning her legs to be less sparkly so as not to distract the squatch from his new toy.

On their internal relay he asked, "What is it, Charlotte? A gift? A bribe?" Billy wondered at what made her want to provide a copy of herself to this large hairy fellow.

"A bit of both, really. I think they like shiny things, and so what better gift than a small, shiny version of myself?" She laughed grandmotherly as Billy did the spider equivalent of shaking his head.

The squatch, sated in his rage, stood while scooping up its large bone club and turned to enter the copse of trees the trio was situated by. It paused, looking back at them before nodding for them to follow. Billy, ever the curious type, followed behind. The other squatch, ranging between six feet and eight feet tall, cautiously watched from behind trees as the trio passed. The copse was not large, a little less than half a mile in diameter, but it hid this rather large tribe of squatch. In the center of the copse of trees there was a small clearing with a fire burning. The fire was burning low, and produced no smoke. This gave Billy pause, as he knew that the wood would have needed to be collected and allowed to dry before burning to rescue smoke. This process reduced smoke by quite a bit if done properly, and this was shown true by the quaint campfire burning merrily with practically none visible.

Over the fire hung a comically large pot, bubbling away. If Billy could smell properly, he would smell cooking meats and spices, with a hint of bacon tossed in. As it was, he saw several corpses strung up, being cleaned out by other squatch. The corpses, to Billy's horror, were also squatches, but with slightly off color fur. The others were busy cutting and cleaning the bodies for meat, bone and hides, which were hanging near the fire on a setup designed to let the heat from the fire bake the skin under the fur.

"Well," Billy said. "This looks lovely. I wonder who's for dinner," he finished, feeling queasy.

"It is likely they consume their elders, or perhaps rival tribes. It is a common enough thing among other species," Charlotte said nonchalantly.

Billy, not knowing exactly how he felt with cannibalism quite yet, let the topic drop. He wasn't alive, nor did he have the need to eat anymore. He required some water and maintenance, but not food. Then again, he did produce bots, and he figured he technically consumed them when he used his Dissembler. He let this thought drop as he followed the large being so that he could pay attention to what was going on.

Following the large squatch around the fire, Billy was led to a spot of cleared ground where the large creature sat with his new toy, which he sat in his lap. The large bone club was laid next to him in arms reach. It grumbled some sounds, and the other squatch nearby dispersed, leaving the trio alone by the fire.

The big beasty started making sounds, grumbles and clicks, none of which Billy understood, but he waited patiently for the grumbling to stop. He took in all the hand waving, the pointing, and the sounds, having no clue what was being discussed. After 10 solid minutes of this, the squatch making noise and Billy sitting patiently, Billy interrupted the squatch by holding out his hand.

Billy consciously focused on wanting to learn the squatch language as the large thing gently took Billy's manipulator in its massive paw and blinked stupidly. It harrumphed, then let go as Billy received the alert telling him his trade to learn the language was completed.

You have successfully learned the Language of the Siguramaku Tribe of Gijja for the cost of 10 Experience points.

Billy then held up a manipulator in a pleading manner, asking the squatch, the Gijja he mentally corrected himself, to wait a moment. He replayed the last few minutes in his mind while translating everything the Gijja had said. The long and the short of it was that

Billy had slain the hounds the Gijja used to protect their copse of trees, and for hunting. They were thankful he had not killed them all, and was accepting of the trade for damages to his caiman. Billy scratched his chin with a manipulator as he replayed this, inwardly cringing at his actions. He had basically killed these people's guard dogs, but it was alright because he had paid them for those damages.

In the language of the Gijja, Billy did his best to reproduce the sounds as he spoke to the large creature. "I am sorry for doing what I did, Gnoosh. I was not aware those were your pets. I hope you like the totem. It should last a long time if taken care of properly." Billy paused as he listened to his own translation.

Most of the Gijja language did not have direct translations to what he'd intended to say, but he was intelligent enough to extract context and reform it into the appropriate concepts. He knew the gist of what he wanted to express was understood, as Gnoosh grunted in approval, so he let the subject drop.

"What brings you to our home?" Gnoosh asked at last.

Billy cleaned one of his feet, "I am traveling to some friends. They are far."

"Ah. Can you not use a tree to move?"

"Move?" Billy was confused by what this meant, so he asked for clarification.

The large Gijja held up his arm, then motioned with his other hand by moving behind his arm, then switching it up, moving that arm from behind the other.

"Teleportation using trees?"

The Gijja clicked its tongue somehow, and Billy got the feeling this was the Gijja equivalent of a chuckle.

"Right. No, I cannot travel by the tree."

The Gijja shrugged its large shoulders in acceptance, then indicated the large pot, grunting.

"No, I do not need food. Thanks for the invitation, though," Billy said, inwardly shuddering at the thought of eating intelligent food. The Gijja huffed in response, then waved its hand toward the trees.

"Yes, I think I will go now," Billy said in response. "It was nice meeting you Gnoosh." Billy stood as Gnoosh did the same.

Before he turned to leave, Gnoosh said, "Don't trust the deep dwellers. They're full of lies."

Not knowing what to say to that, Billy again turned to leave.

Gnoosh grumbled his farewell, thanking Billy once again for the lovely payment, and returned to sitting and admiring it. Billy moved through the small copse, not seeing a single Gijja. He thought he saw a small metal craft of some sort, but he caught it out of the corner of his corner eye and when he turned to look, there was nothing but the trees.

"What do you think he meant, Charlotte?" Billy asked as they walked.

"I don't know dear. He didn't say who these deep dwellers were. It could mean anything," was all she said, and Billy let the matter drop.

Billy exited the small copse in line with his trek to the elves, and rapidly sped up his pace as he got out into the open. He did some quick math here, estimating another couple of days before he reached his destination, if he took his time. He did not wish to, however. He wanted to meet the elves, figure out what they had to say, determine what the humes wanted, somehow, and then deal with that. The mystery of the city, the Dungeons, and whatever else was going on here would have to sit on the back burner. As much as he wanted to investigate everything, he had to keep reminding himself that he was here to save the world, not explore it.

Billy cranked up his boiler and practically launched forward into the grassland. He dashed past the rocks that stuck up here and there, only noting them long enough to move around them. His legs blurred as the pistons and cogsprings rammed forward and drew back, other planetary gears inside him jerking smoothly as the accelerations changed with the angle of his legs, clever switches resetting the whole process. Billy's weight was also perfectly dispersed over the area of his foot pads, preventing any one foot from sinking too far in the soft soil the grass stabbed up through. He saw himself as a tarantula moving across the land, but much faster.

The blades of grass did their best to scour Billy's legs and undercarriage. If he'd been made of flesh, he would have been having a bad day. As it was, he was slowly being covered in tiny scratches and bits of grass he'd sliced through as he moved. The one good thing, Billy thought as he ran on, was that he was just tall enough that the grass was barely tickling his belly. The tightly contoured skid plate under there would keep any of his sensitive joints from catching anything that could cause damage, but he would definitely need to stop after a time to clean out the stuff he was already feeling was collecting up under the edges.

Billy closely watched his map as he traveled, the elevation almost imperceptibly changing as time passed. Where he'd come from was at a decent elevation to begin with, and now the grasslands were steadily dropping. Several times Billy had passed some of the herd animals he had seen before and as he approached, the larger ones would turn and face him, large horny heads lowering threateningly. He ignored them and focused on covering as much distance before dark as he could instead.

The evening of his fifth day out from the Lair of the Fey saw Billy coming over a great hill. Far off in the distance Billy saw a faint reddish-tan line smudging the edge of the horizon. He couldn't tell exactly how far away the line was, it could be five or 25 miles away. To the north Billy could just make out the dark gray and white caps of absolutely immense mountains. From where he stood, he could see a cloud line very low near the base, and that nothing green grew anywhere near that line. Those mountains could be miles tall from his perspective. Towards the south, Billy could also see a mountain range, but much smaller than the ones in the north.

The perch Billy found himself on appeared to be the point where everything dropped in elevation. For the next however many miles, the grasslands angled down until it reached what looked like desert sands. The longer he thought about it, the more sure he was that the reddish line was the edge of a sandy region. It was difficult to tell, but it looked like he would have to descend several miles in elevation to get to the area ahead of him, and all of it seemed to be covered in grasses and large boulders haphazardly scattered between him and the sand.

"Charlotte, we might have a problem soon."

"What is it dear?" She asked.

"Up ahead of us, it looks like the land dips down into a desert. The problem would, therefore, be the lack of water."

"Why would that be an issue now, dear?"

Billy, not knowing if Charlotte were being serious or not, struggled to respond for a moment. "I need water to both mitigate the heat I create and I create heat to propel myself around," he said.

"Yes, but have you seen your reserves since this morning?"

Her question gave Billy pause, and he checked. According to his gauges, he was topped off with water.

"That can't be right, I haven't stopped by a water source since yesterday."

"Dear, your reclamation system is working much more efficiently since your upgrade. Those blue hairs you are covered with aren't just giving you humidity levels, they are drawing in water from the air, including the steam you blast over yourself. " She rubbed the fine hairs over his face and Billy just knew her legs contained no water, on contact.

"And how much humidity do you figure a desert would have?"

"Billy, dear, that likely won't matter. If you look at the map here, the elve's rendezvous point is right there where the sand begins." She pointed down the great hill, toward some invisible point Billy could only see thanks to his map overlay.

"I wonder why they're meeting at this desert, and not up here in the rocks." Billy scratched at his chin for a moment before pulling out his cloak from his storage compartment and donning it.

Instead of responding, Charlotte climbed to her position and settled down for the journey. Billy waited until she was done adjusting her legs, double checked his cloak with a few leg pats, and started down the hill. He thought about quickly making a tophat for his outfit, but then discarded the notion as that would probably come across as too posh for the setting.

The hill that Billy descended was miles long and steadily dropped in elevation. Along the way, large house-sized boulders lay embedded in the hillside. Billy wasn't exactly sure how heavy any individual rock was, but the tonnage had to be closing on the triple digits. He wanted to investigate some of the rocks, as there were some which were eroded quite strangely, and others looked fresh off of the side of a mountain with plenty of sharp edges and little signs of erosion. He didn't, however, but he snapped some photos of his approaches and departures from them so he could at least look closer at them later.

Billy kept an eye out for any signs of elves, but he spotted nothing. He did, however, see plenty of evidence of insects. Large mounds of dirt stretching up a dozen feet or more marked the locations for termites. There were hundreds of mounds Billy could spot from any location. It seemed whatever was in the soil here fostered the growth of these peculiar insects, which also filled the air in places with clouds of themselves flying around. He tested the soil at one point, and found it to be exactly the same as the soil he'd tested in other places, with similar dirt and organic material contents. It was very strange, but he let that slide because he was on a mission.

After several hours of walking downhill, Billy arrived at the edge of the desert. He was at the rendezvous, but there was no sign of any elves.

Billy slowly looked across the horizon for any sign of deception, any edges to illusion, anything at all that could indicate a hidden redout. He saw only the shifting sands ahead, which seemed to roll up and down in the winds like the waves of an ocean. There were waves, in fact, of sand crashing on the rocks just like water would. The sand scoured the landscape of all dirt and organic soil, leaving only bare, polished gray rock for the sand to slide back down from whenever it receded. The hissing of uncountable granules of sand grinding against one another was deafening, even when heard from so far away. Fortunately, the gentle wind carried away all the fine dust, creating what looked like a low level mist of red just above the lapping sand.

Holding up a manipulator to shield his eyes, he asked, "Charlotte, do you see anything at all out here?" He had to send the message on his internal relay due to the growing noise of the sand.

"I see quite a bit of cleaning I must do at some point, dear." Her sense of humor had Billy chuckling to himself at her response.

Of course she would only be concerned with the maintenance work. That was mostly her purpose here. In an effort to wrest his sanity from the monotonous sound of the sand, Billy made his way back up the land a few hundred yards until the grinding of the sand faded enough for his liking. He walked along the hillside to a large, dark gray rock and moved to the side that placed the rock between himself and the wind, and squatted down to think. The rock wasn't large, only a few feet tall, but it was wide enough to create a pocket for him to hunker down in. The constant northern wind created piles of sand, not large ones, beside these large boulders which were close to the beach itself.

"I think we will just have to wait for a little while, Charlotte," Billy said while preparing to make camp.

Charlotte dismounted from her perch around Billy's head. The sand blowing around them occasionally tinkled off of her crystalline legs.

"I will see what I can do for your joints, dear, but I fear this sand will be getting in places it shouldn't, unless we can make some shelter." She tapped several places along Billy's abdomen and flat sections popped off. These flat sections then morphed into the new bots much like origami. Charlotte carefully wound the shiny brass key on each, then directed them to go about collecting rocks and fashioning a very crude stone enclosure.

Billy let Charlotte handle the shelter organization while he reviewed his logs. Tapping one of the many options, he'd organized them by days. He counted them up, and learned he'd only been on this quest to save the world for a almost two months. In that time, he'd started off as a half ton, ancient magical steam-powered machine and is currently resembling something almost entirely different; a dark blue haired jumping spider which was almost indistinguishable from a living blue haired jumping spider. Thinking about this, Billy sent one of his bots to sit on the large rock they were huddled beside to keep an eye out, and to be visible. It held onto a bright blue bit of cloth in two of its legs, letting it flap in the constant wind.

While he reviewed his logs, Billy found himself subconsciously removing the dust caught in the hair covering his body with his manipulators. Charlotte was doing this as well, but she was also checking joints, cracks and crannies for the tiny granules of sand and then removing them. Billy saw she never complained about her work, even when it was as meticulous as plucking single grains of sand from a crack, but she steadfastly did it and only complained when she could not do so immediately. It was almost as if she found joy in servitude, and this revelation gave Billy some pause.

Before he could move a leg to waggle and mention his feelings on this subject, Billy heard the bot he'd set up on the rock tapping a foot loudly. It had spotted movement.

"Alright, Charlotte, pack em up. Someone's here." He positioned himself for the bots to reconnect to his abdomen, or to re-enter the storage compartments they were withdrawn from, and in a couple of minutes they were all in place and under his leathery cloak. For some reason, he wanted to wear a tophat, but it'd have to be set on his eyes, and Charlotte sat there already. The stray thought came and went yet again while he took the time to remove some of the shelter of rocks, which served to protect them from the wind and sand, down to make a doorway. He then cautiously stepped outside.

The wind pulled at his leathers, and the sand did its best to try and scratch the acrylic lenses of his eyes, and both tangled in the short but fine hair of his body. He felt all of this try to push him sideways as he stepped into the wind from behind the small boulder.

A lone figure, dressed much like a western cowboy in leather pants, leather vest and a rather striking five gallon hat, casually walked around the rock Billy had sheltered next to. The individual had a bit of cloth covering most of the nose and mouth, and this bandana was tied around the neck, also like cowboys used to do back in the wild west on Earth. They didn't have gun holsters on their belt, but what this person carried was almost as lethal at short ranges. Billy took in the appearance quickly as he followed the figure's approach. Gloves covered hands, leather covered most of the body, and the head was covered with the bandana and the hat, so it was difficult to know if this was the elf he was waiting for, or someone else.

"Hello there, Mr. Billy I presume?" The voice, masculine, was someone muffled by the wind and dust covering, but Billy heard him clearly.

"You are?" Billy let the question hang in the air between them.

"Ah yes, I am the messenger sent to meet you here, on behalf of Captain Aurora. She sent me ahead of her arrival to meet with you and prepare you for the journey." The person, possibly an elf, stood with one hand casually on his belt near his sheathed knife, and the other hand holding onto his hat to keep it from flying away in the constant wind.

Chapter 20

"What journey?" Billy, not really feeling good about this situation, prepared himself to leave if he was not given any more explanation.

The elf, sensing Billy's hesitation, took his hand from his knife and motioned to the makeshift shelter.

"May we speak outside of this wind? It is rather cumbersome to have to shout over the wind and having to deal with the sand going everywhere."

Billy stepped aside, leaving room for the elf to duck into the former exit, now entrance, to get out of the weather. Inside, there was barely enough space for the two of them. Billy let the elf duck in first, but did not immediately follow after. He carefully scanned all directions to see if there was anyone else, but spotted nothing.

Inside, the elf had removed his hat and was busy knocking dust off his leathers and out of his very fine, gray feathered hair, while squatting down under the rocky roof. That roof was nearly five feet from the ground, but this would have been uncomfortable for anyone taller than that, and Billy was not. The gentlemanly elf pulled down the bandana to reveal an aged face covered in the bark-like skin of his people, craggy lines showing the features of an old, but active man. His eyes were a deep green color, and they looked very similar to goat eyes, which had horizontal pupils instead of round.

"I am Acooshin Ta'Rinelle, First Mate to the vile Captain Aurora of the Sandsparay." Acooshin bowed slightly at his introduction, and if it weren't for the seriousness of the quest he was undertaking Billy would have turned and left right then.

"I'm Billy. Nice to meet you Acooshin." Billy refrained from holding out a hand, he knew that if this elf had access to the System he could probably identify Billy by touch. This didn't mean such contact had to be consensual, but Billy did not want to accelerate introductions beyond what he could control for the moment.

Acooshin squatted down on his heels, and his boots creaked a little as he did so.

"We are going to wait for an hour or so for the ship to arrive, then we are going to take my skiff out in the sands and meet up with her. Once aboard, the Captain will take you to her cabins and explain things there. I want your word you will not endanger the ship, or her crew, while you are onboard. If you do, you will be tied to heavy stones and tossed into the sands." The almost dead, animal eyes of Acooshin looked at Billy for his response, and Billy got the feeling that if he did not agree, he would be going anyway, just not with as much freedom as he had now.

Rocking side to side slightly, Billy said, "Sure, I can do that much. I have plenty of questions, I hope Aurora,"

"Captain Aurora," Acooshin interrupted.

"Captain Aurora, then, will answer. I will, of course, answer any questions I am able to as well. I would rather, however, not board that ship if at all possible." Billy watched Acooshin to see if he would react to this, but he only seemed to be watching Billy.

"I am afraid the ship is a requirement for the meeting. The Captain is only stopping here to pick you up because you went looking for her." Acooshin pulled on one of the leather straps crossing his shoulder, and this tugged a small pack around for him to access. He untied a string holding it closed, and pulled out some things that looked like food. He also pulled another strap and this brought around a leather sack that likely held something to drink, as it sloshed a little when it moved.

"That's fine, then. I need answers and if she has them, all the better." Billy watched as Acooshin took out food and ate, then watched as he sipped from his waterskin.

Acooshin didn't ask if Billy wanted anything to eat or drink, but that was likely because he already knew Billy wasn't alive to begin with. The refreshments were quickly consumed, and Acooshin corked his skin, and weaved closed his knapsack of food, and slid both around his hip to rest on his back as he sat and looked over Billy.

Acooshin didn't know what to make of the hume weapon in front of him. He had, of course, seen plenty of these weapons during his tenure as First Mate on the Sandspray. Quite often his Captain would get word of some unfortunate group uncovering a hume research facility, only to release the weapons from ages past. These weapons weren't always arachnoidal, but they were insectile and absolutely ruthless in their slaughtering of everything in front of them. Yet, here sat one such machine not a foot in front of him. It had first appeared in the Lair of the Fey weeks ago, but looked nothing like it did now. His Ability, though, did not lie. This was the mechanoid by the name of Billy that he'd spoken to nearly a week past.

Billy looked more alive now than just a week ago, and this was probably due to the fact this machine somehow has access to the System. As far as he was aware, only things with souls could use the System, it seemed a requirement. As Acooshin watched Billy, he saw small tells that the machine wasn't in some kind of standby, ready to react. He was thinking, adjusting, and doing life processes. As he listened, Acooshin thought he could hear Billy breathing, or at least taking air into his body, and occasionally exhaling after a few moments. He was also adjusting his weight, as if his legs were getting cramped, or he was nervous.

The motion of his pedipalps was also something actual spiders did, constantly feeling around the environment and cleaning the feet and eyes. Billy was doing this seemingly subconsciously, and this helped with Acooshin's nerves. He was fairly certain he was safe with Billy, and that Billy would not kill him unexpectedly. Acooshin really was quite surprised that the information he'd collected about the machine was accurate. He'd followed Billy here, of course, and had watched him go through his own personal evolutions after clearing the unnamed Dungeon just the other day. He had seen Billy go in looking like a machine, and he'd come out looking almost alive, then he'd applied more changes not long after.

Acooshin had gone into the Dungeon a little ways after Billy had left it, and realized the place would require a small army to clear, and yet Billy had done so on his own. This worried the elf. Yet he knew that once they were out in the sand waves, no amount of power Billy had would be able to save him if he were tossed in with stones tied around his feet. And that would happen if the Captain thought the machine would turn on them.

Reaching into a pocket under his vest, Acooshin pulled out a small metal watch, popped open the cover, and checked the time it displayed. Billy watched this, and was mildly interested in the device, but said nothing. Acooshin then replaced the watch and patted the pocket it rested in.

"We have only another 20 minutes or so before the Sandspray arrives. I think we should prepare to leave. The skiff I brought here is a few hundred yards away, and we need to board and move out to meet the ship. It is difficult to tell, but there are razor-sharp rocks hiding in the sandwaves. We need to move beyond those and wait for the Captain to arrive." The elf held out a hand indicating Billy exit first, so he got up and shuffled out of the entrance, back into the wind and sand.

Billy turned and watched Acooshin exit, tug on his hat, and pull up his bandana to cover his nose and mouth. Acooshin then turned to face the sand ocean, and moved to the right, somewhat southerly, and began walking. Billy followed at a short distance, then moved up beside Acooshin to talk.

Speaking loud enough to be heard over the wind, Billy asked, "Do you think your skiff can hold us both? I weigh a bit more than you, I think."

The elf turned and observed Billy's footsteps in the sandy grass, and, seeing next to no marks of passage, looked back up at Billy.

"It is mostly a matter of balance, Mr. Billy. And based on how carefully you walk without leaving much trace of your passage, I feel confident in saying you are perfectly able to center yourself on a boat floating on the sands. And that's what sailing is all about, staying balanced."

Billy took this information in stride. He knew he was going for this ride, and would prefer not to be crushed in this strange, alien sand ocean, which seemed to violate everything he knew about fluid dynamics and physics. He knew very little of both, but it was getting increasingly difficult not thinking about how this ocean existed like water when he was soon to be sailing on some kind of boat over it.

"I will take your word on that, Acooshin. I've never been sailing before, so this will be a new experience for me."

Acooshin looked over at Billy, ducking his head to allow his wide-brimmed hat to deflect the blowing sands as he did so. Billy caught the side-eye and would have shrugged but had no actual shoulders.

"What?" Billy asked. "I know about sailing, sort of, but I have not had the opportunity to do so. I'm looking forward to it."

The elf said nothing as he turned back into the wind, mildly disturbed the machine seemed to read his expression, his eyes scanning for something ahead. In a few minutes Billy saw something moving on the grass, and he realized it was a cloth tarp covering a long boat of some sort. It looked quite small for what he was expecting.

Acooshin went to the tarped boat and tugged the cover off, carefully folding it as he did so, and wrapping it with a tie string. He collected the spikes and rope used to hold the tarp in place, and tossed the rolled tarp with them into the bottom of the skiff. The boat itself was only about 12 feet long, give or take, made of some kind of metal Billy could not easily identify, and saw it had some things attached to it he did not recognize.

Acooshin moved around the skiff and pulled on something lying in the boat, and round orbs fashioned onto the ends of swinging arms locked into place outside the skiff, and were held in place with several locking pins. There were four such devices which hung over the sides of the boat, and at the back was a rudder of metal, wide and vertically flat, hanging from a ring which would likely serve as a means to guide the boat once out in the ocean of sand.

What Billy couldn't figure out was how the boat would float on sand.

"How does it not sink?" He decided to ask instead of waiting to figure it out.

"These," Acooshin shouted, tapping on the strange orbs suspended off of the sides.

"Right, that clarifies wonderfully," Billy shouted back as he moved to the back of the boat, preparing to help push.

"Ah, there is no need for your help, Billy. Why don't you go ahead and hop in. I will get us out on the sands," Acooshin shouted, indicating the interior of the skiff near the front.

Billy turned to look into the boat, and saw there was very little space for someone like himself, and he would have to be sitting exactly in the middle and hold onto the sides with all eight of his legs. There were several boards placed just to be seats, but none of the bits of wood would be able to support Billy's mass by themselves.

As Billy was trying to figure out how he would maneuver into the boat, he heard a hum building up from the orbs. After a few seconds, the grass under the orbs began waving fiercely away from the orbs. Then, to Billy's astonishment, the boat lifted itself from the ground about an inch, and hung there.

Acooshin went around Billy, and deftly hopped over the side, into the boat and settled down on the bench with the rudder. He smiled over to Billy, and waved him aboard.

"Come, Billy. We need to catch the tide," Acooshin shouted over the wind. His strange goat eyes were alight with the joy of getting back out on the sea of sands.

With that, Billy climbed aboard the skiff and settled over the bottom of the boat, near the front, supporting himself by holding onto the sides with four of his eight feet, his other food resting on the bottom of the boat. He lowered his abdomen so that it was in the boat and not above it, and then slowly settled himself down until he was barely sitting on one of the benches. Once there, he locked his legs into place with a thought, and watched Acooshin.

"You should face the way we are going, Billy. It will be quite the sight!" Acooshin twisted the handle of the rudder and the orbs somehow rotated back, and the skiff slowly floated from the grass into the sandy waves. The sound of countless grains of sand lapping against the sides of the boat, along with the "mist" of dust made the experience quite mysterious. Somehow, Acooshin could navigate this environment. Billy could, of course, see where they were going, but could not figure out how Acooshin knew.

"Charlotte, how does Acooshin know where he's going? I can't see five feet past the bow," he sent this on his internal relay, and it took a moment for Charlotte to reply.

"I think, dear, you are forgetting that Navigation is a Talent, and such an Ability would, of course, allow those who master it to, I dare say, Navigate." Her tone was almost condescending, but Billy knew she was only teasing him. He was still new to this whole "everyone can use magical interfaces to interact with their reality" thing.

"Good point, Charlotte. I forgot about that." He remained silent as Acooshin pushed left or right on the rudder, moving the nose of the boat right or left respectively. He wondered why Acooshin was going on such a roundabout path when he saw dark blades of jagged rock poking through some of the waves they slid past. The red sand quickly hid the razor sharp rocks as they were sloshed over in waves, and soon they were past the rocks and out into a calmer sea.

Billy felt and saw them moving out into the 'open seas' when the fine dust vanished, and the waves of sand were much longer and more difficult to distinguish from one another, except from the sound the sand made as it slid across the bottom of the skiff. The orbs were keeping the boat from sinking in the sand, the hull of the skiff kept the sand from filling the inside, and the sound was amazing, like a million pieces of sandpaper scratching an endless supply of lumber. Billy, of course, had been taking pictures of the whole trip out. He would have quite the tale to tell once he returned to Earth.

Acooshin held the rudder steady for almost exactly 20 minutes. The hum of the orbs, and the scratching of the sands prevented nearly all verbal communications, so Billy sat calmly and enjoyed the adventure. He'd heard of stories of worlds with oceans consisting of moving sand, but he had never thought to see the actual thing. It was quite daunting, knowing that if someone fell into this they would sink almost immediately, never to be recovered. At least, that is what he thought would happen. He wasn't really sure.

Acooshin pointed ahead of them, and Billy turned a little to look. He saw dark, triangular sails stabbing into the sky, moving swiftly towards them. Acooshin angled the small skiff to reach the Sandspray quicker, and the hum of the orbs which propelled the boat increased in pitch as the skiff slid forward with a slight twist of his wrist. Billy held still over his bench, feeling the sand resist the boat's motion by trying to push up the bow.

As the small boat bobbed slowly on the sandy ocean, Billy kept an eye out for anything in the sand which might mean them harm. He had no idea if anything actually lived in the sand, but being on both an alien world and a world where magic existed, he thought anything could be possible.

"Does anything live in the sand?" Billy shouted to be heard over the grinding sand.

Acooshin saw Billy moving his manipulators, and he must have heard the question, as he responded, "Yes, but not in this part of the sea. At least, not this time of year." He said no more as he returned his eyes forward toward his approaching home. Billy had so many questions, but no time to ask.

Billy watched as the ship, the massive ship, approached their little, tiny, bobbing craft. As it got closer, Billy realized he was unaware of the scale of the Sandspray when seen from a distance. He'd had an image in his mind of a three masted boat, like what sailed long ago on Earth, but what he was seeing now, it gave him pause.

The ship was close to 300 yards long, if not longer. It looked like it was almost 50 yards wide at its widest point. It was shaped like the outline of a whale from Earth, but without the flapping tail part. The front was rounded up and back, creating a large, solid shield against the winds and sand, and it looked all to be made of some kind of wood, or plant. It was difficult to describe as the whole thing resembled a partial submarine with sails, and looked like it was made of some mix of tree, not wood, but a growing plant the size of a great tree, and with machines worked into the tree to give it the qualities of a giant cargo vessel.

And every so often, ports on the side of the ship would open up and blast sand from the interior out into the sand sea because unlike the little skiff, the Sandspray rode on the sand itself.

"The Sandspray!" Acooshin shouted as the giant ship drew upon them very quickly, then blasted past. The sand being sprayed out washed over the duo in the skiff as the ship's wake threatened to throw them into the sea as well.

In moments, someone aboard Sandspray had thrown something at the little skiff Billy was on, and that thing had somehow caught onto the skiff, and then they were rapidly pulled into a docking bay that opened up on the port side, near the stern. The wall quickly closed on the bay, and some kind of pump system pulled the sand that had followed them into this hold back out, and Billy realized the skiff had settled into a rack built into the bottom of the hold itself, perfectly.

"This way, Mr. Billy, if you will. The Captain is already waiting to speak with you." Acooshin adjusted the sleeves of his coat, and checked his hat, before moving to the middle of the skiff to prepare to leave.

Billy had a difficult time discerning what Acooshin was saying, as the hold they were in was filled with many sounds new to Billy.

Several sailors were shouting to one another as they secured ropes to the skiff and began pulling it out of the rack set in the floor. They were doing this while Billy and Acooshin were still in it, and once they stepped off the boat onto the walkway Billy saw the boat sliding on some rack system in the ceiling with pulleys on wheels riding rails, being pulled by ropes. The noise of the sand pumps was also quite new to Billy, as it sounded like massive vacuums going on.

"Mr. Billy, this way please," Acooshin said again, pulling Billy from his observations.

Billy followed Acooshin up some steps, and had to reorient his legs so that he could more easily fit into the narrow halls. The hallways were only a few feet wide, and about six feet tall. Billy's body was almost three feet wide, so a couple of steps into the hallway Billy found it necessary to transition to the walls to walk, which was almost as uncomfortable. Acooshin turned back and watched as Billy worked out the most efficient way to walk in the narrow halls and Billy thought he heard the elf chuckle to himself, but let it slide. He was the outsider, and possibly the danger to them, there was no reason for him to expect them to change the interior of the whole ship to accommodate him alone.

The passageways were mostly made of some kind of wood, and were straight, with intersecting rooms, and other passageways going off in different directions. There were places where ladders cut up or down through the floors, but these accesses were in alcoves set into places in the wall, and none of these would accommodate Billy. They were very narrow. Likely, this design was intentional but Billy wasn't sure.

Eventually, even with so many sailors moving through the hallways every once in a while, Acooshin managed to lead Billy to a set of stairs somewhere near the rear of the ship, and this gave Billy enough room to navigate upward. Billy passed floors of laughing and talking sailors, who went silent as he ambled by, then carried on in whispers once he was past. This bothered Billy a little, but only because he didn't want people to think he was some kind of monster, and that if they gave him some time to talk with them he could convince them he was on a mission to help this world recover from whatever catastrophe had befallen it.

After several flights of cramped but passable stairs, Billy was led into a large storage room that had more stairs going up the outside of the ship to an exterior upper deck. Looking back, Billy watched as the strange ship's rear undulated in the sands, providing some form of thrust for the ship to sail with. Looking forward on the ship, and up, Billy saw the body of the craft on the exterior here was riddled with several openings which all connected with an intricate array of stairs leading up and down.

Acooshin shouted at Billy to follow, and he did so, going up several more sets of stairs behind the First Mate. There were numerous elves on the rear of the ship going about their business, and all of them paused in their work to watch Billy and Acooshin pass. Billy continued to follow the First Mate upwards, and snapped the occasional picture for reference later. He also mapped his entire journey through the ship, simply because he was interested in how the ship worked. It was interesting to see the large numbers of elves living in such an alien vessel. Then again, he was on a different world from his own, and this understanding gave Billy more perspective.

It didn't take long before Acooshin finally led Billy to the helm of the ship, where Captain Aurora was standing by a large, spoked wheel.

"Mr. Acooshin. If you will, take the helm. I need a word with Mr. Billy," Aurora, now clad just like Billy imagined a pirate captain from Earth would be, in pantaloons, a clean white shirt, a fine vest, and with a very large, feathered tricorn hat, ushered Billy to follow her. She looked every bit the Jack Sparrow, but wasn't human, had actual feathers for hair, and had pale skin that had the contour of tree bark. She had large, horizontally slit eyes, which were a stunning shade of yellow, almost gold. And she had quite strange ears, something a little off from what he expected. He'd seen a large number of elves in the last few weeks, but none of them had their ears exposed. Most wore some kind of coverings, or their own feathery hair concealed them. Now, seeing as Aurora had hers purposefully uncovered, Billy could see they were small, round holes not unlike that of birds.

Aurora caught Billy looking at her, and she seemed to take this as some kind of insult.

"I said, Mr. Billy, this way to my office," she said, still holding out her hand to an open door behind the wheelhouse.

Billy shook himself out of his study of Aurora, and said, "Sorry, you just look much different from last we met. I didn't mean to offend," he finished, leading the way through the door to the Captain's room.

The room itself was quite large, with a bed along one wall, and a screen set up near a dresser. The walls looked like they were polished wood, and had many pictures stuck to it. There were also several maps in various places. The rear of the room had several large windows, and opened these led out to a balcony. The center of the room was dominated by a large, rectangular table of ancient looking, polished wood. Behind this, near the windows, was a large wooden desk. It was all very well organized and clean.

Taking this all in as he moved inside, Billy noticed there were small orbs in the ceiling and along the walls which provided a soft but strong white light that lit the room entirely. Billy wondered if this was similar to electric lights, but he then recalled magic existed and it could be that these were magical lights instead. He stepped to the side, and turned to watch the Captain enter, and she closed the door behind her and removed her very large hat, tossing it onto a hatrack beside the screen on the port side of the room.

She walked past Billy, who turned to watch her walk. She went to her large desk on the other side of the round table, lifted up a leg to place her foot on the desk, then removed her boot. First one, then the other, and she tossed these beside her desk before moving behind it and setting in the large, cushioned chair.

"Mr. Billy, I need to know what you know of the humes. Their base locations. Their plans for invading. I need to know how many machines they plan to bring this time, and what their goals are." Aurora leaned forward as she made her demands, placing her elbows on the desk and resting her chin on the tips of her fingers.

Billy, for his part, had no idea what Aurora was talking about. He wasn't part of the hume's military, he had no idea what their goals are, or were. Instead of immediately answering, he moved around the table looking at the maps, scratching his chin with his manipulator.

"I don't know anything about the humes, Aurora,"

"Captain Aurora, Mr. Billy," Aurora corrected.

"Aurora, I don't know," he began again.

"I said you will refer to me as Captain Aurora, Mr. Billy," Aurora emphasized by slapping her hand on the table, hard.

"Look, I will make this very, very clear. I am not from this world, Aurora. I have no idea who, or even what, humes are. I came to this world with knowledge from mine, and an example of how that means nothing is thus; we have stories about elves, long hair, who are good with bows, and they have pointy ears. You have, as far as I can tell, none of those qualities."

"Get to the point, Mr. Billy, you are wasting my very valuable time," Aurora once again interrupted.

"I don't know anything about humes. I don't know what they look like, where they are, what they want, or why they're doing what they're doing," he said in a rush, before getting interrupted again.

"I don't believe you, Mr. Billy. You have five minutes to convince me otherwise, or I will have large rocks tied to your limbs and toss you into the sea." Aurora sat back in her chair and crossed her legs.

Billy thought for a minute about what he could say to convince Aurora he was not a tool for the humes. He checked his inventory for an object which could convince her, but he did not wish to relinquish any of his things. He thought of information he could give her, but he knew nothing of this world, and knew much of what he knew of Earth was useless here. In fact, some folks here didn't think Earth, in their lore, was even real.

Then he had an idea, piecing together bits and pieces of information he'd collected while out and about. He reached forward, and in his mind held the intent to give Aurora 10 Experience points. His strange, blue haired, mechanical hand hung suspended over the top of Aurora's desk and she just looked at it. Then, after a moment, she reached forward with her own hand, and took Billy's into hers. Then her eyes widened as she received a prompt asking her if she would like to receive a gift of 10 Experience points.

Not quite believing her eyes, she chose *Yes*, and then she let out a small gasp in surprise, and released Billy's hand.

"It's true then. You have access to the System, and can expend the Experience you acquire. Machines cannot do this." She sat back, somewhat perplexed about being wrong. Then she stood up, and went to a series of weighted ropes, and pulled one. A moment later, a sailor knocked on the door, and poked their head inside.

"Captain?"

"Yes, bring refreshments. Call off the guard. Put us on course for the Isles."

"Captain?" The elf said.

"I said all is well, Lieutenant. Now carry out my orders."

"Yes, Captain," And the elf closed the door.

Apparently the good Captain Aurora had intended to toss Billy into the ocean of sand regardless of what he had to say, but giving her evidence she could not refute had changed her mind.

Captain Aurora stood from behind her desk and picked up her boots, and put them back on the same way she removed them. Billy watched, not really knowing what was going to happen now that he had told yet another native he was not native himself.

"If I may ask, Captain, what do humes look like? I have heard of them from everyone, but I have not seen anything to distinguish them from anyone else." He waited while she tied her last boot on, and then she stood, straightening her shirt and vest.

Then, she passed Billy and went to a chest on the starboard side of the room, and opened it, removing a portrait. Then she closed the lid, and returned to hand it to Billy. What he saw, as a rough drawing in what could be pencil, was something not much unlike a velociraptor, but very feathered, with three fingered hands, short tails, and sky-blue scales. The one in the picture had goggles on, and wore complex looking clothing like would be worn by a modern Earth construction worker back home. It had a belt with straps that went over narrow shoulders, which held up pants that had various pockets and tools clipped on. The raptor, the hume he had to remind himself, carried what looked an awful lot like a machine gun, and extra bullets hung from bandoliers. It also appeared to carry a sidearm, and its feet had toeless boots that allowed its claws, both front and back, to protrude unhindered.

The hume looked fierce, and was much like an earthling would predict intelligent life could have evolved into if dinosaurs continued to live and not go extinct. They would have evolved language, and tools, and the written word, and technology. Mammals would not have had the chance to exist, and would likely have been either food or pets, or made extinct themselves as pests.

Billy took snapshots of the portrait, and after only a minute of looking at it, handed it back to Captain Aurora. She returned it to the chest, and then went to the large rectangular table, a finger tapping on a section of its edge.

To Billy's surprise, the table began doing things. He turned to face it, and squinted as he watched the surface morph into a textured map of the area around the Sandspray, with its replica centered. All around the ship was reddish colored sand, long waves pulsating through it much like it would have if the ocean of sand were water instead. Then, Captain Aurora motioned at the projection and it zoomed out. It kept zooming out until the vast majority of the table was sand, except part of the eastern edge of the map.

A shard of land, much like a scar, rose above the ocean of sand, and cut a swathe across the world. As Aurora continued to zoom the map out, Billy saw other scars, one far to the north and another far to the south of the land he had awoken on. He paid very close attention, and saw that his personal map was updating with this information as he saw it.

Captain Aurora kept zooming out the map until most of the features on land were pale smears of color, surrounded by a planet-covering ocean of red sand. Then, Billy saw the curvature of the world he was on, and realized it was much, much larger than Earth. The scars, which were land stabbing through the sand ocean, looked like something unimaginably massive scratched the planet with its three claws, and the result was that the ground rose and hardened. And the scratches went most of the way around the massive world.

And everything else, every millimeter of the world that wasn't part of those three bands, was red shifting sand.

"This is our world, Mr. Billy. As you can see, it is almost entirely covered in sand, except for these three strips of land which nearly circumnavigate the world. They are all approximately 2,000 miles wide, and more than 30,000 miles long. We aren't sure of the exact dimensions. The sands obfuscate the borders."

Curious, and because this looked unnatural, Billy wondered aloud, "How long has it been like this?"

"It has been like this for the last 4,000 years, give or take," Aurora said with sadness tinging her voice.

Captain Aurora's answer to what he thought was an idle thought brought Billy back into the moment.

"There are records that go back far enough to prove this?" Billy's question had Captain Aurora hesitate before responding.

"You truly don't know?" Captain Aurora looked mildly surprised at his question, as if she expected he'd made up his mad story of not being from this world, whatever that meant.

"I did say I am not from this world, Captain. I have no idea what the history of this world is like, and nobody back in the Lair of the Fey knew either. None that I spoke with, anyways." Billy moved around the map so he could get clear pictures of the planet, now fully floating above the surface of the table.

Aurora's cool voice said, "Noone from the Lairs can be trusted, Billy. They're monsters."

Billy looked past the image of the world into Captain Aurora's eyes. She seemed quite serious about this statement.

"What about the elves there? Are they monsters, too?"

"Yes, Billy. All of them are, except for those of us who venture there looking for clues on how to conquer the humes influence over our world. All of the Dungeons, Lairs, and other places which can be delved by adventuresome folk, contain clues about the invasion, and also give us the power to overcome the obstacles which are in our way." She tapped the edge of the round table, and the globe collapsed into pale, glittering dust that settled invisibly onto the surface of the table once again.

"What invasion?" Billy asked in confusion.

Chapter 21

"How many times do I have to say this, Mr. Billy. The humes are invaders. They are not from this world. They came long ago, put the scars on the world, and buried the rest of it in impenetrable sand. The only things that survive now either live on ships like this, or have migrated onto the scars and fight against the monsters seeking a means to repulse these monstrosities." Captain Aurora seemed on the point of exhaustion all of a sudden, as if she had a hope that Billy could provide some information she desperately needed, but he didn't seem to have it.

Billy, on the other hand, was getting a very clear picture of what was going on, if not why. Aliens have invaded this planet, and are in the midst of terraforming it. Some of the native life, the elves, survived the initial impact, and are doing everything in their power to use the Experience provided by these invaders to overcome them.

"Is there any record of anyone speaking with the humes about why they came here to terraform this particular world?" Billy moved away from the table as he watched Captain Aurora walk back to her chair and practically collapse into it with a huff.

"If there were, we do not have them. Does that really matter, though?" Captain Aurora's voice sounded weary talking about the past.

"That depends. If anyone has opened a dialogue with these humes to explain anything at all, perhaps that dialogue mentioned what the humes came here for." Billy walked slowly to the window overlooking the balcony as he organized his thoughts. "If these aliens came here to find a new home, they inadvertently destroyed yours. If they came to take over resources you had, they succeeded. If they were fleeing some calamity, it could be on its way here. Any number of things could be going on, none of which we are prepared to deal with at any scale," Billy said as he turned to see Captain Aurora was watching him carefully. "Did elves, or any of the other beings on this world, have access to the System before the humes arrived?"

This question brought a wrinkle to Captain Aurora's already wrinkled brow. "Yes, why? Didn't you have access back on the world you came from?"

Billy rubbed his manipulators together before answering. "No, we had nothing like this System you have in this world. We understood the fantasy of having such a thing aid us in our lives, in fictional stories, but not in actuality."

Captain Aurora seemed confused at this admission. "So, you gained access to the System after you came to this world?"

"I did, and I think that when the humes arrived, if they also did not have access to the System, something here allowed them to have access as well. And this likely changed them in some way unexpected by anyone." Billy scratched at his chin while letting all the implications filter through his mind.

As he did this, Charlotte moved, and Captain Aurora caught sight of the motion. She stood quickly, and drew a saber from somewhere and leveled it at Billy's eyes.

"What is that on your head, Mr. Billy. I saw it move, so don't lie and tell me it is nothing."

Billy slowly held open his hands to indicate he meant no harm and said, "This is my personal assistant, Charlotte. She takes care of my body when I require maintenance." On his internal relay he sent a message to Charlotte to dismount and introduce herself.

Captain Aurora watched as crystalline limbs unfurled from around Billy's head and eyes, and straightened to stand beside Billy. She was much smaller in the stature, but had very long, clear limbs, each at least four feet long, perhaps more.

Charlotte's grandmotherly voice was calm and collected as she introduced herself, "Hello, Captain Aurora. I am Charlotte, Billy's personal assistant. As he has mentioned, I take care of him periodically."

Captain Aurora, only now realizing she was outnumbered, but not being threatened, lowered her blade. "Is there anyone else hiding on your person I should know about, Mr. Billy? Shall I expect," She trailed off as Billy, with Charlotte's assistance, began to shed thick plates of metal from his frame, laying them in a pile on the decking.

"These are bots of mine. They perform simple tasks for a short time, and require rewinding often to keep them operating." He picked up one of the flat plates, and pressed on it, and it popped into the rough shape of a spider, but not as finely detailed as either himself or Charlotte. On top of the thing was a shiny brass key, which Billy turned before setting the blue-haired bot on the ground.

"What is it doing?" Captain Aurora asked, watching the thing carefully.

"I have set it to accept simple commands from you for a short time, if you wish to order it around." Billy waved a manipulator forward, and the bot made its normal bot sounds as it trundled forward.

"Dance," She said, the first thing which came to mind. To her surprise, the bot began doing some form of dance, legs lifting and sliding across the floor, doing pirouettes and spins, like an arachnoidal ballerina. It did this for a few seconds, then finished with a spidery bow.

"Oh wow, that was very nice dancing. What else can they do, Mr. Billy? And, if I may ask, can I have one?"

Billy scratched his spider chin again and thought about that. After a moment, he shrugged as best he could and scooped up the bot. He removed a particular internal component, and replaced it with another he pulled from his Assembler, which Captain Aurora hadn't seen him do, and pulled the key out. The bot collapsed back into its plate shape in an instant, and he stuffed a different key back in.

"Pull this key and it will revert to its standby shape, wind the key and tell it what to do, and it will do what it can as long as its wound up. It'll run for about 25 minutes or so before it needs winding again. It will also need cleaning, occasionally." He reached back under his cloak and pulled a small box he had just made and handed this to Captain Aurora as well. "And this has the tools, and instructions, on how to maintain the lil guy."

Captain Aurora, truly surprised Billy would give her such advanced technology for nothing, was skeptical.

"Is this a spy of some sort?" She asked with skepticism.

Billy chuckled at this. "No, Captain Aurora. Its link to my communications relay was severed. That's what this thing was," He said, holding up the component he had removed a moment ago. "I installed a new component coded to you specifically, and it will only listen to you from now on. It won't even take instructions from me any more." He pocketed the component as she took the toolbox from him.

She opened the small tin box and looked at the strange tools inside but then turned and set the box on the table. "How do I order the, what did you call it, bot? How do I order the bot around?"

"Just give it a designation, bot will do if you want, and then tell it what you want it to do."

"Bot," Captain Aurora tested the word, looking directly at the plate now lying on the floor.

"You have to wind it up first," Billy said with a chuckle, pointing a manipulator digit at the brass key.

Blushing, Captain Aurora leaned down and gave the key a few turns, then set it back down and watched as the machine unfurled itself.

"Bot, go fold my laundry in that basket over there," She said, pointing to the basket near her bunk.

The little bot began moving to the basket, dumped it out onto the floor, and then began to examine and fold each article of clothing. It then placed each folded article on the bed. After a few minutes watching, Captain Aurora saw the little bot pick up the basket and return it to its initial position, and returned to her. She heard its tiny, complicated gears whirring away as it waited, and the little brass key very slowly rotated.

"When you want it to stop doing anything, push down on the key until it clicks, and the bot will revert to its standby shape."

Captain Aurora pushed down, hard, on the brass key until it clicked. The bot popped and whirred and reshaped itself into a thick metal plate and went silent.

"This is amazing, Mr. Billy. Is there any limit to the number of these you or I can manage?"

Billy thought for a moment before he answered. "Are you aware of the Talent, Leadership?"

"Yes, of course. It is how I can manage such a large ship with a crew of over 1,000 sailors," She said, waving her hand dismissively.

"That is the limit. These are treated like followers, or friends, or whatever. Your command limit for these falls under that Talent."

"Ah, this makes some sense. They must be somewhat intelligent, then?" Her question was one Billy had not expected.

Billy paused for a moment before answering. "I don't think so? I mean, if I lift a rock, does the rock 'know' that when I let go of it that it has to fall?"

"Of course it does," Captain Aurora said immediately. "How else would it know to fall down?"

"Ah, well. It is not intelligent, Captain. It is a machine with a limited number of functions. For example, these bots cannot fly if you command them to. They cannot swim either. Or write, even though they comprehend commands."

"So they are the perfect slave?"

"No," Billy said. "These are not slaves. They have no thoughts, no feelings. No requirements for entertainment, reproduction, or sustenance. They're machines. You command it to do a thing, and so long as you rewind it often, it will do that thing forever if it can."

Captain Aurora reached down and picked up the thick plate and grunted at its heft. She turned and placed it on her desk and waved Billy around to the front of her desk.

"So, you are not a hume infiltrator, or an assassin. You are as much an alien as they are. Why are you here, then?" Captain Aurora was paying very close attention to Billy as he walked around the desk to sit in front of it. She noted he did not answer immediately, but waited patiently for him to reply.

"Back on my world, not even two months ago, I found an object." As Billy began his explanation, Charlotte worked her way around Billy, performing his regular maintenance. After an hour of explaining how he'd ended up on this world, of which he still did not know the name of, he rushed through his time in the Lair of the

Fey, his discoveries in there, what he learned of the history of this world from Orgar, and the trip to the rendezvous point.

Captain Aurora listened patiently and, at one point, had one of her mates bring in more refreshments. She opened a book when Billy began and took notes of his story, often asking clarifying questions and writing those responses down for future reference. She had many questions about where he erupted from the underground facility, and he managed to share his map data with the table. He walked her through his travels, marking the places and events as best he could on the strange map. He detailed as much of the history of the world as he could recall of his conversations with Orgar.

Captain Aurora was astounded by the degree of fidelity his mapping provided. She knew almost immediately he was telling the truth when he perfectly mapped his route from the Lair of the Fey to the rendezvous point. Her First Mate had already sent her this very same information the day before. She thought Billy would lie at some point, but he hid absolutely nothing, as far as she could tell.

"I have plenty of my own questions about this world, first and foremost is, what is this world called?"

Captain Aurora finished writing something in her book and then looked up at Billy with a small smile on her face. "Let me say this first before we get sidetracked, Billy. The history of the world you learned from the dwarf, Orgar, is false. Ask any monsters in the Liars or Dungeons and you will get nothing but wild tales inconsistent with one another. Second, this world was once called Harmony. It has since been changed to Calamity."

Billy had been prepared to hear this, so he instead responded to the world's name. "Harmony? That is a wonderful name, Captain. Would it be alright if I call it that instead of Calamity? I like to see the positive in things, not focus on the negative."

Captain Aurora ran a hand through her long, feathery hair. "It doesn't matter, Mr. Billy. None of this may matter, anyway."

Billy looked up to Aurora. She looked exhausted, right on the cusp of giving up. She must have received some bad news before they boarded. "What happened?"

"There was only one other vessel our people had, apart from Sandspray here, and we only heard just this morning the ship went down in a storm. There were no survivors." Tears began to slide from her strange golden eyes.

"I'm sorry to hear that, Captain. I didn't realize how desperate things were, or I would have come sooner."

"It wouldn't have mattered, Mr. Billy. They were on the opposite side of Calamity when it happened. There was nothing we could have done from here." She let a few tears fall in silence, and Billy let her have her moment. She opened a drawer and, withdrew a handkerchief and wiped her face dry, gathering herself. "What matters now is that we find a way to end this disaster. And we must do it soon before the news spreads through the crew. We are the last free people on Calamity, Mr. Billy. And if you can't help us break free of the humes, we will perish forever."

Billy sat there, taking in all of the information he had about this situation.

"Where do the Dungeons and Lairs come into this? Are these natural phenomena, or are they artificial?" He felt he could possibly help these elves, apparently the last of the native race of this world, but he had to know so much. Too much, he feared, to make a clear decision.

"What do you mean? There have always been Dungeons on Calamity. Dungeons and Lairs and Hives. They have always been." Captain Aurora looked somewhat confused about the question.

"Alright, Captain, alright. But were they present before The Calamity?" Billy emphasized the event.

"I don't see what this has to do with the present situation, Mr. Billy."

"It could be a symptom, is all I'm saying. A reaction to whatever caused the scarring on this world and covered its surface in sand." Billy thought about what he'd just suggested, and this brought to mind several instances of Dungeons from anime back on Earth. Some genres of stories had Dungeons with an object at their hearts, and if you removed this thing, the Dungeons vanished. This usually didn't stop other Dungeons or their like from appearing, but preventing them from perpetuating was like lancing boils and letting whatever the Dungeons were taking from the land leak back out into the world so things could settle down.

Looking back up to Captain Aurora, Billy scratched his chin, "Is there a Dungeon, or a Lair or whatever, nearby that we could perhaps explore?"

"You want to harvest Experience?" she looked almost disgusted at the prospect.

"No, I want to see if we can sever whatever is linking the places to this world. I just don't know if it's either possible or if it will do anything positive or negative. Has nobody any ideas on what to do? Do you have any ideas, Captain?"

Captain Aurora poured another drink from a porcelain bottle and took a long swallow. Carefully setting down the cup, the Captain looked back over to her chest and sighed.

"We have had some ideas over the centuries about what to do. The problem is that anyone who goes into those places for very long is corrupted by the place. If they stay too long, they don't come back out."

Curious, he asked, "Is that why you didn't stay very long in the Lair of the Fey?"

"Yes, we can only stay for a short time to see if we can find any of our brethren and perhaps free them from the place. I was doing that when we caught sight of you and left shortly after you escaped us." Captain Aurora sighed again, and she seemed to deflate a little, collapsing back into her large chair. "Sorry about that, by the way."

Billy waved the apology away with a manipulator. Instead he asked, "Do Dungeons, or whatever, have anything in them which can be destroyed to close down the thing?"

"Yes. Yes, there is something called a shard in them, and if destroyed, the Dungeon will cease to produce monsters."

Leaning forward, Billy asked, "What are the repercussions of doing that?"

Sighing, she said, "Nothing. Once the shard is destroyed, whatever powers the Dungeons dies."

"What happens to the monsters in those Dungeons?"

Captain Aurora looked up to Billy, her eyes carrying a great sadness in them. "The shards give unholy power to all beings it maintains. Take that power away, and.." she trailed off.

"They die, don't they?" Billy knew this was the case before the Captain even nodded. Billy thought about all of the people in the Lair of the Fey. He felt a deep sadness building inside himself, thinking about all of those people, the dwarves, elves, beastkin, all of them enraptured by the power flooding the entire city. It was doing something to them; it was changing them.

"What are the poles outside the Lair of the Fey for?" Billy inquired.

"Poles?" Captain Aurora wrinkled her brow. "They just mark where the Lair can be entered or exited from.

"Any idea where that place exists relative to the rest of the world?"

Confused, she said, "As far as I know, it doesn't exist anywhere. It is its own place."

Billy pulled up his Status, and tapped the tab which listed his maps. He had maps from when he was on Earth, but the longer he was on this world the lower the fidelity was getting back there. There was a little gauge handily providing that tidbit of information for Billy. There was also a map of this world, which had been updated with the name Calamity. He also had a selection for the maps of the Dungeons and Lairs he had personally visited himself. But they weren't individual maps for the Dungeons and Lairs, it was one giant map, and the different Dungeons or Lairs were marked much like a city or town would be on any other map. They had a distance between them, with black between. Nothing. What was in the nothing outside those places? Outside of them, but not in this world?

Looking at the Lair of the Fey, Billy tapped, zoomed in and out, and rotated what he had recorded while he was there, and something caught his attention, near the places he had entered and exited. The poles were there, the city was there, the blocks were there, but what was also there, was an area past them.

Billy flipped to his map of Calamity and saw that all of the places he had ventured through, which occupied what he thought of as the Lair's boundary, were not only passable, but also part of Calamity, showing his route through the area on his map just as he'd made it.

On his week long jaunt to try and circumnavigate the Lair on the inside, Billy had stumbled across multiple poles leading out into the world, which he'd poked his head between to get his map updated then, and he looked at those places now. He compared the scales and found that no matter how he rotated or altered the size of the city, it wouldn't line up with the points he had collected on Calamity.

Then he looked around the room, at the maps there and caught sight of his reflection on a mirror near Captain Aurora's bed, and a thought hit him. He focused once more on his markers for the Lair of the Fey, and inverted the markers, and adjusted the scale, and the poles snapped over one another, and he froze as he received a prompt.

Congratulations! You have discovered an anomaly caused by the calamity that has struck this world, which none before you has realized. The world Harmony has come into contact with a reality which exists in reflection to its own laws of nature, and this has created rifts between the two worlds which are trying to exist in the same place at the same time.

The intersection of the two realities has created Heart Shards which serve as anchors, holding the two realities in place. This has forced the two realities to try to occupy the same space at the same time, with opposing physics warring to destroy one or the other. The longer this happens, the sooner the two realities will connect, letting physics play out. Seek the Heart Shards of the Dungeons, Lairs and Hives around the world and sever their ties to Harmony, or the calamity of two opposing realities colliding will annihilate both.

Heart Shards remaining: 5

Billy stumbled back as he read the quest update. He had a goal now. He had a progress bar.

"What is it, Mr. Billy?" Captain Aurora had seen Billy freeze all motion as he had realized something, and she wanted to know what happened.

"I think I know what to do to fix Harmony," He said after taking a moment to collect himself. "But it will take some time."

"What can we do?" The Captain nearly begged.

"Do you know of any Dungeon locations?"

"Of course, we know of all of them. Over the centuries, my people scoured the lands as they've grown. We have done all in our power to seal them off, or to destroy them if at all possible." Captain Aurora went to her chest once more and rifled around in it before bringing out a large, leather bound book back to the desk and opening it. She turned the pages of the old book, its worn pages covered in fading ink. She read some of the writing a few pages in, and flipped to near the back, which Billy saw contained several iterations of the scars of the world, with markings.

Tapping small marks on the last map, Captain Aurora looked at Billy and said, "This map has every place we have ever discovered marked." She flipped back a few pages and Billy saw the scars were smaller and the ocean of sand was larger. "These older maps were made every few hundred years as we began to notice the land was changing. We did not know at the time what was happening but we kept track, as best we could, of each one we encountered and the few we managed to close."

The Captain slid the book over to Billy, and he carefully turned the ancient parchment to capture an image of every page. He could not read any of the text, but he would take care of this momentarily.

"I need you to tell me what all of the symbols mean, and the words, as best you can, Captain. I want to get the best idea of what was going on from the source, if you will." Billy carefully turned from the back of the book to the front, and turned the book so Captain Aurora could teach him the language.

"I will do my best, Billy. This will take a while, but first we need to set a new course."

"Take us to the nearest, known Dungeon that isn't the Lair of the Fey, and then we can get started," Billy suggested.

Dust stained the lower hull red as the Sandspray moved over the ocean of shifting red granules. A constant, steady gust carried the ship many miles every hour as the survivors of Harmony did their best to go about their daily lives. Billy spent most of his time with Captain Aurora, learning the true history from the books in her care. She would often bring in various people from around the ship to provide their own family history to the best of their knowledge. During that time, Billy slowly, but meticulously built up a mental map of the shifting world which was Harmony, now Calamity, and a guide to the history of the people of Harmony.

From many voices came stories of strife and desperation passed down through the generations. Huge armies sent to fend off the monsters spraying from Dungeons across a growing landscape surrounded by endless sand. Tales of death on a grand scale as harrowing battles to close the pits spewing forth seemingly alien power, mixed with the draw of youth to explore the unknown and returning with more power than was reasonable, steadily ruined the world's populations.

Throughout these stories Billy learned the humes, who had appeared at the same time as the scars did, had at first tried to aid the elves in their battle against the Dungeons. But something changed shortly after their arrival and the humes broke from the elves to do something of their own design. Nobody on the ship knew what that design was, nor did they know of their goal, but since they broke from the elves in their fight against the Dungeons, the elves began losing ground.

The ships the elves were using now were developed in partnership with the humes in an effort to search the world over for whatever was left that wasn't sand, or to reach the strange growing scars which contained all the land remaining on Calamity. After the humes separated from the elves, the ships were left to the elves in totality, practically abandoned once the world had been completely covered and mapped. The hume's last known location was on the very landmass Billy himself had appeared on. He had seen none of them, but supposed they were on the other side of the gigantic lake from where he'd been. The maps seemed to agree, as well as that of the tales from the various elves who had been on missions in those parts.

Billy's journey had taken him away from the humes, and closer to the other shard of land. He knew the tip of the continental strip he had arrived on was likely to be a fluke, but he felt deep down that he was placed in that location for a reason, and he had not placed in some random body elsewhere to save the world. He, therefore, decided that he would be dealing with the Lair of the Fey last. It would be the hardest thing to take care of, as his friends whom he'd spent most of a month with were there, and were apparently monsters, and not actual people. They were manifestations of the link between two realities mixing, embodied undoubtedly by the presence of a Heart Shard. He was not looking forward to dealing with that can of beans any time soon.

By the time the Sandspray crossed the sands to the next continental scar, Billy had learned the elven language as written, as well as several dialects of it. He was even able to get eyes on a book written by a hume named Zyser-gan, a scientist who spent most of his life researching a Dungeon he had labeled "Abyssal Bore" who eventually became corrupted from spending so much time in it. The journal was a copy of a copy of a copy, and itself was almost falling apart, but it showed the gradual shift in mentality of Zyser-gan from a sane being to an insane monster. He was thought to have been killed by his peers, who barely managed to escape with some of his work. This book contained many of the research notes, but not all of them, and the only reason anyone knew of the poor scientist's fate was because someone had made a note in the back about it.

The reason Billy was interested in the work of Zyser-gan was because the course Captain Aurora set was towards this particular Dungeon. Once they reached land, it would be several days of travel through monster infested land, thanks to the overflow state of nearly all of the remaining Dungeons, Lairs and Hives.

Weeks after Billy had departed land, he finally heard that the ship had sighted land once again. He went to the helm, at the back of the ship that faced forward, which looked over the whole of the population of elves. The helm was busy sending messages to the ships guidance, preparing everyone for the arrival to land. People were going all over the place, preparing parties to go overland to scavenge food, water and other necessities. Billy stood near the Captain's chair, waiting for her to make the decision to send out skiffs.

Turning to Billy, Captain Aurora asked once again, "Are you sure you will be alright going alone, Mr. Billy? I can't convince you to take a few guards?"

Captain Aurora had asked this of Billy several times over the last couple of days, but Billy just turned to her and said, "You know none of them will be able to keep up with me, Captain. And I think speed is of the essence. The sooner I get there, the sooner I can clear the place and get back."

Struggling to maintain her composure, she tried again by saying, "Yes, but I would still prefer it if someone went with you."

For the hundredth time, Billy said, "Captain, if I take anyone with me, it will take me 10 times longer to get to the Abyssal Bore, and that much again coming back. I have explained this already."

Captain Aurora rubbed a hand over her face, the strange skin of her people making an odd sound as she did this.

"Fine, but we will be waiting here until you get back. Our holds are mostly full, and we will only be sending out small groups a few times a week. The important thing is that if one of the sand beasts comes, we will have to move and you might not have an easy means to contact us."

Billy thought for a moment, then he queued up a quick few sticks of chemicals. The extruder only took a few minutes to make the things, and when he was done Billy handed Aurora the special flares.

"After the second week, launch this towards land. Red tells me you went south. Green tells me you went north. Yellow tells me you went west. Blue tells me you went east. If you move the ship, send one of these out, and I'll decide what to do then if I see them. Try and stick close to the land if possible. With luck I will be able to find you once I'm done." He handed her each of the color coded sticks and showed her how to use them. She took the flares and placed them in a satchel she kept at her waist, which sat on her lap while she was in her chair.

"Thank you, Billy. If you succeed, we shall hopefully meet again in a few weeks. If you fail, well. Don't. That's an order Mr. Billy." Her serious look, with her golden eyes looking hard at Billy would have made him swallow, if he was capable.

"Aye aye, Captain Aurora," was all he said.

Captain Aurora waved to a nearby sailor, and gave him swift directions to take Billy to Hold 4. "Once there, he is to be taken to land as swiftly as possible, then the skiff is to return with haste." She gave Billy one last nod, and turned back to her crew to give out still more orders.

Billy followed the sailor through the ship, across the deck, and down through the bowels to Hold 4. Once there, he boarded the small boat, and it was released to float atop the sandy waves of the ocean. It took almost an hour for the craft to take Billy to land, at which time Billy helped turn the craft around and then pushed it back out to float in the sand. He waved to the sailor, pulled up his map, and turned to face the climb up the side of the continental scar.

"Charlotte?" Billy spoke aloud.

"Yes, dear?" She replied from her position between his main eyes.

"What do you think our chances are?"

He felt her moving her legs around his head as she thought for a moment.

"I think we have about a 50/50 chance, dear. We will either succeed, or we will not," She said, wisely.

Without saying another word, Billy cranked up his boiler power, and started running up the long, boulder covered slope.

It took them a couple of hours to reach the top of the slope, at which point Billy was able to see the land ahead. Out at sea, the land was several miles up in relative elevation to the sand and remained hidden from below. Billy knew it would have a similar look to the other scar though, and was not very surprised to see the strange bladed grasses growing as far as he could see. Far in the distance, perhaps 20 miles or so, a line of mountains cut across this part of the continent. There was a pass in the middle, however, and that would lead right to the entrance of his destination.

The Abyssal Bore was a doorway on the side of the mountain range. Its interior supposedly resembled that of a bore hole with stairs spiraling around its edges, leading from one floor of chaos to the next as it continued deep into the world. The pass itself was basically a canyon. There was a narrow river which cut deep through the range, and was traversable on either side. The Bore was located, from this direction, on the left side. Once Billy reached the canyon pass after nearly a week of monster dodging later, he stopped. From what he'd learned from Captain Aurora, it had not been explored in centuries, now.

"Charlotte, there's gold in this river," Billy said when they arrived outside the canyon.

"There is gold in most rivers, dear. The water draws it from.."

"I know, Charlotte," Billy reached down and plucked up a grape-sized orb of pure gold, "But is there this much?"

Charlotte looked down at the large glob of gold, and her legs twitched a little.

"This is the first time we have come into contact with non-Dungeon gold, dear. We definitely require this for one of the upgrades you have postponed for a number of weeks." Charlotte carefully dismounted from her place and stepped into the water. Her own manipulators came up with her, and she held an apple-sized ball of gold she could barely hold to.

Billy quickly snagged the valuable metal and set it on the ground. Pulling up his Status page, he went to check his Experience points. He had much more than he thought he should have. Digging through his logs, he found he had received a portion of the Experience he had accumulated from his apartments back in the Lair of the Fey.

He wondered at this, and scratched at his spider chin as he scanned his logs. At some point during his absence, Sharea had gained access to the Administrator column again, and she opened the park and the store. She and Elsie had made quite a bit of Experience and coins from the abundant greenhouses, which they had also upgraded to increase productivity in his absence.

Then he saw that a little over a week ago she had used a chunk of his bank there to purchase another block and two more parks. She had basically copied them, and had linked them all together. Between Sharea and Elsie, they had made thousands upon thousands of Experience points from sales, and tens of thousands in coins. Billy was rolling in the one resource he needed a nearly endless supply of. As it was, his absence had still granted him an allotment of about 2% after everything was taxed by the city for maintenance and other costs, but that was still a chunk of Experience points exceeding 100,000, and he was in dire need of performing the one upgrade he had wanted since the day after he'd arrived in Calamity.

Chapter 22

"Alright, Charlotte. Let's get the bots out and looking for the precious metals in this river, then we will begin the upgrade process. It shouldn't take too long thanks to the gains from the city property I own. I can use some of the Experience to decrease the upgrade period to a quarter what it is without, and the gold, Gloopos and gemstones will make everything else possible."

Charlotte was already moving around Billy and winding the bots as he deployed them from his abdomen and compartments. While she did this, Billy shed most of his inventory, except the Gloopos population, and set it all on the rocky ground beside the river. On a whim, Billy decided to name this nameless river El Dorado. He chuckled to himself as he did this, but then went back to arranging his possessions.

Rubbing his manipulators together, he said, "Alright, Charlotte, I already have the schema for this upgrade, and I hope the System lets me do this. It's going to be a massive upgrade to my ability to do combat." He set the last pile of ingots he'd had in storage on the ground, then began to clear a space around himself for the necessary rituals.

Billy looked over as Charlotte waved to get his attention. "Dear, if this works, I want you to do the same for me. If I am to assist you, it would be best if we operated in the same manner."

Billy got the hint, and queued up the schema which would modify her after he was done upgrading himself. He kept this tidbit of information from her, but she would see it if she went looking.

Once a large enough area was cleared of rubble, Billy waited while his bots scoured the river for the gold he would need soon, and for night. He was incredibly lucky when they brought in gems of various types, from jasper to diamond. The powdery grit in the bottom of the river had polished many of these jewels and gems, and they would come in handy for himself and for Charlotte.

He was also lucky enough to locate platinum nuggets, along with some silver. It seemed wherever this river had traveled through it had cut through large swathes of metal rich veins and carried it to the end of the canyon. Billy let his bots roam for a little over an hour before the sun began to set on the horizon. Once he reached what he figured was the appropriate time, he called to Charlotte, "We have everything, now. Are you ready for some fun?"

Charlotte looked giddy at this news, and Billy knew she had already inspected his Assembler queue. Her legs were waving all over the place in happiness.

"Yes, dear. I am ready as ever," she said stoically.

Billy looked over his Status one last time, making sure every necessary point into his Attributes was present, and the few

Abilities he'd needed were also selected. He looked at his internal clock to mark the time, and his *Apply*. The world went black.

The old man was sitting at a small, round table at a quaint looking coffee shop. There were no other people, just Billy and the old man. They were in a place that looked familiar to Billy, he thought he almost recognized it, but the thought vanished too quickly and he couldn't nail it down.

The old man was sitting there, in one of those wrought iron chairs with the soft cushion and the hard, metal back for support. The table was also wrought iron, round, with a glass top. Two cups sat opposite one another, full of what appeared to be a rich, dark brew. The old man was wearing his white toga, the same as the last few times Billy had seen him. Billy could smell the rich brew as he had appeared and it smelled like home.

The old man held forward a hand, indicating Billy take a seat, and it took Billy a moment to realize he wasn't a spider this time around. He pulled the chair out, and saw that his hands weren't quite like he thought they should look. He thought for a moment and they shifted to something he more expected, and sat down.

Billy sat, watching the old man sip at his cup of coffee, and Billy reached forward to grab his cup and do the same. He couldn't remember the last time he'd had coffee. Bringing it to his nose, Billy drew a shallow breath through his nose and smelled the rich coffee bean steeped in the boiled water. It had a hint of sweetness, and nothing else. Cautiously, he took a sip, and the flavor exploded over his tongue as if he'd never had coffee before.

Lips tingling, and tongue still sending signals to his brain talking about how awesome this stuff in the cup was, Billy settled back in the chair and looked up at the old man.

"I see you have finally taken the necessary steps, my boy. I thought you would never start solving the problem out there," He said, waving a hand, out there.

Chuckling, he said, "I got sidetracked, old man. You didn't leave very many clues for me to follow." Billy watched as the old man scoffed.

"I left no such clues." The old man sat silently for a moment before smiling. "But I am glad you did find the information."

Billy pondered the meaning of the change in expression the old man gave. He thought, perhaps the old man had nothing to do with anything at all. Perhaps he was just someone who observed.

"In either case, I did find the information I needed to get things going. I just don't think I can do this by myself." Billy sipped his coffee again, drinking more now that it had cooled some.

"Yes, well, none of us can do everything alone," He said, indicating Billy and himself. "After all, here you are, and here I am."

Billy smiled at this game. He knew what the old man meant, but he also knew it wasn't exactly what he'd meant.

"Is there anyone who can help me? Is there something I could be missing which would assist me in finding assistance?" Billy sat with both hands around his coffee, suddenly feeling the chill in the air around them.

"Assistant, you say?" The old man smirked as he said this, and took another sip of his own coffee.

"Do…" The world blinked before he could finish his question, and his other eyes started working in the other world.

Billy felt his boiler heating up rapidly, as was usual when he awoke from these upgrade periods. This time, however, he did not feel the boiler in its usual location inside himself, and for a moment he felt almost panicked thinking something had gone wrong. Then, as he became more and more aware of himself, he recognized the prompts in his mind, manifested in the form of multiple blue screens much like computer monitors of various sizes, one for each of his eight eyes.

The first thing Billy focused on was the time, however. Time was of the essence, and he saw that he had been unconscious for just over 14 hours. It was currently morning. Next Billy checked his prompts, which provided step by step updates on the upgrades Charlotte had performed on him. His body, once that of a mechanoid spider, was now that of a mechanoid hybrid human-spider.

He saw the model of his new body in his mind, and he smiled to himself. His eight limbs, plus two manipulators, had been shifted to provide him with two very powerful legs, two equally powerful arms, and an extra pair of arms tucked behind his back. His abdomen had been repositioned to where his human butt would have been, and it hung back like a wide, thick cape where a tail could have been. This connected to his torso with powerful cabling and gizmos, providing him exceptional balance and strength.

The largest change was his own head, which had been reconstructed from the wide, spider version with eight large eyes wrapping around it, to that of a very human head, but with eight eyes instead of two. He now also had a mouth, which still functioned as his Dissembler port, but was very human now, with teeth, lips and everything else. He could now feel himself smiling. He'd opted to cover swathes of his body with the dense, dark blue hair, optimized his frame for power and performance, and ended up being close to seven feet tall, and just shy of 450 pounds of dense steel, brass, titanium, and other special metals.

He was human again, or as close to one as he could be and still be a Mechanoid. His boiler was in his torso now, along with his massively modified alchemist's pot. As for his head, he had to have that constructed from scratch, hoping beyond hope the information he had downloaded on the day he awoke from the strange computer deep underground was accurate. It had given him many forms to choose from, but in the end he had spent his off time modifying it. The only thing that had prevented him from doing this sooner was the large requirements of non-Dungeon gold. He'd needed to feed hundreds of pounds of raw, non-Dungeon gold, along with several of the Gloopos, into his alchemy pot to upgrade it so it would be able to produce the brain he was now using to observe the world with.

Many of the schemas had not allowed him to make a frame much less than nine feet tall, but he'd brought back with him some knowledge of complicated gear combinations from his time on Earth and had been able to incorporate this into this body after developing the schema for them.

Looking at his status now, Billy saw his Attributes reflected his new strengths and weaknesses. He had many strengths, and few weaknesses, and he'd done everything he could think of to mitigate those weaknesses with ingenuity, and a few searches on the universal store. That, and the Gloopos he'd acquired had been harvested. He only had a dozen of the little blobs left, now, and had no intention of using any more of them. He was going to leave them on the ship with Captain Aurora, but decided it would be best if he just kept them with himself for now.

Once he made sure the numbers were correct with his remaining stock, Billy fired up his Assembler and began to make the components for Charlotte's upgrade. Once that process began, Billy opened his eyes, and stood up.

At first Billy was expecting for his perspective to halt once he was about four feet from the ground, but it continued as he straightened himself to his full height and for a moment he felt a smidgen of vertigo. This passed very quickly, for which Billy was inwardly thankful, thanks to the powerful and accurate gyros he now had in his head. It also took a moment for his new eyes to adjust, and still having eight of those gave him momentary pause as the new machines each quickly adjusted.

Looking over himself as his Assembler worked, Billy could feel his new balance. On eight legs for nearly two months now, he had never been off kilter, so to speak. He was stable in every environment, but now that he was on two feet, he knew the abdominal extension acting like a lower back cape also acted like a secondary stabilizer. He would subconsciously adjust this, which connected where, say, a cat-person's tail extended from the lower spine, and its subtle motions would act to further steady him on his feet like a counter-weight.

Billy ran his hands, with five fingers now, over his new arms. The metallic framework he had for a skeleton was covered in special hydraulic systems which functioned exactly like muscles, but with fewer limitations of the meat version. This was covered in a skein of material which acted to protect the systems underneath from debris and the environment, and this was covered in a fine layer of ultramarine blue hair.

His hands were metallic, as well as the lower part of his legs and feet. His chest and torso were covered in the fine hair as well, and he had created armor plates, which were replaceable, that mimicked the human torso of a superhero that the hair attached to. The fine hair covered these plates, but did not diminish the basically ripped body he had on display now. As he ran his hands over himself, he could feel his hands moving through the hair on his body, but he could not feel in the same way any of the exposed metal parts themselves. He felt pressure there, but nothing much else. He also felt the new antennae he had on top of his head, stiff, two-section, narrow stalks which looked very similar to that ants would have. These would function to send commands to either his bots, or to Charlotte using a new signaling system.

Charlotte watched Billy examine his new form, and he got the sense she was jealous. Fortunately, she would not have to wait long for her own form which, by necessity, would be smaller and more utilitarian. She was his assistant, and his mechanic, after all, not his equal.

Smiling, he said, "Alright, Charlotte, time for you to take a nap. Your parts are just about ready, and I want to get this done quickly." Billy bent down and scooped Charlotte up with one hand, and she just hung limply over his hand.

"I look forward to the improvements, dear. And do be careful. I have delicate parts." Her tiny limbs hung limp, prepared to be powered off.

Billy chuckled, which sounded very close to his own voice from Earth, and he reached behind Charlotte's own head and tapped a tiny plate. This popped open, revealing a small switch, and he flicked it. Charlotte instantly went limp in his hand. He then began to Dissemble her one leg at a time, the last part being her head.

Several hours later, Billy was sitting in the early morning light listening to the rushing of the river over the rocks nearby, when he twisted the head of his new assistant on, and flicked some switches. He reached inside her back and his fingers connected a cable there, feeding the information which was all Charlotte was in digital format, into her new upgraded brain. This took a few minutes, and while he did this he produced a preselected-by-Charlotte outfit. This took next to no time, as it was all cloth, and as his one hand was uploading Charlotte into her body, his two free hands dressed the doll body. Once he was done uploading Charlotte into her new form, he reached to the back of the doll, located the switch and pushed it twice, then replaced its cover, which reformed seamlessly into the back.

The doll was female, to match Charlotte's request. Billy had his hangups on the design Charlotte had chosen herself previously, but in the end the doll ended up being female in design, or at least feminine. There was no human analog for her appearance, as her initial body was incorporated into the design, much like his own. She had eight limbs, but they were bound similarly to his with each leg formed of two spidery limbs, and she also had an extra pair of arms, her pedipalps, which she decided to keep actively available. Her form was sleek, but not slender. She would need to lift and remove heavy objects, such as himself, during maintenance cycles, so she had well defined musculature, again like his own. She also had her own version of antennae similar to Billy's, for silent communication to him and his bots.

One of the major upgrades she was given was her very own Dissembler component. Her doll did not get the Assembler, as Billy could not reproduce the alchemy pot which provided the magical means to produce components. He did not really want her to have the option, however, so he did not push himself to solve this particular problem. His own mind was based on his soul link to this mechanical body with magic, and as far as he could tell Charlotte was the result of magical programming. She was purely a machine, a living intelligence without conscience. He felt better knowing she could not glitch out and then run around making copies of herself until the planet just consisted of a collection of her.

The miniature furnace and boiler in Charlotte powered up, and Charlotte's limbs twitched as pressure and fluids moved into her limbs, and her mind adapted to the new form. This only took seconds, and when she finally opened her own set of human eyes, all eight of them which could be closed and opened with a thought, she smiled up at Billy with actual lips. He looked down at her with his own smile and straightened up.

"Welcome to the world of bipedal intelligences, Charlotte. How do you feel?" Billy watched as Charlotte took several careful steps. She then went through a strange routine to test her physical balance and reach. She looked like a little kung-fu fighter in a pale blue dress, made of metal and pipes, gears and cogs, irregular fingers and extra joints included.

"You know, dear, neither you nor I feel anything. However, this new form does allow me to operate more efficiently." She held up a hand and her fingers cycled through a number of tool bits, like a swiss army hand.

Her face, as alien as Billy's, looked almost excited at the prospects of using new tools. Billy knew that feeling himself, he'd seen it in the faces of many of his customers from the old hardware store back on Earth when they came in to purchase a new tool.

"Yes, well, I can see you are at the very least excited, if not happy, with the new form. For now, we need to clear up this mess and start down into the bore." Saying this, he sent commands to his bots to stow themselves using the new antennae on his head, and the small army obediently complied and collapsed into their flat forms and Billy scooped them up and placed them into storage compartments. They were useful as tools, but not much else.

Once the area around them had been restored to its natural beauty, all of the debris and leftover material from the upgrading process scavenged and stored in compartments, Billy looked into the morning sky and saw that it might rain soon.

"Come on, Charlotte. We have far to go, and no way of knowing how long we will be traveling down the Bore." Billy looked down on his new assistant, and she looked up to him, her strange clothing floating slightly in the light breeze.

She looked at him in turn, and smiled. Billy suppressed the shudder he almost felt at the alien face making the gesture, and he smiled back.

"Ready when you are, dear," She said giggling. "Lead the way and I shall follow."

The stony shore of the canyon river eventually met face to face with the walls of the pass through the mountains after a few minutes hiking. The pads of both Billy and Charlotte's feet softened their steps and provided firm grips as they easily navigated the shoreline. After a half an hour, the canyon opened up to a wide S-bend, which the burbling river followed. This split in the rock formed an arch on the one side, and when Billy moved to look inside he saw the shadows hid a set of ancient stairs leading around a massive hole hidden under the mountain.

"Do you intend to fight without a weapon, dear?" Charlotte asked Billy when he ducked under the arch formed by the rock.

"I think with all of the Experience I have allocated into fighting with natural weapons, and the points purchased in other Proficiencies as well, it would be better if I just used myself as a weapon." Billy glanced again at his Status just to make sure he was good to go.

"Yes, well," She started to move her arms and legs in the language of the spiders and stopped mid-step before continuing with her antennae. "Are you sure that is wise?"

Billy, still having eyes in the back of his head, saw her antennae twitching. He interpreted the question and pondered for a second before responding.

"Sure, after all, I made most of the parts of my hand and some sections of my legs out of that mithril we were able to produce, thanks to all of that gold. It wasn't much, Charlotte, but having almost indestructible knuckles and shins should be quite useful so long as I don't stress my joints too much." He held out a hand and flexed to show off his shiny knuckles.

Charlotte, her big eyes wide, almost tripped seeing this. She had replaced his hands herself, but to see he had upgraded them without her knowing meant he had done this while he was in the process of remaking her new body.

"Let's hope, then, the cleanup and maintenance will be easy. I would not like to have to replace your whole arm because the hand has gears or cogs that cannot be lubricated and they lock up."

"That would be a tricky thing to do," he replied mysteriously.

Turning to the arch cut into the side of this mountain, the cave-like hole hid all. Billy had to duck only a little to get into the entrance, and once he stepped foot inside, he received a prompt.

Congratulations! You have discovered a new Dungeon, the Abyssal Bore! What secrets are hidden within? What treasures await? Only the brave may find out!

Rank:S

Status: Overflowing

Threat: Apocalyptic

Experience for Discovery: +2,000

Do you wish to challenge the Abyssal Bore with your current Party? Yes. No.

Billy dismissed the Experience gain window and paused as he looked at the Status and Threat information.

Billy recalled what he'd learned the first time he had cleared a Dungeon, and knew most would require a small army of powerful individuals to clear. He also knew this Threat level was vastly beyond what he'd dealt with before, which was only Dangerous. This time, he had Charlotte, and the Threat level was Apocalyptic, and he only had one shot to clear this thing.

"What is it, dear?" Billy caught a strange expression on Charlotte's face as she spoke to him.

"The Status of this Dungeon is Overflowing, and the Threat level is Apocalyptic. It's also a Rank S Dungeon. Is the Rank important?" Billy turned to look down at Charlotte as her antennae started jittering.

"Oh dear, this is bad news. The Rank determines the voracity of the monsters inside the Dungeon. A Rank F Dungeon, or Lair like the first one you cleared, would have only a dozen monsters at the most, with a single boss. The monsters are usually alone, and will not attack on sight or when you get within a certain proximity. There are also few, if any, traps. The rewards are very poor, but have the chance to be decent."

She paused as she squatted down, and Billy did the same, looking around to make sure things were safe enough.

"Each Rank up increases the number of monsters by an order of magnitude, most times. The monsters become more aggressive, and more deadly. The treasures become greater as well."

Charlotte pushed a pebble around with one of her new fingers as she put her thoughts together, before continuing.

"Rank S Dungeons break the mold. There could be as few as one single super-Boss, or as much as 100,000 monsters and dozens of bosses. There will be traps, every one of them lethal in the extreme. The monsters will have strange Abilities, and rather unnerving intellect. They could work in groups, lay ambushes, create more traps, or build fortifications. It's really a nightmare land in there. We could spend years in there, Billy. Years, and never locate the final boss." Her tiny face looked troubled as she said this.

Billy watched Charlotte as she told him these things, and her little antennae drooped as she finished explaining. Billy himself had a few plans in mind, something Charlotte did not seem to be aware of, which he was sure she was not, if only from movies back on Earth.

He tried to console her by saying, "That shouldn't be a problem, Charlotte. I think we can get this done in as little as a month, if things get really bad."

Something in Billy's voice had Charlotte look up, and she saw determination in his strange, mechanical, spidery eyes.

"Alright, I have several ideas, Charlotte. We need to get in there," He said, pointing down into the Bore, "and see what we have to deal with. If you're worried, just know I do not plan to fail here. We have everything we need to do this. All I need from you is to be brave, and listen to my directions, and be quiet. Can you do this?"

Charlotte's little antennae stood up as he saw her confidence build with his words, and when he fell silent she stood and saluted with one of her little antennae.

"Yes. I can do this, dear. I can be brave, listen to your directions, and be quiet. We can do this!" She said finally.

"Good. Let's get going, then," he said, standing up, turning to the steps leading deep into the ground and selecting *Yes*.

The Abyssal Bore was oriented like a pitch black, cylindrical hole cut straight into the ground. Around the inside of the Bore were stairs carved to allow adventuresome people the opportunity to enter. This long climb down also gave them plenty of time to rethink their decision to enter, and leave. Billy did not hesitate as he confidently took each step downward, his eyes easily giving him access to the layout of the place with their magically mechanical power.

The Bore entrance itself was about 20 feet in diameter, and the dark, stone steps were comfortable enough even for Billy's seven foot height. Charlotte seemed not to have any issue either, even though she was so short. She didn't complain, though, and Billy was glad for this. He did not want her to ask him to leave. He knew if she asked him, he would let her return to the entrance, and he would continue on alone. He just didn't want to do that.

Down they spiraled into the ground, the deep steps leading onward into the pitch dark hole as their soft footsteps echoed downward forever. Nearly an hour they both silently tread, the slow boil of their mechanical hearts powering their cogworks and pistons. Looking up, Billy saw an endless spiral of stairs when, suddenly, Charlotte stopped behind him.

"What is it?" Billy sent with his own antennae, while crouching down.

"There's a door over there," Charlotte signaled, a metallic finger pointing across the way and down.

Looking the dozen or so steps ahead, Billy saw an archway cut into the dark wall of the Bore. The entrance was lined with square-cut blocks of dull, tan stone. Squinting, Billy could just make out the faint gray lines limning the frame that he expected to see.

"I think magic is in the doorway. I can just make it out surrounding the frame of the rock." Billy took the last few steps to approach the doorway, and saw there was an actual door. The solid wood was a rich, black of very fine texture. The blocks of rock that served as the frame for the door had markings cut into them. Billy could barely make them out.

"Ah, yes. These are markings which indicate Floors. I don't think we can go further unless we clear this Floor. Inside, there should be something we will need to continue." Billy watched Charlotte signal the message, and shrugged to himself.

"Are you ready?" He asked her.

"Yes." Was all she signaled back.

Billy opened the door, and crossed the threshold.

The deep, black darkness and quiet of the Bore was immediately replaced with a hot, humid, dim jungle. Billy stepped from what appeared to be a solid block of rock, which he turned to look at as Charlotte appeared from it in a gray flash of invisible light. She looked around at the dim lighting, whatever served as a sun hidden by tall, thick vegetation.

Billy's new senses caught several scents in the air, dank, musty smells from rotting plants and bog water. There were bugs making noises that he could not see, and things not very far away making predatory sounds during their now interrupted hunt.

Billy crouched and turned as he heard something thumping hard on the soft ground nearby. Thick roots crisscrossed the area around Billy, some a couple of feet tall, coming from trees 100 feet tall. Billy placed a hand on the ground to help try to determine which direction the threat was coming from. He felt the thumping for a few moments, then suddenly it all ceased.

Signaling Charlotte to be on the lookout for trouble, Billy moved next to the nearest tree. His boiler was beginning to heat up, and his strange dark-blue hair was already pulling moisture from the air to keep him topped up. He was ready for whatever was to come.

He was, in fact, not ready for what came.

The rumbling in the ground had gone silent, the strange thumping sounds of an approaching threat gone mysteriously silent. Then a massive, four foot wide, four foot tall, 12 foot long brown monstrosity slid over a large root, leaving a trail of gooey slime. It had a pair of eye stalks that stuck up three feet, with dead black eye spots locked right onto Billy.

It was a huge slug, and its mouth was gaping open with lamprey teeth, and a hissing sound blasting saliva and slime ahead of it as it oozed toward Billy with frightening speed. The long slug bore down on Billy, ignoring the roots as if the ground were flat. Almost too fast it lunged its gaping maw full of teeth right at Billy's legs. Quick as a whip Billy lashed out with a leg, snap kicking the side of its head.

Billy was almost twice the height of the slug, which made its head at the perfect level for his kick. With a blur, Billy's reinforced leg smashed into the slug, and he spun to a stop as its whole body rolled over with the hit as the ripple from the impact traced back to its tail end. Fast as his kick was, Billy returned to a forward stance, left foot forward with his right leg back, both knees slightly bent, his two hands up in a boxer's stance prepared to block or attack in a blink.

The giant slug rolled several times before it stopped, and then quivered. As Billy watched, the slug righted itself, and then turned its hellish maw back on him and immediately began to slide at him again.

Billy took a moment to look around for Charlotte, and he noticed she had moved up one of the large trees nearby. He glanced up and cursed. Another giant slug was making its way down that tree from above while Charlotte was watching Billy from around the side. A quick twitch of his antennae and Charlotte's bulky form lunged from the tree she was on to roll across the complicated terrain just as the giant slug slid around the trunk of the tree to take a chunk out of the tree where she had just been.

"Keep mobile, Charlotte. Kite them if you can," he sent to her as he turned back to his attacker. "Run around and get their attention, I'll take them out one at a time," He clarified when he saw the questioning quirk of an antennae.

Charlotte took off through the jungle brush, the myriad plants knocked out of her way as she dashed through the leaves. Billy turned to face the oncoming giant slug, which was already hissing in rage as it came onward. It had no complex form of attack, no plan, and just came right to Billy and tried to bite him while also trying to crush him. Instead of letting this happen, Billy sidestepped the slug's lunge and kicked at it again, harder than last time. The slug again slammed to the side, but this time Billy had positioned himself so the slug would smash into the side of a tree.

With a *Whomp*, the slug crashed into the trunk of the large tree, and it shivered, small sticks and leaves falling on it from above, and a few vines falling loose to hang over the scene. Billy did not stop moving, and he stepped forward to backhand the large eye stalk lifting from the slug's head trying to locate him. His mithril hand blurred and the eyestalk exploded on contact. The stem of the stalk instantly retracted, spurting ichor, and the slug swung its head violently in pain.

Billy lept straight up as the slug rolled and slid past, then as he came down, he lifted a leg and slammed it down onto the slug's head. His weight, combined with the short fall, made for a powerful attack on the monster's head. Goo and slime flew out of the slug as its head compressed, and it simultaneously pulled its head back into its main body and pulled its body toward its head. As it made this attempt to save itself, Billy leaned forward to put as much weight as possible on his heel, which, unmoving, ripped into the slug's squishy brain. Blood and viscera spilled from the head wound, and the monster fell limp almost instantly. It twitched twice, then its entire body relaxed as it let out its last gurgle.

Looking around, Billy heard more slugs slamming through the thick jungle brush. Movement caught his eye as he saw Charlotte dashing from one tree to the next, leaping and using thick vines to extend her reach. Several slugs lunged up at her as she clambered to one of the nearby large trees, and other slugs rushed to chase.

"Keep it up!" Billy sent to Charlotte as he moved with purpose to the tree three slugs were trying to surround as she was climbing it.

With a heave, Billy jumped with the intent of pulling a Mario on the buggers by stomping their heads in. Unfortunately, the strange slugs seemed to have their own danger sense, and the one Billy was targeting wobbled to the side. Billy crashed down in between two of the large, slime-covered monstrosities, but didn't hesitate. He rotated and performed a palm strike on one slug, and he kicked backward with his opposite foot to stun the other slug, pushing against both as he made simultaneous contact with them.

Without pausing, Billy stepped into his palm strike and spun in a full circle, swinging hard at the eye stalks of this slug. He got lucky, and both of the angry monster's eyes popped one after the other, splattering trees with eye goo. Leaving that monster to writhe blind on the ground, Billy jumped horizontally across the ground and performed a powerful straight punch into the side of the other slug.

This large slug tried to curl in on itself as Billy's fist impacted it once, twice, three and four times in rapid succession. The eyes on this monster bobbed all over the place as Billy's mass moved its mass aggressively. While he was punching the one slug, a third slug was already up the other side of the tree, but Billy still managed to see Charlotte running across a large branch above, and jumping to yet another tree. As she did this, the slug's mouth tried to follow her, and it ended up leaping off of the tree while it was 20 feet up. Its body reached out into open air, trying to bite Charlotte as she flashed away, then it fell to the ground, partially landing on the blind slug behind Billy.

In desperation now, Billy dropped to a knee and quickly dug for a good sized rock while all of the slugs were overcoming their own confusion. Finding one, Billy spun on the same knee and threw the softball sized rock at the blind slug's head.

To Billy's amazement, the rock blasted through the head of the slug and continued off into the jungle, smashing through and smacking off of several trees as it went. The blind slug went limp as its head imploded on impact, and Billy winced. He'd not wanted to use projectiles to fight. It was too easy to forgo physical combat with ranged, and then get lazy and die to some normal attacker. However, this was effective, and he didn't have to make anything, so Billy performed a combat roll to get away from the slugs he was beginning to get entangled with to gain a little distance.

Once a couple of feet away, Billy watched as the slug that fell from the tree turned to continue its search for Charlotte. Looking around, Billy's sensors located a number of useful rocks in the brush. Acting fast, Billy shuffled through the plant life and grabbed a handful of good rocks.

The slug he had been punching was now turning to Billy as he came up with rocks, and it began sliming its way to him, its terrible mouth open to devour him. Billy cocked back his arm and threw the rock as hard as he could at the thing. To his dismay, the rock flew right into the ground next to the slug, which seemed not to even notice what had happened. But, Billy still had a moment and so he tried again, this time aiming for the giant body instead of the head. The effect was spectacular.

Chapter 23

As Billy released the rock from his insane grip, the rock simply vanished as it passed through the body of the slug. It did not take the shortest path from side to side of the slug, no, it went through it diagonally. The rock impacted the ground on the other side of the slug almost silently, but the eight foot long hole he'd made through it noisily gushed hot internal fluids and pieces of organs. It was quite the sight for Billy, who took a second to appreciate his own strength.

Turning, Billy almost casually threw the next rock at the chasing slug, and it did the same thing, passing length ways through the slug, ending it in a single shot. Billy stood, his knuckles covered in slime from his epic, but useless punching, and shook his head in annoyance. He had really been hoping not to bring guns to knife fights, but then again, it had ended all of the threats.

A few seconds later, with the area quieting, Charlotte tumbled through the air in a feat of acrobatics, and landed next to Billy, her strange, alien eyes wide with excitement, or fear.

"Are you alright, Charlotte?" Billy spoke aloud. "You're not hurt or anything are you?" He crouched down to look at her as she turned to look at the devastation Billy had wrought on the slugs.

"I am fine, dear. Perfectly fine." She had sent her reply silently, but Billy got the message just the same.

Chuckling, Billy signaled, "Well, I didn't want to go around throwing things to kill them, but it seems like it will be more efficient that way." He turned to scan the foliage, and began going around scooping up heavy rocks, and then opening his mouth to stuff them into his Dissembler.

"What are you doing?" Charlotte asked as she watched him walk around chewing rocks, curious.

"Making better ammunition," He said, not stopping in his search and seizure.

"What is that? Ammunition?"

Billy paused in his search, but continued Disembling the rocks he had in hand. "It's a term from my old world, used to describe objects propelled at high speeds with lethal force."

"Like an arrow or bolt?" She asked, curious, but now helping locate rocks for Billy to consume.

"Not really, no. The biggest difference is the speed at which the object goes through the air. Bolts and arrows go fast, but the ammunition I'm talking about is the kind that has the potential to go many times faster than the speed of sound, making it silent to the enemies, until the soundwave catches up. I mean," He continued as he started walking around again, "Technically arrows and bolts are ammunition for the bow and crossbow that fires them.

But I am not using either of those tools. I will just throw them, instead. I could make a rifle, but that requires more chemistry than I can.."

Billy opened up his status while he chewed on some rocks. He went to his Ability tab, and scrolled around for a little while. He noticed he had received some Experience points, and decided that he might as well spend them. He didn't want to make a gun, the gunpowder and the casings would just be a pain to produce, assuming he managed to create the schema for it. However, he could use powerful air pressure, along with some youtube ingenuity, and make something which could launch a certain kind of object at ridiculous velocity.

Turning back from this thought, Billy spent a few minutes playing the strange game required to manifest the proper schema based on his design input. The game had ever changing rules, and he often failed to procure the schema he wanted, wasting time and some minor resources in the prototyping process. This time, however, Billy already had many schema for what he wanted, and he just needed to simplify it, and make it more complex in another way.

After 30 nerve wracking minutes of gameplay, Billy finally achieved the schema for an attachment he could use on his arm. It would be awkward, but absolutely devastating. And, thanks to his storage stocks, Billy had everything he needed to make one in a few more minutes.

"Charlotte, I have a design in production now, I need you to attach the cabling and hoses in a few minutes, if that's alright. I won't be using rocks either. Just drop those there." He dropped the few he'd had himself, and Charlotte came over to wait. Both kept watch as Billy's Assembler extruded part after part for Charlotte to affix to Billy's right arm under his direction.

As the arm mechanism was attached, the schema for the device to provide extra power was completed, Assembled and prepared to be installed on his back with Charlotte's help. She did so after completing installation of the arm piece.

"What is this supposed to do, exactly?" She asked as she bolted the framework to Billy's back plating.

"It uses some of the steam from my boiler to turn some components to help create compressed air. The pressure takes a few moments to build, but it grows to incredible levels. That air is fed down this line here," He tapped the reinforced flexible red hose leading to the contraption on his arm, "To this chamber, where it builds up. Once it gets to a certain pressure, the line is shut off by this valve here, and the compressor keeps building up spare air in the tank here," He reached up with one of his extra arms and tapped the long blue tank.

"Yes, but why all of this to throw a rock?" Charlotte continued to assemble the parts on Billy's back as the components were extruded from the Assembler.

"I'll show you why when you finish." Billy said nothing else about this until Charlotte finally connected the last copper tube, and high-pressure steam was switched on to spin up his turbines and gears.

With a loud whining sound, Billy's magical steam-powered compressor rapidly charged the tank on his arm, then the tank on his back. It only took about five seconds, and he was amazed at the raw power of his internal systems. He only hoped the release valves would hold up to the pressure.

Once the system was charged, Billy opened up his Status and queued up the nine millimeter lead pellets he'd designed with the help of the System to work with his new rifle. It only took moments for his Assembler to drop a few hundred into his storage, and he then produced the strange aluminum clips to hold them.

"Take a bunch of these here, Charlotte, and load them into these magazines like this," Billy said, showing Charlotte how to load the pellets in the right direction in the narrow, spring loaded clips. Each one only held 12 pellets, but he was already spitting out clip after clip from his abdomen into his inventory.

Charlotte helped load up some 20 of the clips with pellets, and then Billy took one of them and placed it into the port of the arm-mounted rifle. He could easily see the gauge both with his eyes and with his Status screen, and it was reading almost 1,000 P.S.I. This was a monstrous amount of pressure, but he might want more.

"Watch this," Billy said, as he took aim at one of the trees. With a thought, the system released compressed air which slammed the lead pellet down the barrel, and into the tree with a snap. Billy scratched his chin with his free hand as steam billowed from the end of the short barrel.

"Was that it?" Charlotte asked, going over to the tree and seeing the lead pellet stuck in the bark.

"No, that was just a test fire, to see if the barrel was good to go. Now we crank up the pressure to the max." As he said this, the pack on Billy's back screamed into life as gargantuan air pressure was rammed into the mithril tank, which also had mithril valves.

The magical metal was nigh indestructible, and would likely be able to take thousands of pounds of pressure before deforming, but Billy had faith in the exotic metal. He put 1,000, then 4,000, then 10,000 P.S.I. into the canister. When it hit 25,000 pounds per square inch, Billy shut off the compressor, and steam erupted from the shutoff backflow, and the jungle fell silent.

"Now, watch this," Said Billy with a smile as he mentally pulled the trigger again.

Air exploded out of the barrel, forcing the lead pellet out of the way by blasting it down the barrel. Billy's arm visibly kicked back as a cloud of air expanded out of the barrel that the pellet left. The pellet vanished into the trunk of the tree, leaving a small hole as evidence it had struck.

Charlotte poked a finger at the hole, while Billy checked over the system. The barrel was not very heavy, and did not interfere with his motion, being attached to his triceps as it was. He could still move his arm around, but noticed the barrel sticking out at a very odd angle. With a thought, Billy caused the barrel to fold back and attach itself to the top of the weapon frame, making it well clear of catching on something.

"This doesn't seem very impressive," Charlotte said as she examined the hole. "It's very loud and only does a little bit of damage." She turned to look at Billy as he fiddled with something on the back of the weapon.

"Yeah, I have some ideas on how to fix that, but I don't have the schema right now. Besides, this thing could probably hit something accurately up to a few hundred yards away. Also, if you check the trees on the other side, it likely went through some of those as well." Something clicked on Billy's arm, and he seemed satisfied.

Billy reached back to his Assembler, pulled from it a long, curved magazine, and began stuffing pellets into it as quickly as he could.

He wanted them to come pre-loaded, but his Assembler would not perform that particular task. The schema did not provide it with those kinds of directions.

The long clip held many more pellets, and once it was loaded, Billy replaced the 12 round magazine with the new one. Then he had the barrel swing and lock back into place, and there was a quick hiss of evacuating air as the barrel emptied of air, creating a small vacuum.

"Now, this should do something worthwhile," Billy said as he lifted his arm to aim at the same tree. Then he activated the system, and air snapped dozens of times as he swung his arm slowly across the trunk of the tree in a straight line.

Holes appeared, one beside another, in a long line all the way across the tree's trunk, from one side all the way to the other. Small splinters of wood were shooting out the longer Billy shot at the tree, and the jungle echoed with the sounds of pellets rocketing through hard wood. Midway through the trunk Billy's compressor kicked back on to supply the necessary air pressure, and when his weapon fell silent, the compressor remained on for only a couple of seconds before silence once again spread through the jungle.

Charlotte looked poleaxed in surprise and fear as she watched the massive tree, now cut all the way through, slowly lean over and crash to the jungle floor. Leaves, vines, and broken branches fell to land all over the area around the tree, and Billy just stood there smiling at his new tool. Charlotte saw Billy looking with satisfaction at the thing on his arm, and she held back her own shudder. She had no records of any such machine ever being made or even conceived of in all her long recorded history. It was horrifying to see how only a few dozen tiny lead things could slice through a 1,000-year-old tree with almost no effort.

Billy, unlike Charlotte, was somewhat disappointed in how the rifle functioned. He did not want to manage gunpowder, so he would have to worry about efficiency later. As it was, this would do some major damage to crowds of smaller creatures.

"This will work for now," Billy said as he reloaded several more of the longer magazines. He removed the expended one and replaced it with a short one. On his waist, Billy opened a compartment and dropped in all of his full magazines for quick reloading.

Charlotte watched Billy in growing wonder. She had been aware, almost as soon as she was activated, that Billy was not her original master to whom she was supposed to serve. He was something special, something this world had never seen. He was bringing with him strange ideas, a total lack of understanding of how the world works or its history, but most of all, he was bringing with him new technology she had never thought to use. His greenhouses were something to behold, as they easily and efficiently grew food indoors. His jewelry production brought in enormous wealth in a very short time, in a monster Lair, no less. He wasn't even aware they had been in a monster Lair either, which was something she was afraid to tell him when they went back to the city. She knew he was aware of this, but she got the feeling he had not yet come to terms with the data.

"Let's go. We have to find the goal of this place."

Billy's voice jerked Charlotte out of her thoughts, and she spoke without thinking.

"Are we going to loot the monsters?"

Her question brought Billy up short, and he facepalmed himself. Shaking his head, Billy returned to the sight of the still stinking corpses of the giant slugs, reached down to poke them, and looted the bodies one after the other.

Congratulations! You have looted Giant Jungle Slug. You have acquired:

+90 Experience Points.

+36 Slug Pelt.

+3 Slug Tooth.

+10 Jar of Slug slime.

+25 Slug Steak.

"Gross, slug steaks? That sounds disgusting," Billy said to himself as the pile of treasures, sans Experience points, plopped onto the ground in front of him. "And why didn't this stuff get sent to me in the mail after we cleared the place?"

Charlotte said after a moment of thought, "I'm not sure; perhaps it is because this place acts differently while it houses a Heart Shard?"

"Yeah, I guess. I hadn't checked on that when we were in the Lair of the Fey, so it could be," Billy said with a shrug.

"Also, according to my records, dear, those steaks are very hardy, full of protein and flavor well enough to sell for nearly one silver coin each," Charlotte said as she inspected the pile of meat by gently poking it with a finger.

"I'm not very worried about money, Charlotte. I still have several pounds of gold left from that river outside, which I could turn into coins easily." Billy wasn't happy about the meat; he had nobody on hand to feed it to. He looted all three bodies, and then checked his status to see how much of this he could put into storage and what would need to fill his compartments, and saw he had the option to toggle on or off the *Delayed Loot Delivery* option here.

Tapping to turn it on, he received another prompt.

Warning: this option may only be changed once while inside the Dungeon. It may not be changed again until after you clear the Dungeon or escape. Continue? Yes. No.

Billy shrugged and selected *No*, then went to check his storage options. To his surprise, Billy found he could store everything here easily, if he just Dissembled it. He could deconstruct things and use the material to make other things, or he could deconstruct things and reconstruct that exact thing at a small cost of one Experience point per replication cycle. The material that he would Dissemble would be stored inside the magical alchemy pot inside himself, and that had no limit to what it could store. These new capabilities were all thanks to his latest upgrades to the magical component.

"Looks like I need to Dissemble everything, Charlotte, to save on space. I can reproduce it later if we don't use its materials to make anything else." That said, Billy stuffed one item after the other into his Dissembler. It took him a few minutes, but with Charlotte helping, he had everything stuffed into his Dissembler hole in no time.

"That was fun," Charlotte said. "I thought for a moment there you would choke on those pelts." Her sense of humor showed with the angle of her antennae, and Billy couldn't help but do the same and chuckle to himself.

"Yeah, nothing like stuffing long rolls of slug skin into someone's face, one after the other, nonstop, to make that almost happen," He said, shaking his head with a smirk.

The jungle was full of monsters, from Jungle Mosquito Swarms to a terrifying lizard called a Relkifin Spine Dragon, which used its tail to launch barbed bone spikes. It looked like a bearded dragon from Earth but was about 30 feet long, made from plants, and had a scorpion-like tail that produced bony spikes it used as projectiles by flinging them. Billy ended up having to rip the tail off, then each of its legs, before he could take care of the biting end. His own brute strength was barely able to get the job done, but in the end, he had stuffed the barrel of his pellet rifle into the monster's eye and emptied the entire 12-round clip into its brain at full power. It died the instant the nearly shotgun blast of lead punctured its brain cavity.

The jungle was full of large, venomous snakes that came at him by the dozens. Not being a biological lifeform, Billy simply let the six, eight, and ten-foot nope-ropes nibble on his metal frame as he casually went around kicking heads off or stomping their backs in half. Charlotte did a fair job of luring large groups around in circles, giving Billy the time he needed to pick them off in smaller groups one stomp at a time.

The Experience and loot were not all that great for individual monsters but the numbers were slowly adding up over time. Whenever Charlotte felt the need to perform some minor maintenance, she and Billy would find a very large tree and climb it, and he would lock onto the trunk with his powerful hands and feet, and she would walk around and over him to pull out spines, teeth and broken twigs from his joints, before brushing his fur clean and oiling any joint which seemed even an iota low on lubricant. Then, she did the same for herself.

After what Billy knew was almost a full day, he realized that the light in the "sky" had never changed, and he mentioned this to Charlotte.

"Yes, dear, if you recall from previous conversations, the Dungeon provides the setting, which includes any day or night cycles, if it has one, as well as all of the terrain and monsters." She said this while working on gathering monster corpses for Billy while he slowly looted one after another.

"I know, it's just so weird that I know it's the dawn of our second day here, but it's been daytime the whole time." He tapped bodies to loot them, then stuffed the rewards into his Dissembler one at a time.

Charlotte did the spider equivalent of a shrug, which looked quite odd coming from a humanoid and kept on collecting bodies.

It was another two days of slogging through marshes and jungle before they came upon a ruin. It looked like some of the images from South America that Billy had seen on the internet back home when people were mapping the jungles there with L.I.D.A.R. and discovering the jungle had grown over ancient cities en masse. This was like that, a gigantic, irregular mound of cut stone blocks, nearly completely overgrown with jungle vegetation, vines and even massive trees.

And the entire thing was covered with dozens of car-sized snails pulling around huge, spiky shells on their backs.

"This is a very animal-centric floor, Charlotte. Are all Dungeons like this?" His antennae quirked at the end, forming the question.

"Sometimes, dear. Most often, the magic creating them latches on to the local flora and fauna that inhabits the area and it manifests monsters related to them. It isn't always like that, though, and it could create almost anything in any scenario." Her own antennae barely moved to twitch out the reply. "We are, after all, in a jungle baked by the sunlight buried deep in the side of a cliff, which we teleported to by walking into a magical doorway."

Billy chuckled as he said, "Let's take a look around the area, then. I think we need a special kind of weapon for these big fellas."

Both of the mechanoids moved around the perimeter of the large, overgrown structure. The snails crawled all over the stone, using their mouths to scrape clean its surface of rapidly growing plant life. Looking around the area, Billy found nothing that could be useful in combating the snails except the plants themselves. There was a large variety of plants, many with thorns and sticky traps. Billy assumed some of them were toxic, but he knew next to nothing about the plants in this jungle.

After circling the large structure once and finding nothing, both Billy and Charlotte found a small space to formulate a plan.

"Do you think we can lure them?" Charlotte asked.

"I don't think so. I think we have to find the entrance. It will be a small break in the rocks, likely at the bottom of one of the sides or near the middle. The top, well, if it's at the top, we will have to hope it's open." The sound of snails crunching into solid rock interrupted the two for a moment until the jungle became quiet again.

"First, we need to know how tough one of those snails is." Billy commanded his weapon barrel to rotate and lock into place with a thought, and the gears around it spun silently and then softly clicked into place. Next, Billy carefully opened up his back tank to fill the chamber of his rifle system and waited for the gauge to show full. Taking careful aim at the closest snail's shell, Billy sent the signal for his weapon to discharge.

A blast of steam propelled the five-gram lead pellet to several thousand feet per second, and in almost no time at all, the pellet went from Billy's barrel to the stone on the opposite side of the snail shell. The snail instantly stopped moving as its heart exploded and sprayed out of its side onto the rock, out of Billy's view. None of the other snails so much as reacted to the felling of one of their number.

"That was far too easy, Charlotte." Billy checked his rifle, but did not stow it yet.

Struggling to find an appropriate response, Charlotte said, "Well, you are quite strong, dear. And you bring technology this world has never known."

Billy thought about this for a minute as he waited to see what the snails would do. As they waited, he saw one of the large snails had found the dead one, and it slid over to it as if to inspect. Billy thought at first it might look around for enemies. But, to no real surprise, the snail began eating the corpse of the fallen snail instead. Satisfied that the monsters were not at all curious or even aware of his action yet, Billy slowly began taking them out, one at a time.

Most of Billy's shots hit their mark. A few took two, but as he was able to see the snails very clearly as he circled the structure, and he had no problems sending another pellet at the monsters with impunity. It only took about an hour to eliminate each of the monsters surrounding the place, and when the last monster ceased moving, Billy stood and approached them to loot.

Pausing a few steps forward, Billy turned to look back at Charlotte, who was just standing there staring at him in awe.

"I have never seen, nor heard, of anything happening like this before, Billy. You are truly frightening, did you know that?" Her large, machine eyes were wide open as she watched him, and Billy got the feeling she was issuing some form of reverence towards him.

"Things like this here," He said, tapping his right arm, "Are very common, if not to the same degree, on the world I come from. Most weapons like this from my world don't use super compressed air to launch pellets like this. They use small explosions to do that instead. It's louder, most often, but doesn't require the pack like I have on my back."

She was practically quivering in glee as she said, "It's still amazing, Billy. Absolutely amazing."

Billy, not comfortable with this level of adoration, shrugged. "Come on, let's loot these monsters and clear this floor. This Dungeon isn't going to end itself."

As the duo circled the structure again, looting as they went, Billy kept an eye out in the rocks for any possible entrances. When there were only two more monsters to loot, Charlotte made the discovery of a sealed entrance partially opened by the roots of a huge tree root.

With an erratic twitch of her antennae to catch my eye, she signaled, "It's here, I think. This large rock is pushed out of the wall here, and I can see inside."

"Good work, Charlotte. Let's get these last two monsters and then open it the rest of the way." Billy tapped the shell of the still snail and it crumbled into a small pile of loot at his feet as he received the prompts showing him his new gains.

Congratulations! You have looted a Giant Jungle Snail. You have gained:

+45 Experience.

+5 gallons of slime.

+2 Giant Snail eye stalks.

+4 bolts of snail hide.

+1 Giant Snail stomach.

+3 phials of Giant Snail venom.

+4 plates of Giant Snail shell.

Stuffing the last piece of unstorable loot into his Dissembler, Billy descended to the large stone blocking the entrance. Charlotte had worked on clearing some of the roots out of the way while he looted, which was a big help. Currently, only a single fallen stone remained that was blocking the way in.

"Alright, Charlotte, watch out. I'll push this thing out of the way so we can get a better look." Billy wedged his arm into the crack made by the roots, and twisted hard. The rock ground against the rest of its neighbors for a few seconds as Billy grunted in exertion, and then it grated out of its place. With a last grunt of effort, Billy pulled the great stone free and tossed it down the side of the structure, where it quickly became lodged in another tree root.

"Excellent, but it looks a bit too small for me to walk in," He said while waving a hand at the small hole that was revealed. "Time to go spider again, I suppose." Billy bent over, and his limbs separated themselves, each arm and leg unlocking into two, and in seconds, Billy was once again a spider, albeit a strange-looking one with a more humanoid head. Charlotte did not change, as she was more than small enough to fit in the confines of the ruin.

With no effort at all, Billy swiftly moved into the short corridor through the crack in the structure, Charlotte walking right in behind him. Billy had his optics shifting to the low light settings, adjusting it as he went in further. As he moved into a large, square chamber, he saw he had room enough to stand again. Seconds passed as he shifted back to his humanoid form, then he looked around to see what the room revealed.

Charlotte silently walked around the room, her steps nearly imperceptible. She studied the walls and floors, looking for any clues or traps. Billy had not moved further into the chamber than it took him to realize he could stand, and so when he heard the faint sound of rock sliding on rock, he knew he was safe.

"Charlotte!" That was all Billy barked out when the floor in front of him vanished, Charlotte along with it. She didn't make a sound as the floor fell away, but Billy saw the fear in her eyes as she spun and looked at him on her way down into the darkness, arms and legs splayed to find purchase on something stable.

Quick as lightning, Billy twisted and pointed his abdomen into the hole and blasted out as much webbing, as hard as he could, into the hole. Thick, sticky strands of webbing erupted from him, lancing into the dark in a horizontal fan. A second later Billy felt something catching on the web, and he planted his powerful legs and held on to the entrance with both hands.

"That was close, dear," Charlotte called up to him. "Give me a moment and I'll climb back up."

Billy watched over his shoulder as her not insignificant mass pulled awkwardly on him, but he simply stood there, waiting for her to reach him. It only took a couple of minutes of maneuvering, but when she finally grabbed onto his planted leg and pulled herself out of the web, he felt relief.

Turning to help her up, he said seriously, "Gotta be more careful, Charlotte. You did say these places would be full of lethal traps. Next time, let's go slower, alright?"

To Charlotte's credit, she did not look ashamed of her actions, instead focusing on the positives. "With reflexes like that, dear, I think we need not worry about these kinds of traps."

"Until it's something like magical dragon fire, anyways," Billy said, and that made Charlotte pause.

All she said was, "I'll be more careful in the future." While she was back there, she tore free the webbing from Billy, and stuck it to the ground under him. If they forgot coming back out, and fell, this would hopefully save them.

Looking around the entrance Billy had paused at, he saw their shadow cast on the opposite wall. He also saw the blocks circling the room which now served as the new floor for getting around.

The walls themselves were carved, showcasing an ancient beast on the left wall. It was lion shaped, but based on the tiny figures surrounding it with spears, it was also quite large. The other two walls showed similar, but different monstrosities. Out of habit, Billy looked up, and there he found what he was looking for, the boss of this floor. Of course, it was a massive, enormous, leech looking monster. The rock carving showed the beast with tiny figures hanging out of its maw, tiny spears sticking all over its body.

As he studied the artwork, Billy signaled, "Charlotte, do you think we can just go straight to the boss?"

"Unlikely, dear. It will probably have a door requiring certain keys to enter. So, we will have to take out each of the other bosses before getting to the chief." She looked up as Billy had and saw the giant beast as well, but she seemed unconcerned with its appearance.

"I need salt," Billy said this quietly but with authority.

"Yes, it would seem so," Charlotte silently signaled back.

Shrugging, he signaled, "Perhaps somewhere in here we will find what we need. Dungeons want to be cleared, don't they?"

This statement caused Charlotte to stop, her motion catching Billy's attention as he circled around the walls of the room to the lion carving.

She deliberately twitched her antennae, asking, "Why do you think that?"

Without looking back he continued, "I have been thinking about what these places are doing to the world, is all. And I think they want to be cleared. I think nature itself might be doing what it can to entice people from either world, whichever one is available, to seek the Heart Shards to separate the two worlds. Otherwise, why would they provide Experience, and lovely loot?"

Charlotte continued behind Billy, and stopped when he reached the place in front of the giant lion carving. Billy ran his hands over the carving carefully, looking for the latch that would open a door. It took a few moments, but he did locate a portion of the wall which pressed in as his fingers found it.

"I have never heard of such a reasoning, Billy. What made you reach this conclusion?" Charlotte watched as Billy pushed open the section of the wall he'd just unlocked. It swung in with a rock on rock grinding sound, and Billy ducked into the new hallway.

The tunnel was short, and led to a tube cutting down into the ground, with handles carved into the wall to act as rungs. As the two went head first down the makeshift ladder, Billy signaled his thoughts.

"Back on Earth, I found something. It took me to a place, and while there an old man told me the thing I found would give me the chance to do something. Are you following me?" He waited for a response before continuing.

"I'm following you," He saw her reply.

"Right, so, after I was told that," H started to signal.

"Told what?" He saw Charlotte twitch.

"Are you not receiving all of our conversations?" Billy signaled with a questioning bend of an antennae, unable to turn and look at her as he asked.

"I am, dear. I just don't know who told you anything in particular. You were saying that you were going to explain something, and said nothing until you asked if I was following you. I am following. Then you said you were told something, and here we are." Charlotte's explanation of the conversation had the gaping hole involving the quest item, and the conversation with the old man.

"You have no record of any of our conversations about an old man?"

Billy continued climbing down the ladder as he waited for her reply. But she sent nothing.

Chapter 24

Concerned, Billy signaled aggressively, "Charlotte?"

"Yes, dear?" She replied immediately.

Thinking quickly, Billy revised what he was going to mention, "Alright, so, Aurora said two worlds collided for some reason, which is yet to be explained. These worlds are touching inside the Dungeons, Lairs and Hives that spawned all over the scars left by the connection of two worlds. These places entice people to explore them by doling out lots of Experience and loot, and they were explored for a long time. But something changed, and people stopped exploring them, and yet these places kept making monsters and treasures for people to come collect but nobody was showing up. It seems to me, Charlotte, these places need to be explored, and reality itself is bribing the population to do this."

"You think these places are aware?" Charlotte finally signaled just as Billy reached the bottom of the long shaft.

"No, but whatever is in control of the System has to be, peripherally at least. It must have some mechanism to self correct to prevent things like this, otherwise, how would it even be possible for two separate worlds to overlap?" Billy stood upright and looked around the black-walled chamber they were in. He could see a trough running through the middle of the floor, carrying with it a stream of water. The trough was lined with strange algae patches which glowed faintly, a pale green.

"None of that information is in my records, Billy. I have no idea how any of this could have been possible. The most I have is that many people, our creators, studied the phenomena in what remained of the land. Most of the population was dropped into the Sand Sea during that period, perishing without any chance to realize what was happening to them. Those who lived found places like these almost immediately, and began exploration.

"The System aided by giving vital information to the explorers at the time, and some even managed to locate strange objects known as Heart Shards," She finished, her twitching antennae halting as she followed Billy out of the shaft to stand beside him.

"You're just now telling me this?" Billy saw her flinch at this, for which he knew he would have to apologize to her for seeming so angry.

She seemed to understand he was not angry with her, however, and signaled to him, "This is the first time I have been able to access the information, dear. We have not had any conversations about the nature of these places inside of a Dungeon with a Heart Shard known to be in it before."

Billy carefully studied the floors and wall where he stood, Charlotte standing behind him in the ladder shaft.

"What?" Billy signaled, perplexed by what she sent.

"This is the first in depth conversation we have had about the state of the world, inside a Dungeon known to have a Heart Shard, dear," Charlotte signaled behind him.

Thinking quickly, Billy realized that whatever was going on in her head was linked in some way to the place they occupied right now, even as he knew she was probably right as well. It was as if she was accessing some network information not available anywhere else. Thinking back to their previous conversations however, he knew he had tried to speak to her about how he got this quest, but she had never responded to it before. He only realized now how odd those conversations had been. But here, something was different. It was as if there was some kind of network.

"Charlotte, are you and I a part of this world? Not this Dungeon, but the world outside." Billy kept looking around the room with his enhanced optical vision, trying to see any designs or patterns, but finding nothing, while watching for her antennae to twitch a response.

"I," Charlotte paused, and Billy turned slightly to look directly at her.

"What? You don't know?"

"No, I don't know, Billy. Are we... are we the invaders here?" Her antenna quivered a little as she asked.

Billy had no idea, but that didn't matter to him, not really. He was here to save the world, not necessarily live in it once he was done.

"It doesn't matter, Charlotte. What is important is that while in here, you have some of your records back, right?" This time he turned and squatted down to look at Charlotte directly, his antennae conveying his question.

"Correct. I think I have access to most of them now. But I don't think any of this will help us here." She looked Billy in the eyes, and he nodded.

"Very true, Charlotte. So," He once again turned to look about the room, deciding to change the subject, "What sort of traps do you think are in this room?"

"Why not send a bot?" She signaled, and Billy almost smacked himself in the face.

Without saying a word, Billy's abdomen, flat as it has been relative to its previous arrangement, swelled a little and opened a compartment and out slid a thick plate a few inches wide and long. Billy plucked at the brass key lying flat on the thing, oriented it properly, and turned the key and pulled at the same time. As he wound the little bot, it unfolded all eight of its legs and popped into shape. He sent a quick order in the dim light with his antennae, and the bot responded by moving forward.

The happy bot scuttled all over the floor of the room, and after a minute of wandering around looking at the cool rock walls, it returned to Billy. Scooping it up, Billy removed the cylindrical recording device they all now had and stuffed it into a port on his chest where gears whirred for a moment to download what it had recorded, then returned the small component to the bot.

"It looks safe, I think." Billy carefully took one step into the room, his potent optics in the faint light providing their own pale blue lines detailing every surface in his mind. The room wasn't large, some 40 feet by 30 feet, and almost 10 feet high, but it was relatively empty apart from the trough. As Billy took this step, the pale light from the plants growing in the trough running long ways through the room was shifted to a reddish hue. A grating sound had

Billy turning around, But Charlotte was faster as she simply leapt up and wedged herself into the space a block of stone was trying to move into to block off the ladder access.

"Charlotte, will you be alright there?" Billy warily watched the room as he heard Charlotte settle into place as stone continued to ground stone.

"Yes, dear. It's not pushing hard, and I can move out of the way easily if I need to." She spoke aloud, but did not sound strained at all, so the counterweight must not be too heavy.

Billy dropped the bot he had and ordered it to assist Charlotte with finding something to wedge into a crack somewhere to hold open their escape route, and then he moved further into the room.

"Alright, but tuck your legs up so nothing out here sees you in such a vulnerable position." He had to speak aloud as she could not see his antennae, nor he hers, but he saw her lift her legs and he knew she understood him. They had been communicating with their antennae, but continuous communication was more important than stealth at this point. He also knew she was built tough, not delicate by any means, though she could appear so in the way she moved sometimes.

Once Billy reached the trough in the room, he found himself almost in the middle, and the light had changed with every step until it had become a dull white light, illuminating the ancient, gray stone block walls. Billy turned a full circle slowly, and nothing seemed to happen. The ladder access was a shaft cutting through the long wall of the room, just off center, and the trough in the floor separated the room with the ladder access on one side of it, and the rest of the room on the other. Billy lifted his foot carefully, and stepped over the trough.

As soon as his foot touched the floor, a section of the room several yards in front of him dropped away into darkness.

"Crap!" He shouted, and backed up a step.

In front of him, the whole other side of the room dropped away into 40 foot wide steps. This opened into a massive room easily 10 times as large as the one he was in. The new room ran under the wall in front of him, and the floor level he was on was the ceiling height in the new room. Carefully he looked into the room, and more than 100 yards ahead of him stood a massive, eight foot tall lion.

Turning back to the hole, Billy called to Charlotte, "Come on down, Charlotte, it's just a big cat."

A moment later he heard Charlotte drop to the ground and walk up beside him. The light from the part of the chamber they were in spilled down into the large room, but it did not touch the far walls. The light just lit up the lion, which was standing in the center of that chamber, its tail slowly swishing side to side watching them.

Billy waved Charlotte to wait as he took to the steps and dropped down several feet at a time with each one until he was level with the lion. Carefully, he locked his rifle into position and opened up the compressor valves to quietly charge the chamber with a thought and moved forward. Looking left and right, he saw the strange slice of light making a rhombus shape of light on the floor. The rest of the room appeared to be empty, the lion the only thing in here.

"Do you speak?" Billy called out, and he saw a giant ear twitch.

"Welcome, adventurer. Welcome, at long last," The deep baritone voice of the lion called out in some tongue Billy was able to understand despite not really knowing the language itself.

Billy continued toward the lion, until he was a dozen feet from it, and his eyes shifted on their own to observe a net of thick, gray, non-light lines surrounding the lion in front of him. The lines of gray were pulsing slowly, and sporadically twisting one way or another as it seemed to try and make contact with the animal before him, similarly to slow-moving lightning.

"What are you?" Billy asked, beginning to walk around the lion. It did not turn to watch him, it stood almost frozen in place, its tail, ears and mouth all that moved.

"I am the roar of existence. I am the call to arms. I am the predator on the plains. I am the finality of all." The force of the voice pushed at Billy while he was so close, and as he circled the lion, he saw that as it spoke the gray lines were trying all the harder to crush down on it, as if speaking were showing a weakness.

Returning to face the large cat, Billy tried to look into its eyes, but his mind would not allow him to make direct eye contact, and nothing he did to force himself to do so would allow him to. The best he could do was look at its face in a general sort of way. The large cat seemed strong, impossibly strong. It gave Billy the feeling of being watched, hunted, and that there would never be any escape. As he took in the visage as much as he could, Billy found himself taking a step back, his boiler for a heart almost missing a pulse.

In English, so that Charlotte would not hopefully understand, he said, "Are you some kind of god?"

The lion looked down upon Billy, and his mind felt the weight of worlds try to crush him down. Out of instinct Billy stiffened his spine and legs, and held himself uptight. After a moment, the feeling passed.

"Yes, adventurer. And you," It replied in perfect English as it blew a gust of air that washed over Billy, "are an adventurer that is not an adventurer."

"Yes, well, now that we haven't made introductions, I am Billy. I was sent here.."

Its growl interrupted him, "To save a world, yes. It was I who submitted the request to That Which Is Above for aid. It is you that has come, then. Good."

Billy doubted that this powerful being could be a god or that it would be able to make a quest that could bring him from one reality to another.

Turning to Charlotte, he saw she was far back, standing at the top of the steps, well out of earshot of this conversation. It was alright, Billy thought, as she would unlikely be able to comprehend what was going on anyways.

"Why are you here, then?" Billy asked instead of many of his other questions. Here he was, standing in front of a self-professed deity, and all he wanted to know was why it was here. It was an odd sensation.

"To the point, my conqueror. This is good. Focus will do you well, dwelling on the dross is unbecoming." The lion god, for the first time, moved and slashed out with a massive claw, and the gray lines flared to life as the claw collided with them.

Billy fell back a few steps as power unlike anything he'd ever experienced lashed out around him with the flaring of those alien gray lines, and he had to hold a hand up to shield his many eyes.

"Is this stuff sealing you here? Is it imprisoning or siphoning power from you?" Those were the only things Billy could think a trap like this would be used for.

"No, this is the compression of my purpose to act, it is the collision of two worlds unable to accept change." The god before Billy looked upon him, and Billy did everything he could to just look at its nose. His eyes wanted to flee from the form of the lion, so close up, but he forced his mind to do his bidding. Then the words sunk in, and Billy thought he understood.

"Is there another god of creation in here?"

"Very clever, adventurer. Yes. There is another. It is unlike me, but like me. We are too much the same, and not enough alike. We are both bound, one to another, that we stave off the end of all. It is not the time, but that time is upon all." The booming voice crashed down on Billy with the absolute knowledge of things. Staggering at such truth spoken by this being almost crushed Billy flat, but his magical frame, his human will to do, to succeed, would not let him think of anything but standing and listening.

"What must I do here? Free you both?" Billy was trying to figure out where all of this was going, and he considered the other murals on the walls of the first vestibule, the three other beasts, and Aurora's advice.

"That cannot be, adventurer. We three have trapped ourselves to fend off finality itself. Only one of us has refused. And she is not here." The lion ended this with a deep growl that vibrated reality around Billy, and he felt parts of himself want to separate into nothing, but he still somehow managed to hold on to sanity.

"We have to fight, don't we? I have to defeat each of you, take something from each, and use that to defeat some great evil or something?" Billy recalled his gaming days, and the few times he'd played games with gods involved in the world's problems, the player would have to fight a weak version of the god in combat to receive some mcguffin that would solve the problem ahead. And, he knew, that solution was almost never obvious.

"What a curious question. You come here, recognize me for what I am. You are an adventurer, that much I can see. And you expect to be able to fight me? Do you expect to win?" The voice practically snapped at Billy, the deep bass vibrating the stones of the floor.

Thinking fast, Billy took a step forward, fairly certain in his observations.

"I think you need me to fight you. I think you know that. I also think that you not only want me to win, you need me to. Why else would this," He waved around the lion's body, "Would these lines be here, if not to make this encounter viable?"

"Hahahahah! Yes! I need you to fight! I live for the fight, adventurer. And you live for the Experience, the loot, the adventure! Your struggle is not so different from mine, adventurer." The tail of the lion swished with its own impatience. "But, you see, I cannot fight you from here. I am imprisoned." The growl that followed this admission caused the hairs on Billy's body to arc with static electricity.

Still, Billy stood firm, his eyes squinting hard to trace the barely visible gray non-light of the lines surrounding the lion. Then, he found what he was looking for and, as quick as a flash, he pointed the barrel of his rifle and fired.

The crack of super pressurized air snapped around the stone chamber, and the pellet practically teleported from Billy to the point in the strange web around the lion, the expanding air rapidly creating a frozen cloud of slowly falling air. There was a spark of impact, and Billy saw the lion flinch as if it had been surprised. Then the strange, alien gray non-light crackled, and the even lines developed odd curves, and the lion winced in visible pain.

"What have you done!" The shout knocked Billy back a half dozen yards, but his powerful legs and gekko-like padded feet gripped the stone and halted his backward slide while he leaned forward.

"If I am correct, I think I messed up that little spell you were working on. I don't think it was a prison. I think it was a trap," Billy said, with just enough confidence to seem believable.

The lion was crouching, the writhing lines breaking apart around it, and then slowly they vanished as their pattern was disrupted. In seconds, the strange lines completely separated from each other, and the whole thing faded out of existence. Once the lines were gone, the oppressive feeling of overwhelming power faded as well, and Billy knew he was correct. This was no god. This was a Boss.

The lion roared in rage, and Billy could now see Charlotte moving in his direction, sticking to his own shadow so the lion would not easily see her. Billy crouched forward, preparing to act when the lion did while signaling to Charlotte to be careful. To his annoyance, the lion began to circle him, focused intently on him as it stalked. It was prowling, and to keep things fair Billy circled with it, his footsteps only a little heavier than the great cat's.

Charlotte circled around with Billy, accelerating her pace to keep in position. To further distract the lion, Billy cranked up his compressor, which screamed to life on his back, and the lion's ears laid back, its eyes narrowing in the sudden pitch change.

Billy's targeting systems were showing no weaknesses on the lion. Its head was protected, its chest was as well. The side facing him was also well defended, as were its legs. The lion was moving too strangely to target the eyes, which were both too large and small at the same time, and his targeting system would not lock onto them for some reason. Then an idea hit Billy, and he grinned.

Suddenly stopping, he straightened and faced the lion. A quick twitch of his antennae and he signaled to Charlotte, "He's about to attack, get ready to move right." This caused the monstrous beast to bare its teeth. Then it began trotting to Billy with purpose, and Billy prepared himself for what was to come.

Billy could feel the moment coming, it was building quickly, and he noticed Charlotte not following his orders. He cursed to himself as his Perception of the battle began to accelerate as the moment he was waiting for came. Time suddenly seemed to slow to a crawl as the moment arrived.

The lion leapt, its mouth open in a silent roar, its left paw raised to strike, six inch claws exposed. Billy saw Charlotte moving left, but couldn't do anything at this point. Carefully, Billy brought his targeting mark up, waited for the perfect moment to strike, then commanded his rifle to release its remaining payload of 11 supersonic pellets.

With a ripping sound, the pellets lanced out from the barrel, one practically behind the other, and every one aimed directly for the gap in the pads of the raised paw coming toward him frighteningly fast. Hoarfrost instantly formed on the barrel, which he saw the same time the lion screeched out a roar of pain and tumbled onto the ground, its powerful paw curling painfully under the big cat as it bowled over itself to roll past Billy. Dodging aside, Billy watched as blood sprayed in a wide arc as the now useless limb smacked the stone floor, and Billy could hear bone break under the weight of the cat as it rolled a second time before skidding to a stop.

As fast as he could, Billy ejected the spent magazine and locked in one of the larger ones, his compressor furiously pressing more air into the chamber of the rifle to recharge it. He had dumped most of the pressure in that continuous stream of fire, but his magical compressor was up for the task and in seconds his weapon was recharged and he was venting excess overpressure in a short blast.

Billy watched the cat struggle to stand. Its ruined front paw would not allow the lion to put any weight on it, and Billy could see something come into the eyes of the beast that wasn't there before. He saw fear, and he knew this was likely the first time the Boss had ever felt this sensation.

"You are not from the outside world, are you?" Billy stood firm as he watched the cat examine its bleeding, broken limb. It seemed unable to comprehend what had happened. "Charlotte, get back. It's still dangerous," He sent with his antennae, and was annoyed when she just stood there.

"Neither are you, adventurer. Your progenitors are from the world I brought into existence." The cat tried to hold back a yowl of pain as it spoke, but Billy ignored this attempted bravado.

"Was your world responsible for the intersection of these worlds? Were you a part of that?"

"Foolish adventurer. Did you not hear me? We are a product of their collision."

Billy let the clear insult pass, again, and wasn't really paying attention because he could feel the pressure capping in the chamber while he watched his gauges max out. After another few seconds, the compressor cut off, and the sound of its screams echoed into nothingness in the great stone room.

"I need the key, or whatever it is that this place has, to get to the final Boss here. And when I take care of that guy, I will be destroying the Heart Shard."

The lion growled fiercely at Billy's statement. "You would dare! Foolish adventurer, you know not what you do. What lies have you been told!?"

The lion did not give Billy the opportunity to reply, instead leaping forward on its powerful hind legs. The lion opened its mouth wide, intent to crush Billy's head in one decisive attack.

Billy raised the barrel of his rifle and emptied the large magazine right into the lions' mouth. It happened in a half a second. The lion was leaping, eyes alight with the need to kill, the next second its face was cut in half as more than 100 supersonic pellets sliced it open from the inside of the mouth to the top of its head. Somehow, the pelt of the cat prevented the pellets from passing clean through, which inadvertently caused even more damage as they bounced around inside the cat's body.

The body of the great cat flopped to the ground in front of Billy, sliding the six feet from its point of contact to his feet with a smear of blood. Billy casually replaced the spent magazine with another, but did not recharge the compressor tank immediately. The tank was covered in a thick film of frozen condensation, and he needed to wait a minute to let that evaporate. He walked up to the somehow still alive lion, which looked up at him with one unfocused eye.

"You can't.. You can't destroy.. shard. Must.. you must…" It breathed out its last and fell still.

Billy looked to his prompts to see if he'd received anything from the encounter, and checked his logs as well. They showed nothing.

Charlotte moved beside him, toward the body, and Billy put out a hand to stop her. Billy's eyes narrowed as he looked around the large, shadowed room. On impulse, he initiated the compressor cycle, and it screamed to life in the apparently empty room, recharging the canister and the rifle's chamber in moments. Heat radiated from Billy's chest, his boiler running on overdrive at this point. His abdomen, once in its flat configuration, swelled as he prepared to act once again. The air lines running to his rifle cracked when the ice broke as he moved.

Charlotte reacted to Billy's actions, crouching and looking around the room while attempting to identify the danger to Billy. He knew she would see none.

Billy slowly walked around the body of the great lion. He saw the paw he'd shot first, blood pooling around it on the floor. The head of the great beast was almost split in half, the pieces held together by its hide. The fur, once pristine and golden yellow, was now smeared with dark, red blood. The shadow of the beast cast by the light from the entrance hid nothing from Billy. The smear of blood was several feet long from where it slid to his feet. The tail lay limp, the chest unmoving, the ears still, the eyes glazed in death.

Billy's abdomen silently pulsed as he walked around the body, its motion like ocean waves as it rolled over the air causing a hissing sound that even Billy himself could not detect.

Charlotte spoke as Billy came back around to the head of the lion, her glittering limbs sparkling as she slowly turned and watched Billy circle it, "Are you going to loot this, dear?" Her voice was faint, and echoed strangely in the room.

Billy said nothing, but reached out a foot and tapped the corpse. He reviewed the prompt that came up, and shook his head in the negative and kept looking around the room into the shadows. He saw movement, or pretended he did, but said nothing as he focused on what his abdomen was producing.

Once Billy returned to the front of the corpse he carefully looked at the steps leading into the large room, eyes squinting. He could barely detect the lines, but he did see a wall of gray non-light lines criss-crossing the entire section separating the steps from this large room. Then he paused a few feet from Charlotte, who was also looking around, and he squinted harder. And then he saw the gray lines around Charlotte.

Charlotte caught Billy's look, and as she looked up at him, she took a step back. He saw fear in her demeanor, and in her antennae motions. He cocked his head at her reaction, but still said nothing. Diving into his mind, Billy reviewed the conversations over the last few minutes, since they had entered the room from the steps. This was when he noticed that everything he had said to Charlotte through signally was being ignored. He had spoken aloud to the lion, but down here he only signaled her and she never responded.

He sent her a message using his own antennae again, "Charlotte, do you understand what is going on here?" He waited a moment, but she did not seem to react. Her own antennae reflexively laid back, and her eyes seemed to sparkle.

"Who are you?" Billy asked aloud. "What have you done with Charlotte?" He stood firm, several feet from the body of the lion, and watched her.

"I... I'm your assistant, Billy. Is something wrong?" She even went so far as to look afraid for him, and Billy had to hold in his laughter at the ruse.

He had tried one more time to communicate with his antennae while she spoke, but she did not respond to the odd twitching of his antennae. Instead of responding to Charlotte, Billy walked past her, his abdomen slowly pulsing as he did so. Billy thought to himself that it was odd Charlotte did not understand what he was doing, even though she had seen him do this before.

Billy slowly circled Charlotte as he waited for her to act, but she stood still, watching him with her eight eyes instead of actually turning to face him. He continued to lay his trap, which she seemed totally unaware of.

"I see on my map here," Billy pointed into empty space, "That my companion, Charlotte, is in the other room over there. And you, well, you are a red dot. I hadn't noticed until now because of the cat here," He tapped the body as he passed it, his pad getting a little blood on it from doing so. "And once I realized how easy it was to kill a self-proclaimed god, I thought to myself, 'Self? If I were a god, would I drop so easily? No, I say to myself. I would set a trap, obviously.' Then I check my map to see what appears, and there you are, Charlotte. In two places at once, and one of you is a nice, red dot on my map."

He stopped in front of her after circling three times. His abdomen ceased its pulsing, and he brought up his rifle, its frozen tip inches from Charlotte's face.

In a burst of effort, the Charlotte clone tried to move, but immediately found itself unable to. The vicious look that came into her eyes became a red glow, and Billy saw the hydraulic musculature bulging with the effort to move. She was trapped, though, in an ultra-fine net of super strong silken web. Three layers of it, only now shimmering since she moved.

"You will fail, adventurer!" The voice coming from Charlotte was now very similar to the once lion god. It boomed into existence, struggling to force away the web from its body, but failing to do so.

"Ah, see? I won't fail. I can't, not now." Billy fiddled with the chamber of his rifle while the figure that looked like Charlotte struggled mightily to free itself.

"You cannot destroy the Heart Shards, fool! You doom us all in your ignorance! How could you possibly think you are wiser than the very gods that created everything here?!" Charlotte's body vibrated with the effort to break free of the webbing, but she was not built to do these things.

"I can, whoever you are. They're anchors, holding both of these worlds together. Get rid of the anchors, and the worlds continue on away from each other, back to where they came from." Billy wasn't sure why he was explaining the obvious to something he knew he was going to destroy in a moment, but perhaps he could get more clues if it kept talking, even if he knew it was lying about something.

"Those aren't anchors, fool! They are the result of the two worlds colliding. They are the explosion, the pressure, the result, not the cause." Charlotte, which wasn't Charlotte, pulled mightily at her bonds, and Billy could see some of the tiny threads stretching.

"Then tell me, what should I do? Leave them? I can't do that, and you know it. They must be pulled free so the two can separate. Otherwise, they'll both be destroyed." Out of caution, Billy raised his weapon to point at Charlotte, and this motion caused fear once again to come onto the face of what he was fairly certain was a god, or at least a god-like being.

"You can't succeed, adventurer. There are thousands, tens of thousands of those Heart Shards. The worlds are contacted in more than one place. You will need help. Yes! I can help you separate them without destroying them. If they are allowed to grow, I can.."

Billy unloaded the magazine of his rifle into Charlotte's head and chest. The resounding sound of supersonic pellets obliterating the metallic body filled the chamber. Bits and pieces of metal gears flew everywhere, pinging off of Billy, the floors and walls as he dismantled her in seconds. He didn't pause after emptying the magazine, and reloaded as the form of Charlotte fell to pieces in front of him. He walked around the pieces, eyes squinting to try and see what was happening.

Perception check Successful! You have detected remnant magical emanations from this pile of parts lingering in the chamber.

With a foot, Billy tapped a chunk of a metal frame that was the Charlotte bot, and he received a notification.

Billy felt the weight of the parts settle into his compartments while he recharged his rifle and compressor tank. The whining sound quieted once the tank was filled, and all the while he searched the dark recesses of the room for motion. Frost continued forming along the length of the barrel thanks to the compressed air sucking the heat from it as it rapidly expanded under such high pressure.

"Hahaha! Foolish adventurer! You cannot hope to win, not now. You will not leave this room, much less disable the Heart Shards. It will not be much longer before a new god is born, and nothing you do will matter." The alien cackle smacked the walls of the room as the voice spoke.

Billy slowly spun around, trying to locate the source of the voice, but all he saw was the rock of the floor and walls. As Billy searched, the hairs on his shoulders began to feel weird, like he was about to be struck by lightning, and his head twitched to look above him, but he was too slow. An arm of solid rock slammed into Billy's head, and he went flipping head over heels like a rag doll for dozens of yards, where he smacked with a crunch into the stone wall.

His body stuttered as his head rang like a bell. The reinforced skull he had felt like it deformed, but placing a hand to it only told him part of the hair covering his head was now missing. Billy barely noticed the 'whomp' of something very heavy dropping to the floor when he was partially depressed in the stone wall.

Grapple check failed. You are stuck, immobile, in the wall.

Movement Penalty: -100%.

With a thought, Billy slipped into his menus to check his Status, and to his amazement he saw he'd only lost a little Durability, spread almost evenly over several of his parts. His legs took a few points of Durability Damage, and his head did as well. His left arm took a couple points of damage, and his shoulder also took a couple of points of damage, but other than the stunning effect, and the grappled effect caused by being stuck in the wall, he was fine.

Pushing awkwardly back with his limbs, Billy forced himself from the crevice his body had made in the wall, and he regained his footing, losing the grappled status.

Strength check successful. You have freed yourself from the grip of the wall.

Movement Penalty: 0

Looking up, Billy saw ahead of him, back where he had stood moments before, a large, stone golem silhouetted by the pale white light behind it. The dark mass of stone was six feet wide and tall, its blocky edges looking familiar from Billy's gaming days.

Billy looked down to his right arm and the high powered pellet rifle attached there, then back up to the slowly approaching stone golem, and shook his head. With a quick tail wag, the abdomen he had partially inflated again began dropping his bots, which clattered onto the stone floor. Swiftly scooping them up a few at a time, Billy turned the brass keys on one after another until he had a dozen bots powered up. He then dropped his two larger scavenger bots, and wound these up, but placed them onto his back instead of back on the floor. He fed them instructions using his antennae and they awaited his command to act.

Chapter 25

A twitch of his antennae sent all of his smaller bots up the wall behind him, and they moved into place on the ceiling. These little guys shadowed Billy up there as he moved forward, keeping position just ahead of him but doing so on the ceiling. He knew he was going to be in for a fight, if this golem were anything like those in game lore from Earth. It would be very strong, immune to most status effects, and it would have a high physical defense. He also knew in this world, with its weird rules, golems were not alive in that they have no Life points to subtract from with damage. Golems would have Durability which, when reduced, would reduce it to smaller disconnected components, or pieces. It would break.

This thing was a giant, mobile rock, and all he had to do was break the right part. "Easy peasy", he thought to himself. Flexing his fists, Billy cranked up his boiler in preparation for a fight as he closed in on the mobile rock stomping its way towards him in turn.

"What's your plan, rock man?" Billy said with bravado. He felt he needed to entice the thing to define more of its plan, if it had one.

"Do you think that by destroying this world you can make a new one, or do you think it'll take two worlds instead?"

The stone golem thumped to a halt as it cocked its lumpy head, and the gravely rock-on-rock voice spoke. "It won't matter if I tell you, as you won't leave this place. But I will humor you, adventurer. The collision of the two worlds created the Heart Shards. Those Heart Shards represent the new order. All that needs to be done is to let them be. You see," It lifted a large stony limb with a lump of rocks grinding together into a fist, "All I have to do is nothing. And all I need to do is to prevent you from interfering."

"Yeah, I can't do that, sorry," Billy said as he stepped forward, not sorry, to begin dismantling the golem before him.

Charlotte looked around the strangely glowing room she was in. She waited for Billy to call for her, as he'd indicated prior to descending the steps into the room ahead. She was not impatient, nor was she worried. Her friend was quite durable, and unlikely to fall to some caged beast. She knew this. She had reviewed Billy's Status many times, even though much of it was hidden from her. She did not mind this, however. It was intrinsic for individuals to keep some aspects of themselves to themselves. It was a matter of privacy. She knew Billy had the authority to monitor her Status, and thus all her Attributes and Abilities, but he kept out of this, and had long since allowed her to disperse her own scant Experience points as she desired. She had never asked for this permission, and he had never mentioned it. It was just something he had assumed from day one and it had been thus ever since.

She was curious about this temple they were in. She did not know what it was for, or exactly why they needed to do anything here, but Billy was on a mission of some sort, and it was her job to assist him in accomplishing all that he desired. That was, after all, why she existed. It was her purpose. And she was fine with this arrangement. It kept things simple.

As the days had rolled into weeks, then into months, Charlotte had built up a small collection of useful Experience points. She was restricted to gaining these by performing specific actions for Billy, not for anything else. Every little request he made provided some Experience once the tasks were finished. She was sure he was unaware of this transaction, but he did know she was gaining Experience for herself, never mentioned it, and never ordered her to spend them in any particular way.

Now, after months of existence, and any number of adventures, she had quite a pool to draw from. She had spent some of this early on to increase her own Intelligence and Wisdom by increasing her memory, processing capacity and speed. Billy was even gracious enough to build her the components she required to upgrade herself, which she had never really needed to ask of him.

Billy gave her clothing and ornaments as if she were her own person, which was unusual for reasons Charlotte herself did not fully understand, but accepted nonetheless. She understood she was a machine whose sole purpose was to fulfill Billy's desires and commands, and he seemed to quietly command her to be her own person. This was something Charlotte was unfamiliar with. Her programming and construction did not provide direction with how to be more than just something to follow orders, much less order of her own design, but time and again she found herself free of task or command and she was given no direction but her own during those times.

As she watched Billy do whatever it was he was doing down the steps, she noticed that he was trying to communicate with her. She comprehended the commands, but it also appeared as if he were commanding someone else in the room with him. She saw no one, but that did not seem to be the case for Billy. At one point she tried to signal Billy that she was in fact not down there, but he did not react to her signals.

Charlotte tried to descend the steps herself but found some barrier she could not move past and instead had to endure waiting for Billy to retrieve her.

"I wonder what he is seeing in there," Charlotte said to herself after a few minutes. She saw Billy moving and acting as if he were interacting with something in the room, but she saw nothing and nobody else but him. She waited another moment to see if her Perception could pierce whatever veil was there, but she had not succeeded, thus knowing she was unlikely to verify her conclusion that some form of illusion was active. Illusions required Mental Reflex checks, something that would snap the mind into reinterpreting what information it was receiving. What she saw was nothing, and what she could not see was the illusion she knew was there.

Stepping back into the room, Charlotte carefully examined it once again. Opposite the steps leading down, she saw the tube cut into the wall with the ladder going up. That was currently partially blocked, with a small bot preventing it from sealing completely. Going from left to right in the room was a small trough about a foot wide, and a few inches deep. This had a small stream of water going through it, with some strange plant or growth, which was providing the now white light.

Carefully, she reached into the water, and tested it. It was as pure as she could possibly determine. Her sensors tested the conductivity and it showed, within a margin of error quite small, the purity was very high. It was water, but absent almost all minerals found in regular flowing water.

Such pure water provided no nutrients to plants, which she had learned during her time setting up the hydroponics back in the Lair of the Fey. The plants required special fertilizer to grow. The strange plant emitting the light was on bare stone, and stone had no nutritional value. Again, she had learned this from Billy, who had used that knowledge to create barriers plants could not cross to spread to other places plants grew in their facility back in the Lair of the Fey. He called them planters, which housed individual plants such that they would not compete for nutrients. They could not consume the containers as they had no nutritional value, and being made of a hard material Billy termed pottery, their roots could not force their way through them either.

Carefully, Charlotte dipped a finger underneath a small patch of a glowing plant, and plucked it from the stone. It immediately went dark as it lost contact with the water. Placing it back in the spot she had removed it from caused the plant to begin emitting light again, but somehow out of sync with the rest of the plants.

Looking back to the room Billy was in, she saw the shadows had shifted some, and an idea began to take form. Without a second thought, Charlotte ran her hand along the stone trough and started scraping off the moss glowing there. As she did this, she saw a significant change in the room below. Billy was punching and kicking at the air, occasionally flying backward to avoid something, and then rolling in and around as if dodging something else, but the lighting seemed to subtly change as well.

As she removed the plants, the light in the room changed, creating pockets of visibility surrounded by total darkness. As fast as she could, because Billy looked to be getting beaten up by something that was apparently not really there, Charlotte continued to remove the plants from the trough. The room was dozens of yards wide, and it took her a few minutes to clear one side, and then went to the other side. She scooped the plants out of the water, and plopped them in piles as her hands got full.

Down the steps, Charlotte saw Billy dramatically fighting the air in front of him, and he appeared to be doing some damage, though nothing was there except someone else's imaginary monster. Stepping up her game, Charlotte quickly scraped and removed all of the plants along the other side, and as her hand passed one last time to scrape off the last bit of glowing plant, the last bit of visible light flickered away, and both the room downstairs and the room she occupied went pitch black. A split second later Charlotte heard the telltale sign of Billy's boiler dumping excess pressure in a sharp hiss that cut off a couple of seconds later.

"About time, Charlotte. I thought you'd never figure out what was going on," Charlotte heard Billy call up to her.

With a flick of her attention, Charlotte switched to another optical light sensor, and she saw the pale blue outline of Billy approaching. He was scooping up several of his bots and she noticed almost a dozen of them were completely destroyed. The pile of parts was scooped up by other bots while Billy picked them up and he stored them in their compartments. Apparently the illusion was more real than she had thought at first glance.

"I wasn't sure exactly what you were trying to do, dear. You were sending signals that weren't making much sense for a little while, and when you started shooting your rifle I knew there was a problem." She moved toward Billy in the hopes she could inspect him for damages as she spoke.

"It's fine, Charlotte. I'm just glad you figured out how to turn the thing off. Besides, it all worked out in the end, and I did get some nice loot," he paused mid-step and checked his inventory. Yes, he did have the rewards he had collected. He also had an update to his quest.

You have discovered more of the truth of the world you have chosen to save, though this information leads you to the task of eliminating an unknown number of Heart Shards. You have noted a number of remaining and known Dungeons which have yet to be cleared, compiled by yourself and Aurora, the Captain of the Sandspray; this represents the estimated number of sites to visit and secure.

+1,000 Experience points.

You have acquired a new Special Ability: Insight. This Special Ability activates in areas inhabited with the Heart Shard's presence, allowing you to pierce the veil into the new realm being fashioned at a new fundamental level, and interact with it on that level. Removing the threat caused by the Heart Shard will deactivate this Special Ability, granting the only evidence available to prove the Heart Shard has been disconnected from the local setting.

Increase the Mental Reflex: Illusion Resistance +10.

"And, it appears we were awarded with the ability to determine if or when we deactivate the Heard Shard in the Dungeon. As it so happens, we have succeeded here already." Billy picked up the last bot, which also held the pieces of another bot, and placed it in his compartment to work on later.

"Does that mean we are finished here?" Charlotte asked, hoping to get some time to perform maintenance on Billy's frame.

"No," He sighed. "We need to finish this Dungeon and remove it from the overflow state it's in. I think that the shards grow in strength as the population exceeds the Dungeon's capacity to hold them. It could be possible that if we left another one could try and form with the help from the current overflow." He ran a hand over the portion of his head that was now hairless and chuckled. "Although, I would still like to take the time to fix my head. I'm missing a big patch of hair."

Charlotte sighed, realizing that she would have to replace each hair individually, and he had quite a lot of hair on his head now. She took a few minutes to examine Billy as they both sat beside the still flowing pure water, and then spent the next half an hour on maintenance. While Charlotte happily worked on Billy, he worked on repairing his damaged bots.

Slapping the last bot back into its compartment, Billy stood with Charlotte. Together, in the total darkness, they collected the strange plants that had piled along the trough of water.

Congratulations! You have collected 100 unknown plants.

Take them to a Botanist to identify them.

Billy dismissed the notification, knowing already he had no idea what kind of plants these were. He wasn't a botanist himself.

Dungeon Heart Shard has been unanchored from this reality. Its absence will now begin to stabilize the local region.

"That's odd," Billy signaled as he saw the next notification.

"What is it, dear?" Charlotte wiggled her antennae his way.

"I got a second notification after we collected the plants stating the Heart Shard has been unanchored from this reality. It seems the Special Ability helps me identify the danger, and the removal of it entirely denotes the cessation of its effect on the world."

"That's unusual, isn't it?" she signaled back to him. Neither were actually speaking, instead using their antennae to communicate, but Billy still somehow heard the confusion in her question.

"A little," He said. "The Ability is like a danger sense, letting me know it is close but not what it is. The notification about its status only happens when it is removed from the Dungeon. 'It' being whatever the Heart Shard is. Apparently," He began, scratching his chin, "It does not have to be an actual heart, or a shard. The only thing left to do now is to clear the place of monsters, and leave, I guess."

"And get loot!" Charlotte replied back, excitement evident in her following that up with a fist pump.

"Yes, and get loot," Billy replied, shaking his head.

Four days later, Billy and Charlotte found themselves standing in the valley of rock, a few feet back from the Abyssal Bore's entrance. Both were covered in blood and viscera, with ropes of organs, along with treasures, plopping to the ground once they appeared outside of the place.

"That was much rougher than I figured it would be," Billy said aloud to Charlotte, shaking his arms in an attempt to remove some of the mess from the monsters they had defeated. "Who knew the salt would explode on contact with that leech dragon?"

"We can clean up at the river, dear. And take some time to do a little repair work as well," Charlotte said, her own frame stained green from the bile of the giant leech dragon that had tried to eat her whole just before it had exploded.

Shrugging, he said, "Let's do that." Billy gave up trying to free the goop and bile from himself and gave in to getting a bath instead. Twenty minutes of splashing around saw him getting out to dry on the rocks.

Dropping onto his butt by the stream of water, Billy waved away all of his notifications as he sat quietly while Charlotte moved around him. She lifted arms and legs, and even his abdomen, checking for necessary repairs and maintenance while Billy thought things over with himself.

"What am I going to do now? When I got here, I made my way to the Lair of the Fey. There, I met some nice folks after fleeing Aurora's attempt to capture me. I learned from Orgar a little of the history of the world from his lore. Later, I learned a little more from Sharea and Elsie, but not much. I helped all three unlock the System, which let them level Attributes and Abilities with Experience, and all was well until I finally met up with Aurora again, only to be told everything they said about their history was a lie and not to trust them.

"The illusion monster, the lion, kept calling me 'adventurer' while we fought. That was a bit disturbing. Nobody in this world has yet referred to anyone else as an adventure, a term I am definitely familiar with back home. There's no way it could have known anything about that concept; I have no actual mind to read, it isn't written down anywhere, and I have never mentioned the concept aloud to anyone, so how could it know about the term? What does this all mean? Can I trust it said what it said, or was Aurora wrong about something?

"The lion had been right about one thing, I was here for the Experience, loot and the adventure. It was why I picked up that Quest Prompt to begin with and accepted it. And I got so much Experience and loot I'm not sure what I'm going to do with it. That isn't even considering I now have a complete set of parts to build a second Charlotte in his pocket, so to speak. What would it mean, having two digital assistants at the same time? Was that even possible? How would Charlotte react? How would I?

"The biggest problem I have is not knowing who to trust. The monsters in the Dungeons and the Elves, along with Aurora, seem to agree on one thing while calling each other liars about everything they say. Did Aurora's people really exist on Harmony prior to the cataclysm that scarred this world? Or are they just remnants, evolved monsters that exist only as overflow that had spent enough time outside to diverge from the monsters inside?

"The illusion boss I fought the other day said something about doing nothing and letting the Heart Shards grow, and this would release some new god on the world, and it really had seemed content to do nothing until I had come along to interfere. But what does that even mean? Are there gods out there vying for power or trying to come into existence thanks to the opportunities brought about through the collision of two overlapping worlds? Can I even trust this information? And why did Aurora know and talk about the humes, and the monster never even mentioned them? Why did it not know that most of the Heart Shards had already been destroyed? There are so many unanswered questions here, and every time I get even a little piece of the puzzle, it seems to conflict with other information.

"I think the System, in this case, may be my only clue as to what is true or false. It seems to be pointing me in the direction of eliminating the Heart Shards, although it is very clear that I am here to save a world. Which one, though? If there are two worlds that have collided and now this one here is the result, what of the places the Dungeons and Lairs and Hives exist? It's clearly a different place, and all of those places are linked. Man, what am I going to do, huh? I guess for now, I will head back to Aurora and let her know what I've discovered here and see where this quest tree leads me." His thoughts were suddenly interrupted when he heard a sound.

"Billy, dear? Did you hear me? I said I have completed the maintenance." Charlotte tapped Billy's head, the metal on metal tapping causing the sound that snapped him out of his thoughts.

"What? Yes, thank you, Charlotte. I was just thinking over all we've learned so far. And trying to figure out what we are going to do next." Billy held up his right arm, examined the attachment there, and let it drop again.

"Yes, well, we took far less time to clear out the Abyssal Bore than originally planned. We have a couple of days ahead of us to return to the Sandspray rendezvous point through monster-infested land." Charlotte finished washing off a cloth she had used to wipe Billy free of dust before tapping one of the compartment doors on Billy's abdomen and placing it inside.

"Let's go then, Charlotte. Those Dungeons aren't getting any closer while we sit here." Billy stood up, flexed his mechanical muscles, and flattened his abdomen, so it hung behind his legs like a tailcoat. His blue hair twisted and turned to a deeper black, then went almost clear in the early morning light. His exoskeleton was dark underneath the hair, showing the powerful physique that was his body. And with one step following another, the two began to jog back the way they'd come less than a week ago to meet the Sandspray.

To Be Continued...